Also by John Case

THE FIRST HORSEMAN
THE GENESIS CODE

the syndrome

john case

FAWCETT BOOKS • NEW YORK

A Fawcett Book
Published by The Random House Publishing Group
Copyright © 2001 by John Case
Excerpt from *The Eighth Day* copyright © 2002 by John Case

www.ballantinebooks.com

ISBN 0-345-43310-6

Manufactured in the United States of America

First Hardcover Edition: May 2001
First International Mass Market Edition: April 2002
First Fawcett Books Mass Market Edition: November 2002

OPM 10 9 8 7 6 5 4 3 2

(S)ome other power, some third class of individuals aside from the leaders and the scholars must exist, and this third class must have the task of thwarting mistakes, and nipping the causes of potential disturbances in the bud. There must be a body of men whose task it is to throw out the rotten apples as soon as the first spots of decay appear . . .

A body of this nature must exist undercover. It must either be a power unto itself, or be given the broadest discretionary powers by the highest human authorities . . .

From "The Invisible Empire," an after-Action report of Carleton Coon to OSS Chief William Donovan, quoted in *The Last Hero* by Anthony Cave Brown.

THE SYNDROME

PROLOGUE

Zurich
June 16, 1996

It wasn't the Grande Jatte. Not exactly. It wasn't even the afternoon. Not quite. But it felt that way—just like the picture—as if nothing could ever go wrong. The placid park. The bright and dozy day. The neon-blue lake, shimmering in the breeze.

Lew McBride was on a long run through the narrow park that follows the shoreline of the Zurichsee from busy Bellevueplatz out to the suburbs. He'd already gone about three miles, and was on his way back, jogging through the dappled shade, thinking idly of Seurat.

The pointillist's great canvas was peopled with respectable-looking men in top hats, docile children, and women in bustles carrying parasols. But the age it captured was two world wars ago, before *Seinfeld*, the Internet, and "ethnic cleansing." People were different now, and so were Sunday afternoons (even, or especially, when they were the same).

To begin with, it seemed as if half the girls he saw were on cell phones, Rollerblades, or both. They had pierced navels and mischievous eyes, and cruised, giggling, past kids with soccer balls, dozing "guest-workers," and lovers making out in the lush grass. The air was fresh from the Alps, sunny, cool and sweet, its soft edge tainted now and then with whiffs of marijuana.

He liked Zurich. Being there gave him a chance to practice his German. It was the first language he'd studied, chosen in high school because he'd had a crush on an exchange student. Later, he'd acquired Spanish, picked up a little French, and

1

even some Creole, but German was first—thanks to Ingrid. He smiled at the thought of her—Ingrid of the amazing body—cruising past a marina where sailboats rocked at their moorings, halyards clanking.

He could barely hear them. He had the volume turned up on his Walkman, listening to Margo Timmons sing an old Lou Reed song about someone called

". . . Jane . . .
Sweet Jane . . ."

Music, books, and running were McBride's secret nicotine and, without them, he became restless and unhappy. They were the reason he did not own (could not afford) a sailboat—which he wanted very much. His apartment in San Francisco was a testament to these obsessions. Near the windows, the stereo and the oversized sofa, stacks of books and CDs stood like dolmens: blues, *mornas,* DeLillo, and opera. *Konpa,* rock, and gospel. Chatwin on Patagonia, Ogburn on Shakespeare. And a dozen books on chess, which McBride would rather read about than play (except, perhaps, in Haiti, where he and Petit Pierre sometimes sat for hours in the Oloffson, hunched over a battered chessboard, sipping rum).

Thinking about it made him miss it—the place, the chess, his friends . . .

As he ran, he glanced at his wristwatch and, seeing the time, picked up the pace. He had about an hour and twenty minutes until his appointment at the Institute, and he didn't like to be late. (In fact, being late drove him crazy.)

Headquartered in Küssnacht, about twenty minutes from McBride's hotel, the Institute of Global Studies was a small, but venerable, think tank funded by old money flowing from tributaries on both sides of the Atlantic. Like so many foundations established in the aftermath of the Second World War, the Institute was dedicated to the idea—the vague and elusive idea—of world peace. Toward that end, it hosted conferences and awarded fellowships each year to a handful of brilliant youths whose research interests coincided with the Foundation's own.

These included topics as diverse as "the rise of paramilitary formations in Central Africa," "Islam and the Internet," "Deforestation in Nepal," and McBride's own study—which concerned the therapeutic components of animist religions. With the Cold War a thing of the past, the Foundation's directors had formed the opinion that future conflicts would be "low-intensity" struggles fueled, in most cases, by ethnic and religious differences.

With advanced degrees in clinical psychology and modern history, McBride had been traveling for nearly two years. During that time, he'd produced reports on, among other things, the mass-conversion techniques of faith healers in Brazil, the induction of trance states in Haitian voodoo ceremonies, and the role of "forest herbs" in the rites of Candomblé.

Two of these reports had been published in the *New York Times Magazine*, and this had led to a book contract. In three months, his fellowship would be up for renewal and, after thinking it over, he'd decided to take a pass. He was a little tired of living out of suitcases, and ready to focus on writing a book. And since the Foundation had summoned him to Zurich for their annual "chat," it was the perfect opportunity to let them know of his decision in advance.

All of which was just another way of saying that life was good—and getting better. If McBride's meeting went as planned, he could catch the six o'clock flight to London, arriving in time for dinner with Jane herself—the real Jane, whom he hadn't seen in months.

"Sweet Jane, Sweet Jane . . ."

It was this prospect that spurred his pace, so that he got back to his hotel—the Florida—nearly ten minutes earlier than he'd expected. This gave him plenty of time to shower, shave, and dress, as well as to pack his only bag—a canvas duffel that had seen better days.

His meeting was with the Foundation's Director, Gunnar Opdahl, a wealthy and cosmopolitan Norwegian surgeon who had given up medicine for philanthropy. Having spoken with Opdahl by telephone from California, McBride knew that the director wanted him to re-up for a third year. He was glad that he had this opportunity to meet with Opdahl face-to-face. It would give him the chance to discuss the reasons behind his decision to leave, while at the same time expressing his gratitude to the Institute.

And, while he was at it, he could visit Jane on the way home.

The Institute was headquartered in a turn-of-the-century townhouse, a brooding pile of granite built by a Swiss industrialist who had later hanged himself from a chandelier in the foyer (damaging it in the process). The building was three stories tall, with mullioned windows and wavy antique glass. There were copper gutters with gargoyles at the downspouts, a trio of chimneys poking through the tiled roof, and half a dozen window boxes, dripping with flowers.

A small brass plaque beside the massive front door declared the Foundation's identity in German, French, and English. Above the leaded glass transom, a closed-circuit television camera stared down as he rang the doorbell once, twice, and—

"Lew!" The door swung open, and Gunnar Opdahl surged into view, eclipsing the room behind him. Taller even than the six foot one McBride, the Institute's director was impeccably dressed in an expensive business suit that had a hand-tailored look, and a Hermes tie that McBride recognized from the duty free shops at Heathrow.

Rangy yet solidly built, the fiftyish Opdahl moved with the grace and languor of an aging athlete—which, in fact, he was, having won a bronze medal in the downhill decades earlier. It came up in conversation one time—the strange co-incidence that McBride's father had medalled in the same

Games (Sapporo, 1972), taking a silver in the biathlon (the first American ever to place in the event). Opdahl had winced good-naturedly, complaining that "Norway *owns* the biathlon—at least, we're supposed to!"

Now, Opdahl shook his hand and clapped a friendly arm around McBride's shoulder. "So how was your trip?" he asked. "No problems?" The older man ushered McBride inside, then pushed the door shut behind them.

"A little jet lag," McBride replied. "But, no. The flight was fine."

"And the Florida?" Opdahl asked, looking bemused as he took McBride's duffel and set it beside the door.

"The Florida's great!"

Opdahl chuckled. "Large rooms, yes. But, great? I don't think so."

McBride laughed. "Well, it's cheap, anyway."

Opdahl shook his head, and clucked. "Next time, stay at the Zum Storchen, and let the Foundation worry about the money. I've told you: that's what we *do*!"

McBride made a gesture that was something between a shrug and a nod, and glanced around. The Institute's quarters were more or less as he remembered them, with Persian carpets scattered across the marble floors, coffered ceilings and oak wainscotting, oil paintings of flowers and landscapes, and a scattering of blond PCs on antique wooden desks.

Though he'd only been to the Institute twice before, he was surprised to find its headquarters so quiet. Noticing that surprise, Opdahl clapped him on the shoulder, and gestured toward the stairs. "There's just us!" he exclaimed, leading the way.

"Really?"

"Of course. It's Saturday! No one comes to work on Saturday—except the boss. And that's only because I don't have a choice!"

"Why not?" McBride asked, as they began to mount the steps. "If you're 'the boss'—"

"Because I live here," Opdahl told him.

They ascended the stairs in tandem, heading toward the third floor. "I always assumed you lived in the city," McBride remarked.

Opdahl shook his head, and winced. "No. This is . . . what do you say? 'My home-*away*-from-home.' " He paused on the landing, and turned to explain. "My wife lives in Oslo—hates Switzerland. Says it's too bourgeois."

"Well," McBride said, "that's its charm."

"Of course, but—one can't argue these things."

"And your children?"

"All over the place. One boy's at Harvard, another's in Dubai. Daughter's in Rolle."

"School?"

"Mmmnn. I spend half my life on airplanes, rocketing through the void."

"And the rest of the time?"

Opdahl flashed a grin, and resumed climbing. "The rest of the time I'm raising money for the Foundation, or sticking pins in maps, trying to keep track of people like *you*."

It was McBride's turn to smile and, as they climbed, he made a joke about being breathless. "I thought there was an elevator," he remarked.

"There is, but I don't like to use it on weekends," Opdahl replied. "If there were a power failure . . . well, you can imagine."

On his previous visits, McBride had met with Opdahl and his assistants in a conference room on the second floor—so he was at least mildly curious about the living quarters overhead. Arriving on the third floor, they came to a door that seemed entirely out of keeping with the building they were in. Made of steel rather than wood, it was unusually thick and sported a brushed aluminum keypad that governed its opening.

Opdahl punched three or four numbers, and the door sprung open with a metallic click. The foundation director rolled his eyes. "Ugly, isn't it?"

"Well, it's . . . big," McBride remarked.

Opdahl chuckled. "The previous tenants were a private bank," he explained. "From what I've heard about their clientele, a big door was probably well advised."

The office itself was large and comfortable, brightly lighted and furnished in a modern style—unlike the rooms below. There was a wall of books and a leather sofa. A Plexiglas coffee table was laden with a silver tray that held a steaming pot of tea, two cups and saucers, milk and sugar, and a little pile of madeleines.

"Tea?" Opdahl asked.

McBride nodded—"Please"—and walked to the windows behind the desk, where he marveled at the view. Seen through the trees, the lake was the color of Windex, and glittered like broken glass. "Spectacular," he said.

Opdahl acknowledged the compliment with a tilt of his head, pouring the while. "Sugar?"

"Just a little milk," McBride replied. And, then, noticing the computer on the director's desk, he cocked his head and frowned.

"Where's the A-drive?" he asked.

"What's an 'A-drive'?"

"For your floppies."

"Oh, that!" Opdahl replied. "There isn't one."

McBride was genuinely puzzled. "How come?"

Opdahl shrugged. "We like to keep our data confidential and, this way, we can be sure it stays in-house." He handed McBride a cup of tea and, sitting down behind the desk, gestured for the young American to take a seat on the couch. Then he sipped, and exclaimed, "So!" A pause. "You've been doing a wonderful job!"

"Well . . . thanks," McBride replied.

"I mean it, Lewis. I know how difficult it can be to work in places like Haiti. They're filthy, and if you don't know what you're doing, they can be dangerous."

"I got my shots."

"Still . . ." Opdahl leaned forward, and cleared his throat. "You must be wondering what this is all about. . . ."

McBride shifted in his seat, and smiled. "Not really," he said. "I just *assumed*. The fellowship ends in a couple of months. . . ."

Opdahl nodded in a way that confirmed the observation even as he dismissed its relevance. "Well, yes, you're right—of course, but . . . that's not the reason you're here."

"No?" McBride gave him a puzzled look.

"No." A whirring sound came from the hall outside the office and, hearing it, the two men looked in its direction.

"Is that the elevator?" McBride asked.

The director nodded, his brow creasing in a frown.

"But—"

"It's one of the staff," Opdahl supposed. "He probably forgot something." Then the whirring stopped, and they could hear the doors rolling back. A moment later, there was a knock. "Would you mind?" the director asked, gesturing toward the door.

McBride frowned. Hadn't Opdahl said, "There's just us"? And something about not using the elevator. But he did as he was asked. "No problem," he said, and, getting to his feet, stepped to the door and opened it.

There was only a fraction of a second to take things in, and no time at all to make sense of it. What he saw was this: a man in surgical scrubs with a gas mask over his face. Then a cloud of spray, and the floor rising toward him. A shower of lights. Darkness.

He was in an ambulance. He was sure that he was in an ambulance because he could see the lights on the ceiling, reflected red lights, going around and around. Nearby, a man in surgical scrubs watched him with a look of mild curiosity.

McBride wanted to ask what was wrong with him, but it was difficult to speak. His mouth was dry, his tongue like wood. When he tried to talk, his voice was slurred, as if he were drunk. After a while, he gave up trying to talk, and tried to concentrate on what had happened. *There was a man in a mask. An emergency worker of some kind. Which meant a gas leak, or something like it.*

And the aerosol? What was that?

He tried to raise his head—tried to sit up—but it wasn't possible. He was strapped to a gurney, flat on his back, and soaked in lassitude. A tranquilizer, then, and by the feel of it, a powerful one. Thorazine, maybe. He closed his eyes, thinking, *I should be frightened . . . it would be healthier to be frightened.*

They must have been riding for an hour or more, and never once did the driver use the siren—just the lights. Every so often, McBride's eyes fluttered open, and there they were, rotating over the ceiling: *Red . . . yellow . . . red . . .*

It was so strange. Wherever the ambulance was, wherever they'd been, there wasn't any traffic. The ambulance cruised at a comfortable speed that seldom varied—as if they were on a highway, or driving through the country. Which didn't make sense. There were lots of hospitals in Zurich—so why leave town? If it was an emergency—and it *had* to be an emergency, because . . . if it wasn't . . .

The tranquilizer was beginning to wear off, and as it did, he could feel the first stirrings of anxiety, deep within his chest.

Then they were there—wherever "there" was. The ambulance crunched to a stop on what sounded like gravel, and the lights winked off on the ceiling. Then the car door slammed, and the walls trembled. People talking in Swiss-German, and the rear doors opening with a yank. A rush of fresh air, and then the gurney began to move underneath him.

"Where'm I?" A funny building, barely glimpsed—but modern. Then a face, looming in front of his own.

"Not to talk."

And then they were inside. Down a long hallway, and into a brightly lighted room. Where he was left for nearly half an hour, his mouth getting drier and drier as he stared at the clock, high up on a glazed, ceramic wall.

"You're very brave."

The voice came from the end of the gurney. It was

Opdahl's voice under Opdahl's eyes, staring at him over the edge of a surgical mask.

The tranquilizer was history by now, and McBride found himself able to speak without much difficulty. "What's happening?" he asked. And then, when no reply was forthcoming: "What are you *doing*?"

"Vec," Opdahl said—but not to him.

A needle appeared—McBride saw it for the best part of a second, then felt the sting just below his elbow. Instantly, everything began to slow down. His heart seemed to start and stop, as if he'd been punched in the chest. And, suddenly, he couldn't get his breath. He was suffocating, and the realization made him panic. And as the panic rose inside him, he lunged, lunged reflexively against the straps that bound him. He was determined to stand. If he could stand, he could breathe. But the straps wouldn't budge, or—not that. It wasn't the straps. It was him. He was paralyzed, as immobile as a butterfly under glass.

Opdahl leaned closer to him, so close that McBride could feel the older man's breath on his face. Then the point of a scalpel touched his throat, just above the breastplate, and he felt the knife cut through the skin. "Sh-sh-sh-sh-sh," Opdahl whispered, though McBride had not made a sound. "It's going to be all right."

But it wasn't.

He was dying. He might as well have been underwater, encased in concrete, or buried alive. Airless and frantic, he felt something enter the wound in his throat. Whatever it was, it tore at the tissues in his neck as Opdahl worked it into him. Then a machine began to pump from somewhere behind him and, suddenly, he was breathing again—or the machine was breathing for him. He couldn't tell.

The older man checked the pupils of McBride's eyes, shining a penlight into the back of his head, oblivious to McBride himself. Then McBride felt himself being cranked into what was almost a sitting position. A moment later, a large machine was rolled to the side of the operating table, even as a second machine—itself about the size of a refrigerator—whirred into operation. McBride recognized the first device as an operating microscope, and guessed that the second was a fluoroscope, capable of generating live X rays throughout an operation.

Opdahl hove into view again, as someone wheeled a television monitor up to the operating table. It rested on a little stand, glowing brightly, and McBride's eyes were drawn to it. With a sickening sensation, he realized that the man on the screen with a trache tube in his throat was himself.

"You're going to be all right," Opdahl promised. "Not to worry." Then he reached for one of the surgical instruments that lay in a steel tray at his side. "We've given you eight milligrams of Vecuronium—that's why you can't move. It's a paralytic." He paused. "But not, I'm afraid, an anaesthetic."

Then he nodded at the small monitor next to the table. "I'm sorry you have to watch this," Opdahl told McBride, "but it's a part of the procedure." With that, he turned to the nurse, and nodded. Wordlessly, she stepped behind McBride and, reaching toward him, seized his upper lip between her thumbs and forefingers. Then she pulled it back, exposing his upper gum.

Opdahl leaned in, and drew his scalpel across the bit of tissue that held McBride's lip to the gum beneath his nose. This done, and as the paralyzed McBride stared in terror at the monitor, Opdahl began the procedure known as "degloving," delicately prying the younger man's face away from the skull, peeling the skin back to reveal a direct passage into his brain.

1

She was in a kind of road-trance, coasting south with her eyes on the horizon, not quite listening to the radio—that was, in any case, playing songs from her infancy. The car was a cherry-red BMW convertible, a Z-3 with new Michelins and a killer radio that seemed to be tuned to the past. Removing her sunglasses, Nico put the car on cruise-control—she didn't want to speed—she knew *better* than to speed—and hit the *seek* button.

Easy listenin'. Country. Oldies. Salsa.

A riot of oleanders divided the highway, which unfurled across a sunbaked landscape that was flat as a pool table, seedy and glamorous, all at once. Dilapidated double-wides hunkered beside the road under canopies of live oaks strung with Spanish moss. Here and there: confederate flags and pink flamingos. Mortuaries and nursing homes. A roadside stand selling boiled peanuts, Cajun and plain.

Florida, she thought, then shook her head and rolled her eyes behind her Ray•Bans.

What glamour there was, was in the light, and in the Dodger-blue sky. It was in the pastel promise of the Gulf coast, a few miles west, and it was in Nico, too. Like the car she drove, Nico was a masterpiece, fast and expensive.

She'd come down by train from Washington to Orlando, where the BMW was waiting for her in a parking lot at the train station. (She'd have preferred to fly—she liked to fly—but, under the circumstances, what with her baggage and all, flying wasn't practical, flying wasn't even an option.) Taking the I-4 to the Tamiami Trail, she'd turned south just outside of Tampa. This was Florida, trashy side up, all strip malls and trailer camps, parking lots and gas stations.

But all that began to change when she left the Trail, heading west toward the causeway that connected Anna Maria Island to the mainland. At first, it was the same-old/same-old, a constellation of Shoney's, Wal-Marts and Exxons. Stopped at a traffic light, she glanced to her right and saw, with a shock of surprise, an unkempt woman lounging on the pavement next to a shopping cart piled high with plastic bags of what looked like trash. Hanging from the side of the cart was a hand-lettered, cardboard sign that read:

> SECRET SERVICE MAFIA SCUM
> MURDERED DIANA—JACK—ADLAI
> DAG! MASER WHORES AND ELF
> SLAVES! YOU TOO!

Once Nico pulled away from the light, she left the craziness behind—or, at least, the crazy lady—and, with it, the down-at-the-heels world of the Inland.

Her destination was a rich man's redoubt, a barrier island just a few miles north of Sarasota, a lush sandspit dappled with turquoise swimming pools and emerald-green golf courses. This was a place where million-dollar villas and high-rise condos stood their ground on a shimmering blond beach that, seen from the sky, made the island look as if it had been outlined with a yellow highlighting pen.

Or so she thought. She'd never actually been there. At least, she didn't *think* she had. But she'd seen the pictures and brochures. And the place was beautiful. Longboat Key—the Florida that old money dreamed of.

Seeing a sign for La Resort, Nico turned into a boulevard of palm trees, which took her to the front door of a low-slung villa with apricot walls. Killing the engine, she unfolded her long legs, and climbed out into the rapt gaze of the bellboy.

"Checking in?"

"Hope so," she said and, tossing him the keys, bounded up the steps to the office.

Inside, a big "Hi there!" from the clerk behind the desk, who, unlike Nico, was dressed for air-conditioning: white shirt and tie, khakis, and a blazer.

"Brrrr," she replied, with a wince of a smile.

The clerk laughed, and pushed a registration card across the desk. Like the bellboy, he was a nice-looking young man with closely cropped blond hair and sparkling blue eyes. Over the pocket on the left breast of his blazer was La Resort's logo, a pink-and-cream orchid flanked by palm fronds.

"Do you have a reservation?"

"Unh-huh," she said. "It's Nico Sullivan. Nicole."

"If you'll fill that out," he told her, "I'll take an imprint of your credit card—and we'll get Travis to help you with your luggage." Taking a brochure from a Lucite display stand, he turned it upside down, and sketched a line in ballpoint from *You Are Here* to a building marked *Flagler Tower*. Then he typed something on his computer, reached under the desk, and produced a white plastic card with Nico's name embossed upon the resort's logo.

"This is your key," he said. "It's a charge card, too. So you can use it for anything at the resort—drinks, clothes, golf lessons—you name it! Just show the key, and it's yours."

"Thanks!" Nico replied, reaching for the card with a bright smile. But the clerk held onto it for just a second too long, flirting with her.

"Any questions?" he asked.

Nico laughed, a musical giggle. She gave the card a little tug, and he let go. "If I think of anything," she said, "I'll give you a call."

"I'd like that," he replied.

She ran her fingers over the embossment of her name, and looked up. "This looks out over the beach, right?"

"Absolutely."

"So it faces west . . . ?"

The clerk nodded.

"Oh, good," she said, "because I'm really looking forward to the sunsets."

"Well, you won't be disappointed," he told her.

A moment later, she emerged from the office to find the bellboy waiting with her luggage on a trolley. Nearby, the BMW sat in the shade under an arbor of bougainvillea.

"Nice ride," the kid remarked.

"Thanks."

Together, they followed the sidewalk to the Flagler Building, making small talk about real estate and the weather. When they got to the elevator, they had to wait and, as they did, Nico's wristwatch began to chime, an insistent electronic flutter that reminded her to take her medication. The bellhop smiled. "Throw it away," he suggested.

"I wish I could!"

"Hey, this is Florida! We don't have appointments here! You just . . . go with the flow."

She laughed politely, but the truth was, she *did* have appointments. There was the appointment with her laptop every afternoon at four, and the appointment with her meds, twice a day. The meds were a lithium compound prescribed by the Clinic. Duran said they were used to treat "bipolar disorder," or manic-depression, which meant that she had a problem with her moods. Like everyone else, she had her highs and lows except, in her case, the highs were in orbit and the lows could give you black lung. The lithium kept her on an even keel—which was good, if you liked even keels.

But she didn't, really. She was a girl who liked to fly. And, as a matter of fact, she was feeling pretty good right now, standing next to good ole Travis, waiting for the elevator.

Which raised the question: why not do as the natives do, and just . . . go with the flow? Like the bellboy said. Accentuate the positive—eliminate the negative. *And only the negative.* It wouldn't be the first time. . . .

She touched the little button on her wristwatch, killing the alarm. A moment later, the doors slid open with a clatter, and the two of them got in. Slowly, the elevator began to rise until it came to a shuddering stop on the eighth floor. A couple of turns down the open-air corridor brought them to a door marked 806-E. The bellboy inserted the key-card in the lock, and waited for the diode to flash green. When it did, he pushed the door open and held it for her.

"Oh, wow!" she gushed, sweeping into the living room, and doing a little turn. "It's great!"

And so it was. The suite was large and airy, a choir of pale blues and soft pinks, with a long balcony, lots of rattan and a high-rise view across the water toward Mexico. Nico unlocked the French doors to the balcony, pushed them open and stepped into the sunshine.

"You want me to show you around?" the bellboy asked, placing her baggage on a luggage rack, just inside the door.

"That's okay," she said, returning inside. "I'll figure it out."

The bellboy shrugged, and flashed a boyish grin that had a little too much practice in it. "Whatever." The question had been rhetorical, a way of keeping the conversation going. He knew the kinds of guests that enjoyed a tour of the amenities, and this one, cool as a popsicle in her sherbert-green sundress, was definitely not the type.

Nico smiled, pushed a fiver into his hand and walked him to the door. "Thanks for the help," she said, as she closed the door behind him. Then she turned on her heel, and went to the computer carrying case in which she kept her meds.

Opening it, she rummaged through its interior until she found what she was looking for—sort of. There were two little orange bottles made of plastic. The first, which held a month's supply of lithium, was almost empty.

The second bottle held a drug she called "Placebo #1." A joke—she'd even written it on the label right below the printed information, which read: 326 NICOLE SULLIVAN: TAKE AS DIRECTED. Because the drug was experimental and wasn't even manufactured in the States, the stuff didn't have a name, just a number. You couldn't look it up in the *Merck Index* or buy it at the pharmacy. You had to get it abroad, or through the mail, and so she did—three or four times a year, depending . . .

It had a way of putting her at a distance from herself, as if her body were an actor in a play she'd come to watch. Supposedly, it was therapeutic—a way of letting her see herself as others saw her. And not only that: Placebo #1 enabled her to do some remarkable things. Without affect, her body and emotions were entirely within her own control. Every reaction was appropriate and measured (or seemed to be) so that, if she'd wanted to, she could have walked an I-beam between the suite she was in and the building across the way. And she'd have enjoyed it, too, because when she was like this, she was free in a way that "normal people" almost never were. It was a strange and interesting way to be.

And unlike the lithium (which could make you fat, if you weren't careful), the side effects were minor. Although it could mess with your memory. Oh, she was okay minute-to-minute and hour-to-hour, but day-to-day could be a problem. Though whether that was a bug or a feature, she couldn't say.

Opening the minibar, Nico took out a bottle of Evian water, and unscrewed the cap. Shaking a pill from each bottle into the palm of her hand, she washed them down with a sip of water, and had a look around the suite.

And it was fine: big, clean, crisp, and stylish. She approved of everything: the welcome basket, filled with fruit; the heavy white bathrobe and translucent soap; the little sewing kit, and the split of champagne that lay on its side in the refrigerator. It was California champagne, but even so—it was the good stuff. Domaine Carneros. A nice wine.

Inventory taken, she unpacked her clothes and put them away. Undressing, she tried on each of the swimming suits she'd brought, twisting and turning in the floor-to-ceiling mirrors in the alcove, just outside the bath. She'd almost decided on the black one, a classic maillot that didn't show too much cheek, when she changed her mind, opting instead for a lemon-yellow bikini. *It's not like I have anything to hide,* she thought, slipping into a pair of leather sandals.

Crossing the living room, she went out to the balcony and

stood at the railing overlooking the beach. Directly below was the patio-pool complex, with its Jacuzzi and swim-up bar, beach umbrellas and tables. Between the pool and the Gulf, a line of palm trees thrashed in the wind while out to sea the water's surface shimmered and flashed.

Standing there, she could feel the pills kicking in, softening the air at the edge of her skin. Leaning out over the railing, hands at her sides, she remembered—vaguely—that she was afraid of heights. But, not now. Now, there was nothing. She might as well be standing in her own living room.

On the beach below, attendants were methodically folding and stacking a row of bright blue cabanas that belonged to the resort. Nico gazed, mesmerized, at the patterning and repatterning of the surf, the lacy white foam curling and uncurling with a muffled roar. Every so often, a child's voice floated up to her, squealing from the pool.

Returning inside, she removed her laptop computer from its leather case, and set it down beside the telephone on the table in the living room. Using an RJ-11 jack, she connected the computer to the phone, adjusted the monitor to cut the glare, and pushed the *On* switch. It took about a minute for the CPU to go through its routine. When it was done, she clicked on the AOL logo, and waited yet again. Finally, there was the familiar rush of noise and bleat of horns, the farcical handshake of the modem exchanging protocols with the server. And then she was on.

You've got mail!

Out of habit, she clicked on the mailbox to see who it was.

10-7	*Adrienne*	*Where are ya, Nikki!?*

Little sister.

Ignoring the message, she went to the Internet connection, and in the box for the Web address, typed *www.theprogram.org*

and waited.

A moment later, Web Site Found appeared in a box in the lower left-hand corner of the screen. And then

Transferring document
1%   2%   12%   33%

Why did it take so long?

Opening Page

And then: a nearly blank screen with its oh-so-familiar, black-on-white inscription.

Unknown Host
        Description: Could not resolve the host
    "www.theprogram.org" in the URL
"http://www.theprogram.org/".
                Traffic Server version 1.1.7

Reaching into the computer's carrying case, she took out a transparent plastic overlay, and fitted it over the monitor's screen—whose size it duplicated perfectly. A calendar of sorts, the overlay had two axes—a vertical one, divided into twelfths, and a horizontal axis with thirty-one gradations. Together, they created a grid with 372 boxes, one for every day of the year, with seven left over. Using her mouse, Nico slid the cursor over to the box that corresponded to that day's date (October 7th), clicked, and moved on to a second box, the one that corresponded to her birthday (February 11th). And clicked again. Instantly, a tiny hourglass appeared, floating behind the overlay, which Nico then removed.

It always took a minute for the site to load. She watched the blue bar crawl across the page and then she was on:

Hello, Nico

The cursor blinked beneath the greeting, awaiting her instructions. Taking a deep breath, she touched *Ctrl-F5*, and— pictures and words and . . . something else, a sound she couldn't quite hear, but *felt*. Pictures and words, scrolling and flipping, moving so fast you wouldn't believe she could take it all in. But she did. She sat there in the room, unmoving, eyes bright with the turmoil on the monitor.

She had been at the resort for three nights, and he still hadn't shown. Each evening, she went down to the beach and waited for him, just to get a look—but he was never there. And the pills were beginning to get to her. If she took them for too many days running, she started to . . .

What?

Lose track of herself.

That was the only way to put it. There were long periods of time when . . . there was nothing. And then, quite suddenly, she'd be herself again—except at a distance, always at a distance, as if her identity were a phantom limb. You wouldn't think a little pill could grab you like that, but—

Not to worry. They said he'd be here, and they were always right. It was just a matter of time.

She glanced at her watch (it was 7:15), then looked out the window to where the sky had just begun to blush. Her fourth sunset.

Grabbing a towel, she took the elevator to the ground floor, and walked through the pool area toward the little boardwalk that led to the beach.

It wasn't exactly the season yet, only the beginning of October, so there weren't that many people around. A couple of kids in the pool, attacking each other with what looked like big, Styrofoam noodles. Mom on a chaise lounge, reading, and over there, two oiled, teenaged girls lying on their stomachs, bikini tops undone. Nico thought maybe they were asleep because, really, there wasn't much sun left to bathe in.

The area around the pool was already in shadow, the underwater lights glowing eerily. Lamps were beginning to flicker on the periphery of the terrace. The attendant who sold hats and sunglasses, sand toys and sunscreen was busy putting away things at his little stand, closing up for the night. As Nico walked past, a fiftyish woman in a purple bathing suit lowered herself carefully into the Jacuzzi beside the pool, her mouth releasing a soft *Ooof* of pleasure.

The beach was even less crowded. Most people seemed to be at dinner, or dressing for dinner.

And then she saw him—

An old man, sitting in a wheelchair at the end of the boardwalk, where it broadened into a platform above a flight of steps leading down to the sand. He had a shawl over his shoulders, and his eyes were fixed on the reddening horizon. Nearby, the old man's dreadlocked Jamaican caretaker leaned on a railing, listening raptly to the music blasting through the earphones of his Walkman. Reggae, Nico thought, catching the rhythm as she passed, the sound a remote, tinny whine.

There was no one else, really. Apart from the Jamaican and the old man, the only other people in sight were a lone jogger, running in the wet sand along the surf line—and a couple, walking with their heads down, looking for shells.

And that was it. Everybody else was . . . somewhere else. Which left Nico with Nico, one on one, watching her towel fall to the sand as she waded into the warm Gulf waters. In front of her, the sun seemed balanced on the horizon's dark rim, turning the sky the color of a million postcards.

She's in heaven, Nico thought, watching herself move through the water. Which was shallow here, no more than knee-deep for upwards of a mile offshore. Wading farther and farther out to sea, she could see herself dwindling in the old man's eyes. Finally, she slowed, stopped, and sank to her knees. Leaning back on her arms, she luxuriated in the warm bath of the Gulf, listening to the cry of gulls wheeling overhead. She remained this way for what seemed a long time, eyes shut, face turned toward the sky. Then she pivoted on her left arm, and spun to her feet in a single move that would have been startling if anyone other than she had seen it.

Slogging back to the beach, she picked up her towel and climbed the steps to the little boardwalk. As she passed the old man, she gave him a shy smile and a meek "hello," and kept on going. The Jamaican didn't even notice. He was up to his ears in Bob Marley, eyes closed, shoulders swaying, quietly singing the words

"No, woman, no cry;"

At the footbath inside the gate, Nico rinsed her feet, slipped on her flip-flops and crossed the terrace to the elevator.

Back in her room, she removed the little bottle of champagne from the refrigerator, and opened it with a soft pop. Then she filled a flute from the kitchen cabinet, and took a single sip. It was nice, she thought, very nice.

Moving to the couch, she set the champagne glass down on the glass-and-rattan coffee table, and got out her laptop. Connecting it to the phone, she waited for the CPU to boot up, then got out the plastic overlay, and went to the hidden URL she'd accessed the day before (and the day before that). She moved the cursor to today's rectangle, and then to the one that represented her birthdate:

Hello, Nico

The cursor blinked silently.

Resting her fingertips on the keyboard, she typed

Picture, please

Instantly, an hourglass appeared in the center of the screen, and hung there, like a bug in the air at the end of an invisible thread. After a while, an image began to form, one line after another until, in the end, there was a snapshot of an old man, the same old man who was sitting in the wheelchair eight floors below.

Certain now that she had the right man, Nico went to the folding luggage rack that held her baggage. These were a battered leather pullman in which she kept her clothes, and a waterproofed case made of lime-green, high-impact plastic with a customized, foam interior. Turning the numbered wheels of the combination lock on the second bag, she sprung the catch, opened the case and checked her tools.

These were nestled in a complex of foam compartments and, once assembled, constituted the finest sniping system money could buy. There was a bolt-action, M-24 barrel that coupled with a reassuring *cliick* to a Kevlar-reinforced, fiberglass stock with a matte-black finish. A Leupold scope was mounted to the barrel on steel rings and bases, in tandem with a B-Square Laser. Support came from a Harris bipod, and silence from a Belgian-made helical suppressor that threaded onto the maw of the rifle's twenty-inch barrel.

Nico assembled the weapon system with practiced ease, taking about thirty seconds, and tested the trigger's three-pound pull. Then she inserted a single round of Teflon-coated, .308 ammunition, and rammed it home. With the silencer, scope, and laser, the rifle weighed almost eleven pounds— which made the bipod essential for accuracy.

Walking out onto the balcony, she saw that the sun was almost underwater, the horizon hemorrhaging as the sky darkened to a blue-black bruise. Backlighted from below, a dozen palm trees trembled in the evening breeze.

But the old man was right where he was supposed to be, sitting in the twilight, enjoying the day's last gasp.

Lying on her stomach, Nico slid the muzzle between the pink balustrades at the edge of the balcony, its barrel resting on the bipod, taking the weight off her arms. Then she looked through the scope, and flicked on the laser, which cast a wafer of bloodred light between the old man's fourth and sixth vertebrae. From the end of the barrel to the edge of his skin was less than two hundred yards, an easy shot for her, even in the gloaming. Still, she could see the light tremble on her target's back as her finger curled on the trigger, drawing it toward her for what seemed like forever. Then the rifle spasmed, and she heard a sound like a champagne cork going off in another room. The old man jerked upright and stiffened, as if an electric shock was moving through him. Then his body slumped, sinking into itself in such a way that she knew she'd cut his spine in two.

There was no smoke, really, and no flash that anyone was likely to have seen. The cartridge she'd fired was subsonic, so the only sound that could have given things away was the noise of the slug as it slapped into the old man's back.

Not that it mattered. No one was paying attention— certainly not the Jamaican, who was lost to Bob Marley, and certainly not the children in the pool, whose laughter hung in the air like music.

Nico sat up, and broke down the gun. *No muss, no fuss.*

Then she got to her feet, and returned the rifle's components to the Underwater Kinetics case in which they belonged. Finally, she spun the custom-fitted, little brass wheels that locked the suitcase, and topped off her champagne. Then she walked out onto the balcony with her glass, sat down and waited for all hell to break loose.

There was still no reaction to what she'd done. The Jamaican was nodding in time to the Walkman's lonely concert, eyes half-closed. The shell seekers and jogger were long gone, and the teenaged girls had packed it in. That left the woman who'd been in the Jacuzzi, who was shuffling toward the elevators, the kids and their mom. The kids were still there, splashing in the pool even as their mom stood over them, holding towels, pleading with them to get out. A minute went by. Then five. The sun was below the horizon now, so that there were only a few faint streaks of red left in the sky. Finally, as if he'd just realized that the night was almost upon them, the Jamaican removed the headphones from his ears, grasped the back of the wheelchair and, slowly, began to push the old man up the boardwalk, never noticing that his charge was dead.

But when they reached the pool, the kids saw it. And Nico saw what they saw: the old man, lifeless beyond sleep, slumped in his chair with whitewashed eyes. And the bloom on his chest where the bullet had tumbled out into his lap, tearing a hole in his shawl.

One of the little girls began to scream, and her mother admonished her, thinking the kids were fighting. Standing at the edge of the balcony, sipping her champagne, Nico could hear the woman, warning her daughter: "That's it, Jessie, that's really *it*, that's the last time—"

Then her voice evaporated, the wind died, and a frightened whoop cut through the air. Then a second whoop, as if someone were gathering the strength to scream. And, finally, the scream itself, cutting through the night.

Leaving the balcony, Nico stepped inside and picked up the remote. Turning on the TV, she sat down on the couch and surfed among the channels until she found her favorite show. Channel 67. MTV. *The Real World.*

An ambulance and three police cars arrived about ten minutes later, sirens blaring. A TV camera crew came soon after that, running through the lobby to the terrace, where they got some good shots of the bloodstained wheelchair, the old man being taken away on a gurney, and the Jamaican nursemaid, sitting in a deck chair with his face in his hands. Nearby, a dozen guests stood with tropical drinks in their hands, whispering among themselves and frowning.

More than an hour went by before a policeman knocked on Nico's door to ask if she'd seen or heard anything unusual. She told him that she hadn't, and asked what the commotion was all about.

"A man was shot," the policeman told her. "Down on the boardwalk."

"You're kidding!"

"No."

"But I didn't hear anything—I mean, not until the ambulance came."

"Nobody did," the policeman said. "Not so far, anyway."

"But he'll be all right, won't he? The man who was shot?" The cop shook his head.

"You mean, he's *dead*?" she asked.

"I'm afraid so," the policeman said. "Murdered. You might even say 'gunned down.' "

"*Here?* That's horrible!"

The policeman snorted, as if she'd told a joke. " 'Horrible' ain't the half of it."

"What do you mean?"

The policeman looked embarrassed. "I shouldn't say, but . . . it's stupid."

"What is?"

"Shooting that guy."

"Why?"

"Guy's name is Crane. He's eighty-two years old. Cancer patient. Everybody knows him. Real prominent guy."

"So?"

"So his nurse says, he's got about six months to live when he's shot. Maybe a year if he's real lucky. I mean—" The cop shook his head with a rueful chuckle. "What's the point?"

2 Talk about "flying"—she had so much energy! And not just today. It was the same way as the day before, and the day before that. Basically, ever since she'd gotten back from—wherever.

Florida! She'd been in Florida.

This morning, she'd gotten up at five (it was impossible to sleep when she was like this), reorganized the kitchen cabinets and defrosted the refrigerator. She'd cleaned the oven after that, and washed and waxed the floors. Going into the bathroom, she'd emptied the medicine cabinet with a couple of sweeps of her hand, dumping its contents in a shopping bag. Then she'd cleaned the mirror and the shelves, thinking, *I don't need any of it, anymore. Not the Vicks, not the lithium, not the aspirin.* This was the new Nico, clean and clear and energetic as an Evian waterfall.

Today was her day to see Duran.

His office was in Cleveland Park. To get there from Georgetown, she had to walk down M Street to the Key Bridge, cross the Potomac to Rosslyn, and take the Metro. It was a hike, but seeing Duran was about as optional as breathing. It wasn't like the lithium. It was really important, so important that it never occurred to her not to go. Duran was her anchor, shrink and exorcist, all in one. He brought her face-to-face with the demons that bedeviled her and, with his help, she'd drive them out. He'd make her well. He'd promised.

Entering the subway, she was struck by the smell that floated up the stairs, a mixture of the cave and the vacuum cleaner. This was the underground scent that darkness gave off, the perfume of hidden places. Subways, tunnels, basements. The root cellar in South Carolina. Shenandoah Caverns in Virginia—where the whole family went once on vacation, and Adrienne got yelled at for touching a stalagmite. She could still remember the guard's snotty voice: *It takes tens of thousands of years for a stalagmite to grow a quarter-inch and some selfish people just cannot keep their hands off. Please respect nature's majesty! Thank you.*

That underground smell was the subway's olfactory background, like the bass line in music or the set on a sitcom. But there were brighter aromas, too. Coffee, sweat, tobacco, dust. A whiff of urine, a flash of perfume—or was it hair spray?

And the ride! The ride was a massage that left her almost dreamy. She liked the sound of it, the rush of air, the rhythmic sway of the segmented train hurtling through the tunnel. She liked the way her body felt as it made a series of intricate adjustments, compensating for every change in velocity and direction, reacting instantly to Newtonian forces that were as real as they were unseen.

When the train got to Cleveland Park, she took the escalator up to the street, where the Juice Man was waiting, three doors down. As she always did, she bought a papaya smoothie and sucked it down so fast that it gave her an ice-cream headache. Even that was okay, though, because when her brain unclenched from the freeze, there was a moment— there was always a moment—when her mind felt so *clean*. It was worth the pain, almost, to feel it, that sweet blur of relief.

Once, she'd asked Adrienne if she had the same reaction— if she knew what she meant, but . . . no. Of course she didn't. Her sister just got this weird, worried look, and made a joke of it.

Unlike Duran.

Who understood her—

To a *T.*

His building was a block north of the Metro stop, on the east side of Connecticut. It was a nice neighborhood (if you didn't mind the constant surf of traffic). Moms pushed strollers past the firehouse. Joggers zigzagged down the sidewalk, sidestepping businessmen on their way to lunch. Outside Starbucks, a young couple did their best to ignore a schizophrenic black man, wheedling for change.

And then there were the old people.

They sat on the benches in front of Ivy's Indo-Thai place, feeding the pigeons. One of them was there every week. She recognized him by the fisherman's cap he wore, rain or shine. And by his hands, which were as big as dinner plates, but clumsy with arthritis, so that he fed the birds by tumbling popcorn at them from a brown paper bag.

Duran's building was an old one and, while everything worked, it worked on its own terms. Which meant, among other things, that when the intercom buzzed, it really *buzzed*—as if to announce that the apartment's occupant had gotten an important question dead wrong. But since no question had been posed, the noise was always unexpected, and sometimes startling—especially when, as now, Duran was watching television.

So when Nico buzzed, he jumped—and just as quickly, acted to compose himself. Took a deep breath, and blew it out. Then he pushed a button on the TV's remote and watched the image in front of him implode in a swirl of sparks. (The sparks were what was left of Oprah, who'd been leaning forward to refine a question.)

Closing the door to the bedroom, Duran walked toward the intercom, knowing it was Nico, but knowing also that formalities had to be observed. He spoke into the metal grid.

"Yes?"

The reply came back an instant later, light and musical. "It's Nico—Nico, Nico, Nico!"

He could tell by her voice that she hadn't been taking her lithium. She was so full of herself, you could hear it in her tone. "You're right on time," Duran told her. "Come on up."

While he waited for her, he found himself wondering what Oprah had been about to ask when the intercom buzzed. The image of her face remained in his mind—lips pursed, head inclined, brow slightly furrowed. Eyes narrowed. The Look. The one she adopted when she was about to ask a really prying question. It was a look that combined mischief with apology, inviting the person before her to enter into a kind of conspiracy. *These questions—your answers—our pact. If I dare to ask, will you dare to answer?* It was a brilliant look, much better than Barbara Walters's po-faced ooze of sympathetic understanding, or Diane Sawyer's wincing compassion.

He waited for Nico beside the door, imagining the change in air pressure when he heard the elevator doors open with a swoosh on the sixth floor. And then he heard her footsteps on the tiles in the hall, a soft *click-click-click* that grew louder and louder until, suddenly, there was nothing. And then the doorbell rang, a single note, clear and round, as if from a xylophone. It reminded him of the public address system in department stores like Macy's and Saks.

Not that he went to department stores—or not often, anyway.

Duran opened the door at the sound of the bell and, as he did, Nico stepped back, a little surprised by the absence of any delay.

"Nico!"

"Oooh!" she exclaimed. "God, Doc, you made me jump!" Then she smiled. Relaxed. And came in.

"You're looking great," Duran told her, closing the door behind them. "Tanned and healthy. Though I guess 'pale and healthy' is the new paradigm." He paused for a moment, and looked her up and down, trying not to be sexist about it—an impossible task, under the circumstances (the "circumstances" being high heels and a pink tube skirt about the size of a handkerchief.) "Where have you been?"

She shrugged. "Just the beach."

"No kidding. Which one?"

She shook her head. "One of the beaches. I forget what they call it."

Together, they walked through the living room to his office. "Is that new?" she asked. Paused and pointed.

Duran followed her eyes to a bloodred Kirman that lay on the floor in front of the fireplace. Then he nodded. "Yeah," he said. "I just got it."

"You've been *shopping*?"

Duran smiled ruefully, and shook his head. "It's from a catalog."

"I thought so. You know, you ought to get out more, Doc. You're pale as a ghost."

Duran shrugged. "I don't have time. And, anyway, it's like I said—a new paradigm."

The "office" was a lot like the living room, but with recessed lighting and windows hung with heavy drapes. Neutral colors dominated—the walls a buttery cream, the furniture slipcovered in beige linen. Watercolor landscapes hung from the walls in tortoiseshell frames.

And so did Duran's credentials. Like the oversized furniture and kilim-covered pillows on the couch, his bona fides were there to reassure his clients. There was a Bachelor's degree from Brown, and a doctoral degree in Clinical Psychology from the University of Wisconsin. Flanking the diplomas were certificates from the American Board of Psychological Hypnosis and the Society of Cognitive Therapists.

"Why don't you make yourself comfortable?" Duran asked, as he sat down behind the desk. "I want to take a look at my notes—and we can start the tape."

"Do we *have* to tape?" Nico complained, tipping off her shoes as she flopped down on the couch.

"Yeah," Duran said with a chuckle. "We have to. We really do." Inserting a cassette in the tape recorder, he hit the *Record* button and, turning to his computer, began to type. "It's not my idea, y'know—it's the insurance company's."

"*I'm* not going to sue you, Doc."

"Riii-ight," Duran replied. "That's what they all say."

* * *

He had her in a light trance, reclining on her back with her limbs slack, eyes shut, expression neutral. Duran took her through the usual imagery-progression, his deep and soothing voice guiding her into and through an imaginary landscape.

"You're on a soft, dirt path beside a cool stream, and you pause for a bit to listen to the water splashing over the rocks," he said. "You see a leaf, caught on the surface of the water— it's like a tiny ship—and you follow its progress as it sails downstream, caught for an instant against a rock, and then spinning free into the current. You watch it until it disappears around a bend and then look at the water—its miraculous texture, so smooth and silky as it rolls over the pebbles of the streambed."

Nico frowned momentarily as he led her away from the stream, and winced slightly as she followed his instruction to crouch and duck under some "spiky" branches. Her brow furrowed with effort as she made her way through the "dense" vegetation. And then her faint and blissful smile returned as she crossed a meadow on a path that was "soft and spongy" under her feet.

"There's a light breeze on your cheeks. It lifts your hair and bends the grass . . ."

As she was told, she opened a small white gate and walked down several flights of lichen-covered steps, descending through a dappled shade to a secluded pool. There, she sat on a fallen trunk of a moss-encrusted oak, watching the sunlight "sift through the trees and dance on the water." Nico's left hand rolled over the side of the couch, trailing against the rug, dipping into the cool water.

She was in her "safe place," where nothing and no one could hurt her. Duran watched her chest rise and fall as he began to regress her. "Let's go back," he said. "To when you were a girl."

"I *am* a girl."

"A *little* girl. Twelve ... eleven ... ten. Do you remember?"

She shifted uncomfortably on the couch, and nodded. Duran was a few feet away, leaning forward in a wing chair, amazed at the way her face had changed, the wised-up and guarded neutrality giving way to a look of sweet and energetic innocence. She was a child again, and even her voice was childlike.

"Where are we?" he asked.

"South Carolina."

"At your foster parents'?"

"Umm-hmmm. In our house. It's a big white house, way out in the boonies."

"Tell me about it."

"*You* know."

"Tell me again."

Her brow furrowed. "It has columns. Big old white columns. Like rich people. Only the paint's all peeling and you can see they're not really solid—just slats of wood, glued together. And now they're coming apart. So maybe—maybe it's going to fall down."

"What is?" Duran asked.

"The porch."

"Okay ... what else?"

"Trees."

"What trees?"

"There are *trees*. Live oaks. The house is at the end of a little road—"

"A long driveway," he corrected.

" 'A long driveway,' with life oaks on both sides."

"*Live* oaks," he corrected.

"Right. That's what they call them—except they don't really look alive. They look old and dead. And everybody thinks they're wonderful. Except me."

"You don't like them?"

"No. I'm scared of them!"

"Why?"

"Because . . ."

"Because of what?"

"They're creepy."

" 'Creepy'? What do you mean, they're creepy?"

"On account of the cobwebs."

"You mean the Spanish moss," Duran told her.

"Unh-huh."

"And what else?" he asked.

Nico's brows furrowed as she thought about it. Finally, she shook her head.

"Didn't Deck do something with the moss?" Duran asked.

Once again, she shifted on the couch. After a moment, she nodded. "Mmmm-hmmm."

"What did he do?"

She turned her head toward the cushions. "He put it in his hair on the shadow-nights."

Duran nodded. " 'And it was like'—what was it like?"

"Cobwebs."

He leaned closer to her. "Tell me about Deck," he said.

"I don't *like* Deck," she exclaimed. Suddenly, her eyes flew open, and she started to sit up. "But—you can't *tell* him!"

"I won't."

"Promise!"

"I will. I do. Now, lay back. Close your eyes. You're safe here." Duran could see that she was beginning to hyperventilate. "It's just you and me, and the wind and the stream and . . . Okay?"

She nodded.

After a while, he returned to the subject. "Why don't you like Deck?"

She was silent for upwards of a minute, her chest rising and falling. Duran waited patiently for the answer, his eyes on her lips. Finally, she blurted out the words: "Because of what he does!"

"And what's that?"

Nico squirmed. "He pretends we're going to church with our friends, but it isn't a church that we go to—it's just a tunnel under the basement—"

"And what happens there?"

Nico's body became very still. Then she shook her head.

"Didn't you make movies, sometimes?"

She nodded.

"Tell me about the movies," Duran said.

Nico frowned, then rolled over onto her side, so that she was facing away from Duran, with her eyes on the back of the couch. "I can't," she said.

"You can't?"

She shook her head.

"Why not?" Duran asked.

"Because I just can't."

"You can't remember *any* of them?"

Once again, she shook her head.

"But . . . I remember one," Duran told her. "Wasn't there one where . . . where you got married?"

Reluctantly, Nico nodded and, as she did, Duran saw her stubbornness dissolve into a mix of apprehension and unhappiness.

"So let's go back to that," Duran suggested. "The wedding. Tell me about the wedding."

And so she did. Under Duran's guidance, Nico recounted her older sister's death in a pornographic film that starred the two of them, with a younger sister playing a supportive role. This was territory that Nico and Duran had visited often. It was the heart of the matter for Nico, and coming to grips with it was vital.

"I'm all in white," she said breathlessly. "Dressed as a bride with a long train, and a bouquet of flowers."

"What kind of flowers?"

"Baby's breath and red roses," she answered without hesitation. "And ferns. Rosanna is the groom—which is silly, because she's a girl."

"What's she wearing?" Duran asked.

"A black tuxedo with a red carnation. She looks so beautiful! Adrienne is the ring bearer."

"And how is Adrienne dressed?"

"She's *not* dressed. She has a garland of flowers in her hair, that's all."

"And you walk down some kind of aisle?"

"Ummmhmmmn."

"Are there candles?"

"Yes. Candles and chanting. And then the minister stands before us, asking, 'Do you take this man . . . ?' " Her voice faded, and she seemed to lose concentration.

Duran prompted her. "The minister asks, 'Do you take this man'—and then what? As I recall, that was your cue—"

"Right," Nico said.

"That was your cue to—what?"

"Kneel down."

"And?"

"Open my mouth."

Nico's discomfort was palpable now, and Duran was worried that the discomfort would devolve into hysteria, as it had on some earlier occasions. So he changed tack. "Tell me about Rosanna," he said. "Who is she?"

"The groom."

Duran waved the answer away, as if it were a fruit fly. "Right. In the movie, she's the groom. But . . . who *was* she—really?"

"You mean, outside the movie?"

"Unh-huh."

"She was my sister. Rosanna was my big sister, and then there's Adrienne. Adrienne is my little sister."

"I see . . ."

"Because when I was ten, Adrienne was only five. So that meant I was *a lot* older!"

"You have two sisters, then."

Nico shook her head. "No," she said. "Just Adrienne. I don't have Rosanna anymore."

"Why not?"

"She died."

"Oh . . . I'm sorry," Duran told her, and fell silent for a moment. Then: "How?"

"How what?"

"How did she *die*?"

"She died in the movie!" Nico whispered.

"Ohhh, that's right," Duran said. "She died *in the movie*! But it was just a movie."

"Nunh-unh. It was real!"

"What was?"

"The movie!"

"How do you mean?"

"It was real! They pulled back her hair and—"

"Who?"

"A man."

"What man?"

"The man in the red hood. He was wearing a robe, and there was a hood on it."

"A robe?"

"*Everyone* was wearing a robe—except me. And Rosanna. Adrienne and Deck."

"What was Deck wearing?"

Nico frowned with childlike concentration. Finally, she said, "Straps."

"What?"

"He was supposed to be the priest—a really important priest! But he wasn't dressed like a priest."

"What was he dressed like?"

"I don't know," Nico said. "He was just wearing straps. Leather straps. And the cobwebs."

"Okay," Duran told her, "but . . . you said they pulled Rosanna's hair back."

Nico nodded. "Unh-huh."

"And . . . when this happened—where was she?"

"On the floor."

"What was she doing?"

"She was just . . . on her hands and knees."

"Why?"

"Because there was sex!"

"She was having sex?"

Another nod.

"With who?" Duran asked.

"Some men."

"But . . . wasn't she very young?"

Nico shrugged. "Twelve."

"Okay. She was having sex, and—then what?"

"I told you. The man in the red hood pulled her hair back . . ."

"And?"

"He cut her."

"Where did he cut her?" Duran asked.

She touched a finger to her throat. "There . . ."

"And then?"

Nico made a keening sound, and turned her face toward the cushions.

"Don't look away, Nico. You have to face it. Just tell me what happened."

"Rosanna's eyes got so big—she was so scared! Because the blood was *foaming* out of her, and she couldn't even say anything—she just made a noise—"

"And where were you when this was happening?"

"Under Deck."

"Okay, but . . . if it was just a movie—if it was just pretend—"

Nico shook her head, violently. "No," she insisted, pushing up on her elbows, her voice swelling with panic. "It *wasn't* 'just pretend.' It was real. It was *really* real! Deck kept the movie in a special box—with a lock. And, sometimes, he made me watch it with him, but—you couldn't see Rosanna anymore—except in the movie. Because Rosanna was gone. Rosanna died in the tunnel, the tunnel they said was a church . . ."

Duran tried to calm her, shushing softly. "Sshhhhhh . . . it's okay. You're here with *me*, now. Nothing bad is going to happen."

Slowly, the tension seeped out of her, and her head fell back on the cushions. Duran could see that she was exhausted.

Talking quietly, he guided her slowly out of the trance, retracing the steps they'd taken through the imaginary terrain that was so familiar to them both. The path. The stream. The trailhead.

"Take a deep breath," he told her. "The air is delicious. So sweet and crisp and cool."

Her chest rose and fell. And rose again.

"When I count to five," he said, "you'll wake up, and you'll feel relaxed and refreshed, okay?" Without waiting for a reply, he began to count: "One . . . two . . . three . . ."

Nico's eyes fluttered and opened, revealing dark, unfocused pupils that dwindled in the light. Duran handed her a Kleenex.

"You've done some really good work, Nico. I'm proud of you."

She blinked furiously at the light, until Duran came into focus. Then she swung her feet off the couch, sat up, and cleared her throat. Her face was flushed, but her eyes were shining and clear.

"So it was okay?" she asked.

He nodded. "Absolutely. And we'll talk again on Friday." With that, he helped her up, and showed her to the door, where she gave him a big smile, and a lingering kiss on the cheek.

"You really make my day, Doc."

"Yeah, well, that's why I'm here," he joked. Then he got serious. "There's one thing, though."

"What?"

"Your lithium—*take* it, Nico."

She rolled her eyes, and looked away.

"Promise me," he repeated.

Reluctantly, she nodded. "I hate it," she said. "It makes me feel dead."

"It keeps you grounded. And you need that. You want to be on a roller-coaster all the time?"

She shook her head.

"Then take your medication."

When the door closed behind her, Duran went back to his desk and typed a brief summary of the afternoon's session.

> *October 16. Sullivan, Nicole, 30*
>
> *Hypnotherapy and guided imagery continue to elicit classic allegations of Satanic Ritual Abuse (SRA), allegedly suffered as a child (8-10) in a South Carolina foster home. Sisters, Rosanna and Adrienne, similarly abused. Rosanna supposedly killed by foster father, Declan, while making pornographic film. Client's narrative includes occasional references to politically prominent persons and celebrities, implicating them in the activities of the cult.*
>
> *Episodes of manic-depression and compulsive behavior currently managed by medication (Lithium salts), though client continues to encourage the manic phase by skipping doses. . . .*

When he'd finished his summary, Duran attended to the tape recording that he'd made. Removing the cassette from the machine, he wrapped it in a length of bubble wrap, which he then secured with rubber bands. This done, he slid the package into a JetPak, and addressed it to the Mutual General Assurance Company in New York City.

Then he sat back in his chair. The nearest mailbox was a block away, a *long* block away, at the corner of Porter and Connecticut. He'd have to take the elevator down, and—

He didn't like to leave the building.

There it was. He didn't like to leave the building. But of course, he had to.

Package in hand, he went into the hallway and pressed the button for the elevator, thinking that the best thing to do was to think about something else.

Like SRA. (Talk about a mess . . .)

Nico's story was shocking, of course—but it was wholly unoriginal. If you read the literature, there were hundreds of accounts of "organized" child abuse. And almost all of them were the same—a lurid narrative that strained credulity to the breaking point.

The elevator arrived. The doors drew apart, and Duran stepped inside. Pressed 1. Began riding down.

Depending on the therapist you talked to, or the paper that you read, SRA was either a mass delusion or something less probable, but even worse—an epidemic set in motion by a demonic underground whose perversions centered upon, and were ignited by, the ritual murder of children.

The elevator doors opened, and Duran stepped into the lobby. Looking neither left nor right, but concentrating on the monologue inside his head, he took the revolving doors to the outside and strode briskly toward the mailbox on the corner. It was one of those cool and windy days that made it seem as if the whole world was air-conditioned. Overhead, the branches of trees rocked in the gusting air, even as the windows of storefronts rattled up and down the avenue.

He thought about the feminists—who had become entangled in the Satanic Ritual Abuse controversy. Many of them believed that denying the reality of SRA was the first step in disavowing more pedestrian forms of sexual abuse. Which made every skeptic an "enabler," or even worse, a collaborator in the sexual destruction of innocent women and children.

And yet . . .

If there really *was* a Satanic underground whose sacraments included human sacrifice, cannibalism, and pedophilia— where was the evidence? Where were the bodies, the bloodstains, the bones?

This had always seemed like a good question to Duran, but there were consequences to asking it aloud. For many, it was the sexual equivalent of denying the reality of the Holocaust. And, in fact, SRA *was* a kind of latterday holocaust—or so it was claimed.

He looked up at the wide-open sky and for a moment, thought that he was going to faint. The words in his head— *bloodstains, bones*—seemed disconnected.

Nico, he reminded himself. You are thinking about Nico. No matter what she told him, Duran kept a lid on his own feelings. No shock, no doubt. Just his own, helpful neutrality, his informed sympathy and concern. *Something* had happened to her, he told himself, and this story, this fable—if it was a fable—was her way of dealing with her own dysfunction, her own dissociation. She'd plucked it out of the culture, out of the air, and fixed on it as an explanation for her problems. Somehow, it helped her to function, and his job as her therapist—was to . . .

But he'd arrived at the mailbox. He slid the JetPak into the mail slot and turned around and began to walk home. At least he told himself to walk—just *walk*—but after a few steps, and almost imperceptibly, his pace began to increase so that, by the time he got back to the Towers, he was practically running. The security guard—today it was the kid with the Buddy Holly glasses—gave him a funny look as he came crashing into the lobby, but then the kid recognized him and lost interest. Duran managed a smile. A nonchalant salute. And then the elevator took him back to his sanctuary.

3 For a guy who didn't get out much, Jeff Duran was in very good shape.

This was owing, in part, to his determination to stay in shape, and in part to the fact that he lived in a building with a health club on the top floor. Since membership in the "club" came with residence in the Towers, the facility was undersized and not quite state-of-the-art. But it had all the basics, the treadmills and Nautilus, Stairmasters and free weights, and in addition boasted a terrific view of Georgetown and the National Cathedral.

Duran was there every morning at six-thirty. His body was well-muscled and flexible, and he kept it that way with a demanding regimen of stretches, cycling, jogging, and weights. His midsection was flat and hard, the result of a punishing routine of sit-ups and crunches. Five days a week, he ran six miles on one of the treadmills that stood in front of the windows, looking out across the city. From that vantage point, he could see Georgetown University's spires and, beyond it, the curling band of light that was the Potomac.

He always did the first mile at an eight-minute pace, warming up to the next five, which he covered in thirty-seven minutes. It was always the same. When he was done with his run, forty-five minutes had transpired (give or take a minute, here and there).

He could have run faster, but there were two reasons that he didn't. First, he'd reached the point of diminishing returns:

neither his VO-max nor his pulse rate would benefit from speeding up.

Second . . . Well, the second reason was idiosyncratic. It was, simply, that when the treadmill exceeded eight and a half miles an hour, it gave out a high-pitched whine that most people couldn't hear, but which Duran found extremely disagreeable. So he took it a little slower than he might have.

Today was like any other. He arrived at the club a little after dawn, stretched, jogged, and lifted without saying much of anything to anyone. Then he returned to his apartment, showered and shaved.

Standing before the mirror, drying his hair with a towel, he caught a glimpse of himself, and remembered Nico's remark of the day before: *You oughta get out more, Doc. You're pale as a ghost.*

And so he was. And so he *would* be—unless he overcame the peculiar phobia that was keeping him indoors. *You need a shrink,* Duran told himself, chuckling silently, but not with much conviction. He *was* pale. Not sickly looking, but white—*like a vampire in his prime,* he joked to himself.

Returning to his bedroom, Duran strapped his watch onto his wrist, and noticed the time. It was 8:35, which meant that he had less than half an hour to prepare for his meeting with the day's first client, Henrik de Groot. Dressing hurriedly, he strode into his office, sat down at the desk and turned on the computer.

Once the machine had booted up, he went into the caseload folder, and opened the file on the Dutchman.

At twenty-eight, de Groot was a successful and sophisticated businessman, commuting between the U.S. and Europe. His firm, one of the world's largest in the field, designed and installed fire suppression systems for hotels and office buildings, specializing, as De Groot put it, in "human occupied facilities." The company had pioneered a method of retrofitting halon-based systems in a way that minimized costs. ("Halon," de Groot explained, "is being phased out in the same way as freon and for the same reason: it's destroying the ozone.") Although Duran had not asked, the Dutchman had explained how "his" fire suppression system worked. When triggered by smoke or heat, a series of nozzles emitted inert gases which lowered the level of oxygen to a point where combustion became impossible—but not to the point that human beings suffocated.

Recently, de Groot's firm had signed a contract with a major hotel chain in the mid-Atlantic region. This was why Duran had the Dutchman as a client—de Groot had relocated to Washington so that he could oversee the work.

Handsome and powerfully built, Duran's client spoke four languages fluently and claimed to be "conversant" in Portuguese and Thai, as well. Duran didn't doubt him.

When de Groot wasn't working or visiting his therapist, he had one other passion: "trance music." When asked, the Dutchman described this with a disciple's enthusiasm. "It's synthesized stuff, you know—upbeat, fast 4/4 beat. It energizes you, you get lost in the sound, you dance and you go into another dimension. Your mind . . . kind of explodes." The Dutchman, jerking and spinning, had launched into an amazing imitation of a synthesizer playing a weird techno version of "Joshua Fit the Battle of Jericho."

"Wow."

De Groot had smiled. "It's great! You ought to try it, Doc." He'd named a couple of D.C. clubs. Duran had said he wasn't much of a dancer and then he'd warned de Groot against using any of the drugs common to the club scene. (Given the medications de Groot was on, recreational drug use would be a big mistake.)

But the image de Groot projected—that of a capable and cosmopolitan businessman, multilingual and hip—was an illusion. Or not an *illusion*, really, but a gloss upon something so dangerous that his other qualities dwindled into irrelevance. Public persona aside, the businessman was in the grip of "command hallucinations." Specifically, the Dutchman believed that "a worm" had taken residence in his heart and that, as his heart pumped, the worm whispered to him, counseling de Groot on all manner of things, from politics to finance.

In fact, de Groot exhibited most of the diagnostic criteria listed under paranoid schizophrenia in the *DSM-IV*, the maroon-jacketed tome that served as the shrink's bible.

Under the circumstances, there was only so much that Duran could do. The psychopharmacology was straightforward enough—Clozaril was the drug of choice—and it was prescribed by the Dutchman's psychiatrist in Europe, who communicated occasionally with Duran by e-mail. Using hypnosis and regression therapy, Duran's task was to uncover any trauma contributing to de Groot's dysfunction, and to help him confront it. Only then would he have any chance of a sustained recovery.

It was, in many ways, a curious case. Among other things, Duran found it interesting that the Dutchman interpreted his illness as a kind of possession—with the instrument of possession being a worm. That the worm was a demon, rather than a parasite, was self-evident even to de Groot: parasites didn't issue orders—incubae did.

At first, Duran had theorized that the worm was indicative of a multiple personality, with the Dutchman suffering from dissociation rather than schizophrenia. But, no. The Worm was an invader (in de Groot's eyes), and not an alter ego.

Another disturbing element in de Groot's personality was his overt racism. In an age of political correctness, it was startling to encounter someone who said the kind of things the Dutchman did. "I don't know how you live in this city with all these niggers." Duran was offended by comments like this and always and immediately objected; it was one of the things he and the Dutchman were working on, although so far they hadn't succeeded in discovering the roots of de Groot's bigotry. Holland had a small population of blacks—mostly Moluccans—but people of color did not seem to have played any significant role in his client's life. Duran shook his head, wondering how the Dutchman got by in the business world—particularly in D.C.—if he tossed off racist comments with any regularity.

Duran looked down at his notes and picked out a word that he'd underlined: *mandala*.

It was a term that figured prominently in de Groot's fantasy world, with the Dutchman insisting at every session that the mandala was evil, and had to be destroyed. Duran recalled that a mandala was some kind of geometric design but still, he'd looked up the term in hopes of parsing its significance for his client. But the encyclopedia wasn't very helpful. According to it, a mandala was (variously) a representation of the universe; a symbolic painting (consisting of a square, enclosed by a circle); and/or a field of power in constant flux. Buddhists used the figures for meditative purposes, but what they meant to de Groot was anyone's guess.

Two weeks earlier, he'd shown the Dutchman a collection of Tibetan mandalas that he'd found on the Internet. De Groot's reaction had been a soft shrug, and the polite remark, "How interesting . . ." The figures had not seemed to engage him at all.

What *was* interesting was what Duran had learned through his research—that visual hallucinations of mandalas were quite common in schizophrenics, who found in the rigid symmetries of the figures a kind of order and stability that did not exist elsewhere in their minds. Most schizophrenics found *solace* in mandalas whereas de Groot . . .

Bizzzzzzzzzzzzttt!

The intercom startled Duran, as it always did, but his client was right on time. Closing the folder, he got to his feet, went into the living room, and pressed the switch on the intercom. "Henrik?"

The Dutchman was almost as handsome as he was crazy. His hair was yellow, rather than blond, spiky and glistening, like the pelt of a wet animal. High cheekbones and the palest of blue eyes flared and glittered on either side of a long, straight nose. A deeply cleft chin completed the picture.

Or not quite. There was something else about de Groot's appearance that turned heads on the street. It was, for lack of a better term, an aura of athleticism—a nimbus of physical power and grace that his expensive business suits did nothing to conceal. And, somehow, that made his illness seem all the more tragic.

Henrik was humming to himself as he came in. It was the same tune the Dutchman always hummed and Duran had long ago discerned its melody: "Joshua Fit the Battle of Jericho." He'd inquired several times if the song had some special significance. Had de Groot, for instance, been especially religious? A churchgoer in his youth? That might have explained quite a bit, but de Groot denied it. "Church?" He'd frowned, pronouncing the word as if it were foreign to him and slightly distasteful. "No."

Escorting the Dutchman to the easy chair that he preferred to the couch, Duran put his client in a light trance, and softened him up with guided imagery. "We're sitting together on a rock," he said, "in a little harbor that no one else can see. There's just you and me, and the waves, and the birds. And a light wind that smells of the sea. It's our safe place, Henrik."

"Yes."

"And nothing can hurt you here. Nothing and no one."

De Groot nodded. "No one," he repeated.

"Now, I want you to tell about the Worm," Duran suggested. "Tell me about the Worm."

"The Worm is boss," de Groot mumbled.

"We know that, Henrik, but—how did you come by it?"

De Groot frowned, and shook his head. "This is not to be discussed."

"Of course it is," Duran replied. "That's why we're here. And, anyway, we've spoken of it before—many times."

"No . . . I think not."

"There was a light," Duran reminded him. "A bright light. Remember? You were driving. . . ."

The Dutchman's expression changed from a look of defensive certainty to apprehension. "No," he said, "not today."

Suddenly, he began to lean forward and sit up, as if he were about to get out of the chair.

Duran laid his fingertips on de Groot's wrist, restraining him with the softest touch. "It's okay, Henrik," he said. "You're with me. We're in the safe place."

His client sagged, and touching his tongue to his palate, made a soft *tsk*. "All right," he said. "I remember."

"What do you remember?"

"There was a light—on the road—"

Duran shook his head. "There was a light—in the *sky*."

"Yes . . . of course, *it was in the sky,* but . . . I was driving. I was on a farm road."

"In America?"

"Yes—here, in America!"

"Where?" Duran asked.

De Groot shrugged. "Watkins Glen."

"And then what?"

"The light was in the road," the Dutchman said, suddenly agitated. "It was all around me. So brilliant! And blinding— like a flash that doesn't go away. I can't see!"

"But you can, Henrik. You *can* see. I want you to see."

"It's absorbing me!" De Groot shuddered, his body flattening into the chair.

"What do you mean?"

"It's like a sponge. The light is like a sponge! I'm pulled into it."

"And what color is the light?"

De Groot shook his head, fiercely.

"Isn't it blue?" Duran asked. "Blueish?"

"Yes, *blue!* And I'm *bathed* in it. Inside and out. It passes through me—like a ghost."

"What do you mean, 'like a ghost'?"

"Like a ghost, moving through a wall."

"That's good, Henrik. That's very good. Now, I want you to do something courageous. I want you to remember what happens when the light goes through you. Can you do that?"

"No!"

"It's your safe place, Henrik. Remember that. You're *safe* here. Now, breathe in. Slowly. *Verrry* slowly. In . . . and out. In and . . . out. Again! In . . . and out. In . . . riiiight. That's it. Now, let your breath expand all the way to the surface of your skin. I want it to fill you up, so you can let it go." Duran watched the Dutchman breathe for a while. Then he prompted him. "Okay . . . when the light passes through you . . ."

"It takes me up. I go up in the light."

"What do you mean?" Duran asked.

"The light pulls me into it. It's like . . . like an elevator without walls, an escalator without stairs."

"And then what?"

"I'm in a room . . . in the sky."

"What kind of room?"

"Like . . . an auditorium."

"And what are you doing?"

"Nothing."

"Why not?"

"I can't move," the Dutchman said. "I'm turning in the air—"

"What?"

"I'm slowly . . . turning in the air."

"Why?"

"I'm on display . . . like a bug . . . in a case. A glass case."

"Are you alone?" Duran asked.

The Dutchman shook his head. "There are seats all around—and they go up, row after row."

"Are there people in the seats?" Duran asked.

De Groot shook his head. "I can't see. The light is so bright—they're just shapes." Suddenly, de Groot stiffened, and thrashed.

"What's the matter?" Duran asked.

De Groot answered through gritted teeth: "I am being interfered with."

Duran looked puzzled. "What do you mean?"

"I've told you! I am *interfered* with."

"How?"

"I am examined by . . . I don't know who . . . I don't know *what* they are."

"Doctors?"

"No!" de Groot shot back, his voice suddenly loud and scared. "Not doctors. *Figures!* Shapes. I don't want to look."

"Then . . . why don't you run away?" Duran asked.

"I can't move. The light won't *let* me move. It holds me in the air."

"And what are the shapes doing? What's happening?"

"They . . . insert instruments."

"Where?"

"In my nose. Mouth. Every *hole*." De Groot winced, and his eyes slammed shut.

"Yes?"

"It feels bad!"

"What does?"

"I'm not to remember," de Groot muttered. "For my own *welfare*. I am not to remember."

Duran pushed.

"It's all right to remember, Henrik." He laid a hand on his client's shoulder. "It is good to remember. But you have to relax. You have to breathe. Thaaaaat's it. Now, just concentrate on breathing. It's safe here. You're not in the light anymore: you're on a rock at the edge of the water. You can hear the waves lapping at the rock. There's a breeze. And seagulls wheeling overhead . . ." Duran let him think about this for a while, and then: "Now, let's go back to the other place, the place in the light. But don't be frightened—I'm with you. I want you to tell me about the instruments . . . what do they look like?"

"Tubes."

"And what are they made of?"

"Glass. Metal." Once again, de Groot shuddered.

"What's the matter?" Duran asked.

"They're cold. *So* cold . . . they stick to my skin—and they burn."

"And what are they doing with . . . the instruments?"

De Groot took a deep breath, and shuddered. "They put them in me."

"Where?"

"No."

"Henrik—it's for your own good."

"But you know!"

"Of course, I know—but you have to tell me."

De Groot shook his head.

"Where?" Duran insisted.

"My willy! My . . . arse."

"But why? Why are they doing that, Henrik? Do you know?"

The Dutchman nodded. "They're feeding the Worm," he said. Suddenly, de Groot whimpered, and his face clenched with a mixture of sadness and pain.

Duran glanced at his watch. To his surprise, he saw that fifty minutes had gone by. "Okay, Henrik, that's enough. That's enough for now."

He brought the Dutchman back to wakeful consciousness, disappointed that he was still unable to surface the trauma underlying de Groot's delusion. He needed to help de Groot *push through*, reversing the process of sublimation which had generated this absurd story of alien abduction (if, indeed, that is what it was). As things now stood, de Groot was being tortured by an event that his mind had encrypted, repressing the memory by transforming it into something else.

The Dutchman sat up, blinked and looked around. "What happened?" he asked, his voice thick with suspicion.

"You did great," Duran told him. Then he switched off the tape recorder, and got to his feet. "We made real progress."

To Duran's surprise, de Groot remained where he was, tapping his fingertips together, listening or thinking or both. Finally, he pushed himself to his feet, and smiled. "That's funny," he said. "I don't feel any better."

4 Nico lived in a two-bedroom apartment in The Watermill, a Georgetown condominium just below M Street, where the C&O Canal begins its journey out to the Maryland suburbs and beyond. The building was a modern and elegant one with decent security, a nice view of the Potomac, and capacious balconies brimming with plants.

That morning, she'd slept late, and by the time she'd climbed out of bed, Jack was practically crossing his legs. He reproached her with a series of stiff little barks as she quickly dressed, then ran a brush through her hair, using a scrunchie to corral it in an untidy ponytail. Finally, she grabbed a plastic grocery bag, stuffed it into her pocket and headed toward the elevator with Jack lurching ahead on his leash, scrabbling along the carpeted hallway.

"Mawnin' Miz Sullivan."

The doorman, Ramon, was an aspiring actor who tried out a different accent each week. His latest affectation was to mimic the speech and mannerisms of a southern butler, a not entirely successful undertaking that suggested an unlikely hybrid of Vivian Leigh and Antonio Banderas.

"Hey, Ramon!"

"And to you, too, Master Kerouac." The doorman leaned down to pet the dog, a Jack Russell terrier who rewarded Ramon's attention by launching himself in a series of impressive vertical leaps.

"Whoa," Nico said. "Take it easy, Jacko."

"Vigorous animal," Ramon remarked, still in his plantation accent.

Nico smiled. "He is, indeed. What's up?"

Ramon segued into himself. "Did I *tell* you, I got a part in the Scorsese movie, the one they're shooting in the District!"

"That's terrific. Congratulations!"

"Well, it's not *so* terrific. I mean, it's just a walk-on. But guess what the part is—I'm a *doorman*."

Nico wasn't sure what to say, so she said, "Heyyy!" Jack was straining at the leash, pulling her toward the door. "Congratulations are definitely in order."

"The thing is, I don't know whether to *take* it. I'm gonna miss three, maybe four days work. Probably, I get fired. So whatta you think, Neek? Should I do it?" He gave her a beseeching look.

"Jack!" she said. "Do you mind?" In point of fact, Jack had already settled down, sitting quietly between them. She wasn't sure what to say, and used the dog as a distraction to avoid the doorman's eyes. Should he risk his job for a bit part that might not even make the final cut? Ramon took his career as an actor very seriously, but the truth was, he didn't seem to be very good at it. So playing a doorman might not be a bad idea. Then again, was it worth giving up his real job so he could *pretend* to do the same thing on camera? Finally, she said: "Go for it."

"Really?"

"Definitely. I saw this whole thing on TV once, and this guy is saying, you know, you can't go wrong if you follow your bliss."

"My bliss? You mean, like, what makes me happy? Like acting?"

"Exactly."

Ramon winced. "I don't know. I like my job, too. The tips aren't bad, you know? And Christmas is coming—not too long now. Coupla months."

Nico shrugged. "Maybe you can get somebody to fill in—

make it worth their while. And, anyway, where are they going to find someone as reliable as you? What I think? You get someone to cover—they won't touch you."

"You think?"

"Yeah."

"Okayyy! So that's what I'm gonna do. I'm gonna follow my bliss."

"Now you've got it!"

He held the door open for them. "You think—I ask Victor, you think he'll cover for me?"

"Sure. He's a friend of yours, right?"

"Yeah, I guess . . ."

"Well, there you go . . ."

Once outside, Nico and Jack mounted the steps to the broad dirt path that ran beside the canal. Jack indulged in his complicated, almost frantic, ritual of sniffing and peeing, while Nico let her mind drift, eyes on the turbid water.

On the way back, she tied Jack up outside Dean & DeLuca's and went in to buy cheese and a baguette—and a single, perfect tomato. Returning a minute later with her little bag of groceries, she found a woman in a maroon suit talking to Jack, whose leash she'd tied to a parking meter.

"Heeza guh-boy," the woman mewed, "waiting for Mommy. Yes he izzzz. Whatta guh-boy." Suddenly, she straightened up, and looked sharply at Nico. "I hope you clean up after him."

"Oh," Nico said, taken aback. "I do. Absolutely." Stooping, she freed Jack from the parking meter, and headed back toward her apartment.

Inside, she set to work on a tomato and brie sandwich, lightly toasting slices of the baguette. Using an Appalachian bread knife that resembled a fiddler's bow, she began to cut paper-thin slices from her perfect tomato. And as she did, and much to her surprise, she found herself crying. She could feel the tears rolling down her cheeks, hot, wet, and senseless. It was almost as if she was slicing an onion instead of a tomato, because there were lots of tears—and they came from no-where, as irrelevant as snot because they had no emotional content. They were just . . . tears.

She wasn't sad. She wasn't unhappy. She wasn't . . . anything. It was the woman outside Dean & DeLuca's who'd brought it on, the one who was so friendly to Jack, and yet . . . people like that made your heart sink. *I hope you clean up after him!* she'd said, as if there was something wrong with *her*, something about Nico that was unclean or contemptible. You could see it in the woman's eyes, hear it in her suspicious tone.

When the sandwich was made, she went into the living room and sat down in front of the TV. Jack composed himself at her feet, waiting for her to eat, waiting for her to share—which she did, tearing off a part of the sandwich that was runny with cheese. She wasn't hungry anymore. Just . . . gray.

Pushing the sandwich away, she lay back on the rose-velvet sofa and flicked on the remote. Jack finished his little wedge of brie and, with a regretful glance at its source, jumped up beside her, curled into a ring and went to sleep. Idly, Nico scratched behind his ear as the morning bled into afternoon, talk shows giving way to soap operas and peculiar sports. *Oprah! One Life to Live. The BMX Challenge . . .*

It was odd the way these things came and went. One minute, she was on fire, the next—she didn't feel like doing anything. Wherever her energy had come from over the last few days, it was gone now. All she wanted to do, all she felt able to do, was lie there in front of the TV. And it really didn't matter what was on. *NASCAR. The Weather Channel. Seinfeld* reruns. It was depressing.

And tiring. And not just physically. The exhaustion she felt came as much from her heart as it did from her body. *I hope you clean up after him!* Why were people like that? It was enough to make you weep.

* * *

The sandwich was gone.

Jack must have eaten it—which was fine, because she'd been lying there on the couch for fifteen or twenty hours, gazing at the television, half-asleep, watching anything and everything, seeing nothing. And now, after all that rest, she was even more tired than when she'd first lain down. It was all she could do to sit up, and once she had, she regretted doing it because the back of her head was pounding.

Walking into the kitchen, she stood for a minute in front of the little espresso machine, rehearsing in her mind everything she'd have to do to make herself a cup of coffee. In the end, she gave up on the idea, and wandered out onto the balcony. It was a chilly day, and overcast, as if her mood had been projected on the world around her. Every once in a while, a gust of wind rattled the wrought iron rods on the balcony and the ferns thrashed. They looked a little peaked, and it occurred to her that she should give them some water and, maybe some plant food. Or bring them inside—it was almost time. But she didn't feel like doing that. She didn't feel like doing *chores*. She felt like—

Suddenly, the alarm went off on her wrist, reminding her to take her meds, and "call home." Crossing the room to the table that held her portable computer, she picked up the carrying case in which she kept her medication. Unzipping one of the side compartments, she found the little orange bottles she was looking for, but the one in which the lithium had been was empty. She'd forgotten to refill the prescription in . . . wherever the fuck she'd been when she was taking Placebo 1.

Somewhere hot. Sunny. Palm trees. California!

But why was she in California? To see someone. Find someone. But who? Why? She couldn't remember. Which was the whole trouble with Placebo 1. It really messed with your memory. Seating herself at the table, she opened the computer, and slid the *On* button forward. When the machine had gone through its routine, she sent the browser to the requisite URL, and waited for the page to load. Soon, the familiar words appeared:

Unknown Host
Description: Could not resolve the host

Removing the overlay from the carrying case, she began to affix it to the monitor—and hesitated. For a long while, she sat there in front of the computer, staring at the nearly empty screen. And then, impulsively and, somehow, defiantly, she switched the computer off, and stood up. Crossing the room to the hall closet, she grabbed her inline skates, and left the apartment with the vague idea of refilling her prescription. But when the time came, she glided past the pharmacy on M Street, and kept on going.

She didn't know it, but a part of her was coming to a decision, answering a question that Nico herself hadn't had the courage to ask, using a part of her mind that she would have sworn wasn't there. In her soul or subconscious, an argument was raging, and that argument was generating all the energy she needed to move faster than traffic, sweeping past Georgetown's chichi restaurants and slick bars, stores selling books and Japanese prints, artisanal toys and love potions.

She loved blading, the glide and grace of it, the way faces, trees and buildings slid by in a kind of montage, half glimpsed and never quite remembered. Somehow, this smooth ride took all the edges of the city away.

Approaching the Four Seasons Hotel, she swung south and descended into Rock Creek Park. There, she swept past the Kennedy Center, turned around, and went back the other way, moving like a speed skater with her right arm swinging in a rhythmic cadence. By the time she reached the old mill, just above Porter Street, the argument within her had come to an end, and the relief that it brought was palpable. *Enough,* she thought. *It's over.*

Reversing direction, she turned for home, elated by the prospect of a warm bath. *I'll use the rosemary bath gel,* she thought, imagining the spice and tang of it.

* * *

Her headache was gone.

While the bath filled, she telephoned Adrienne at home, knowing her sister would still be at work, and left a message on the machine.

"Hey 'A'," she said. "It's Nikki. I hope you haven't forgotten about dinner tonight—it's rainbow *importante* . . ."

The two of them dined together every other Tuesday, alternating venues—unless, as sometimes happened, one of them was really busy (as Adrienne had been of late) or under the weather (as Nico sometimes was).

Rainbow was a family code word, invented by Adrienne herself when she was a really little kid, maybe four or five, and persisting in conversation between the two of them to this day. Used as an adjective, the word added urgency or veracity or weight to anything it modified. (You like that guy— *rainbow* like? Yeah. I am *really* going to flunk that math test. *Rainbow* flunk? You bet. . . .)

She frowned. It wasn't enough. What if Adrienne came and knocked and . . .

She scribbled a note to her sister and took it downstairs. Ramon was out front helping Mrs. Parkhurst out of a taxi, so she just ducked behind the desk and stuck the note into the slot for her apartment. If Adrienne came, Ramon would look there. He was very responsible.

Back upstairs, she went out to the balcony and made a little fire in the *chiminea*. The sun was going down now, splashing the sky with a swirl of violet and orange that reminded her of a Gauguin. As she stuffed some twisted-up newspapers into the *chiminea*'s belly, she tried to remember *which* Gauguin, but couldn't. Atop the newspapers, she crisscrossed a few pieces of Georgia fatwood, and crowned it all with a length of piñon wood. Then she lit a match and watched her construction bloom into flame. *I'm practically a Boy Scout,* she told herself.

Returning inside, she checked the bath. It really did smell fabulous, and she saw with satisfaction that the froth of bubbles was deep and luxurious, and almost to the top. She turned off the water and stuck a finger in—*hot hot*, as Marlena used to say.

Then she left the bathroom.

Getting a step stool from the broom closet in the kitchen, she went into the bedroom and, with the help of the stool, retrieved an old scrapbook from its hiding place at the back of the closet's top shelf. Climbing down, she carried the book out to the balcony and, seating herself beside the crackling *chiminea*, opened it.

There were maybe a hundred snapshots in the album, each affixed to the page by little dabs of glue in the corners. They were family pictures, mostly, showing herself and Adrienne, Deck and Marlena, over a number of years. There was a picture on the first page of herself in a swing, hair flying, as Marlena pushed her from behind, her own face alight with laughter. In the background, a redbrick rancher.

Elsewhere on the same page—a snapshot of Adrienne at the free throw line, her eight-year-old face frowning in concentration; Deck, standing beside the barbeque in the backyard, a spatula in one hand, a Bud in the other; Nico and Adrienne at the beach, building sand castles; Adrienne, putting the finishing touches on a gingerbread house; Nico sitting next to Deck, with her arms around the pumpkin that she'd carved; and so on. There was even a photo of Nico in her prom dress, just before she went to Europe and all hell broke loose.

If you judged the family by the album, it was very nearly perfect, and about as wholesome as a Minnesota spring. But Nico saw what was not in the album as well as the people who were. And what was missing was the nightmare, manifest in the absence of Rosanna—whose face she couldn't even recall.

There were no pictures of her older sister, not a one. It was as if she'd never existed. Which meant that the album in Nico's hands was a part of the deception. Forget what had happened to *her*. She, at least, was alive. At least *she* had a past. But her sister—her sister didn't even exist as a memory. First, she'd been slaughtered, and then she'd been erased—

like a Moscow apparatchik whose existence was suddenly, terminally inconvenient.

Nico removed the photo of herself and Marlena at the swing, and turned it over. Written on the back in her foster mother's spidery hand were the words:

Swingin' with my honey!
July 4, 1980
Denton, Del.

Even that was a lie, Nico thought. The ranch style house in the background was nothing like the peeling and dilapidated mansion she'd known in South Carolina. Had she ever even *been* to Delaware? She didn't think so.

Crumpling the picture in half, she laid it on the fire in the *chiminea*, then watched the paper flatten, even as the faces faded to black. Finally, the snapshot flared into flame, and sparks snapped from its surface, swirling into the chimney above it. One by one, Nico fed the fire with pictures from the album until, in the end, the only photos left were of herself and her surviving sister. Then she got to her feet, blinking the tears from her eyes. And as much to the walls as to herself, she muttered, "Ding dong, the witch is dead."

It was almost dark now, or as dark as it got in D.C., the winking lights of planes standing in for the myriad, invisible stars. She got a wire whisk from the kitchen and when the fire had subsided to a smolder, smashed up the ashes.

This done, she went into the living room and removed an envelope from the top drawer of her desk. Written more than a month before, it had lain out of sight until the time was right—and that was now. Going into the kitchen, she glanced around for a place to leave it, and finally settled on the refrigerator. Clearing the door of everything on its surface—cartoons and take-out menus, a recipe for chicken sate and a picture of Jack—she tossed it all in the trash. Then she centered the envelope to Adrienne, and affixed it to the door with a magnet shaped like a tiny bottle of Tanqueray gin. She looked at her watch. Six-thirty. There was still more than an hour before Adrienne was due, so there was no hurry.

Standing at the kitchen counter, she poured herself a cold glass of Russian River Chardonnay, and put on a Miles Davis CD. *Sketches of Spain.*

Sipping the wine, she felt a shiver run through her as she walked into the bathroom. All that time on the balcony, sorting through the album had given her a chill. Removing the space heater from the linen closet next to the bath, she plugged it in and set it on the ledge that encased the tub.

Flicking on the heater, she luxuriated for a moment in its bright and sudden warmth, then undressed slowly, tossing her clothes into the hamper. Standing there in the nude, she took a sip of wine, and, swaying slightly, gave herself over to the viscous, haunting slur of the trumpet, as Miles soared through "Concerto de Aranjuez." Finally, she stepped into the water and, ever so slowly, eased herself into the cloud of bubbles that lay on its surface.

The water was perfect. So hot she could just barely tolerate it. So hot, the warmth seemed to suffuse her. So hot it was just at the perfect intersection of pleasure and pain—in other words, just over the pleasure edge. She thought about that phrase—the pleasure edge—and smiled as she continued her glacial slide into the water. She could hear the tiny explosions of the bubbles, collapsing under the pressure of her back. She could feel them in the hair at the nape of her neck.

Languidly, she sipped her wine and watched the coils of the space heater turn a deeper and deeper shade of orange. Then Miles hit a note so heartbreakingly pure that it brought a film of moisture to her eyes—and gently, almost tenderly, she extended her foot, and tipped the heater in.

5 Duran's apartment complex, the Capitol Towers, included an underground shopping center that made it more or less unnecessary for anyone who lived in the building to ever leave home. There was a supermarket, a drug store, a dry cleaners, a newsstand, and a travel agency, as well as a Starbucks. Each Sunday, an ad in the *Washington Post* featured a photo of the building above a cutline that read: "Capitol Towers—the Convenience of a Village in a Sophisticated Urban Setting!"

Returning upstairs from the underground Safeway, Duran hefted three plastic bags of groceries with his left hand, while he struggled to open the door to his apartment with his right. Finally, the door swung open and, as soon as it did, he knew the telephone was about to ring.

It was a trick of his. Or something.

For whatever reason, he was peculiarly attuned to the pitches and hums of machines—the whir and chink of the icemaker, the somnolent hum of the air conditioner, the gush and gurgle of water in the dishwasher. Any change in the acoustics of his appliances, no matter how subtle, struck him immediately, the malfunction as apparent as a burglar's sneeze at midnight.

It wasn't a particularly useful trait, and he didn't know how he'd acquired it. But that it was real was certain. Kicking the door closed behind him, he sensed a kind of tension in the room as soon as he entered it. For a moment, he stood there, frozen, just inside the doorway, listening to the air. Then, he stepped toward the phone.

And it rang.

It was uncanny, and unquantifiable. If anything, it suggested that he was more in tune with his appliances, with refrigerators and phones, than he was with people—an unfortunate characteristic in a therapist. Still, he thought, reaching for the receiver, there was no mistaking a room in which the telephone was about to ring. The air trembled with expectation, like an auditorium on the brink of thunderous applause.

"Hello!"

"Jeff?"

He didn't recognize the voice. And the question—no one really called him that. He was always *Duran*, or *Doctor Duran*.

"*Hel-lo-oh?* Anyone there?"

"Yeah! Sorry, I—this is Jeff."

"Well, hi-iii! It's Bunny Kaufman Winkleman? I'm so glad I got you! Mostly, I get machines."

"Really . . ."

"Almost always, but . . . I didn't really know you? At Sidwell? We were in the same class. Not English or anything, but—the class of '87? I was just plain Bunny Kaufman then." She paused, then hurried on. "You must have been one of those quiet guys."

Duran thought about it. Had he been? Maybe. And Bunny? Who was *she*? A face didn't come to mind—but then he hadn't kept in touch. High school was ancient history. "Yeah, I guess," Duran replied. "So . . . what's up? What can I do for you, Bunny?"

"Two things. You can promise me you'll respond to the query I'm sending. You know, one of those 'where-are-they-now' things?"

"Okay."

"And the second thing is: you could come to the reunion. Reunion *avec* homecoming, you know. You got the alumni newsletter, right? I'm calling to remind you—we need every *body* we can get."

"Well . . ." He picked up a matchbook—de Groot had left his cigarettes behind at their last session—and rotated it through his fingers. The matchbook was embossed with concentric silver and black circles. An eye stared out at him from the center of the design. He flipped the matchbook over. The back showed the same concentric silver and black circles but instead of the eye, the center held the words:

> *trance klub*
> *davos platz*

He opened the cover to see that the matches inside were European, made of thin flexible wood instead of paper, with bright green tips.

"Jehh-eff?" said the voice on the telephone. "You still there?"

Pay attention. "Absolutely."

"Well how about it?" Bunny said in her wheedling voice. "Come *on*. Just *do* it! *Come.* It isn't just *our* class—there are two others. And there's a sort of competition to see who has the best turn out. It's dumb, but—can I count on you?"

"I'll try."

"Well, I guess I'll have to *settle* for that. 'I'll try' is better than 'I'll think about it' (which, as we all know, means, 'No way.') So, *put it on your calendar,* okay?"

"Will do."

"October 23rd."

"Got it."

"Great. And, Jeff?"

"Yeah?"

"If you *can't* come to the reunion? I *will not* understand!"

When they'd hung up, he repeated her name aloud, turning it over in his mind as he put away the groceries, half expecting a face to well up in his memory. But there was nothing. Not an image or an anecdote.

High school was a long time ago, he reflected, putting the lemons into the vegetable bin. Even so: his class was only a hundred strong, half boys, half girls. So you'd think he'd remember *something* about her.

He emptied the ground coffee into the Starbucks canister and pushed his thumb down on the metal clip to close it. Bunny Kaufman. When he shut his eyes and thought about it, he imagined a short, blond, featureless girl. And that was it. It was odd, in a way. After four years of classes and games, track meets and banquets, science fairs, dances, and field trips—the best he could do was 'short and blond'?

It was depressing. And the more he thought about it, the more he realized how little he remembered about school. Almost nothing, really. A couple of names and faces. The headmaster, Andrew Pierce Vaughn, his jovial face frozen in laughter. The front of the school. Commencement in the garden behind Zartman House. But of the friends he'd had, and the teachers . . . there was nothing.

It was a little unsettling, actually. Enough so that, even though it wasn't at all his kind of thing, he wrote the date on a Post-it and stuck it to his computer monitor: *Sidwell reunion: Sat. Oct. 23.* What the hell . . .

His four P.M. appointment with Nico came and went—without her. He thought about calling, but decided against it. The responsibility for maintaining the connection between them had to be hers, or the relationship wouldn't work. Like many children who'd been orphaned at a young age, Nico had a long history of dependence, of seeking parental surrogates who would care for her. As an adult, she needed to take responsibility for her own life, rather than relying on authority figures. Otherwise, she'd fall into new patterns of abuse, confusing sex with love, debasement with penance.

So. When she didn't show up, Duran wondered about it—but he didn't call. Autonomy was important for Nico and he'd made a point of establishing from the very start that she, and she alone, was responsible for getting well. He could help her. But he was not her father, her husband, or her caretaker.

And so he watched Ricki Lake until it became time for dinner. Going into the kitchen, he glanced around with a sense of hopelessness. The room was well outfitted, with pine cabinets and tumbled marble countertops, a magnetized bar holding a dozen sharp knives, and a queue of food processors and other appliances. But cooking wasn't something that he did—or, at least, he didn't do it much. Most of the time, he just ordered out.

There was a small CD player on the counter, and he peered through its glass top to see what it held. Cowboy Junkies. He forwarded to the fifth song, pressed *Play*, and flipped through a sheaf of take-out menus as the singer lamented that she'd

> *"rather smoke, and listen to Coltrane,*
> *than go through all that shit again . . ."*

He could order Thai food—that would be okay. But only if he had some beer and, preferably, Singha. Pulling open the door to the refrigerator, he glanced from shelf to shelf. There was Perrier, milk and Coca Cola, and a bottle of Pinot Grigio, but no beer.

He looked at his watch and frowned. He'd just been shopping. Why hadn't he remembered beer? It was a little after seven, which meant that the Safeway in the basement was closed, and that if he wanted beer, he'd have to walk to the 7-Eleven. The thought made him queasy, as if in the corner of his eye he'd seen something skitter under the couch. Something dark and fast. A toxic sensation passed through him like a chill.

With a sigh, he removed the Pinot Grigio from the refrigerator, pulled the cork, and poured himself a glass. Then he pushed the button on the telephone that automatically dialed Chiang Mai Garden. He gave his order, and the man on the other end converted it.

"One numbah foh, one numbah twenny-two. Very good. Fifteen minute!"

He tried to tell himself that wine was just as good with Thai food as beer. But the truth was, it wasn't. As good as the Pinot Grigio was, he could almost *taste* the cold, hoppy beer that he longed for.

It was only three blocks to the 7-Eleven. He ought to go, but . . . *This is ridiculous,* he thought. Sitting down at the kitchen table, he sipped his wine and shook his head.

Had he always been like this?

No. At least, he didn't think so.

Since when, then? When had it begun?

He ministered to people with cognitive problems so he knew his own symptoms well enough. According to the *DSM-IV,* he suffered from agoraphobia. Or to be exact, because agoraphobia itself was not codable, he suffered from the malady listed in the *DSM-IV* as 300.27: *Agoraphobia with panic disorder. Situations are avoided or endured with marked distress.*

In its most debilitating form, agoraphobes were prisoners of their fears, unable to venture out of their homes. Duran's malady was less severe. If the need was great enough, he could resist it. He could go out, and he did. But less and less frequently, it seemed, and never with much enjoyment. In point of fact, if he were not living and working in an "urban village" like the Capitol Towers, the phobia might have been crippling.

So it worried him. And not just the phobia, but the way he was handling it. In essence, he was ignoring the problem because it made him uncomfortable to think about it—which was ironic, given his profession. Indeed, it made him wonder if he was even functional. Could a therapist live an unexamined life, and still help others? Did he have any business dealing with patients as disturbed as Nico and de Groot? He drained the wine and poured himself another glass.

A voice in the back of his head whispered, *Therapist, heal thyself.* And a second voice replied, *Later . . .*

6 Nico's sister, Adrienne, had made a pact with the Devil. It was as simple as that.

Having graduated from Georgetown Law the year before, she'd made a Faustian bargain with Slough, Hawley, in the interests of paying down a mountain of student debt. In return for a whopping salary and the inside-rail on what everyone said was "the fast track," Adrienne was expected to work eighty-hour weeks, doing mostly shitwork, in what amounted to a two-year bootcamp for baby lawyers. If, at the end of this period, she was still "viable"—which is to say, neither burned out nor canned—she'd be named an associate. Whereupon, things would get a lot easier, or if not easier, at least more interesting.

For now, however, life was hell. That was the deal.

At the moment, she was working on a memo for Himself. This was Curtis Slough, the name partner who was supposed to be her mentor, and the only one for whom she actually did any work. The client was Amalgamated Paving, a Maryland-based company in the business of building parking lots and roads.

Four years earlier, Amalgamated had been sued by the District of Columbia, which contended that its work on the 14th Street Bridge had been shoddy. Specifically, the pavement had begun to crumble only six months into a projected, ten-year life span. Large and dangerous potholes had opened up, causing accidents and letters to the editor. Litigation was inevitable.

When the District filed suit against Amalgamated, Slough, Hawley countered on behalf of the beleaguered paver by filing a continuum of hopeful motions. Each of these was accompanied by a memorandum of law in which it was argued that the facts did not entitle the plaintiff to relief. That the roadway had crumbled was not at issue; it was a mess. But it was not (necessarily) Amalgamated's mess. In the considered view of Slough, Hawley the fault rested not with their client, but with the subcontractors and suppliers whose work and materials had been inferior. Or, if that could not be shown, then the fault might be attributed to an Act of God, i.e., to the weather (which everyone agreed had been harsh and bizarre), and/or to an unexpected increase in traffic. Finally, it was suggested that the blame might be ascribed to the salt used by the District's road crews—an unusually corrosive formula whose impurities ate into the asphalt's binder and destroyed "the integrity of the road." That, in short, was the firm's position: one of the above.

Which is to say, they hoped to settle. But after four years of legal maneuvering, the District's attorneys had yet to budge—and the judge had had enough. A court date had been assigned. There would be no further delays.

Panic had ensued.

And so it fell to Adrienne to assist the firm's namesake, Curtis Slough. She'd spent two weeks assembling a document database, spending day and night with a team of paralegals, poring over thousands of documents: memos, reports, correspondence, receipts, and invoices. It was mind-numbing work. Each piece of paper had to be read and categorized, after which it could be stamped with a number and logged in.

Now, they were in the last stages of discovery, and quarreling over which documents should be released to opposing counsel. Some materials were attorney-client work product or proprietary secrets and, as such, privileged from disclosure. But others were not so easily protected, and it was Adrienne's task to identify those, and then to suggest ways in which problematical documents might yet be withheld.

Using her desktop computer, she typed in the corrections that she'd made in pencil on the rough draft of the memo she was writing. Then she added the references that she'd gleaned from *Lexis*, and read it over. There were typos all over the place. She was used to working on a laptop, and much preferred its keyboard to the clunky device in her office. But fixing the typos was easy with the spell-checker, and when it was done, she saved the file, hit the *Print* button, and sat back. As the memo rolled out, she sat back in the chair and closed her eyes . . .

So nice . . . to just . . .

Her eyes flew open. Yesterday, she'd pulled an all-nighter and, if she didn't watch out, she'd zonk out, there and then. The night before, she'd been working at home, almost finished with the memo, when her laptop crashed, wiping out hours of work. She'd ended up going to the office at midnight, where she'd finished the memo on her desktop machine. Now, what she really wanted to do was to go home, soak in the tub until the water cooled, and air-dry on her big, soft bed.

But . . . no. It was the second Tuesday of the month, and after the message Nikki had left on her phone, there was no way she could bag their dinner together.

Sitting up in her chair, she stapled each of the four copies of the memo, and glanced through it one last time, looking for errors. There were three copies for Slough, and one for her file. She hit the speaker button, and tapped the great man's extension, but of course he was gone, along with the secretaries and just about everybody else. So she put the memos into an interoffice envelope and headed upstairs.

Here, no expense had been spared. The reception area that led into the various offices was calculated to create a very particular impression, one of enormous gravitas and means. At once lavish and understated, the area was carpeted in a taupe material so dense that it dragged at the feet, as if the floor had been dusted with matter from a neutron star. A pair of travertine marble columns upheld a fourteen-foot ceiling from which shafts of indirect lighting tunneled to the floor.

Luminist oils hung from the walls within sight of a reception desk that was itself a work of art, a shimmering walnut crescent whose burnished surface glowed amid the blinking diodes of the telephone console. Here and there, some richly-grained leather chairs, a spectacularly tufted Chesterfield couch, a glass-and-brass coffee table with copies of *Granta* and the *Scientific American* on its surface.

Slough's suite was locked, of course, so she put the envelope on the reception desk, and went back to her office for her purse. On the way out, she stuck her head in the cubicle across the hall.

"Hey, Bets—I'm outta here." Bette was a first-year, too, and, like Adrienne immured in work.

With a wince and a moan, Bette got to her feet. "Jesus," she said, "I'm seizing-up. I've got to remind myself to move once an hour." She paused, and a hopeful look dawned on her. "What d'you say, Scout? Want to go out for sushi? I'm dying in here."

Adrienne shook her head. "Got a date with my sister. Our once a month bonding session."

Bette frowned. "How's she doing, anyway?"

Adrienne shrugged. "Still crazy. Seeing a shrink, two or three times a week—though, if you want to know the truth, I think he's as much a part of the problem as the solution. Anyway . . . she wants to talk. Says it's *importante*."

"*Uhhh*-oh."

Adrienne smiled ruefully. "Tell me about it."

Ordinarily, Adrienne walked or used public transportation—as well she might considering that she was almost seventy-grand in the hole to various institutions of higher learning. But tonight, she was so tired, and late, that she looked for a taxi. And, in this, her inexperience showed; it took almost five minutes before her tentative wave was acknowledged as a summons.

The man behind the wheel was an attacking-style driver, and as they rocketed along, Adrienne squeezed her eyes shut for blocks at a time. Then they were there, and the fare was seven bucks, about twice what she'd expected. For a moment, she was inclined to argue with the Nigerian behind the wheel, but there was no point in that. The zonal system that determined cab fares in the District was inscrutable, and meant to be.

As she entered the building, the doorman recognized her—sort of. "Hey—you're Nico's sister, right?"

"Adrienne." She smiled. "Will you buzz her? Let her know I'm on my way up?"

"Sure thing." He waved her past him toward the elevators, which surprised her by wheezing open as soon as she touched the *Up* button. But when she got to the apartment, Nikki didn't answer. Adrienne stood at the door, pushed the doorbell again, and held it down with her thumb, thinking *Maybe she's in the shower* . . . Listening, she thought she could hear Jack barking, faintly, as if he was locked in the kitchen, a steady, distant cadence of *woof, woof, woof*. But from Nikki, there was nothing. Adrienne looked at her watch: it was almost 8:30.

In a way, she was more relieved than annoyed. She was out the cab fare that she'd spent, but she was looking forward— *rainbow* forward—to taking a bath and going to bed. Nikki had either forgotten their date or, what was more likely, she'd gone out for cigarettes or something, and gotten hung up.

Whatever she was doing—Adrienne gave the doorbell yet another long push—she'd given Adrienne a way out. As she walked back to the elevator, she could imagine the telephone conversation that they'd have in the morning.

But I was there—ask your doorman!
I was only gone ten minutes!
I rang and rang!
I ran out of butter!
How was I supposed to know? You didn't leave a note.

Her sister. As much as Adrienne loved her, the truth was that she was never comfortable in her company. She was always waiting for the conversation to take a wrong turn—as it inevitably did in the course of an evening. Being with Nikki was like driving on a tire that had a flat. It worked okay for a little while, however nervous the driver might be, but then everything would start to wobble and . . . you had to pull off the road. Not that she wasn't sympathetic. She was as tender and caring as she could be, and she would have been happy to humor Nikki if her sister's delusions had taken any other form. But the sexual abuse she imagined was so bizarre and theatrical, so patently crazy, that it was impossible to play along. Especially for someone who was supposed to have been victimized by the same unspeakable acts.

If a guy in a hood had screwed me when I was five, Adrienne thought, *I think I'd remember it.* The elevator doors slid open, and she stepped inside, then pressed the button for the ground floor.

The subject was more or less verboten now, a thing between Nikki and her therapist. Adrienne couldn't talk to her about it without losing her temper, a circumstance that was not lost on Nikki. According to her, Adrienne was "in denial." She'd "repressed" it all. And as bad as that was for Adrienne (or so the argument went), it was at least as bad for Nikki. Where was her "validation"?

Gimme a break . . .

Then again, even this craziness wouldn't have been so bad if Nikki had seemed—more like herself. But the Nikki who lived in the Watermill wasn't the glam' and funny sister that Adrienne would have done anything for. This Nikki was *spacy*, and getting more so, day by day.

Because of Berlin, Adrienne thought, *because of what happened there.*

There was a time, just after her sister graduated from high school, when everything was okay with Nikki, even though Adrienne hardly ever saw her. Against Deck and Marlena's advice, Nikki had taken a bus to New York with the dream of becoming a model. Deck said she'd be back in a month, but to everyone's surprise (except Nikki's own), she was successful almost immediately. Within a year of turning nineteen, she had a contract with the Marrakesh Agency and a five-room apartment in Soho. She sent postcards to Adrienne from places like Jamaica, and called every week, where the sound of her voice—*Hey, A!* riding on a quiet giggle—made her little sister's day.

It seemed to Adrienne, then, that Nikki was living the good life, and so she was, but it was a fast life, too. Returning from a shoot in the Cayman Islands, her bags were searched at JFK. A couple of Thai sticks tumbled out, and that was that: two hundred hours of community service, a thousand-dollar fine and no more work with Marrakesh.

Nikki could have stuck it out, of course, but she didn't. She hit the road and kept on going, saying she was "on an adventure." Adrienne got postcards and calls from just about everywhere. In fact, the first thing she asked whenever her sister called was, "Where are you?" She used to pull out the Atlas to see where she was and read up about it in the *Encyclopaedia Britannica*, imagining Austin, Vancouver, and Telluride. Barcelona, Amsterdam, and Berlin.

Then—nothing. Adrienne was a sophomore at the University of Delaware when her sister stopped writing and calling. Deck and Marlena did their best to find her, but there wasn't much they could do, really. They made calls, placed ads, and hired a private investigator—all to no avail. Then Marlena died. Adrienne went to law school, and not long after, Deck, too, passed away. For the first time, Adrienne was truly alone in the world.

Two more years passed before she saw Nikki again, and that was by accident. Adrienne was in the Nine West store at Georgetown Mall, buying a pair of clogs, when she turned to leave—and there she was, as beautiful as ever, standing across the store, twisting her foot to examine the way a pair of sandals looked. For years, Adrienne had dreamed about this reunion—and when it happened, it took her breath away. It was hard to explain how *right* it seemed to see her sister after all those imagined sightings, after all the times when she'd thought it might be Nikki, but it turned out not to be. Finding

Nikki, seeing Nikki—it was a moment that fell perfectly into place, as naturally as the last harmonic chord in a great piece of music.

And there was no doubt that this was her, not a moment's hesitation despite the fact that they hadn't seen each other in nearly ten years. She'd tiptoed hesitantly down the aisle, shoes in hand, and stopped in front of her to ask, "Nikki?" And Nikki had looked up, frowning a little—and then her face had split into the biggest, widest grin. And the two of them were screaming and hugging, Nikki shouting: "This is my baby sister!"

As Nikki told it, she'd been tripping with her boy-toy in Berlin, a German kid named Carsten Riedle, and she overdosed. No Tristan, young Riedle left her for dead, drooling on the floor of the family's townhouse in one of the city's most fashionable neighborhoods.

The Riedles' housekeeper found her in a coma the following morning, and sent for an ambulance. Hospitalized, she remained unconscious for the better part of a week and, when she awoke, remembered almost nothing. Weeks went by, and then a month. Finally, she was removed to a clinic in Switzerland where they had a doctor on staff who'd had success with cases similar to her own. The clinic also treated substance abuse and since Nikki's troubles had started with an overdose, it was considered the ideal place for her rehabilitation.

While her doctors expected the amnesia to pass of its own accord, she remained Patient X to herself and everyone else. Meanwhile, queries to the U.S. Embassy in Bonn—Nikki's English was clearly American—proved fruitless. According to embassy officials, no missing persons reports had been filed that would fit her description. Neither had anyone found a passport with her picture on it. Which meant that her nationality could not be established. *Next!*

And then it happened. On a warm spring day, as she walked from the clinic toward the marina and its restaurants, Nikki saw a poster on the wall emblazoned with an ad for *Far and Away*. Cruise and Kidman were locked in an embrace, and . . . *Nicole*. It all came flooding back. She remembered her name. She remembered Carsten Riedle. She even remembered the music that was playing on the CD when the scumbag shot her up. Alanis Morissette. *Jagged Little Pill*.

Two days later, she had a lawyer, and two weeks after that, a settlement: in exchange for the fräulein's agreement to disappear from their son's life and to forgo legal action against the family, the Riedles would establish a trust fund in her behalf. And so it was done: half-a-million dollars. Exit the Riedles.

The elevator opened on the lobby, and Adrienne stepped out, still thinking about Nikki. She'd always wanted to ask her, *When did you remember me? Was it there, in Switzerland, or later?* And: *why didn't you call? Why didn't you come home?* Not to mention the questions she had for the clinic, such as: *Who was the idiot they talked to at the Embassy?* Because Deck and Marlena had called the State Department repeatedly. Knowing that Nikki's last known address was in Germany, they had made several inquiries, asking if an American woman of her description had run afoul of the police, or been in an accident. Somehow, Nikki's plight had slipped through the cracks. It was infuriating, but there wasn't anything to be done about it.

And, anyway, it wasn't the same Nikki who'd come back—not really. It was like, Nikki-Lite or something.

Almost furtively, Adrienne glanced around the lobby, half expecting to see her sister—and feeling a guilty rush of pleasure when she did not. Crossing the lobby, she reflected on the fact that her affection for her sister was more nostalgic than real, her contacts driven as much by duty as they were by affection. That was wrong, but she wasn't going to beat herself up about it. Nikki wasn't just disturbed; she was *disturbing*.

What was always revealed between the kiss hello and the appetizer was something that Adrienne preferred to forget. Nikki was not getting better, she was getting worse. And this shrink she was seeing was not helping. Quite the opposite, in fact. During the time that Nikki had been seeing him, she'd gotten loopier and loopier, ranting about things that not only had never happened—but never *could* have happened.

And seeing her sister like this, Adrienne wanted to do something about it, but—

"You leaving?" The doorman was holding the door open for her.

Adrienne shrugged. "I guess she went out."

The doorman looked puzzled. Shook his head and frowned. "I don't think so—I would have seen her. You check the laundry room?"

Adrienne paused in front of the door, then turned around. "No—what a good idea." Forcing a smile, she took the stairs down to the basement, where she could smell the room before she saw it. The heated sweetness of the fabric softener, the sharp tang of the bleach. She peered inside, but there was no one, the small room desolate under the fluorescent lights, its banks of machines still, the round eyes of the dryers blank.

So it was back up the stairs, where the doorman was waiting with a chagrined look on his face.

"Hey," he said with an apologetic shrug. "I forgot to look. She left a note for you." He handed it to her.

As Adrienne took the envelope, a feeling of foreboding came over her. Opening it, she felt a surge of adrenaline sparkle through her veins, and the hair stood up on her arms. For a moment, it was almost as if she were standing on a cliff, looking down. And then the note, so short she didn't have to read it.

A—
Couldn't stick it any
longer. Rainbow sorry.
Nikki

7 The doorman's hands were shaking as he inserted a master key in the lock to Nikki's door. Over and over, under his breath, he kept repeating, "Y'never know, y'never know." Then the lock turned, the door swung open, and Adrienne blew past, eyes wild.

"Nikki?" The apartment was dark, the dog barking, somewhere off to the right. "Nikki?"

Ramon's hands felt for the light switch, but nothing happened when he flicked it on. He gave Adrienne a bewildered look. "I think—maybe the fuse blew," he said.

"Fix it," Adrienne ordered as she stepped deeper into the darkness of the apartment.

"Breaker's in the kitchen," Ramon replied, "but I'll need a flashlight. You think she had one?"

Adrienne didn't say anything. She could hardly breathe.

"There's—there's a utility room down the hall." The doorman turned, then broke into a run.

"Nikki?" She could feel the hot tears rolling down her cheeks as she moved, step by step, through the living room, hands extended, just above her waist. She didn't want to trip over . . . "Nikki?"

The only light in the apartment was the ambient, neon glow from outside the windows. That, and the light from the hall. She could make out shapes—the couch and the table, the big leather club chair. But . . . "Nikki!?"

Jack was barking louder now, his feet scrabbling against

the kitchen door. As her eyes began to adjust, she maneuvered her way toward the sound and, finding the door, pulled it open. The dog burst into the room and, yipping, chased his tail in a frantic little circle, then jumped up against her. "Down," she ordered, at once startled and annoyed.

With a yip, Jack bolted through the living room to the hallway where, once again, she could hear him scrabbling at a door—this time trying to get in rather than out. She followed the dog, thinking how silent the apartment was with the electricity out. The only noise was the faint hum of traffic, and the scratching sound that Jack was making. Then he began to bark, and a shaft of light crashed into her eyes.

"I found a flashlight," Ramon told her.

Adrienne raised a hand in front of her eyes, squinted and blinked, helpless as a deer. Ramon swung the light in a figure eight through the rooms, and Adrienne's eyes followed it, afraid of what she'd see. But there was nothing.

"I'll get the dog," she said. "You get the lights."

Ramon nodded, and strode toward the kitchen, taking the flashlight with him. Adrienne felt her way toward the bathroom door, feeling as if she were about to be seasick. "Jack," she said, "c'mon." But his scrabbling became even more frantic, now that she was beside him. Relenting, she opened the door to the bath, and stepped into the pitch-dark.

From habit, she flipped the light switch on and off, then on and off again, but nothing happened. Jack was mewling a few feet away, and the only sound was the *drip*, *drip*, *drip* of water. "Nikki?" Silence. Nothing.

And then, the doorman calling from the kitchen—"Got it!" Suddenly, the lights flashed on, and a lonely trumpet accelerated from 0 to 80 decibels in half a second, pealing through the now bright air above where Nikki lay, drowned and burned in a tub of gray water. Eyes wide in a look of mild surprise.

The moths rose up in her stomach—even as the world fell away from her feet, and Adrienne, sinking, felt a flash of pain at the side of her head. And then it was dark again.

* * *

When she awoke, a policeman was sitting in a chair at her side, talking quietly into a cell phone. The lights were on. Her head was pounding. And she was lying on a couch, with a pillow under her feet.

"Hey," she said, complaining and entreating, all at once. Leaning on an elbow, she sat up. Slowly.

"You hit your head when you fainted," the cop explained.

Fainted? What 'fainted'? She'd been standing in—the bathroom. Suddenly, she remembered the long, peeling jazz horn, and the image of her sister's eyes flashed before her own. A sob rose in her throat.

"There was nothing anyone could do," the cop told her. "It must have been instantaneous."

She made a noise somewhere between a groan and a whimper. Her head dropped into her hands, and the tears rolled.

"The doorman called 911. My partner and I were just up the street."

For the first time, she noticed a second policeman standing near the doorway, talking quietly with Ramon.

"The M.E.'s on the way," the cop added. "And an ambulance. Though . . ."

The M.E., Adrienne thought, turning the initials over in her mind. *The Medical Examiner.* Once again, the image of her sister flashed before her eyes. She was lying in the tub, up to her neck in the ice-cold water. With an appliance—a radio or something—in the water between her legs.

She had to get her out of there.

The blood drained from her head as she got to her feet and stood, suddenly dizzy, swaying on her feet, head pounding like the bass drum in a high school band. She felt the policeman's hand on her arm. "We have to get her out of there," she said, and took a step toward the bathroom.

"No." Ever so gently, he sat her down on the couch.

"She's cold!" Adrienne sobbed.

"No, she's not cold. She's—" The policeman looked wildly

around, as if to find someone who could help him explain. But there was no one else. "She's okay now," he said. "Whatever it was, she isn't hurting anymore."

Adrienne awoke in her own apartment, a little after dawn. To her surprise, she was still dressed and lying on top of the covers on her bed. Just before her eyes opened, she remembered . . .

Getting to her feet, she went into the kitchen and made a cup of strong coffee with the plastic cone and paper filters that she used. Sitting down at the kitchen table, she thought, *That's it. There isn't anyone else. Now, I'm really an orphan.* Tears welled up in her eyes, and she blinked them back, almost angrily. *Who are you sorry for?* she wondered. *Yourself or Nikki?* Then she sipped her coffee and looked at the clock. 6:02. The first gray light of morning.

Her head hurt from where she'd fallen, banging it against her sister's sink. She supposed she was still in shock, and wondered what she was supposed to do. *Make a list,* she told herself. She was big at making lists and, anyway, that's what lawyers always did in a crisis: they made lists. Removing a pen from a Hoya's mug beside the telephone, she found a pad of Post-its, and began to write:

1. Funeral Home

The medical examiner had said there would be an autopsy— probably in the morning. He'd given her his business card, and told her to call that afternoon. Unless something unforeseen arose, they'd release "the remains" later that day. So she'd need to find one.

2. Call the M.E.

3. She hesitated. What was 3.? Then it occurred to her that 3. was the shrink who'd killed her sister. *Duran*—that was his name. *Jeffrey Duran.*

But, no. She'd deal with *that* son of a bitch later. There were more immediate priorities than revenge. So 3. was something else. Like, a memorial service. She sipped her coffee, and wondered what Nikki would have wanted. And then she remembered: a funeral barge, piled high with flowers. They'd talked about it once, half-joking, and that's what she wanted: a burial at sea.

Adrienne sighed. Some kind of service, something simple, but—who should she call? There weren't any other relatives. Just her. Her and Jack.

Jesus Christ, she thought. *Jack!*

There was a key to Nikki's apartment hanging from a hook under the cabinet next to the sink, where she liked to keep her keys so that she'd never have to look for them. *The poor dog!* Adrienne thought. *What about him? What's going to happen to him?*

She left her apartment at 6:35, and walked east on Lamont toward 16th Street, where she could expect to find a cab. The day was brightening now, as early risers came out of Heller's Bakery, attaché cases in one hand, cups of coffee in the other. Half a dozen people waited at the bus stop, while a ragged Hispanic man snored in the doorway of Ernesto's Taquería.

It took her a while to hail a cab, but the ride was a quick one, with the cabbie heading west on Porter, then south on Wisconsin to M. She got out in front of the Watermill, half expecting to find a fleet of squad cars, but there was nothing unusual to mark her sister's death. Just people leaving for work, oblivious to the tragedy of the night before.

She didn't know the doorman on the morning shift but it didn't matter. He was reading the sports section of the *Post,* and merely nodded to her as she passed. The elevator doors opened with a cheerful *ding.* And then she was on the third floor, walking down the silent corridor toward her sister's apartment.

She had almost expected the doorway to be crisscrossed with yellow police tape. But there was nothing. Just the door itself—and her, standing in front of it, looking blank. Only a few hours earlier, they'd carried her sister out on a gurney, her body covered by a sheet. She remembered the water dripping on the floor, a little trail from the bathroom to the front door, but it was gone now. Evaporated. Like Nikki.

She fumbled in her purse for the key and, finding it, opened the door. Standing on the couch, the dog unleashed a stuttering bark that seemed to go on and on, half-warning, half-howl. "Jaa-ck," she said, kneeling to scratch behind his ear as he wiggled over to her side. "Where's your leash?" she asked. "Where'd it go?"

Jack cocked his head, and looked insane, his stubby little tail quivering at attention.

She tried to think where Nikki would put it. There was a closet a few feet from the door, and she opened it. Looked inside. A couple of coats, hanging from hooks. An armload of dry cleaning, still in its plastic bags. A couple of belts. Her sister's Rollerblades. *Things. There were so many things. So many . . . personal effects.* For the first time, it occurred to Adrienne that she would have to do something with it all. The furniture, the clothes, the skates . . .

Maybe the leash was in the kitchen.

Crossing the living room, she went into the kitchen and glanced around. No leash. No dirty dishes. Nothing. If anything, the room was a lot tidier than usual, as if Nikki had cleaned up before she'd killed herself. Even the refrigerator door, a sort of tchotchke art gallery, was empty. Or almost so. There was an envelope pressed to its surface by a magnetized effigy of Tanqueray gin. And Adrienne's name was on it in big, block letters.

Removing the magnet, she took the envelope to the counter in the middle of the room, and sat down with it in front of her, fearful of her sister's last words. After what seemed a long time, she opened the letter, and with a sigh, saw that her fears had been groundless. The envelope contained her sister's last will and testament, a potted document that she'd downloaded from the Internet. Across the top was a four-color, banner-ad with the words:

Beneath that was the declaration that

> *I, Nicole Sullivan, a resident of Washington, D.C., de-*
> *clare that this is my will.*
> *FIRST: I revoke all Wills and Codicils that I have pre-*
> *viously made. SECOND:*

She didn't want to read it now, though she saw at a glance
that she'd been named her sister's executor. Which wasn't surprising. Who else did Nikki have?

Who, indeed?

There must be an address book, somewhere, Adrienne
thought. A Filofax or PalmPilot, some way for Adrienne to
get in touch with Nikki's friends (if she had any). Maybe she
kept it on her laptop, Adrienne thought.

A cold nose nuzzled her ankle, reminding her of the
missing leash. Getting to her feet, Adrienne returned through
the living room to her sister's bedroom—which, like the
kitchen, was quite tidy: bed made, clothes put away. Going
over to the closet, she opened the door to see if the leash was
hanging there, and her eye was immediately caught by a lime-
green, plastic case that she'd never seen before.

Too big for a laptop, and too small for a guitar, the case was
rectangular without being square. Curious, she hefted it and
was surprised by its weight. *Camera equipment?* Removing
the case from the closet, she carried it to the bed and set it
down. A pair of combination locks flanked the carrying
handle, but they were no obstacle at all. Nikki bragged about
using the same combination on everything, one she'd never
forget: 0211, her birthdate. Or, if it was a computer password,
021170, which was just the same, but with the year.

Adrienne spun the little brass wheels until the numbers
matched on either side of the handle, then sprung the locks,
and opened the case.

What she found was so unexpected, and so strange, that it took her breath away. Parts of a gun—a rifle of some kind—lay in foamed compartments that seemed to have been specially made for it. There was a long blue barrel, a matte-black plastic stock, a telescopic lens.

And . . . nestled into the foam below the scope was a carefully-machined, perforated metal tube, that was threaded at one end. Though she'd never seen one before (except, perhaps, at the movies), she knew at once what it was, or must be: "a silencer." Almost as a reflex, she slammed the case shut as if to hide its contents, and spun the little wheels of the combination lock. Then she carried the case back to the closet, and put it back where she'd found it.

For the second time in a day, she felt shocked and guilty. Shocked that Nikki had killed herself, and guilty that she hadn't saved her. Shocked, again, to find a rifle—and not just any rifle, but *such* a rifle—in her sister's closet. And then the guilt welling up—again—at the recognition of her own prurient curiosity.

She closed the closet door with a sigh. *Stop it*, she said to herself. *No one could have saved Nikki (except, perhaps, her shrink). Nikki was doomed. Had always been doomed. And as for going through her sister's things, she was supposed to do that. She was the next of kin. The executor. And the only survivor. If not her, who?*

But it was so bizarre, she thought, looking around to see where else the leash might be. *A gun like that . . . you didn't buy a gun like that for self-protection. And whatever else Nikki might have been, she certainly wasn't a hunter, so . . . it must be someone else's. But whose?*

Returning to the living room, she glanced this way and that, having already decided in the back of her mind that she could substitute a length of cord for the leash. Noticing Nikki's desk for the first time, she went over to it and, much to her surprise, found what she was looking for in the top drawer. The leash itself. And on the desk, Nikki's laptop—with, she supposed, an address book in one of its folders.

(Didn't Microsoft Outlook have some sort of "contact" list?) She'd take it with her when she left.

Closing the desk drawer, she turned toward Jack who suddenly let loose a prolonged and startling bark—then launched himself at the door. To Adrienne's surprise, she saw the doorknob turn and felt a sizzle of apprehension, followed by a defensive need to explain her presence. At such an early hour. In her sister's apartment.

The door swung open, and a man loomed in the entrance, then dropped to a squat and clapped his hands as the dog flew at him. *"Tranquilo, Jack, tranquilo!"*

Ramon.

Adrienne cleared her throat as the doorman rubbed the dog's head with his knuckles, talking to it all the time. But he didn't seem to hear her, and so she raised her voice.

"Hi."

He looked up, startled to find that he wasn't alone. Seeing Adrienne, he straightened and, with a look of embarrassment, smiled. "I was worried about the dog," he told her, closing the door behind him. "I thought maybe I'd feed him, y'know? Take him for a walk . . ."

Adrienne nodded. "Me, too," she said.

Ramon shuffled his feet. "Well . . ." He glanced around, uncertain of what to say. "You're here, so—"

"I really want to thank you for last night," Adrienne said. "I—I really lost it."

Ramon nodded. "It was terrible," he admitted. "The most terrible thing I've ever seen."

"I know."

"I'm just the doorman, but—this lady was my friend, y'know? We used to talk sometimes."

Adrienne nodded.

"So, I guess you'll have a service—" Ramon suggested.

"I suppose so."

"And maybe you could let me know?"

"Of course."

" 'Cause I'd like to be there."

"Okay."

The doorman stepped toward her and, taking out his wallet, produced a ridiculously expensive business card. In the upper right-hand corner were the masks of tragedy and comedy, embossed in gold. In the middle was his name—*Ramon Gutierrez-Navarro*—and a telephone number.

"I'll call you," Adrienne promised. "In fact, that's one of the reasons I came by. To look for an address book. So I can let her friends know . . . what happened."

Ramon nodded thoughtfully, and frowned. "She didn't go out a lot," he said. "Didn't have a lot of people over."

It was Adrienne's turn to nod.

"Someone that pretty, you'd think . . ." He let the thought die, then changed the subject. "What about Jack?" he asked. "What's going to happen to him?"

Adrienne shook her head. "I don't know. My landlady lives upstairs and—she's not real big on dogs."

" 'Cause I was thinkin'," Ramon said. "Maybe I could take him—I mean, if you don't want him—if you can't *have* him. I *like* dogs. And since it's Nikki's dog . . . it would be kind of special."

Adrienne thought it over—for about half a second. "Well, that would be . . . just great!" It occurred to her that Ramon had had a crush on her sister.

"Only . . . if you could keep him for a week or maybe two?" Ramon suggested. "I'm just changing roommates and I got to square it with the new guy. I mean, I can make it a condition. This guy I got lined up, if he doesn't like dogs—I just find someone who does."

Adrienne nodded enthusiastically. "Absolutely! A couple of weeks. No problem."

Ramon looked pleased. "Well, that's great," he said.

She put his business card in her handbag, and the laptop in its case, which was on the floor beside the desk. Then she clipped the leash to Jack's collar, slung the computer case over her shoulder, and stepped out into the corridor. Together, she and Ramon rode the elevator down to the lobby, and went outside.

"You want a taxi?"

Adrienne shook her head. "I'll walk him, first."

The doorman nodded, and they shook hands. "So . . . I'll wait to hear from you," he told her.

She smiled and, at a tug from Jack, lurched toward the curb.

Ramon beamed. "I'm a dog owner," he said to no one in particular. "How about that?"

8 She was standing in the crowd on the platform at Metro Center, waiting for the Red Line train that would take her to Cleveland Park. And the train was going to be there any second. Adrienne knew that because the glass discs at the edge of the platform were beginning to blink, a staccato light show that she could see between the legs of the waiting passengers. Approaching the platform and peering to the left, she saw the train's headlight flickering in the tunnel. Somewhere, a telephone began to ring.

But not in her dream. The phone was real, and the Metro was a phantom. She knew this even as she dreamt about it, but knowing didn't make any difference. The dream still had her in its grip as she fumbled for the receiver on her bedside table.

"Hello?"

The voice at the other end identified itself as "Ms. Neumann," from the Medical Examiner's office. "I'm calling about Nicole Sullivan's remains? Who am I speaking with?"

The word—*remains*—made Adrienne sit up, and the act of sitting up lifted her out of the dream. "This is Nikki's sister. Half sister. Adrienne Cope."

"The police report lists you as the next of kin."

"That's right."

"Well, we need the name of a funeral home—whoever's going to process the rem—"

Adrienne interrupted. "I understand." *Process the remains?* As if Nikki were a kind of cheese or information.

"And?" The clerk's impatience was palpable.

"I've never done this before," Adrienne explained. "So . . . I haven't really decided—"

"I can fax you a list, if you have a machine," the clerk suggested.

"I do," Adrienne replied. "I have one right here." She gave her the number, and the clerk said that she'd wait for a reply.

"There's a release for the remains. So we can send them wherever you tell us."

"Okay."

"If we could have it back this afternoon? That would be good," the clerk added.

"I'll get it to you right away," Adrienne promised, returning the receiver to its hook. Then she got out of bed, threw on some clothes, and attached the leash to Jack's collar. Mrs. Spears didn't allow pets in the house, but "under the circumstances . . ." she'd agreed that Jack could stay until next weekend, by which time Ramon would be able to take him in.

Jack was already at the door, slapping it with his paws, eager to go for his walk.

As the two of them left the house, they entered a patch of garden on the way to the garage, where Adrienne pushed a button that sent the segmented door rattling up from the floor. With the door curling into the roof, Jack yanked her into the alley behind the houses.

Out on the street, Adrienne was thinking that although she didn't have time to take care of the dog, she was going to miss him. It was amazing how many people stopped to talk—ostensibly to her, but actually to Jack. Though it was only a block away, it took her almost ten minutes to get to Heller's Bakery. There, she tied the leash to a parking meter and went in to get a sweet roll, emerging a few minutes later with a croissant for Jack.

By the time she got back to the apartment, the fax machine was disgorging the last page of a multipage fax from the Medical Examiner's office. Jack jumped onto the couch and curled up, as Adrienne retrieved a handful of pages from the floor. At a glance, she saw that they comprised an alphabetized list of establishments providing "mortuary services" in the District of Columbia.

She called the Albion Funeral Home, which was near the top of the list. The man at the other end had the soft and confidential voice of a used-car salesman on Qaaludes. When she interrupted his spiel to make it clear that she wasn't interested in an elaborate service, he offered, without missing a beat, the most "economical" alternative, one that involved no "viewing" or "service" and a "classic," if "basic," coffin. Even so, it was soon clear that even the simplest burial was going to cost thousands of dollars.

In his silky voice, Barrett Albion belittled the amount, noting that "We take most of the major credit cards with the exception of American Express." When Adrienne fell silent at the prospect of the expense, he reminded her that "the estate will often release funds for this purpose."

Once again, she hesitated. She'd imagined a decent funeral for her sister, with her friends and relatives gathered in mourning, there to remember her. But there wasn't any way for that to happen, really. She'd looked in Nikki's computer, and there wasn't anyone, really. Just Adrienne, Ramon, the building superintendent, and her shrink. Amtrak and Avis. Tom Yum Thai.

The truth was, Nikki didn't have any friends. Not really. Not at all.

"What about . . . cremation?" Adrienne sputtered. She could hear the funeral director catch his breath at the other end of the line.

After a moment, he replied, "Well, that *is* an option."

"Fine," Adrienne shot back in a voice so sharp that Jack's ears came to attention. "Let's do that, then."

Albion sighed. "We only cremate twice a week," he told her. "On Tuesdays and Fridays. So it will be Saturday before we can—"

"Saturday's fine."

But even as she selected this "alternative," Adrienne felt queasy about it. *There ought to be a ceremony,* she thought. *Something.*

She and the funeral director nailed down the remaining details, including the number and expiration date of Adrienne's Visa card and the selection of a "receptacle." The most "economical" was a blue cardboard box—"really rather tasteful." Adrienne couldn't face the idea of "a box," and opted for an urn, the "classic." And yes, she would be the one to claim the urn once the "treatment" was completed.

"Will you pick it up in person?" Albion asked. "Or would you rather we had it sent? We could FedEx—"

"I'll get it myself in person," Adrienne replied, thinking, *FedEx? They want to FedEx my sister to me?* As she hung up the phone, she burst into tears. Jack lifted his muzzle from the compact circle that he'd formed, and issued a questioning woof.

Wiping the tears from her eyes, Adrienne went to the kitchen table, and began to make a list.

She had always been a list maker, imposing order on chaos, even if it was only on paper. When Marlena died, Adrienne had helped Deck sort through her foster mother's belongings. She'd come upon Marlena's trove of memorabilia: a fat folder for each child. In Nikki's folder: valentines made of doilies, snippets of fabric lace, faded red construction paper. Wild, even gorgeous, drawings in magic marker. Elaborate and intricate cutout snowflakes. Poems. In Adrienne's folder: a stack of straight-A report cards, some tidy little snowmen, and some of her childhood lists, carefully printed on loose-leaf paper.

1. Brush teeth
2. Make bed
3. Eat breakfast
4. Play

Yes, she had been a child who felt it necessary to remind herself to "play." Unlike the spontaneous and chaotic Nikki, whose motto was, if anything, *Play it as it lays*. She, Adrienne, had been the "good" girl to Nikki's charming and spectacular rogue. Nikki never did her chores without being nagged to death, never came home on time for dinner or from dates, always cajoled her way into getting extensions on her school projects. Nikki was always in trouble, and yet . . . Everyone loved her. She lit up the room, even if she sometimes made you want to roll your eyes. Because you wouldn't believe, you couldn't believe, someone so beautiful and vivacious could be so daring—*and so funny. How did it happen?* Adrienne wondered. *How did someone so . . . glorious . . . turn into a recluse?*

It made her wonder. It made her shudder.

As for her own lists, which were meant to keep everything in order, the last one had included: *Dinner with Nikki*. But it had not included Barrett Albion, a funeral urn, or a sniper rifle.

Adrienne gave her head a quick little shake, as if to clear her mind, and opened the organizer notebook in which she kept her many lists. One by one, she enumerated the things she had to do:

1. Fax release to Neumann.
2. Urn—Albion—Saturday.

3. Amalgamated docs—memo to Slough.
4. Visa: limit?

She thought for a moment. What else? There was something else. And then she remembered.

5. Will.

She hadn't really looked at it. Just the one glance in Nikki's apartment. Enough to tell her that she was the executor.

She looked at her watch, and saw that it was 9:15. She had a meeting that afternoon with Curtis Slough to discuss some "worrisome" documents in the Amalgamated case. And the truth was, she hadn't even finished annotating the papers, much less writing a memo about the ones they should try to protect. She just hadn't had—didn't have—wouldn't have— the time. And yet, she'd have to find it.

She really ought to take a day off, or even two, but how could she when she had this Amalgamated thing hanging over her head? It would take too long to bring anyone else up to speed. And it was the first substantive case she'd worked on for the firm. If she let them down in the middle of discovery . . . well, she might as well look for a job adjudicating parking tickets.

Do it by the numbers, she told herself. *Just do what you have to do, one thing at a time.* And so she did.

She filled out the release for the M.E.'s office, and faxed it to the officious Ms. Neumann. *Cross that off.* Then she dialed the number on the back of her Visa card and listened with gritted teeth to a long and irrelevant spiel on tape. Finally, she heard the option that she wanted, tapped the number eight, and learned that the cost of her sister's cremation would not exceed the limit on her Visa card. In fact, she was surprised to learn that she had more than two thousand dollars in credit— the result of a recent upgrade to Platinum status.

So she crossed that off, too, and began to feel a little better. Going into the bedroom, she pulled on some clothes, tugged a hairbrush through her hair, and did the sixty-second makeup (mascara—lipstick—a dab of foundation on her forehead). Then she grabbed her keys, gave Jack a pat, and rushed out the door.

Only to return an instant later for Nikki's laptop. Because why not use it until the new one was delivered? She hated not having one. *Even so . . .* , she thought as she closed the door behind her, if she was going to take it to court, she'd do well to find a more subdued carrying case than the flaming pink Cordura number that Nikki had used.

When she got to her office, she found that Slough had left a message of his own, saying that he couldn't do lunch after all—so how about tomorrow? That gave her an extra day to deal with the Amalgamated documents. And handle the will.

It was in the laptop's carrying case and, as she took it out, a chord of sadness ran through her. The pathos of her sister's death was impossible to ignore, emblazoned as it was by the banner-ad at the top of her last will and testament.

Wills were not something that she'd ever handled before. She would probably have to file it with the Clerk of Courts, close out her sister's bank accounts, deal with the insurance (if there was any), and . . .

It occurred to her, suddenly and for the first time, that Nikki had not been broke. Her Eurotrash boyfriend (or, more accurately, his parents) had settled a sum of money on her. Half a million dollars. It must have been invested. Even in a money market account, it would have pulled in twenty-five thousand a year. So even with the apartment in Georgetown and the twice-a-week visits to her Cleveland Park shrink, it was hard to see how Nikki could have made too much of a dent in four years. It wasn't like she ever *went* anywhere.

The realization that she might inherit that money, which she then could use to pay down her student loans, sent a frisson of excitement—and a feeling of shame—through her. She didn't want Nikki's *money*. That is, she *did*, but . . . She didn't want her sister's death to be like winning the lottery.

Her eyes drifted down the page:

> *SECOND: I direct that any and all costs of my inter-*
> *ment or cremation should be borne by my estate;*
> *THIRD: I bequeath the sum of $5,000 and my dog,*
> *Jack, to the actor and doorman, Ramon Gutierrez-*
> *Navarro, knowing that he will be as kind to the pooch as*
> *he has been to me;*

Adrienne shook her head, wistfully. Ramon would be happy, both that Nikki and he had been on the same page about Jack and—who wouldn't be?—about the money. She read on. Making a will was so unlike Nikki, and yet . . .

> *FOURTH: I bequeath to my beloved half sister, Adri-*
> *enne Cope, any and all rainbows that may be found*
> *among my possessions, real or imagined;*
> *FIFTH: I direct that the remainder of my estate should*
> *be divided, in equal portions, among my sister, Adrienne*
> *Cope; the Believe the Children Foundation; and my thera-*
> *pist, Dr. Jeffrey Duran, who helped me come to terms with*
> *the secrets of my childhood.*

Adrienne blinked. " 'The secrets of my childhood,' " she muttered. "What 'secrets'?" And then, a moment later: " 'Come to terms'? She *electrocuted* herself!" The will dropped from her hand as Adrienne fell back in her chair, tears springing from her eyes.

A soft knock came at the door, and Bette leaned in. "Are you all right?" she asked. "I was just—"

"I have to go out," Adrienne said, grabbing her handbag and jumping to her feet. "Cover for me."

"But—"

"It's an emergency," she explained, and shot out the door.

9 Henrik de Groot sat slumped in the chair and, at first glance, it might have seemed as if he and Duran were having a casual conversation. The consultation room was a comfortable one, with an array of magazines fanned out on the coffee table between them. A glass of ice-water and a glass of iced tea rested, untouched, on a pair of Sandstone coasters.

Duran regarded the coasters with a look of suspicion. Where had *they* come from? They had a gritty feel, and rasped when he set his glass down. Where had he bought them? What had he been thinking of?

De Groot's cigarettes were on the coffee table, too, along with a pack of matches. There was no ashtray because Duran did not permit smoking in the office. But the Dutchman was a chain-smoker and since abstinence caused him to be anxious, Duran allowed him to *handle* his cigarettes. When not in a trance, he did this constantly, almost obsessively—sliding a cigarette out of the package, tapping its end against the table, stroking its length, even putting it to his lips and pretending to smoke it.

Pay attention, he told himself. Even though he and de Groot had been over this material time and time again, it was important that he pay attention.

It was de Groot's eyes which revealed that he was in a trance. They were open, but slightly out of focus, as if the Dutchman was looking past Duran, past the array of diplomas on the wall, past everything, in fact.

De Groot had been silent for what seemed like a long time, waiting for Duran's cue.

"You're in the car?" Duran suggested.

"Yes—in the car. It's dark in the car and it's dark outside. It's the kind of night where it's overcast and you can feel the moisture in the air. It's going to rain."

Duran found himself leaning forward, puzzled by the stiff, blond bristle that covered the Dutchman's head.

"It's going to rain," de Groot repeated.

Duran pulled back when he realized that what he was doing was trying to get a whiff of the man's hair—trying to discern if the effect was achieved with some kind of mousse or gel. *Pay attention,* he told himself. De Groot was stuck.

"Are there car lights?" he prompted.

On the chair, de Groot squinted and narrowed his eyes, as if the light were shining into them. "Yes. At first, I think it's a car with its bright lights on. I think 'Goddamnit, why doesn't he put his lights down?' "

No, Duran thought. That's what *the driver* thinks. "Did your father maybe say that? He's the one who's driving, right?"

"Yes. Yes, of course, my father. Me—I look away from the lights, but they won't go away. The light—somehow, it's *inside* me. Like a searchlight in my chest."

"And then?"

"I am taken up by the light—and then I am *interfered with.*" He squirmed in his chair. "They put something *into* me."

"What, Henrik? What do they put into you?"

The Dutchman winced. "*The Worm.* Boss Worm."

Duran sat back in his chair and smiled. And then, in one of those instances that he seemed prone to of late, he caught himself up. He didn't understand why he should find the integration of the Worm in de Groot's delusional system . . . somehow *pleasurable.* It ought to be a matter of indifference to him. He shouldn't have a *stake* in it.

And behind that thought—behind the idea that maybe he wasn't maintaining a professional distance from his client—

lurked another, even more insidious notion. *Which was that he'd seen all this on* The X-Files.

Henrik shifted uncomfortably in his chair, grimacing in the subdued way of a person in a trance.

"Who's doing this to you, Henrik?" Duran asked. "Who's responsible—"

At that moment, Duran heard the intercom buzz. And de Groot heard it, too, because he stiffened, and his eyes swelled with fear.

"They're here!" he whispered. "Here!"

The buzzer continued, first a long rasp, and then a staccato series of short ones. It took Duran a second to calm de Groot and, by then, the noise had ceased. The mood, however, was shattered, and although it was a little early, he began to bring the Dutchman out of his trance. Then the front doorbell began to ring, an insistent series of *bings*.

"Goddamnit," Duran muttered, and sprung to his feet. *If this isn't an emergency . . .*

Seconds later, he was standing behind the door, looking through the peephole—and he could have sworn it was Nico, whom he hadn't seen or heard from in a week. Almost as a reflex, he opened the door for a young woman who, as it happened, was not Nico, after all, but someone who looked a whole lot like her—but with darker dirty blond hair in place of Nico's platinum mop. Whoever she was, she was in a highly excited state, almost a rage, and she shocked Duran by pushing him backwards with her two hands in a motion so sudden that he stumbled and almost fell.

"You son of a bitch!" she yelled, coming for him again. "You killed her!" She was shoving him—with surprising force—and he found himself walking backwards in the direction of his consultation room. Reflexively, he put his hands up in a gesture of peace and surrender. "Wait a minute! What are you talking about?" he asked.

She stopped, and glowered, then turned her head away, as if to get control of her temper. Duran could see her chest heaving with emotion as she stared at the wall that held his framed diplomas. Finally, she turned back to him, and he could see that the rage was still intact.

"Nikki!" She spat the name at him.

"You mean . . . Nico?"

"Nikki, Nico—whatever you called her!"

"Where is she?" Duran asked. "I haven't seen her in—who *are* you?"

The question seemed to infuriate her. "I'll tell you who I am! I'm her sister. And I'm going to *put you out of business*, you quack son of a bitch!"

The woman's hostility was like a kleig light, burning in his face. He was stunned by her hatred, and by what she'd said.

"Her sister?" he repeated, sounding stupid even to himself.

"Adrienne."

He flashed onto Nico's voice: *Adrienne was only five.* Suddenly, Duran softened. While he'd never believed that Nico's tales of Satanic abuse were *factual*, he was convinced that in some way she had been abused. And if one child in a family suffered abuse, the others seldom escaped unscathed. In any case, the woman in front of him had suffered a great deal of loss: the unknown father, the junkie mother, the brutal mill of foster care. "Hey," he said, offering his hand. "Nico told me what you've been through," he said.

"She didn't 'tell' you anything! You put it in her head. And it's a crock!" With a gasp of disgust and a shake of her head, Adrienne turned on her heel and strode toward the door. "I just wanted to see the person who did it," she told him. "Because the next time I see you, there'll be a judge in front of us." She had her hand on the doorknob.

"But—wait a second—what did you say? About Nico?"

Adrienne looked at him as if he were a stone. "She killed herself."

It was almost as if she'd slapped him in the face. For a moment, he couldn't find his voice, and when he did, the words that came were senseless. "But . . . why? She was making such good progress," he said.

"Right!" Adrienne snarled. "She was 'making such good progress' that we're having her cremated on Friday."

She wanted to take a swing at him, but all she could manage in her unhappiness and frustration was a feeble push with her left hand. Even so, it staggered him, and he took a step backwards. Anger and grief welled in her eyes. "Did you do it intentionally? For the money?"

"What money?" Duran asked.

Before Adrienne could reply, de Groot was in the doorway behind them. "What's going on?" he demanded. "Who is this person, Doctor Duran?" He seemed dazed and dangerous, all at once, like a big cat waking from a tranquilizer dart.

Adrienne gave the Dutchman a quick glance, up and down. "Wake up!" she shouted. "And if you've got a problem, don't count on this psycho fuck to help you." Then she turned on her heel and was gone.

De Groot jumped as the door slammed behind her.

Duran was staggered. For a long moment, he stood in front of the closed door, woozy with shock. Then the world shuddered back into focus, and he found himself beside the powerful figure of Henrik de Groot. The Dutchman was as alert as Duran had ever seen him, poised on the balls of his feet, bouncing slightly. Slowly, the blond man glanced around. Sniffed the air.

"The Worm was here," he said.

10 Suddenly, Duran couldn't get away from high school reunions. They were everywhere—on HBO,

STARZ!, CBS and Nick at Nite. There was *Grosse Pointe Blank* and *Romy & Michele*, then *Ally McBeal* and some *Seinfeld* reruns. Everyone was going to a reunion, and Duran was no exception. The invitation was right there on his refrigerator.

As a therapist, attending reunions was the kind of thing he *ought* to do. He was in the business of prodding clients to re-connect with the past, stressing time and again that moving on in life was impossible if they didn't do the hard work of in-tegrating what had gone before.

Not that he himself had a lot of "integrating" to do. He re-membered high school as a pleasant interlude—warm, fuzzy and unremarkable. He'd been one of those well-rounded kids who scored points, not only for the basketball team, but for the "It's Academic" squad as well.

So why *not* go? He could kill two birds with one stone. First, it would get him out of the apartment. And while that would no doubt lead to a certain amount of anxiety, it was also the only way he knew to overcome the problem. Like any other bully, phobias had to be confronted—or they could ruin your life.

The other thing was: if he went to the reunion, he might be able to resolve some of the problems he was having with memory. It was one thing not to remember Bunny What's-her-name—that sort of thing happened to everyone. But there was something else going on. At times, it seemed as if his memories were somehow . . . *overexposed,* like photographs that had begun to fade in the sunlight.

Just then, the kettle shrilled, and Duran headed toward the kitchen for a cup of coffee. Passing through the hall, his eye fell on his parents' portraits, displayed in double-hinged frames of heavy silver, resting on a side table.

His father's picture was a head shot. It showed him gazing serenely at the camera, a self-confident smile on his face. His mother was quite a bit younger-looking—perhaps because the photographs had been taken years apart. And she wasn't just smiling—she was laughing. She sat on the porch swing at the beach cottage in Delaware, head slightly thrown back, lips parted over white teeth, eyes crinkling in merriment.

Curious about his own feelings, Duran approached the photograph, picked it up and examined the image more closely: his mother's dark hair and loose curls, her delicately arched eyebrows . . . the old-fashioned dress with its square neckline. *What was it like,* he wondered, *to be held by her?*

And the answer came back: *It was like . . . nothing.*

He'd been staring at the picture for what seemed a long time, waiting for a gut response—but there was nothing. And that, he knew, was evidence of profound alienation.

Maybe it was the way they'd died—so suddenly, he'd been blindsided. A faulty gas heater at a friend's cabin on Nantucket. The silent buildup of carbon monoxide—and then they were photographs.

The event had been as unexpected as an avalanche and, obviously, he was still a long way from closure. The funeral ought to have provided that, but . . . no. In point of fact, he barely remembered the service, even though it had only been six or seven years ago. And while the ceremony should have been engraved upon his memory as deeply as a brand, the truth was otherwise. When he thought of his parents' funeral, the images had a generic quality, cinematic, and spare as a screenplay.

EXT. Rainy day. Mourners . . .

He couldn't remember any real details. He couldn't remember who'd been there—other than "mourners," holding their umbrellas against the rain. He must have been grieving. He must have been overwhelmed. And yet . . .

He put the photograph back on the side table and headed for the kitchen, where the kettle's whistle had turned to an exhausted howl. What did it mean—what did it say about *him*— that he couldn't *remember* his own parents' funeral (except in the most notional way)? And what was worse: when you came right down to it, he didn't remember his parents either. Or, rather: he remembered what they looked like, things they'd said, and things they'd done. But those memories were about as emotion-packed as long division—and that, he knew, was not good.

But what *was* memory, anyway? A jangle of neurons, rinsed in amino acids.

Removing the kettle from the flame, he told himself that he really had to get in touch with himself, with who he was and where he'd been, with what he was doing and where he was going. And where better to begin, he thought, than at his high school reunion?

When the day came, he was jumpy. Even though he'd taken a tranquilizer, he worried that it wouldn't be enough. So he washed down a tab of Unisom, a nonprescription sleeping pill, and waited for the combination to kick in.

As it happened, it was one of those perfect fall afternoons. Overhead, a diamond bright contrail bisected the ballpoint-blue sky.

The taxi was right on time. Climbing into the backseat, he noticed a pair of El Salvadoran flags above the rearview mirror and, without thinking about it, gave the driver directions in Spanish—a language he'd almost forgotten he knew. The driver shot him a smile, showing two front teeth rimmed in silver.

"The Friends' school, no? I never have a fare to this one, but I know it—just north of the cathedral. Chelsea Clinton is attending this school, am I right? Before she is going to California."

Duran nodded. The Buena Vista Social Club was on the radio and, leaning back, he closed his eyes and thought, *It's gonna be okay.* And so it was—even though the traffic was a mess, Wisconsin Avenue snarled with trucks, cars making U-turns amid a chorus of horns, pedestrians bunched at the curbs like startled deer—and the driver yelping "Eee-pahhhh!" at every close encounter.

The banquet table in the Kogod Art Center was manned by a trio of friendly reps from each class at the reunion. Duran didn't recognize any of them, but each had a red-rimmed name tag pressed to the fabric of her blouse. He greeted the woman who looked to be his own age, scrawled his name on an '86 name tag, stripped the backing from it and slapped it on his lapel.

Moving to a paper-covered table, he poured four fingers of watery punch into a Dixie cup, took a bite of a chocolate-chip cookie, and looked over the Schedule of Events. There was a varsity football game at two, an alumni-student soccer match at four, Meeting to Worship, class photographs, workshops on this and that. At six, a buffet dinner.

He talked to a peppy '56 alumnus, then drifted around toward the back of the school, where the athletic fields were. The football game—against the Model School for the Deaf— was already under way. And it was a spectacular day for pigskin, with a light breeze gusting out of the west, trees turning color under an agate-blue sky, temperatures in the fifties. And all around, an affable and stylish crowd lounged on the hillside overlooking the game. Duran was excited. *Crush the Deaf,* he thought, chuckling to himself as he glanced about in search of old chums.

According to the scoreboard, the Deaf were already up by a couple of touchdowns. But so what? He was in a terrific mood, and Sidwell was never very good at football, anyway. Leaning against the trunk of a towering black walnut, he sipped his punch and reflected on the miracle of what was, after all, a quintessentially American afternoon.

He really ought to get out more.

At the end of the quarter, he watched the players trot toward their benches, mouth guards dangling. And standing there in the sunlight, with one impossibly colored leaf after another spinning down to the crisp green lawn, he felt a surge of delight, a connectedness to these people, this place. Even though he himself was more of an observer than a participant in the whoops of recognition and embraces of reunion, everyone was friendly enough. Certainly, lots of smiles came his way.

And it felt good, good to be a part of something larger than himself. Good to feel connected. Good to belong.

A whistle trilled, and the footballers trotted back onto the field, where they lined up against one another, the burgundy against the blue.

Being deaf, the Model students were oblivious to the quarterback's count and the referee's whistle. So a large drum had been brought to the field. Though the deaf couldn't hear it, they could feel its vibrations—which were profound. Duran had noticed the drum—a gigantic thing near the 50-yard line—and guessed that it belonged to the marching band. But, obviously, it was much too big for anyone to carry. A gray-haired man in a powder-blue warm-up suit stood beside the instrument, brandishing a padded mallet whose business-end was as large as a grapefruit.

The Deaf's quarterback, swiveling this way and that, signed a play. The players dropped into the three-point position, and tensed. Then the man in the warm-up suit swung his mallet, and the world trembled. No matter how distracted by the reunion around them, by offspring or urgent cell-phone calls, every spectator turned to the field in astonished unison. The sound was thunderous, a huge concussive boom. And the vibration was massive, a seismic tremor that rose through the soles of Duran's feet, and rushed to his brain—where it reverberated like a tuning fork struck with a hammer.

Offense and defense collided in an explosive rush. Spectators laughed and cheered. But Duran—Duran felt as if he had lost contact with the ground. For whatever reason, the drum's reverberation was like a hammer to his adrenals, sending a surge of panic through his bloodstream. Even as he launched himself toward the nearest door, he knew that his reaction was ridiculous. It was a drum, not an earthquake. But knowing that did nothing to slow his pulse, or quiet his heart.

Fumbling at the screen door to Zartman House, he nearly yanked it off its hinges as he plunged inside, and sank, trembling, into a blueberry-colored wing chair.

Jesus Christ, he thought. *What's going on? Where does it come from?*

Breathing irregularly, he closed his eyes and put himself through the paces of a relaxation exercise. And sure enough, it began to work. Within a minute or two, his breathing was almost normal.

Slowly, he looked around. Zartman was the oldest and most characteristic building on the tiny Sidwell "campus," a modest stone house that had once been the entire school, but which now served as an administrative building.

Looking around, he saw that he was in a large and well-proportioned room, furnished with brass lamps, antiques and oil paintings. Then he heard the women's voices, coming through the open door, volume rising as they approached. He shifted in his seat, as if to stand and greet them, but . . . no. He didn't trust his legs. Not yet.

The screen door slapped shut, and one of the women said, "And he *bites.* He's like a little cannibal!"

The second woman laughed.

"I keep telling him no more breast-feeding if he keeps *that* up, but he's only eight months old—so it isn't as if *threats* mean anything to him. And to tell you the truth . . ." She sighed. "I'm not ready to give it up myself, you know? I mean, not just yet."

The wings of the chair kept him from seeing the women even with his peripheral vision. But he couldn't avoid over-hearing them, and wasn't sure how to declare himself.

"I know exactly what you mean. Nobody told me it would be quite so . . . oh, I don't know—sensual!"

"*Ri-ight!* And—"

A high-pitched whoop cut through the air as the second woman realized that the two of them were not alone. In an instant, Duran was on his feet, hapless with apology. "Sorry! Really, I—I must have fallen asleep . . . I hope I didn't frighten you or anything! Jeff Duran." His hand shot out toward a knife-edged blonde whose name tag identified her as Belinda Carter, '86. Same as he.

"Sorry about the theatrics," she gushed, peering at his name tag. "But you scared the bejesus out of me, Jeffrey Duran." And then, without losing a beat: "Still—it's great seeing you . . . after all this while."

She was beaming at him, and the other woman, a pretty brunette, stepped forward. Her name, he saw, was Judy Binney.

"Didn't mean to break in on your hideout," she told him, a little sheepishly. "I guess we all had the same idea." She cocked her head for a better look at his face. "Were you the strong, silent type?" she asked, her lips bending to a flirtatious grin. "In school, I mean."

Duran shrugged. "Well . . ."

"Because I don't remember you," she explained. "And I think I would."

"I don't think I was as silent then as I was just now," Duran supposed. "I must have dozed off."

"And woke up to Judy and me talking about *breast*-feeding!"

"Not really—what I woke to was a scream."

They had a laugh about that, and spent the next few minutes talking about the oddness of reunions, the fact that twelve years really *was* a long time. Judy commented that despite the small size of the school, and the revved up intensity of emotions during high school—there weren't that many people that she'd remained in touch with.

"It's D.C. Everyone's so transient!" Belinda declared. "And me, too." She kissed Judy, patted Duran's arm. "I have to go."

"I can't believe I don't remember you," Duran told Judy when Belinda had gone. "I mean, you must be some kind of late bloomer."

"Really? Do you think so? Am I finally *blooming*? Wait till I tell Mr. M. He was always waiting for that."

Duran thought she meant her husband, but of course she was talking about their academic adviser, the relentlessly sincere Nubar Mussurlian. Seeing him through the screen door,

Judy tugged Duran outside so that she could tell her old adviser of her newfound efflorescence. Mr. M laughed, and shook hands with Duran, inquiring as to how the world was treating him.

"Pretty well, thanks. No complaints."

"I'm trying to remember," Mr. M said. "Where was it you went?"

"Brown," Duran reminded him.

Mr. M nodded. "Of course."

"And after that—Madison."

"I think I may have had a hand in that. I've always been high on Wisconsin. Economics, wasn't it?"

Duran shook his head. "Clinical psychology."

"Well," Mr. M chuckled, "that's what reunions are for—so we can catch up with one another."

The rest of the afternoon was pleasantly dull. There was Meeting to Worship, during which various alums stood up to share their thoughts on subjects as disparate as the Human Genome project, "sexual responsibility," and efforts to eradicate bilharzia in Egypt.

The photo sessions for each of the three reuning classes were quick and professional, with a no-nonsense photographer manipulating the tableau in such a way that the African Americans were not in little clusters (as they tended to be), but dispersed throughout the crowd.

When the time came, Duran failed to recognize Bunny who, as it happened, looked nothing like the pert blonde that he'd imagined. On the contrary, she was one of the most predatory-looking women that Duran had ever seen, having a long, vulpine face and sharp yellow canines.

"Je-efffff!" she exclaimed, and took him by the arm, dragging him from one knot of Friends to another. "You remember Jeff Duran! Well, here he is!" There was a good bit of forceful handshaking, chummy abrazos, a couple of pecks on the cheek.

"Anyone from basketball around?"

"I don't remember who played *basketball*, Jeff! My God!

Except . . . well, Adam Bowman, of course. He's here." And then her face lit up. "Did you know Adam lost a leg to bone cancer?" She produced the information with the zest of an insider.

Duran shook his head. "No. That's . . . terrible."

She nodded in agreement. "I don't think he's coping well, either." She arched an eyebrow. "Refused an invitation to the Paralympics . . ."

Outside the cafeteria—site of the banquet—the walls displayed a montage of blowups from the yearbooks of classes in attendance. Duran searched for the '86 varsity basketball squad—and there they were, or most of them, anyway. He himself was not in the picture. (As he recalled, he'd had strep throat or something.)

But the rest of the guys were there, standing under the backboard in the New Gym, its ceiling hung with IAC banners from the glory days. There was Sidran and Salzberg, Wagner and McRea. LaBrasca. And Adam Bowman, who went to Rice on a full scholarship, holding the ball in one hand, palm down.

Entering the cafeteria, Duran snagged a glass of red wine. Across the room, he spotted a jet-black giant who had to be Adam Bowman. Slowly, he made his way through the crowd to his old friend.

"Heyyy," Duran said, sticking out his hand.

Bowman peered at his name tag. "Jeff! Great to see you, man!" A ferocious handshake. "Hey, Ron—say hello to Jeff Duran."

Another manly handshake, and a brief exchange of pleasantries. Then Ron McRea turned back to the blonde on his arm, and Bowman resumed his conversation with Mr. M. They seemed to be talking about motivational speaking. After a minute or two, Duran drifted away, vaguely disappointed. It wasn't that they'd been unfriendly. It was just that he'd expected some kind of—what? Camaraderie? Something.

He shrugged it off and sat down next to Judy Binney at the

banquet table. She flirted with him over dinner and wine—
which she drank rather a lot of. Then the coffee came, and
there was a flurry of mercifully short speeches and reminders
of upcoming events and the fall fundraiser ('Friends Stand
Up!').

Eventually, he found himself in the foyer of Zartman
House beside Judy Binney, waiting for a taxi, while she
peered outside for her husband's BMW. Rain tapped at the
windows.

More than a little drunk, Judy whispered into his ear—
maybe *he'd* like to try a little breast-feeding? But then the
BMW appeared, and Judy laughed it off, saying she was
"only kidding." Finally, she pecked him on the cheek, and
promised to see him in 2005.

Five minutes later, his taxi arrived.

Outside the cab, the city slipped by, shiny in the rain. Taillights bled across the wet asphalt, while overhead, streetlights
swarmed with drops of rain. Duran lay back in his seat, feeling out of sorts. The reunion had not been reassuring. Besides
that little business with the drum—which was worrisome—
his efforts to deepen his recall of the past had been a failure.
While everyone had been pleasant and welcoming, he hadn't
been moved by anything he'd seen or anyone he'd met. On the
contrary, he'd felt like an out-of-town guest at his host's
garden party. He was there by invitation, but he didn't belong.
And while the people he'd seen were vaguely familiar, his
memories of them were fuzzy at best—as diffused and indistinct as the blond coronas around the streetlights.

The truth was: when you got right down to it, it wouldn't be
unfair to say that he didn't remember a soul. Not really. Not
at all.

11 Adrienne sat at her hopelessly cluttered desk and yawned. The yawn expanded and deepened until it became painful, and tears seeped into the corners of her eyes. God, she was tired. She took a piece of candy corn from the little plastic jack-o'-lantern on her desk (courtesy of Bette), and bit off the white tip, then ate the orange section, finishing with the kernel's yellow base. Maybe the sugar would help wake her up.

The Amalgamated case was in the deposition phase—with each side conducting what amounted to pretrial examinations of potential witnesses. She now knew far more than she had ever wanted to know about asphalt, thanks to working fifteen-hour days for ten days running, trying to keep up with everything Curtis Slough had been throwing at her.

Nikki had been cremated more than a week ago, and Adrienne had yet to pick up her ashes. The funeral home had called three times. If she didn't come in soon, Barrett Albion informed her, there would be "a storage charge."

The idea of her sister's ashes incurring "a storage charge," as if her funeral urn had been towed for unpaid parking tickets, was unthinkable. She *had* to get down there and pick up the urn. And she had to do it today—despite the fact that she and Slough were scheduled to prep Ace Johnson, a key witness that the opposition was determined to depose. Slough would expect her to have lunch with the two of them, but— they'd just have to do without her.

Mr. Johnson was of interest for having signed off on a

memo estimating the costs, in time and materials, of the road-work that Amalgamated proposed to undertake in the District. Unfortunately, the memo contained a handwritten notation that Mr. Johnson had written in the margin: New mix?

The notation was a problem because, at the time of the bid, Amalgamated was known to have been developing a new asphalt mixture. This "new mix" used a less expensive form of asphalt cement, the black, sticky stuff that held pavement together. Unfortunately, as Amalgamated's own test documents showed, the new mix tended to crumble at low temperatures. Worse, at the time Amalgamated bid the D.C. job, the new mix was experimental and not approved for use. Thanks to the words scribbled in the memo's margin, the District of Columbia was suspicious.

His full name was, improbably enough, Adonis Excellence Johnson. He was thirty-seven years old, and one of Amalgamated's "junior vice presidents." Adrienne had expected Mr. Johnson to be black because, in her experience, most of the boldly named citizens of the world *were* black. In reality, however, Adonis Johnson was a heavy white man, with chalk-colored skin and eyes as blue as a new pair of Levi's. Large and unstylish glasses clung to the bridge of a nose pitted with acne scars. Ushered into the plush confines of Curtis Slough's office, he looked terrified.

Even so, they practiced his deposition for nearly two hours, with the last thirty minutes spent on the memo with the putative notation.

At about 12:30, her boss suggested they go to lunch at the Occidental Grill.

Adrienne affected a crestfallen look, and demurred. "I can't! Remember? I have an errand."

Even though she'd prepared him for the fact that she had to skip lunch, Slough rolled his eyes. "An *errand*?"

She knew what he meant: he didn't want to have lunch with Ace Johnson—not alone. What would they talk about? Asphalt?

"It's just that . . . I've been putting in so many hours, I haven't had time to—"

"Well, Ace and I are *very* disappointed."

She could see her stock falling, but she'd be damned if she'd use her sister as an excuse. And so she shrugged, repeated how sorry she was—and left them there, staring at each other. (Johnson looked hungry. Slough was aghast.)

The Albion funeral home was in Anacostia—she'd chosen it alphabetically, not because it was handy—and the cabbie got lost. When she finally got back to the conference room, an hour and a half had gone by, and she was carrying the urn in a little wooden crate at the bottom of a shopping bag.

Slough glanced at the bag as she rushed in, and raised his eyebrows. *Shopping?* Adrienne felt her face go red.

For the next three hours, they continued to prep their witness. At no point did either of them ask if Amalgamated had actually *used* the new mix. They simply and repeatedly wondered how anyone could be expected to *remember* what he'd been thinking *six years ago*. Was it possible that Mr. Johnson had been, well—*doodling*? Or thinking of some other responsibility?

At about four P.M., a light dawned in Ace Johnson's dungaree eyes. "Y'know," he said, leaning forward with a confidential air. "I'll be honest with ya. I don't remember *what* the hell I was thinking about when I wrote that."

Slough smiled.

Five minutes post-smile, she was back in her cubicle and four hours after that, she was still there, feeling enervated, ragged and bored. Her sister's ashes were in the corner, on the floor beside the shredder, beneath the hat rack that held her coat.

She yawned, put aside the list of questions she'd been preparing, and pulled out her organizer.

Before she went home, she'd have to finish the commentaries that went with each of the questions, print out the file, and leave it on Slough's desk so it would be there when he got in tomorrow morning. Other items on the list included *Call*

Ramon re Jack. The doorman had promised to take him on Saturday—which reminded her: Jack probably had to go out. In fact . . . She took a deep breath and geared herself up to call Mrs. Spears. It was either that or go home, and she couldn't go home—not yet. So she tapped in the number.

"Hiiiiiii . . ." she exclaimed, drawing on the last dregs of "perkiness" that remained to her. "I'm at the office, and—there's a teeny *problem*? With *Jack*?" She hated herself when she talked like this, but—"Oh, you're saving my *life* Mrs. Spears, I just don't know how to thank you, you're an *angel*! No, really! I mean it!"

When she hung up, she sat back in her chair, and swiveled, left to right. Her eyes fell on the urn, and she told herself for the hundredth time that she had to do something with Nikki's ashes. Scatter them on the Potomac . . . or *something*. But where? And how? Did she just stand on the river bank, and sort of . . . *dump* them out? Or should she do it from a bridge? And *which* bridge? Or rent a canoe . . .

With a sigh, she looked at the next entry on her to-do list: Duran

That son of a bitch . . .

She flipped her pen over and bounced the end of it against the corner of her desk. *Duran.* Her threat was turning out to be an idle one. Other than running into his office and shouting at him, she'd done . . . nothing. Too busy.

She was still thinking about Duran when Bette came in with half a dozen little white containers from Tasty Thai. Digging into a heap of Green Curry Noodle, Adrienne remarked that she was going to crucify the shrink who'd killed her sister.

"Well, maybe," Bette said.

" 'Maybe'? The way he twisted her around? What do you want to bet he's got a list of complaints against him a mile long?"

"You think?"

"I'd bet on it," Adrienne told her. "And if I'm right—I'm going to ruin him. I mean it! Nikki may have been spacey—"

"Ummm . . . *Scout:* 'Nikki may have been spacey'?"

"Okay, so she was very spacey. But this fantasy about child abuse—that's why she killed herself. And it had absolutely nothing to do with reality."

"You know that? I mean, you know why she killed herself?"

Adrienne nodded. "It was in her will. Which was what she left instead of a suicide note. And this guy, Duran—who she *names* in the will—invented it all. And then—he makes *her* believe it."

Bette winced.

"It was all she could talk about. And that's supposed to be helping her!?" She dipped into the carton of Pad Thai, tasted it judiciously and shrugged. "Mine's better," she decided.

"So what are you going to do?"

"Nail him."

"How?" Bette asked.

"How do I know? I don't even have time to walk the dog."

"So why not let the city investigate him?"

Adrienne scoffed. "The other day . . . I made a call to the Board of Medicine—they're the licensing authority for clinical psychologists—and you know what they told me? They said I should be wary—they actually used the word 'wary'—about the pitfalls of 'outcome-based malpractice suits' (that's also a quote) in the field of mental health."

Bette rolled her eyes.

"Like I need their legal advice!" Adrienne exclaimed, gritting her teeth.

Bette's chopsticks delivered a morsel of Pad Thai to her mouth, while Adrienne renewed her attack on the curry. Finally, Bette asked, "Why don't you hire Eddie Vanilla?"

Adrienne frowned. Looked up.

"Isn't that what he *does*?" Bette asked. "I mean, isn't that *exactly* his kind of thing?"

Adrienne shook her head slowly. "I guess, but . . . I can't afford that! How much does Eddie charge, anyway? Fifty bucks an hour?"

"Well, there's your sister's money—you're the executor,

aren't you? Under the circumstances, I think you'd be within your rights to hire an investigator."

The idea hadn't occurred to Adrienne, who was so used to being poor that she'd never thought of *hiring* someone to do anything she could do herself—even if she didn't have the time. "Maybe you're right," she conceded.

Edward Bonilla, who was perhaps inevitably known as "Eddie Vanilla," was a retired Army guy who'd spent much of his life as an investigator for the CID. A few years earlier, he'd become a licensed P.I. in the District, listing himself in the *Yellow Pages* under "Bonilla & Associates."

Who the "Associates" were, was anyone's guess. But he'd done pretty well, serving papers, doing asset searches, divorce work, and handling due-diligence investigations for law firms involved in mergers and acquisitions. By all accounts, he was good at tracking down recalcitrant witnesses and doing public records research, though his interviewing skills were considered suspect. (One of the lawyers at the firm called him "Eddie Gorilla"—but not to his face.)

He might be perfect, Adrienne thought.

And he was a neighbor, too, working out of a townhouse on Park Road, just a block from Adrienne's English basement. He was a fixture at Mt. Pleasant neighborhood association meetings. A maven on security issues and a hard-liner where property values were concerned, Bonilla had been instrumental in organizing the Mt. Pleasant Neighborhood Watch. "My posse," he called it, leading bands of orange-vested homeowners on their evening patrols.

"Have some more," Bette said, offering her carton.

Adrienne shook her head, and offered her carton in return. But Bette wasn't interested. Getting up, she dumped her trash in the wastebasket. "Back to the grindstone," she said, and headed the way of her cubicle.

Adrienne sat back in her chair, and had a few more bites of curry. The more she thought about it, the more she liked the idea of hiring Eddie Bonilla. There wasn't any downside that she could see, and there was no way she was going to let this guy, Duran, get away with what he'd done. A little scrutiny would be very much in order. And Bonilla would be perfect. Flamboyant, but still a pro. And even though he was busy as hell—the firm was doing two or three M&A's a month—she knew he'd find the time for her. They were, like, friends. Not really—but sort of.

A year ago, he'd come to her door (this was shortly after she'd moved in), escorted and introduced by Mrs. Spears. "Adrienne, I'd like to introduce Mr. Bonilla."

Her first thought had been that Eddie Bonilla was a trip. He was a short, skinny guy, somewhere in his fifties—who looked like he was still *living* in the Fifties. He wore khakis, but called them "chinos." His hair was slicked back on both sides, while a pompadour crashed and burned on his forehead. Like Elvis, he had magnificent sideburns. Most curiously of all, his clothes seemed slightly too small for him—despite the fact that he was thin—as if he was a kid who'd just gone through a growth spurt.

"Eddie Bonilla," he'd said, peering past her into the apartment. Then his hand shot out, and she shook it. "I make it a point to know who's movin' in."

"Nice to meet you," she'd said.

"I already practically know you—you work down at Slough, Hawley, right? You're the one they call Scout."

This had surprised her. "How do you know that?"

"I know everything," he told her, with a corny wink and a heh-heh cackle. Then he explained who he was and what he did. "I'm one of your 'resources.' "

"Why do they call you 'Scout'?" Mrs. Spears asked.

Adrienne was embarrassed. "I don't know. It's just a nickname."

Bonilla scoffed. "She's being modest," he said. "See, this law firm where Adrienne works, it's stuffed with Georgetown grads. And the way I hear it, there was this big shot professor—"

Adrienne blushed. "I don't think Mrs. Spears—"

But Bonilla held up a hand and gave her a look. "There was

this big shot professor who teaches—what? torts or something, right?"

Adrienne sighed. "Right."

"So one day he's not happy with the class, and he's giving them a lot of grief. 'Cause they didn't do dick—you'll pardon my French. Like they weren't *prepared*. Except for Scout here, who's always prepared!"

Mrs. Spears blinked, uncertain if that was the end of the anecdote.

"Get it?" Bonilla asked. " 'Always prepared.' Like a Boy Scout, except—"

Mrs. Spears lit up with a smile. "Oh!" she said.

"So naturally, the name sticks." He gave Adrienne a fond look. "Scout," he said.

Adrienne shook her head. "You really *do* know everything."

He shot a finger toward her and pulled the trigger. "Better believe it."

After she'd participated in a couple of his neighborhood patrols, they'd become—well, friendly. Eddie helped Mrs. Spears with minor repairs from time to time, and he'd even helped Adrienne fix the windshield wipers on her ancient Subaru (or, as he called it: "the Japmobile").

She called up her address book on the computer, found the number, and left a message on Bonilla's answering machine. He had a pager and a mobile phone as well—Eddie had every gadget in the book—but she didn't bother. He was famous for checking his messages.

Forty-five minutes later, he called back.

"What's up?" he asked, as if he were her only phone call of the day.

"I was just wondering," she said, abandoning a textbook on civil engineering.

"Yeh?"

"Yes. I was wondering if . . . if you could do some work for me."

A short silence. And then: "Like what?"

"Well, it's about my sister—"

"Oh yeah, I heard about that—that was a helluva thing. I meant to tell you how sorry I was, but . . . What do you have in mind? Is it the will, or—"

"No, it's not that. It's—well, there are a couple of things."

"Such as what?"

In the ten days since Nikki had died, Adrienne had used what little spare time she had, or could steal, to put her sister's affairs in order. And very quickly, it had become apparent that rather a lot of money was missing.

"You do asset searches, right?"

"Yeah," Bonilla said. "You lose something?"

"Actually? About half a million dollars."

"Ouch."

"My sister had an accident. (A few years ago—in Germany.) And there was a settlement."

"And you can't find it?"

"I haven't had a lot of time to look—I've been so busy. But . . . no."

"What about her bankbooks?"

"She had a checking account with about two thousand dollars in it, and a savings account with . . . I think there's fifteen K—but that's it. Maybe she had another account—she must have had another account—but I don't know where to look."

"So how do you know she had this money? I mean, half a mil . . . ?"

"She told me about it. It's what she lived on. She didn't have a job. And I was thinking, maybe she had it in stocks, or life insurance—an annuity. Could you find that out, if she did?"

Bonilla clicked the tip of his tongue against his palate, making a sort of clicking sound. Finally, he said, "Yeah. I could do that. No sweat."

"Oh, that's great—"

"You said there were *two* things . . ."

Adrienne hesitated for a moment, and then plunged in. "The other thing is: I'm thinking of bringing suit against her therapist."

Bonilla's grunt had a skeptical tone.

"There are malpractice issues—" Adrienne began, but Bonilla cut her off.

"I gotta be honest with ya, Scout. Sometimes, people get caught up in what they call 'the grief process,' y'know? And they go looking to blame somebody—"

"I'm not *looking* to blame anyone, Eddie. Her fucking therapist killed her."

"Well, 'killed her'—"

"The 'memories' Nikki 'recovered'? There wasn't anything to them. It was all a fantasy. I *know*, because I was there."

Another grunt. "What kinda memories?" Bonilla asked.

Adrienne wasn't sure how to put it. "Crazy stuff."

"Like what?"

She took a deep breath. "Nikki thought she'd been abused."

Adrienne could hear Bonilla thinking about it. Finally, he said, "So? It happens. Even in the best of families."

"By Satanists."

"Oh." When she didn't say anything, he asked, "You mean, with hoods and stuff?"

"Yeah. Hoods and candles and I don't know what—goats' heads."

"Jeez . . ."

"It was supposed to have happened to me, too, but—believe me, you'd remember this stuff."

"And you don't."

"No," Adrienne replied. "I don't."

"And you think her therapist—"

"—invented it all."

"Hunh! And why do you suppose he'd do that?"

"I don't know. But it happens."

"Yeah. That's what I hear," Bonilla said. And then: "I could see how maybe you wouldn't want to *tell*, I mean if it was your old man or something—you'd probably get pretty bent out of shape, on account of the perversion and all. But not

remembering—I got trouble with that. The way I see it, something like that happens, you got trouble *forgetting* it, not the
other way around."

"Exactly, and—"

"The thing is: what's in it for this guy?" Bonilla asked.
"The therapist, I mean. What's *he* get out of it?"

"Two things. First, Nikki left him money in her will. For
helping her, right? Second, I did some searches on the Web.
There's actually a false memory group—parents, mostly, and
family members—who say the accusations against them are
nonsense, that therapists *want* clients to believe this kind of
junk—"

"Why?"

"Because—it means more *therapy*. I want to take this guy
to court—make an example of him."

"And I'm gonna help you . . . how?"

"I want you to investigate him, find out if there are any
complaints on file—that kinda thing."

"So, we're talkin' . . . what? Basic stuff. Credentials, credit
rating? Like that?"

"Exactly."

Bonilla was silent for a moment, and then said. "I can do
that. But—"

"Nikki left me a little money. I can tap into it."

"That's not the point."

"But it is! Of course I'll pay!"

"Yeah, but—"

"Really, Eddie, I insist!"

He waited a few seconds, and then he said, "What I was
gonna ask was: do you have a budget?"

"Oh." She thought about it, suddenly embarrassed. "Would
a thousand dollars—"

Bonilla laughed. "I'm pullin' your leg! I'll do it for expenses." Once again, Adrienne began to protest, but he cut
her off. "So whatta you have on the guy?"

She told him. Name and address. Telephone number.

"You got a Social?"

"No," she replied, "but—I saw his diplomas."

"You *what*?"

"I saw his diplomas."

"You *went* there?"

". . . uh-huh."

A sad sigh on the other end of the line. "What'd you do that for? So you could scream at him?"

"Yes."

"Well, don't do it again."

"I won't."

"You promise?"

"I promise."

"Okay," Bonilla replied. "So where'd this turkey go to school?"

"Brown. And then a doctorate from Wisconsin. Clinical psychology."

"What years?"

"I don't remember."

"Doesn't matter." The line was quiet for a while. Finally, Bonilla said, "Gimme a coupla days."

And then he hung up.

12 Duran felt the air flex just before the phone rang, and thought, *The phone.* Then it rang—and he jumped, despite himself. Pushing the mute button on the remote control (*Oprah* was on), he lifted the receiver.

"Mr. Duran?"

The voice was a woman's, polite and removed. A telemarketer, perhaps, but restrained—not gooey.

"Yes?"

"It's Adrienne Cope."

Oh. His shoulders sagged, and he thought, *The woman's unstable. Don't take it personally.* "Oh, hello." And then, after a short silence, he asked, "What can I do for you?"

"Well," she said. "I'd like to come and see you—if you'd do me the courtesy."

The courtesy? He recalled her voice as she raged through the door—with de Groot in the other room: *You son of a bitch! You killed her!* "I don't know," he said. "I'm not sure that's such a good idea."

"It would only take a few minutes," she promised. "I thought we could talk about Nikki."

Duran winced inside himself. "It's just that . . . I'm not sure there's anything to be gained."

"*Please.* It wouldn't take long, and—it would really help me."

Duran thought about it, the silence thickening. Maybe she wanted to apologize for her behavior. Maybe she wanted to ask him about her sister's problems. Talking to him might bring her to closure. It was never easy, he thought, for the people who were left behind. They often blamed themselves, and needed reassurance.

"It would only take a couple of minutes," she suggested.

Duran heaved a sigh. "Fine."

"Great. When would be good for you?" she asked, her voice suddenly crisp and efficient.

"Let me take a look," Duran replied, and opened his appointments book. Finally, he said, "I could see you tomorrow afternoon. Two o'clock?"

That evening, he timed the arrival of his dinner (a four cheese pizza with artichoke hearts from Pizzeria Luna), so that he could eat it during a PBS documentary about the America's Cup.

Watching the program, Duran felt an almost physical connection to the crew, lowering his head as the boat crested a buoy and came about. The crew's movements seemed spectacularly fast and fluid on a vessel that was heeling over so sharply that water was pouring over the combings.

His pizza sat on the plate untouched as the sight of the boats held him. The spume of spray kicked up by the jutting prow, the way the sails slapped, slack, and then bellied full as the boat took hold of the wind—this sent an arrow of longing through him so sharp that he could not have spoken if he had to. It was very peculiar. Without intending to, he found himself mimicking the motions of the sailors, tensing in synch with the on-screen crew, anticipating its motions with small, shadow actions. *Like a dog,* he thought, *moving its paws in a dream.*

But where does it come from? he wondered. It was all so familiar: the gurgle and slosh of the water, the flash and movement of the crew, the lines, the sails, the salt tang and sparkling sky. He was a sailor. He could feel it. He knew exactly what the crew was doing, and what they were *going* to do, even before they did it. He was able to anticipate every shift in tack, the precise moment when the hull's momentum changed, when the wind filled the sails and the ship surged ahead. *And yet . . .*

He had not a single memory of sailing a boat—or of being in a boat under sail. Still, he could feel that he was a sailor: it was hardwired into him, and there was no mistaking it. And no remembering, either. When he tried to recall even a single moment at sea, his mind went "into irons" as surely as a ship turning into the wind. The sails went slack, and the boat came to rest, dead in the water, luffing, still.

That's me, Duran thought. *My head's in irons.* And for a moment, he wondered, half seriously, if perhaps he hadn't been reincarnated. For how else could he have gained such knowledge, if not from a previous life? *Reincarnation would explain a lot of things,* Duran thought, *but . . . not this.* If true, it might explain life after death, but it could never answer the simpler and even more devastating question that Duran was asking himself:

How is it that I've become so alone in the world, so utterly disconnected from myself, that I can't even recall if I know how to sail, or what it was like to be held by my mother. It's as if I've become a sort of rough sketch of myself . . .

Frustrated by the Jacob's Ladder of his own identity and feelings, he changed channels. There was a "Real World Marathon" on MTV, and he didn't have a client for a couple of hours.

When Nico's sister appeared in his doorway the next afternoon, Duran was surprised to see that she was not alone.

A retro little man was at her side, bouncing on his heels. He seemed to be just this side or that of 50, with laser-trim sideburns and beady eyes. Even without looking, Duran could tell that his fingers were yellowed by nicotine.

"Hi," Duran said, as he opened the door and stepped aside to let them in.

Adrienne tossed him a glance, and entered with her friend right behind her. It was amazing how much she looked like Nico, and yet . . . It was a Snow-White/Rose-Red kind of thing, with Adrienne definitely playing Snow-White. The last time Duran had seen Nico, she'd been wearing a tiny skirt and a skintight top. But her sister was having none of that. She wore a demure green dress that came to midcalf, with a rolled collar that crowded her chin. It was like looking at Nico playing dress-up, pretending to be her kindergarten teacher.

Duran closed the door, and turned to his guests. The man handed him an envelope. Duran looked puzzled. "What's this?"

"You've been served," the man told him.

"I've been what?"

"Served."

"With what?"

A chuckle from Sideburns, who cast a sidelong glance at Adrienne. "Whattaya think?" he asked.

Duran turned to Adrienne, whose cheeks were bright red, though he couldn't tell if embarrassment or venom had put the color there.

"I'm suing you," Adrienne said.

"For what?" Duran replied.

"For the intentional infliction of emotional distress—and fraud." She nodded toward the envelope in his hand. "That's the complaint," she explained, "and a summons to appear in court. You have twenty days to respond."

"Oh, for Christ's sake," Duran exclaimed, shaking his head in disbelief.

"There's more," Adrienne went on. "We've been to the police. They want to talk with you."

Duran shook his head. "Look," he said, "I know what grief can do to people, but . . . your sister was a very troubled woman."

"And you're a very troubled man," Sideburns said. "Or you will be—because you're going to the joint, 'Doc.' "

"Don't be ridiculous," Duran said.

"There's nothing 'ridiculous' about it. You're a fraud," Adrienne told him.

"And we can prove it," Sideburns said.

Duran closed his eyes, and shook his head. Then he opened his eyes, and looked directly into Adrienne's. "I did everything I could for your sister."

"Actually," Sideburns said, "that might be true—but it's not the point. The issue is: you're a quack. You broke the law."

"What law?"

"You got a pencil? Write this down: Chapter 33, Section 2, 3310 dot 1. Check it out."

"Check *what* out?" Duran asked.

"D.C. Criminal Code. You're 'practicing a health occupation without a license.' Not good."

Duran turned to Sideburns, and focused on him for the first time. He looked as if he was made of bone and gristle, one of those wiry guys who got into a lot of fights as a kid—and kept on going. "Not to make too much of a point of it," Duran said, "but who the fuck are you?"

The man smiled, delighted to have gotten Duran's attention. Reaching into his coat, he came up with a business card and handed it to his adversary.

> *Edward Bonilla*
> *Bonilla & Associates*
> *Private Investigations*

There were a lot of numbers for such a small card: telephone, fax, mobile, and pager. In the upper right-hand corner, in what Duran guessed was an attempt at humor, was the detective's logo—a corny fingerprint under a corny magnifying glass.

"Mr. Bonilla is a private investigator," Adrienne explained. "And I'm a lawyer and . . . well, you can see where this is going. We're going to put you away."

Duran shook his head in disbelief. *Put me away!?* "Look," he said. "I understand how you feel about . . . what happened . . . but, you're wrong about me, and you're wrong about my not being licensed. It's in my office—on the wall, next to my diplomas."

Bonilla scoffed. "Lemme show you something," he said, waggling a leather portfolio. "You mind if we sit down for a minute?"

Duran shook his head, and gestured toward the couch in the living room. Once seated, Bonilla made a production of opening his portfolio, then laying it down on the coffee table. "The first thing I did," he said, extracting several sheets of paper, "was check with the District's Medical Board." He donned a pair of reading glasses and peered at the documents in his hand. "And when I ask them about you, what they want to know is, are you a psychotherapist or a psychologist? Because there's a big difference! Turns out, any wacko can hang out a shingle as a 'therapist.' But a clinical *psychologist*, which is what you're supposed to be—that's another story.

Because, one: you got to have a doctoral degree. And two: you gotta complete an internship. After that, you have to do supervised, post-doctoral work. And, finally, you gotta pass a licensing exam. And you, Doc—you ain't done any of this stuff."

Duran was silent for a moment. Then he leaned forward in his chair. "You must not be very good at what you do," he suggested.

"No?"

"No. Because, if you were, you'd know I was magna cum laude—"

"You were magna cum bullshit!" Bonilla interjected. "When the board said it never heard of you, I figured, what the hell— it's probably an oversight. Maybe you're registered somewhere else—Virginia, Maryland—Alaska, for all I know. Or you forgot to renew. So I check with the A.P.A. And guess what? They never heard of you, either. So that's when I thought, *Hmmmnn.* Better check out the diplomas, the ones our friend here saw. Brown, right? And Wisconsin."

"That's right."

"No, Jim—that *ain't* right. For openers, you didn't graduate from Brown. In fact, you never even went there." Bonilla removed a page from his portfolio, and pushed it across the coffee table.

Duran picked it up, and began to read. The letter seemed to be authentic, but . . . it couldn't be. According to the registrar, no one named Jeffrey Duran had attended Brown between 1979 and 1993. A check with academic advisers for the class of 1990 produced not a single transcript, nor did the office of residential life have any records associated with a student by that name. The letter thanked Mr. Bonilla for bringing to the university's attention the inaccurate inclusion of Mr. Duran's name on its "base list" of 1990 graduates.

While we cannot be certain how this error occurred, we have taken steps to improve computer security at the school in general, and at the Registrar's office in particular.

Duran couldn't believe it. "They think—"

"You hacked your way in," Adrienne told him.

"But . . . they're wrong. It's a mistake."

Bonilla's grin revealed small yellow teeth. "Yeah," he said, "it's gotta be a mistake. You went to Brown, only you never took out a library book, registered for a class, or signed up for a food plan. Like I said, 'magna cum bullshit.' " The detective raised his eyebrows, withdrew a second sheet of paper from the portfolio, and slapped it down on the table.

"Wisconsin never heard of you either," he said.

Duran picked up the paper, which bore the school's letterhead with its familiar logo: an eye, surrounded by the words, *Numen Lumen*.

> *Dear Mr. Bonilla:*
> *Re: Duran, Jeffrey A.*
> *Although the name Jeffrey Duran appears on our list of 1994 graduates, a further search of relevant files and databases confirms your doubt about the integrity of that list. Mr. Duran did not earn an advanced degree from the University of Wisconsin. Our search found the records of six individuals named Jeffrey Duran who attended the University during the 1980–95 period. None of these individuals, however, was enrolled in a doctoral program at the University.*

"This is impossible," Duran insisted, wagging his head, as if it were a pendulum. "What *is* this? I mean—" he held up the papers. "Did you write these yourself? Why would you *do* that?"

Bonilla made a little clicking noise with his mouth and shook his head, beaming at Duran with an expression of faked admiration. "You gotta hand it to him, Adrienne. This guy's good. I mean, you don't know better, you'd have to say he's *affronted*!"

"I think you ought to leave," Duran told them, getting wearily to his feet.

"Hear me out," Bonilla insisted, "because I saved the best

for last." There was nothing amused in the man's face now and he looked at Duran with the sharp, malevolent focus of a bird of prey. "All these institutions that never heard of you got me worrying (well, I'm the anxious type, as Miz Cope here will tell you). I had a feeling, y'know? So, knowing your *alleged* name and your *actual* address, I ran a credit check with Experian. Cost me thirty-five bucks. All I was lookin' for was a header—just the top line." He placed another document on the table, and watched as Duran picked it up. "Name, address, and D-O-B. Where you were born. And your Social."

Duran frowned. "My what?"

"Your social security number," Adrienne explained.

"Like I said: it's the top line." Bonilla grinned in a bright, unfriendly way. "And the next thing I do, I get on the Web, and—bim bam boom—I'm at the site for the Social Security Death Index. Takes about thirty seconds. And guess what?"

Duran didn't want to play anymore. "I think you ought to go," he said.

"Not *yet*, Jeff, I'm just getting to the punch line." Bonilla stood up, crouched like a batter and raised his hands to shoulder height. "You didn't attend Brown." His arms came round in an arc, as if he were swinging a bat—and missing. "*Whoosh!* Turns out, you ain't no Badger!" Another swing, and: "*Whoof!* And last, but definitely not least, *you* ain't even Jeffrey Duran." The detective reached into his portfolio, and extracted a piece of paper. "Check it out," he said, and handed it to Duran.

Who saw, at a glance, that it was his own death certificate. A somewhat blurry photocopy, but nonetheless, a Certificate of Death for

Jeffrey Aaron Duran
Date of Birth: Aug. 26, 1968
Place of birth: Washington, D.C.
Date of Death: April 4, 1970
Place of death: Carlisle, Pennsylvania,
Occupation: N/A

The cause of death was listed as "Massive trauma (auto)." The physician of record: Willis Straight, M.D. There was more, but Duran stopped reading.

"In case you're wondering," Bonilla taunted, "you're buried in Rock Creek Cemetery. 'Sometimes Heaven Calls To Its Breast Those Loved Best.' "

Duran was stunned. The only explanation for the documents he'd been shown was that they were a hoax, and yet—who would go to such lengths? Was Adrienne Cope so disturbed that she was trying to kill him off *symbolically*? Maybe, but—what about Bonilla?

"The man you're impersonating never grew up," Adrienne told him. "He died as a baby. But you know that, of course."

"I know you're distraught about your sister's death," Duran said calmly, "and I can make a lot of allowances for that. But this . . . the effort that went into this . . ." He tossed the death certificate onto the coffee table. "You're a very disturbed person. I hope you get some help." Then he turned to Bonilla with a ferocious look. "And *you*—" he began.

" *'Get some help?!' * " Adrienne sputtered. " 'The effort that went into it'—the effort that went into it involved about five hours of Mr. Bonilla's time. And the diplomas took even less. And that's a crime, by the way—having those diplomas on your wall. It's criminal possession of a forged instrument. And for hacking into the universities' computers—that's another crime."

"This is ridiculous," Duran told them. "This goes way beyond providing closure—"

" *'Closure'?!* " Adrienne growled.

Duran took a step back as Adrienne lunged at him, only to be intercepted by Bonilla, who seized her by the arms and murmured, "It's okay . . ."

"Talk about sick!" Adrienne muttered, her voice rising in volume. "You're the one who needs a shrink! The people you see are desperate—they're dying inside—and they come to you for help, and what do they get? Some phony-baloney therapy—"

"Take it easy," Bonilla murmured. "We'll see him in court—and you can write to him in jail. He'll have lots of time to read."

Duran was dumbfounded by her anger. "I feel like I've stepped through the looking glass," he said, to no one in particular.

Bonilla chuckled as he steered Adrienne toward the door. "Is he good or what?" the detective asked. "I mean, you deal with a con man, a little acting talent shouldn't surprise you. But this guy! You gotta hand it to him." He shook his head in a rueful way, stepped into the hallway with his client, and pulled the door closed behind him.

Duran remained where he was, standing in the foyer, staring at the door. In irons.

13 It was insane.

Sitting at the computer, unnerved by his confrontation with Nico's sister and her doberman, Duran read over the last few entries in Nico's file:

15 October
Trance state. Encouraged client to recall "shadow night." Initial resistance overcome, but blocking persisted. Recollection of "black mass" traumatic, even under hypnosis. New detail: participation in Eucharistic ritual with semen and blood.

> 20 October
> *Nicole Sullivan dead. Younger sister, Adrienne Cope, burst into session with de Groot to say she blames me for her sister's suicide. (This grief-to-anger transference may be a healthy one if it facilitates closure for Ms. Cope.)*

Paging down to the bottom of the file, Duran made a new entry:

> 5 November
> *Second visit from Adrienne Cope (accompanied by a P.I. named Bonilla). Served with summons in a $10 million civil action (!), alleging intent. inflict. of mental distress, fraud & imposture.* Incredibly, *the P.I. presented forged letters and docs. in support of allegation.*

It was crazy. If the documents had been genuine, it might have made sense to confront him with them. But they weren't. So what had Nico's sister hoped to accomplish?

It made you wonder about lawyers and private eyes.

Getting up from the computer, Duran crossed the room to an antique wooden cabinet that held a selection of single malt whiskies and a rack of Waterford tumblers. Pouring two fingers of Laphroaig in one of the glasses, he swirled it for a moment, and sipped. You could create any kind of document you wanted with desktop publishing, he thought. Birth certificate. Death certificate. Whatever. But that wasn't the point—that wasn't what was bothering him. What was bothering him was the fact that Bonilla and Cope had nothing to gain by confronting him with phony documents.

Duran took a second sip of Laphroaig, and wandered over to the window. Looking out toward the cathedral, he thought, *Maybe this guy, Bonilla, fabricated it all, and sold the package as a bill of goods to Nico's sister. Maybe he figured he'd make a few bucks, jack up his hours . . .*

It was possible, of course, but . . . how hard up would a guy like that have to be?

He shook his head, uncertain what to think. It was irritating, on the one hand—disconcerting on the other. To have someone get in your face and deny something as fundamental as your own identity—and to do it in your own living room was . . . Well, it put you off-balance.

What was the phrase she'd used? *the man you're impersonating.* A ridiculous accusation but, even so, it made him feel as if she'd shone a flashlight into his soul—and found a structural flaw that ran from his forehead to his feet. She was wrong, obviously, but her accusation went to the heart of what had been bothering him so much of late: the alienation that he felt, and the feeling that . . . how to put it?

In his heart of hearts, there *was* no heart of hearts.

Finishing his scotch, Duran turned from the window and wandered into the hall. There, he picked up the photo of his mother, sitting on the porch swing, head thrown back in laughter. Then he squeezed his eyes shut and tried to remember her as she really was. And what he remembered was . . . *the photograph. Mom in the swing* . . .

Which was the trouble with memory—or *his* memories, at least. There was nothing "eidetic" about them. He'd been reading up about it, and that was the word Ernst Young used to describe memories of a "Proustian" character, referring to the scene in which the bedridden Proust is suddenly immersed in a fully textured past by a single bite of tea-soaked, madeleine.

Not so Duran, whose own long-term memories were almost entirely visual and matter-of-fact. There was no sense of color or smell, no taste or sound. There was just the image, and only the image. Or to put it another way: he remembered his mother in the same way that he remembered . . . Eleanor Roosevelt. (Or Marilyn Monroe—or Pocahontas).

Eddie Bonilla's predatory grin floated before him, like the Cheshire Cat's smile. What was the phrase he'd used? *Magna cum bullshit.*

How could he remember things—words—and not remember his mother's voice? If asked, he could recite chapter and verse of her life: where she was born, the time she got lost in the woods, how she'd fallen from a horse at seventeen and broken her collarbone—which kept her from the senior prom. But the truth was he didn't remember his mother as a mother. She was part of his "database"—along with James Dean, the Baltimore harbor, and long division.

Going over to his desk, he looked up the number for the D.C. Office of Vital Records and punched it out on the telephone keypad. Then he listened through a long and well-organized voice-mail menu outlining procedures for obtaining birth and death certificates. The voice noted that disclosure of these documents was limited under privacy statutes. Birth certificates did not become publicly available for one-hundred years. Death certificates did not become releasable until fifty years had passed. The only exceptions to these rules were the individuals whose records they were, and next of kin.

And, if the recording was to be believed, these people would have to provide a valid photo ID before anything would be released to them. Which proved Bonilla's documents were forgeries. Except . . . he *was* a detective. And from what Duran had seen on television, and read in books, private eyes seemed to make their living through "contacts" and pretexts. That a P.I. should finesse a death certificate out of the Office of Vital Records was not beyond the realm of possibility.

On the other hand, Duran thought, *you'd think I'd know who I am—and whether I'm dead or not.* The predicament would have been amusing, if it weren't for the fact that his client had committed suicide, and now he was being sued for millions.

But there was something else, something that Bonilla had said. It took a moment—then Duran remembered: the Social Security Death Index. The detective had gone to the Office of Vital Records after accessing the Social Security Internet site.

And maybe that explains things, Duran thought. *Maybe the*

private eye found someone with a similar name—or even the
same name—and confused it with me and mine.

Sitting down at the computer, Duran logged onto AOL and searched for the site that lists the names of Social Security recipients who have died. It only took a moment, and then he found it. The page was a link on half a dozen URLs devoted to genealogy. He tried *Ancestry.com*, and was soon connected.

There were three fields of entry in the search engine: first name, last name, and state. Duran typed his names in the appropriate fields, and clicked on the District of Columbia. A few seconds later, the results materialized on the monitor. There was a single entry:

Name	Born	Died	Residence	SSN
Jeffrey Duran	Aug. 25, 1968	April 4, 1970	20010 (WDC)	520-92-0668

It was him.
He almost fainted.

The cabdriver had no idea how to get to Rock Creek Cemetery, even though both of them could see it on the hillside as they cruised along the parkway, gravestones, statues, and vaults stepping down the hill. They tried three exits: Calvert, Cathedral, and Massachusetts Avenue, but as soon as they left the parkway, the cemetery disappeared.

"I'm gon' try P Street," the driver said, heading downtown again. "You got kin buried here?"

Duran nodded. "Yeah."

"Not my *biz-ness*," the cabbie said, scolding himself. "Myself—I lost my mother eight years ago, and I ain't seen her stone for quite a while." He shook his head, and made a clucking sound as he leaned forward. Then he turned on the windshield wipers.

Eight years ago . . . , Duran thought. That was about when his own parents had died—in the summer of '93, when he'd been in grad school.

The driver swung onto the P Street exit ramp, but, once again, there was no sign of the cemetery. Soon, they were back on the parkway.

"Have to be here someplace," the driver said, "you can see it, from time to time." Finally, he pulled into the tiny Exxon station that stood on the corner near the Watergate Hotel. Leaving the car, he went up to the jumpsuited attendant, and clapped him on the shoulder. "Mah man . . . ," he said.

The two of them disappeared into the gas station's office. After a while, the driver emerged with a Post-it in his hand. Sliding behind the wheel, he clapped the yellow slip of paper to the dashboard, and declared, "Now we in bizness."

And so they were. The cemetery's entrance was barely a mile away, though by the time they pulled up to the little building that served as its office, the rain was falling steadily.

"Say, man," the driver asked as Duran paid him. "You want an umbrella?"

"Sorry?"

"No charge or nothin'. Every rainy day, two or three people leave they umbrella in the cab. So what I do, I try to *redistribute* things, know what I mean?"

Duran was so taken aback by the man's spontaneous kindness that he felt a jolt of sadness when the taxi drove away, as if he were bidding farewell to a friend.

The shuffling cemetery attendant looked, to Duran's eye, close to joining the ranks that he himself oversaw. His skin was papery white, his eyes red-rimmed and crusty. He was dressed in work clothes—a dark blue shirt, matching pants, and boots.

"What can I do for you?" he asked.

"I'm looking for a grave."

"Well, you came to the right place. What's the name?"

"Duran," he replied, sounding foolish to himself. "Jeffrey Duran." At the man's request, he spelled it.

The man listlessly punched the information onto a computer keyboard. After a moment, he withdrew a printed map of the cemetery from a shelf, circled an area marked P-3, and handed the sheet to Duran without a word.

The umbrella was nice and big, with a bulbous wooden handle. When he stepped outside and opened it, the rain came down harder, as if on signal, peppering the fabric as he checked the landmarks on the map. He didn't mind that it was raining—if anything, the diminished visibility softened the agoraphobia that was stirring in his gut.

Standing within the umbrella's drip line, studying the map, he could see that finding the grave was not going to be easy. And it wasn't. Even with the map, it took him nearly twenty minutes. And despite the umbrella, his shoes and socks and pant legs were soaked when he finally found it.

Jeffrey Aaron Duran's gravestone sat on a small knoll under a towering Norway spruce. The ground around it was spongy with rain and covered with russet-colored needles that smelled like Christmas. Duran stared:

> *Jeffrey Aaron Duran*
> *B. August 26, 1968*
> *D. April 4, 1970*
> *Sometimes Heaven Calls To*
> *Its Breast Those Loved Best*

The sight of the gravestone was like a body blow. It took his breath away and, for a moment, he was afraid to look around, afraid there would be emptiness on either side of him—that if he looked, he'd find himself stranded in a void with nothing to hang onto but the certainty that the world as he knew it was a mere hallucination, an artifact of his own disordered mind. Destabilized to the core, Duran was helpless as a gust of wind grabbed at the umbrella in his hand, and snatched it away. Reflexively, he turned and watched as the umbrella cartwheeled down the hill, grateful that there *was* a hill, an umbrella, a cemetery.

By then, he was beyond surprise, or thought he was, until

he realized what ought to have been obvious in the first place—that he was standing in a family plot, surrounded by the graves of several Durans. For the second time in a minute, the world lurched as his eyes fell upon a granite plinth from which an angel rose, wings folded, eyes downcast. Beneath the angel, the names of his parents were etched in the stone—and like him, they'd died in 1970.

The words on the death certificate ran through his mind: *Massive trauma (auto)*. Not carbon monoxide, then. And not Nantucket, but *Carlisle, Pennsylvania*.

Turning, he walked slowly through the rain until he arrived, drenched, at the cemetery office, where he asked the attendant if he'd call him a cab.

The man looked up from his desk in a slow, reptilian way and, seeing the look on Duran's face, broke into a toxic grin, ripe with schadenfreude. "What's a matter? Seen a ghost?"

14

It was so unfair.

For the past week, Adrienne had been at the office every night until midnight, preparing for depositions. And just this once, she'd come in late—and Curtis Slough's secretary was all over her voice mail with progressively sarcastic messages. Culminating in: "Uhhh—are you coming in at *all* today?"

Bitch!

Adrienne glanced at her watch. It was ten in the morning—not two in the afternoon. Taking a deep breath, she counted to five, and pushed the button for Slough's extension. The receptionist said that the line was busy, and put her on hold.

While she waited, she looked through the file on Dante Esposito, one of the city's asphalt "experts." From what she could see, it looked as if Esposito was going to testify that the asphalt in question was probably *different* from the mix they usually used. (Not good.)

When Slough finally came on the line, it was obvious from his cheerful tone that he'd forgotten why (or even *that*) he wanted to talk to her. Which put the ball in Adrienne's court, because Slough had a reputation for blaming people for his own shortcomings.

"I got your messages," she told him, "and I have the documents you wanted. Should I send them up?"

"I guess so. Anything useful?"

She hesitated. "Well . . . I found various inspectors' reports—and they're fine for us. As far as the inspectors are concerned, everything about the job was A-OK."

Slough grunted his approval, then qualified it. "Well, that's great," he said, "but we still have Esposito—"

"Yes, but the final inspection was conducted by a man named McEligot. He's retired now, but he's the one who *hired* Esposito in the first place. I talked to him last night, and according to McEligot, the mix was fine. So—"

"Excellent!"

"And since Esposito didn't even *look* at the asphalt until two years after it was laid down—"

"I like it!" Slough boomed. "Makes Esposito look like he's shooting from the hip. Outstanding! We'll kill the bastards."

Eddie Bonilla picked her up for lunch at 12:30. He said he had a "bright idea" that he wanted to discuss with her—and, not only that, he'd buy her lunch.

He was waiting for her in his car, in the courtyard outside Harbor Place, where Slough, Hawley was headquartered. The car was a battered Camaro with a pair of Rubik's Cubes hanging from the rearview mirror, and vanity plates that read

SNUPER. Adrienne climbed in. Eddie gunned the engine and shot out into traffic.

She sat back, and closed her eyes. On the whole, she *liked* being a passenger. It reminded her of the car trips that she took as a kid. She and Nikki. Who used to breathe on the glass so that she could draw on it and they could play tic-tac-toe. It made her think of all those long vacation rides to Lake Sherando, where they went five years in a row, camping out. Deck and Marlena up front, she and Nikki (and all the stuff that wouldn't fit in the trunk) jammed into the back—along with Cupcake, the cat, in her cat carrier.

As they passed the Washington Monument, Adrienne recalled the time Nikki fed Cupcake the remains of her Fishwich—which had been sitting in the sun for hours. The cat got sick, and God how it smelled! They'd pinched their nostrils together, and made noises like *ewwwwww!* and rolled down the windows, and stuck their heads out, pretending to gag. There were a lot of trips like that, and they were always the same: long and boring—and lots of fun. Sometimes, they sang songs, or played word games like the one that went: *I packed my bag and in it I put . . .*

"A gun."

"What?" Bonilla was frowning at her.

She looked around. They were passing the Library of Congress, heading east on Pennsylvania. She hadn't realized she'd been thinking aloud. "My sister had a gun," she said. "A rifle."

Bonilla shrugged. "Lotsa people do. Got one myself. Got a couple, in fact."

Adrienne wasn't surprised. Bonilla struck her as the kind of person who'd have an arsenal. Which made her think that maybe she should show him her sister's gun. Ask him about the silencer—and what she should do with it. She was pretty sure it was illegal to have one. But what she asked instead was: "Where are we going?"

"Mangialardo's. Great subs."

At 9th and Pennsylvania, they got stuck behind a delivery

van and didn't make the light. Bonilla let out a string of curses, drummed his fingertips on the steering wheel, then gunned the engine a couple of times, just out of habit. She looked out the window. They were driving past a kind of demilitarized zone, a down-at-the-heels buffer between black and yuppie ghettos, when she remembered to ask him about "the assets search."

"Oh yeah. I forgot to tell you." He tilted his head from side to side, not quite shaking it. "There's a guy in Florida— 'information broker.' You give him a name or a Social, he'll run it through every bank, brokerage, and insurance company in the country."

"Sounds illegal."

Bonilla shrugged. "Not for me—'cause I don't know how he does it. None of my business. But the point is: he runs your sister—everywhere—and what he comes up with is . . . the same accounts you gave me."

"The ones at Riggs—"

Bonilla nodded. "Checking and savings. Maybe twenty grand, tops, just like you said."

"So he struck out."

"I don't think so. I think the guy found whatever there was to find. I think that's it."

Adrienne shook her head. "It can't be. She had a settlement—"

"That's what you said. So I went through her accounts—all the way back to when she opened them."

"And?" There were half a dozen police cars up ahead, double-parked outside a small store. Bonilla pulled up behind them into a space marked: NO STANDING.

He shrugged. "She opened the Riggs' accounts a couple of years ago. Ever since, she gets a check each month—like a salary—five grand—exactly. Except, sometimes there's more. Like she's got expenses on top of her base."

Adrienne nodded, her eyes on the police cars. "And these checks—where are they from?"

"Jersey."

"New Jersey? Why would she—"

"Not *New* Jersey. Just . . . Jersey! It's an island in the English Channel. Whole lotta banking goin' on."

Adrienne nodded. "Well, that makes sense. It's in Europe. So it's probably the account her settlement was paid into."

"Yeah," Bonilla replied. "That's what I think, too—though I gotta tell ya, if she was banking in the Channel Islands, there might be some tax issues you don't know about. Anyway, I'll fax the address to your office, and you can send the bank a letter. If you show 'em a death certificate, and tell 'em you're the executor . . . they oughta cooperate." He opened his door. "You like subs, right? You mind waiting here?" he asked. He didn't wait for her answer.

He came out a few minutes later with a couple of Oranginas and two sandwiches wrapped in waxy white paper. It was just possible to eat in the car, a pile of napkins between them, without having to change clothes afterwards.

"I meant to ask you," Bonilla said as they headed back toward Slough. "How'd your sister get hooked up with this quack, anyway? She get referred, or what?"

"I don't *know*," Adrienne replied. "It never came up." When she saw his eyebrows lift toward his hairline, she added, "Nikki wasn't exactly forthcoming."

"The reason I ask," Bonilla said, "if I didn't know better, I'd say this guy, Duran, was really knocked on his *ass* by that death certificate. I mean, it looks to me like he's gonna pass out when he sees it. Now, *I grant you,* your conman's a guy who can talk the talk, but this—this was like, I don't know, John Travolta or somethin'! So, I think: you take this guy to court, you got your work cut out for you."

"I don't have any choice," she said. "We both know the police aren't going to do anything. They've got five hundred unsolved homicides on the books. So they're not going to get excited about a misdemeanor that carries a thousand-dollar fine and a one-year sentence—max! That's why I filed the civil suit—which, by the way, took me about an hour to knock out. So it's not like I'm spending all my time on it."

Bonilla shrugged. "Whatever."

Adrienne shook her head. "Don't you get it? This guy, Duran, is supposed to be a *shrink*. Think about that. He uses his credentials to attract people who are—what? Sick. People who don't have anywhere else to turn. And they tell him all their secrets and sins, all their hopes and fears—and what do they get out of it? If they're lucky, nothing. And if they're not? An obituary in the Metro section of the *Post*."

They were quiet for a long while as they drove past the Washington Monument and the Tidal Basin, heading back to Georgetown. Finally, Adrienne asked, "So what's this 'bright idea' you had?"

"Oh *yeah*. I was thinking, maybe you ought to call the guy, and ask him, will he take a polygraph?"

The idea surprised her, and she cocked her head, thinking about it.

"Friend of mine's got a shop in Springfield," Bonilla went on. "I don't know what he charges, but—"

"That's not the point," Adrienne told him. "Duran wouldn't take a polygraph!"

"That *is* the point. 'Cuz he's damned if he does (which he won't), and he's damned if he doesn't. Whattaya think?"

She called Duran from her office, half an hour later, having decided that as a pretext for the call, she'd ask him if he'd gotten a lawyer to represent him in the action. The truth was, she half expected to get a recording, saying that the number was no longer in service. Instead, he answered on the first ring.

"H-hello?"

The tone in his voice surprised her. He sounded stuttery and lost. "It's Adrienne Cope," she told him. "I was calling to see if you'd gotten representation, yet. I have some papers . . ." Silence. "Mr. Duran?" (She was on her best behavior.) "Are you still there?"

More silence, and then: "I went to the cemetery," he said, his voice trailing off.

Adrienne wasn't sure what to say. "Yes . . . ?"

"And I saw the headstone."

"Oh." *Where was he going with this?*

"The only thing I can think is—it's some kind of coincidence."

She couldn't help herself. "Right," she said, "and your parents and *his* parents just *happened* to have the same names. And the registrar at Brown is mistaken, the registrar at Wisconsin is confused, and—is that about right? Is that what you're trying to tell me?"

"No," he said. "I'm not trying to tell you anything. Except . . . well, that I am who I am."

"Then prove it," she told him.

A rueful chuckle. "How?"

"Take a polygraph." Adrienne held her breath for what seemed like a long time, waiting for him to reply.

Finally, Duran cleared his throat. "Okay," he said. "Sure. How soon can you set it up?"

15

Maybe this whole thing is a mistake, Duran thought as he handed the driver a twenty dollar bill. Maybe he should tell the cabbie he'd forgotten something, and ask to be taken home. No skin off the *driver's* nose—he'd double his fare.

But . . . no.

"Keep the change," Duran told him, as he stepped from the taxi in front of a nondescript office building in the Springfield shopping center.

While Adrienne Cope did not have his best interests at heart, they had agreed on the questions he'd be asked (or the relevant ones, at least), and he knew that he could answer each of them truthfully and in the affirmative. He had nothing to hide. And he'd done nothing wrong.

Once she saw that he was telling the truth, she might not be so eager to proceed with the civil suit. As it was, he didn't really blame her for suing him. Her sister was dead, and no matter how you looked at it, this business with the death certificate was disturbing. Even he wasn't sure what it meant—though he did have a theory.

Either he was the victim of an astonishing set of coincidences, *or* . . .

His parents had stolen the identities of Frank and Rose Duran—then given *him* the child's name. That would explain everything (or almost everything: the problem with his university records was in no way explained by his theory, but that, he felt sure, was some kind of database glitch).

Of the two possibilities, coincidence or conspiracy, the latter seemed a lot more likely. Of course, it raised an intriguing question: why would his parents hijack another family's identity? There wasn't any way for Duran to answer that—he wasn't the FBI—but the time frame might be a clue.

When the Durans died, America had been fighting three wars: the Cold War, the war in Vietnam, and "the war at home" (against the war in Vietnam). Any one of those conflicts could have been the source of the predicament in which he now found himself. As crazy as it sounded, his parents might have been Soviet agents—It *happens*, Duran told himself—or, even more likely, antiwar activists on the run. That would explain their adoption of another family's identity. Except . . .

Duran couldn't recall either of his parents ever making a political statement of any kind. Or even hinting at one. Still, Sherlock Holmes's dictum was unassailable: once the impossible has been eliminated, whatever explanation remains—no matter how improbable—must be the truth. Even so . . . he couldn't imagine his mother firebombing the draft board, or his father slinking through Checkpoint Charlie with a false passport and—

Me, Duran thought, as he watched the cab pull away.

On the other hand, look at these women who'd recently surfaced after twenty years underground. To look at newspaper photos of the middle-aged Kathy Soliah, her plain face behind ordinary glasses, you couldn't imagine her driving a getaway car. And yet, she did—she *had*.

Putting these thoughts from his mind, or as far from his mind as he could, Duran entered the lobby, and seeing the building directory, checked for Sutton & Castle, PLC. The polygraph firm was on the fourth floor.

Crossing to the elevator, he pressed the call button and began to wait—until, with a sinking feeling, he realized that he'd begun to hyperventilate. It was impossible to predict when it would happen—except that it never happened at home, in his apartment.

Nearby, a woman in a blue dress was looking at him oddly. She sensed that something was wrong with him and, whatever it was, she didn't want any part of it. He saw her eyes richochet around the lobby, looking for help without calling for it—and finding none, in any case.

It was then that the elevator arrived with a *ding*! The doors pulled back, and the woman in blue quickly stepped inside. Duran took a step after her, but stopped in his tracks when she held out her hand, palm first, signaling him to stay where he was, as if he were a dog. Then the chrome doors drew closed, and she was gone.

By now, the adrenaline was surging through him, and standing still was impossible. Finding the emergency stairwell, he took the stairs two at a time, footsteps thundering on the cold cement. When he arrived at the fourth floor, he was hyperventilating *and* out of breath—which he knew was a perfect recipe for fainting dead away.

Sutton & Castle's door was the old-fashioned kind, with a mesh of wire between the layers of glass, and the name stenciled in gold upon it. He knocked, breathless, and when Eddie Bonilla opened the door, he stepped inside, a little too quickly.

"Well," Bonilla said, "look who's here!" Adrienne Cope got to her feet from a nearby couch, and a third person came over to introduce himself.

"Paul Sutton," he said, extending his hand.

Duran took the hand in his own, and shook it. Then he started to say something—because that's what you did in these situations—but nothing came out.

"You okay?" Sutton asked.

Duran nodded. "Took the stairs," he gasped. "I'm just . . . a little out of breath." The speech took all of the air that was left in his lungs, and when it was gone, the world began to tremble—or perhaps it was his knees. He felt the need to say something—everyone was looking at him anxiously, but nothing came out. The urge to bolt rose within him, but he resisted it—somehow, and barely. Instead, he made his way to a chair next to the window, where he sat down and tried to slow his breathing.

"I think he's having a panic attack," Bonilla said in a voice that was more bemused than sympathetic.

"Oh Jeez," Sutton muttered. "You didn't tell me the guy's a wacko."

"Do you have a paper bag?" Adrienne asked. "He's hyperventilating."

It took a moment, and then a bag was placed over his mouth and nose. Inhaling the woody smell, Duran took his breaths one at a time, listening to Adrienne's encouragement. "That's it . . . just like that. You're going to be okay."

It only took a minute or two for the attack to subside, and when it had, Duran felt mortified. "I don't know what to tell you," he said, looking from Adrienne to Sutton, and then to Bonilla. "I seem to suffer from agoraphobia. Sometimes, when I go out . . . it comes and goes."

Paul Sutton was a short man with a shaved head, a luxuriant mustache and a Boston accent. He regarded Duran with a skeptical eye. "You sure you're all right with this? You sure you want to go on?"

Duran nodded. "Yeah," he said, getting to his feet. "I'm okay. Let's do it."

The polygrapher led him into an adjacent room, where two chairs sat opposite each other across a conference table. On the table was a nineteen-inch monitor, a device that looked like an expensive amplifier—the lie detector, Duran guessed—and an array of attachments that were obviously meant for him. A cable ran from the lie detector to a computer that sat on the floor.

After seating Duran in one of the chairs, the polygrapher instructed him to unbutton his shirt and roll up his sleeve, which he did. Then he fastened a pneumograph tube to his subject's chest, strapped a blood pressure pulse cuff to his right arm, and placed an electrode assembly on Duran's left index finger. Bonilla and Adrienne stood just inside the doorway, watching.

"You know how this works, right?"

Duran shrugged. "I've seen it on television."

"But you're supposed to be a psychiatrist, or something, right?"

"A clinical psychologist," Duran confirmed.

"Then you'll know what I'm talking about when I tell you the machine can't be beat. What we're doing is, we're measuring how your autonomic nervous system responds to the questions we ask and the answers you give. We're talking blood pressure, pulse, respiration, and GSR. Things you can't control."

"What's that last one?" Adrienne asked.

"Galvanic Skin Response," Bonilla volunteered.

Seeing the blank look on Adrienne's face, Sutton explained: "The skin's resistance to electrical currents in the body."

"And what does that tell us?" Adrienne inquired.

"It's an indirect measure," the polygrapher replied, "of cortical arousal. The skin becomes more conductive when the subject tells a lie, so the GSR changes."

"Why is the skin more conductive?" Duran asked.

"Because lying's stressful," Sutton said. "It excites the cortex. And you can measure that."

Then Sutton got to his feet, smiled and ushered Bonilla and Adrienne into the other room.

"What?" Bonilla protested. "We don't get to watch?"

"No, you don't," Sutton told him. "This guy's strung out enough as it is. With you in the room, it's like having a junkyard dog—"

"You're afraid I might give the guy's cortex a hard-on, right?"

Adrienne rolled her eyes.

"Yeah," Sutton replied sarcastically, "that's what I'm afraid of." Then he turned to Adrienne. "I have to tell you: a subject this jumpy? I don't know what we're going to get."

"Oh, fahcrissake, that's what he always says!" Bonilla exclaimed. "Just ask him the questions, would ya?"

Sutton returned to the testing room, and closed the door behind him. Adrienne went over to the window, and looked out. Bonilla ran a hand through his hair and shook his head. "Man," he said, "did you see that guy? I swear, he could hardly breathe."

Adrienne nodded. "I felt sorry for him," she muttered, and it was true. For a moment, it seemed as if he was coming apart at the seams. Then he got it together. Somehow.

"Well, don't get carried away," Bonilla told her. "Just because he's fucked up, that don't make him a good guy."

She nodded a second time. "I know," she replied, and picked up the phone to check the messages at her office. Behind the door, she could hear Duran and the polygrapher talking, but she couldn't tell what was being said.

"Are you sitting in a chair? Wait to answer."

Duran counted to three, and said, "Yes."

"Is today November 8th?"

Again, he waited as he'd been told to do, and then replied, "Yes."

The polygrapher watched the graph being drawn on his monitor. "Am I sitting across from you? Answer 'No.' "

Duran did as he was told. And then they got down to business.

"Is your real name Jeffrey Duran?"

"Yes."

"Are you a licensed clinical psychologist?"

"Yes, I am."

"Just answer the question, yes or no," Sutton scolded. "Are you a licensed clinical psychologist?"

"Yes."

"Was your treatment of Nico Sullivan meant to be in her best interest?"

"Yes."

After Duran had left in a taxi, Adrienne and Bonilla went into the testing room, where Sutton was printing out a copy of the results.

"So?" Bonilla asked, rubbing his hands together. "Whatta we got?"

The polygrapher looked at Adrienne, and shrugged. "What we've 'got' . . . is George Washington."

Bonilla frowned. "Paul . . . don't do this to me. What are you talkin' about?"

"He's Jeffrey Duran."

"No, he's not," Bonilla told him.

"Well, he *thinks* he is," Sutton replied. "And when he says he's a clinical psychologist, he thinks he's telling the truth."

"Get outa here," Bonilla exclaimed. "We *know* he's lying. He's in the Death Index!"

The polygrapher shook his head, sat back in his chair, and turned the palms of his hands upward, as if to say, *What can I tell you?*

Adrienne spoke up. "Just before the test, you suggested the results might not be reliable."

"That's true," Sutton admitted. "But that was because he was so overwrought, so stressed, I was afraid everything he said would look like a lie. But that's not what I got. Look," he said, and beckoned them around to his side of the table.

On the computer screen were four graphs, arranged in tiers, one on top of the other. Using the mouse, Sutton put the cursor on the line marked PNEUMO 1, and clicked. Instantly, the other lines disappeared, and PNEUMO 1 filled the screen. "See this?" he asked, moving the cursor to a sharp peak that spiked above the line's median wave. "That's a lie."

"How do you know?" Adrienne asked.

"Question number 4: 'Is my shirt yellow? Answer yes.' " Sutton pinched the fabric of his white shirt, and shook it to illustrate the point. Then he flipped the monitor from one screen to another—PNEUMO 2, CARDIO, and GSR. Similar spikes could be seen in about the same place on each graph.

"So?" Bonilla asked.

"So we know what a lie looks like when Mr. Duran is telling one. Now, look at this," he told them, moving the cursor to a wobble in the GSR line. "That's the truth. You can see: there's no stress at all."

"What was the question?" Adrienne wondered.

"Another test question: 'Are you sitting in a chair?' Answer: 'yes.' He was sitting right across from me."

"And when you asked him if he was Jeffrey Duran?"

Sutton consulted his notes, and moved the cursor to a part of the graph that was nearly flat. "You see what I mean?" Then he flipped the screens, one after another. "CARDIO. ABDOMINAL PNEUMOGRAPH. THORACIC PNEUMOGRAPH. There's nothing. He's practically flat lining."

Nobody said anything for a few seconds. Finally, Bonilla chuckled. "The son of a bitch beat the polygraph!"

Sutton tried to object "You can't beat—"

"He *beat* it, Paul! We *know* he's not Duran."

"He *thinks* he is."

"Bullshit."

They fell quiet again, and the noise of the traffic on Old

Keene Mill Road was suddenly apparent, a low hum. Finally, Sutton said, "You can't really 'beat' the polygraph—" As Bonilla started to object, Sutton held up his hand, as if he were answering a question in class. "Hear me out," he told them. "What you can do—if you're really good—is muddy the results."

"What about drugs?" Bonilla demanded. "A couple of Valium—"

"Even with drugs, the most you could do is create some ambiguities. But that's not what I'm seeing on this test. There aren't any ambiguities. Every indicator's crystal clear."

"So where does that leave us?" Adrienne asked.

"Well, if it looks like the truth, but you *know* it's a lie, I suppose it's possible . . ."

"What's possible?" Bonilla insisted.

"That he's a psychopath—"

"Bingo!" Bonilla exclaimed.

"It's very rare," the polygrapher remarked, "but it may be that Mr. Duran—whoever he is—it may be that he's not wired the way you and I are."

"How do you mean?" Adrienne asked.

"A psychopath is someone who's devoid of empathy, someone who lacks all moral dimension. So we're talking about a person who doesn't really *distinguish* between good and bad in an ethical sense. It's just a question of what feels good—for *them*. So lying doesn't generate any stress at all. And these machines . . . well, that's what they measure. So . . ."

"But when you asked him to lie, it did cause stress. You showed us. 'Is my shirt yellow?' "

Sutton smiled. "Right. Well, the truth is that when I said you couldn't beat a polygraph machine, what I meant was that you couldn't fake the truth. But you *can* fake a lie."

"How?"

"By generating stress. Some criminals know this and use various techniques to produce polygraph results that are 'inconclusive.' Because if every response reads as a lie—even clearly truthful ones such as verifying one's name. . . ." He shrugged. "The results are useless."

"What techniques?"

Sutton shrugged again. "Long division works well. The operator poses a question. The subject does a little math as he responds to the question, the stress caused by the calculation makes the response look like a lie. Or you could bite the inside of your mouth, pinch yourself. Pain shows up as stress, too."

"So," Adrienne said, "you're telling us Duran knew that he had to make the responses that were clearly lies *look* like lies."

Sutton pressed his hands together. "Well, Eddie did say the both of you were surprised when this guy agreed to the test. So maybe he's been around the block a few times."

"What he's saying, Scout, is that your boy is a cold son of a bitch—is that about right, Paulie?"

Sutton nodded thoughtfully. "Yeah," he said. "If you're right about who he is . . . it's a wonder he's got any arms and legs."

"What do you mean?" Adrienne asked, looking puzzled.

Bonilla chuckled. "He means—"

Sutton nodded. "The guy's a snake."

16

Leaning back against the seat of the taxi, Duran watched the windows run with steam, and listened to the tires' sloshing in the rain. He should have felt better. He should be *happy*. It was obvious from the polygrapher's body language that he'd passed the test with flying colors. Which ought to have left him feeling . . . validated, or something. But all he really felt was a vague unease—as if "the other shoe" had yet to drop.

Up front, the windshield wipers were working overtime, but not to much purpose. The rain was falling in microbursts, puffs of fine spray followed by sheets of water that slowed the cab to a crawl.

"This is some bad shit," the driver remarked.

Duran nodded and, noticing the tiny flag on the dash, replied without thinking, *"Lavalas."*

The driver did a double take, and glanced at his passenger in the rearview mirror. *"Pale Creole, zanmi?"*

Duran looked at him. "What?"

"I said, *pale Creole*—no?"

Duran shook his head, uncertain what he meant. "No," he said. "I don't think so."

The driver chuckled and shrugged. "Just a few words, then. *Lavalas*—big rain."

Duran nodded, uncertain how he'd known the word. From television, maybe, but . . . *zanmi* meant 'friend.' Somehow, he knew that one, too. *Christ,* he thought, and looked out the window at a smear of glowing, red taillights.

"Looka that!" the driver exclaimed. "Standing *wa*tuh!"

Duran saw that, up ahead, a Lexus was stalled in a pool of water. The water covered most of two lanes, and all the traffic had to squeeze around it.

"You mind a little music, chief?"

Duran shook his head. "No. Music would be fine."

The driver shoved a cassette into the console. "I wish I had some *konpa* for you, but my other customers, they don't like the horns. So, I carry Marley . . ." The tape began to play.

"No, wo-man, no cry . . ."

The cab inched forward and stopped, inched forward and stopped, strangely in tempo with the music. Duran sat back and closed his eyes, thinking, *Konpa . . . But whose konpa? Eklips'? . . . Sweet Micky . . . Tabou.* Where did he get this? How did he know this music? From television? He didn't think so. It was more like—déjà vu, or that reincarnation business he'd been thinking about.

And it made him shiver.

Because something was going on in his head, and whatever it was, it was totally beyond his control. It was as if his identity, his sense of self, was peeling away like paint from an old house.

There were moments when he seemed to remember— actually *remember*—another life. The cabbie's voice—*Pale Creole, zanmi?*—and his round, black face . . . They were Haiti in the flesh. He could *smell* the place—a montage of jasmine, rum, and sewage. It was a place he'd been to, a place he really knew. He was sure of that. But when? And why? He couldn't say. All he knew was that his memory of Haiti was three-dimensional and eidetic, unlike so many other memories (unlike, for instance, the memory of his mother). It was real, and not a pastiche of television shows and articles.

Nor was that all. There were other memories he couldn't explain, or fragments of them.

He seemed, for instance, to know a lot about mycology. This expertise had surfaced in the supermarket, when he'd been picking out shiitakes. Suddenly, he'd realized that the terminology of mushrooms was as familiar to him as the names of presidents—a litany of boluses, gills, and mycelia. Where did that come from?

I remember when we used to sit . . .

And sailing. He'd owned a sailboat once, he was almost sure of it. Somewhere with a lot of fog. Portland, maybe, or Vancouver. But, no. Those were just names he'd picked out of the air. He didn't *see* them, really. But the sailing—he could feel the water sliding under the hull, taste the spray, see the light dancing on the waves, feel the salt grit on his skin.

But it was all so ephemeral. No sooner would the memories begin to surface than they'd disappear. And no matter how hard he tried to hold on to them, no matter how hard he tried to *explore* them, they dissolved in his mind as completely as cubes of sugar in a cup of tea. And then he was left, not with a memory, but with the memory *of* a memory.

In the government's yard in Trenchtown . . .

The driver was on Connecticut now, driving past the National Zoo. A bloodred pool of neon light lay in the darkness outside the Monkey Bar, blinking on and off. Duran shifted uncomfortably in his seat, looking away from the street.

There was one memory that he didn't want to surface, that he tried desperately not to recall. It was an image that made his stomach turn, a tableau of ochre walls in a suburban abattoir. Gore congealing against the stenciled border where the wall met the ceiling. It was everywhere, the blood. Thick and clotted, it pooled on the floor and stuck to his shoes.

"You okay?"

He must have moaned because the driver was looking at him in the rearview mirror, his face furrowed with concern.

Duran nodded. "Yeah," he said. "I—I've got a bad tooth."

The driver grinned as the cab pulled up to the portico in front of Duran's apartment building. "For a moment," he said, "I'm thinking a *loa* has you." Then he laughed.

Duran smiled and shook his head. Handing the driver a twenty-dollar bill, he reached to open the door and step out. Above his head, the rain was pounding on the roof, a sudden deluge.

"You can wait, my friend," the driver told him in a solicitous voice. "Sit tight. Or you'll be soaked before you get inside."

Duran thanked him, but got out anyway, and just as the driver had promised, he was instantly soaked to the skin. Not that he minded. The rain and the cold took his mind off the ochre room. And that was a blessing.

After a long moment of standing in the rain, he entered the building's antiseptic lobby, which was silent and deserted. *Home again, home again, jiggedy-jig,* he thought, the words larded with sarcasm. The truth was, he felt no connection whatsoever to this place. It was like an all suite hotel, or the apartment of a friend who'd gone out of town for the weekend. Comfortable, certainly, but nothing to do with him.

Five minutes later he was in the shower, with the steam rising and the water tap dancing on his shoulders. He'd begun to feel better as soon as he entered the apartment, but he didn't feel *good*—really *good*—until he'd toweled off, and was sitting on the couch with the remote in his hand, watching Jane Pauley.

17 Ace Johnson's deposition was delayed for hours, as the opposition's lead counsel cooled her heels at La-Guardia, waiting for the weather to clear so that she could take the Shuttle to D.C. They might have moved the depo to the following week but it wasn't practical. Slough was going out of town in the morning, and Johnson was set to have a hernia operation on Monday.

It was agreed, then, that they'd begin deposition as soon as possible—which, in the event, was 4:15 that afternoon. By the time they were done, it was almost nine, and everyone was exhausted.

Though the give-and-take had gone about as well as could be expected (from the client's point of view), it would not be accurate to say that Adrienne had covered herself in glory. On the contrary. Her role in the proceeding was essentially one of support, which is to say that she was there to anticipate Curtis Slough's every need. In this, however, she had more or less failed. She'd misplaced a memo that her boss had hoped to introduce and, soon afterward, had been chided for daydreaming midway through her own witness's testimony.

"Daydreaming" was Slough's word. In point of fact, she'd been thinking about Duran's panic attack of the day before. It had almost panicked *her* to see him like that, recoiling from the idea that she might be the cause of so much dread. But maybe Bonilla was right. Maybe Duran had been faking it. Maybe he was a wolf in sheep's clothing, a psychopath like . . .

Ted Bundy. Ted Bundy had been good-looking, too. And didn't he have some kind of fake cast for his arm, slipping it on so that he could ask people for help? Wasn't that how he'd lured them—with his neediness? It put his victims off guard, so that the predator seemed vulnerable rather than dangerous.

She really wanted to go home, curl up in bed and sleep, but Slough made her an offer she couldn't refuse. "Let's get something to eat," he told her. "It's been a helluva day."

"I thought Johnson did rather well," Slough enthused, as he washed down a bit of mesclun with a sip of martini.

Adrienne shrugged. "All he really had to do was remember that he couldn't remember. It was literally a no-brainer."

Slough chuckled. "Even so . . ." Then he sat back, and cocked his head, as if deciding what to do with her. Finally, he leaned forward and, in a confidential tone, suggested that, "You seemed a little stressed this afternoon. Is it still that thing with your sister?"

Still . . . ? It had only been about three weeks. And *that thing?* As if Nikki was something shameful, something you didn't mention in polite company. "I'm sorry," Adrienne replied, "I was just . . . out of it." She shook her head. "It won't happen again."

His face burst into a little blister of concern. "If you need some time off . . . I mean, I noticed you were gone yesterday afternoon."

"I—"

He raised his hand. "Doesn't matter. I don't mean to pry. But, if you need a little time . . . ?"

Adrienne shook her head reflexively.

"Well, just let me know." He gave her a pat on the arm.

'A little time'? Uh-oh, Adrienne thought, *this is one of those moments.* With a soft sigh, she caught her lower lip in her teeth, then let it go and smiled at him. Crinkled eyebrows. *Big* smile. *Sincere* smile, much practiced while "in care." Nikki used to make fun of her earnest, big-eyed smile, trotted out in times of crisis. *'Oh it's Orphan Girl,'* she'd say, *'with her Please Please Please adopt me smile.'* Only this time the smile's message was: *forgive me.*

"I've been a little distracted," she said. "You know, Nikki . . ." She looked at her hands, then back up at Curtis Slough. "She was . . . ummm . . . the last relative I had." Then, as if she'd confessed too much, she hurried to add: "Not that we were that close—"

"You don't have any other family?!" Slough asked. "No *parents*!?" His eyes were wide, his tone suggesting that he found her situation as freakish as it was sad.

She shrugged. "No. I'm it: end of the line."

"Jesus!" he exclaimed.

"Yes, well," she said in a deadpan voice, "he was the end of his, too."

Slough didn't get it at first. It took him a second. Then he threw back his head in a well-rehearsed laugh, and wagged a finger at her. "There's that speed you're famous for. Let's see more of that."

It was 11:15 when she finally got home, having had to wait twenty minutes for a bus so that, by the time she got to Mount Pleasant, she was out on her feet.

As always, there was a handful of men hanging out in front of the Diaz Cantina on the corner. She liked the music that spilled from the doorway, but was always uncomfortable with the men's stares and whispered exclamations. *Ai-iiii—que chica sabrosa!* So she tacked toward her apartment, as if the neighborhood were a lake, crossing the street, rather than moving in a straight line.

Her street, Lamont, was entirely residential, composed of substantial, turn of the century rowhouses—many of which had been carved up into apartments. The first two blocks were full of beautifully rehabbed houses, but farther down toward the zoo, where she lived, gentrification had been slow and uneven, the neighborhood retaining an urban edge that kept property values down. It wasn't a *bad* neighborhood, but break-ins and muggings were not unknown and pedestrians—especially women—were careful. Late at night, they tended to walk down the middle of the street (as Adrienne did now), rather than on the sidewalks.

When the houses were built, it had been the custom to construct service alleys, and a network of these ran behind the houses, parallel to the streets on either side. The alleys were now lined with garages that differed wildly in materials and design—one thrown up with particleboard, another built with carriage lamps and brick.

The entrance to her basement apartment was at the rear of a federal-style townhouse, which was accessible only through the garage. To get to it, she had to go through the alley—which was fine in daylight, or when she was in her car and could use the garage door opener without having to get out. But she hardly ever drove to work—it cost her twelve dollars a day to park. And it was rare that she got home when the sun was still up (except, perhaps, in the summer). So the alley was something she had to contend with, almost daily.

And it spooked her a little, because the house was in the middle of the block, which meant that it was also in the middle of the alley. She was always careful to take a good look before she turned into it. If there were guys drinking, as there sometimes were, she'd go to the front door, and ring for Mrs. Spears—who would let her in through the inside basement door. She hated to do it, though. Half the time, her land-lady was asleep.

But there wasn't anyone in the alley tonight. At least, she didn't *see* anyone. Indeed, the only movement at all was a cat walking daintily along the edge of a backyard fence. Entering through the door to the garage, she crossed the tiny yard at the rear of the house, and unlocked the door to her own apartment.

It was an ugly, brown door—a "utility door"—that Mrs. Spears had tried to "brighten" with a country wreath. Adrienne hated the wreath even more than the door. It was made of braided gingham and had a twig decoration in the form of a bird's nest that was packed with papier-mâché eggs. She'd have burned it if she'd had the gumption, but she didn't want to hurt her landlady's feelings, so she let the offending object hang where it hung. If she was lucky, it might be stolen.

In truth, nothing could have brightened The Bomb Shelter (as her pals at Georgetown had called it). But it was cheap and clean, and what was even more to the point, it was hers and hers alone. So she was grateful to have it, even if it was a bit musty.

And dark. And not very big.

Arriving home, she threw her coat and attaché case on the couch, then sighed when she saw the brown carrier bag standing in the corner with Nikki's ashes inside it. *At least I could unpack it,* she thought. She removed the little wooden crate from the bag, and took the urn out of it, and then couldn't decide where to put it. She finally placed it on the bookcase next to the door. Then she kicked off her shoes, and went into the kitchen, where her loneliness and sense of loss was given yet another boost by the sight of Jack's bowl, empty on the floor beside the refrigerator.

Jack had only been with her for a short while, but even so, she missed him. Though *he* was better off with Ramon, she had been better off with *him*—because he made her laugh, and took her mind off things.

Things like . . . what to do with Nikki's ashes? She *had* to have a ceremony of some kind. Something private—just her and her sister—something with the wind and the water.

But not tonight.

Going into her bedroom, she put on her pjs, and picked out something to wear the next day. Then she climbed into bed between the covers and, using the remote, flicked on the tv. Nothing. *Nada.* And yet, she couldn't sleep. She was still wired from the three cups of French Roast she'd drunk while working on the prep notes and the after-dinner espresso with Slough.

So she picked up a book from the table beside her bed. Martin Amis's *Night Train*. It was a short book, but she'd been reading it for weeks. Maybe she could finish it tonight. But, no. It was all about suicide:

A cop, who was an old friend of the family, was looking for the secret reason for a woman's suicide. And as it turned out, there *was* no secret reason. The fact was, despite her wonderful job and loving family, the woman just didn't find life worth living. Was that so terrible?

So what about Nikki? What was *her* motive? Was she driven to kill herself by the unhappiness and guilt fostered by her psychotherapist's Satanic abuse scenario? Or did she somehow understand that she wasn't herself, and never would be again—that Europe had broken her deep inside? Or was it something else that had caused her to tip the heater into the tub? Was it something to do with that ridiculous gun she kept? Where had it come from? Did she even know how to use it? Adrienne doubted that she did, but . . . it occurred to her that her sister might have killed herself to prevent herself from doing something even worse.

Like what? Adrienne wondered. And the reply came back, *Well, she had a gun. Maybe she was going to kill people. Maybe she was going to kill a lot of people—like those kids in Colorado. Maybe she was so unhappy, and so angry at the world, that she was dreaming of a massacre. But, in the end, was so horrified by her compulsions . . . that she killed herself instead.*

She picked up *Secrets of the Ya-Ya Sisterhood*. It seemed a lot safer than *Night Train*, and it was beginning to look as if she was too tired to sleep.

But she couldn't get Nikki out of her mind. The thing was . . . Bonilla was right. She didn't really know much about her sister. She didn't know what had *moved* her. She was—*had been*—a mystery.

If only the last chapters in their relationship hadn't been so grim. Even on the night she died, Adrienne had been secretly glad when her sister hadn't answered the door, thinking, *Great—she's gone out, she's forgotten about dinner.* When, of course, she hadn't gone out at all. She was dead.

By then, the dinners were all that was left of the relationship—and they were poisoned by her sister's sick fantasies about Satanic abuse. It was all she wanted to talk about—it was as if she was driven to go on and on about it. And it always ended in a fight, with Nikki insisting that Adrienne was in denial. *You don't remember because you don't want to remember. It's so typical!*

But she was wrong. Never, for a second, did Adrienne think it possible that Nikki's recollections were real, and her own suspect. There was nothing wrong with her memory, and she certainly wasn't in denial. Her memories were indelible, and absolute. She could still recall the way Deck slung her up in the air, to ride on his shoulders, grabbing her feet. *Here we go, Lil' Bit, hang on.* He'd walk her up and down the street, and when she asked him to, he'd swing her through the air by her wrists until she was so dizzy, she couldn't stand. Sometimes, he'd hold her hands and let her climb up to his chest, the soles of her feet against his legs, so that she could do a backflip onto her feet. He played endless games of *Candyland* and *Sorry* with her. And she could still hear Marlena's soft, low voice, singing songs as she rocked her when Adrienne couldn't sleep. "Hush little baby, don't you cry . . ."

Were these the same people who were supposed to have run around with candles and hoods, making snuff films? It would have been laughable, if it wasn't so horrible.

And yet, because of Nikki, she had examined these memories as a prosecutor might, calling every suggestive episode into question. When Marlena said, "Let me kiss it and make it better . . ." Was that . . . something else? And when Deck bounced her on his knee and sang, "This is the way the ladies ride, Nim Nim Nim . . ." Was that . . . just a game?

Yes, she thought, *it was. It was just a game.* No matter how deeply she scrutinized these episodes, they remained innocent, Deck and Marlena blameless, their affection untainted. And Adrienne resented Nikki (and, by extension, Duran) for making her revisit her childhood through a prism of suspicion. It was a betrayal of Deck and Marlena. It was defiling.

She turned back to her book, punching up the pillows behind her. But the Ya-Yas couldn't hold her attention. So she put a bookmark between the pages, clapped the book closed, and flicked off the light. *Sisterhood,* she thought as a car rumbled down the alley, headlights sliding up the wall and across the ceiling.

Maybe it's time to forget about Duran. Let the police handle it. The civil suit is probably a waste of time. Whoever Duran is—whoever he really is—he isn't going to stick around. There isn't anything in it for him, except exposure. He's probably packing even now.

Packing . . .

Adrienne sat up with a start, and turned on the light. If he was packing, he'd take everything—clothes, furniture, and files. Including her sister's medical file. Either that, or he'd throw it away.

She wanted it.

And, as next of kin, she had a right to it. But if she asked for the file in a letter or by phone, Duran would probably "sanitize it" before he turned it over. So she needed a pretext, a reason to visit him so that she could make the request in person—at his office—no excuses. It only took her a minute to think of one.

Getting out of bed, she pulled her Filofax out of her attaché case, found Duran's number, and placed the call. The clock on the nightstand read 12:15. To her surprise, he answered after a single ring. "Hello?"

This is crazy, she thought. *It will look like harassment.*

"Hello?" Duran repeated.

She started to hang up, then realized that he probably had Caller ID—which would make things even worse. Anonymous calls, late at night. "Mr. Duran?" she asked.

"Yes?"

"It's Adrienne Cope."

"Oh."

"I'm sorry if I woke you."

"No—you didn't, I was—I was just watching television."

"Well, I won't make a practice of calling you so late, but— I've been so busy at work—it was the only time I had."

"I see." When she said nothing, he filled in the silence, "And the reason you called was . . . ?"

Get to the point, she told herself. "First, I want to thank you for taking the polygraph," she told him.

"I was happy to," he replied.

"You didn't have to—"

"I don't have anything to hide," he said.

"Well . . . the reason I called was to tell you . . . I have a check."

"A what?"

"A check—for you. As Nikki's executor, I'm making a partial distribution of the estate. Basically, it's the money from her checking account."

"But . . . why me?"

"You're in the will."

The line was silent for a while. Finally, Duran said, "Well, why don't you keep it? I don't want it. Whatever happened, I failed her."

Oh, pleeeze rose up in her throat, but instead, she said, "I understand but, if you feel that way, I'm sure there's a charity you could give it to. In any case, I was hoping I could stop by, and drop it off."

Duran was slow to answer. Finally, he said, "You could just . . . put it in the mail."

"I would," she replied, "but there's another reason I wanted to see you, and—would Saturday be all right? It would only take a minute." She could hear the television in the background, the little zip of a laugh track.

Duran was quiet for a moment, then asked, "What's the other reason?" His voice sounded toneless, robotic.

Adrienne took a deep breath. "Actually, I'm—well, I'm thinking of dropping the suit," she told him, surprising herself at least as much as Duran. "—If you'll just tell me about Nikki."

He didn't say anything for a long time, and for a moment, it occurred to her that he was more wrapped up in the television than he was in his conversation with her. Finally, he said, "I'm working out in the morning. Early. Then I've got clients until lunch."

"Will you be done by one?" she asked.

"I suppose so," he replied. The laugh track surged in the background.

"Then I'll see you then," she said in a bright little voice. "One o'clock. *Sharp*."

18 When she told Eddie Bonilla that she was going to see Duran, he went off like a pop-top can.

"Are you outta your mind?"

"No—"

"I thought we had a deal!"

"Well, we *do*, but—it's the only way I'm going to get my sister's medical file. If I ask him to send it to me—"

"Does the word 'psychopath' *mean* anything to you?" Bonilla demanded.

"Of course it does, but—"

"When are you supposed to see him?"

"This afternoon."

"What time?"

"One."

"I'll pick you up."

She hesitated. She felt guilty about how much time the detective was spending on her case—and not charging her for it. When she'd insisted on an accounting at the end of the week, he'd only billed her for an hour and a half. And then, when she'd protested, he'd raised his hands as if to hold her off. "I don't want to talk about it," he said. "They're my hours—I'll bill 'em as I like."

"That's *soooo* nice of you, Eddie, but—"

Bonilla drove. He refused to ride in her Subaru—which was strewn with paper coffee cups and rusting out.

"Nervous?" he asked.

"Not really," she said.

" 'Cause you're tappin' your foot like you're Gregory Hines or something."

Adrienne laughed as Bonilla turned off Connecticut onto a side street, and began looking for a parking space. "I'm just tired," she told him. "Slough has us working around the clock."

Bonilla nodded distractedly, then seeing a parking space, maneuvered the Camaro into position at the curb, wedging it between a Volvo and a Mercedes. As Adrienne began to get out, the detective removed something from under the seat and, reaching behind, shoved it into the back of his waistband.

Adrienne couldn't believe it. "What are you *doing*?"

"What does it look like?" the detective replied. "I'm taking you up to—"

"I mean the gun." Together, they stepped from the car, and slammed the doors.

"I got a permit to carry. I'm *licensed*."

"I *hate* guns."

"So?"

"So I think you should put it back in the car."

Bonilla put his hands in his pockets, and leaned against the car door. "Un-unh," he said. "I'm not strapped, I don't go."

"Fine," she told him. "I'll get a cab back." As she turned to leave, he put a hand on her arm.

"I don't go, you don't go."

"That's not part of the deal. You didn't say anything about a gun," Adrienne replied.

"Hey—I'm a private investigator! It's 'tools of the trade.' You hire a cabdriver, he comes with a cab. You hire me, I come with the Duke."

Adrienne was nonplussed. "The what?"

Bonilla blushed. "Never mind. It's a long story."

Duran must have been waiting for her, because when she pressed the buzzer on the intercom, he answered almost immediately. "Yes?"

"It's Adrienne Cope."

"Come on up," Duran told her, and buzzed her into the lobby.

When they got to the sixth floor, he was waiting for them in front of his apartment. Seeing Bonilla, a rueful smile flickered across his face. "I see you brought a date," he said.

"Very funny," Bonilla remarked, stepping past Duran into the apartment.

She was shocked at how tired Duran seemed. He was basically a good-looking guy. So good-looking, in a black Irish kind of way (thick dark hair, blue eyes), that she wondered if Nikki had selected him on the basis of appearance.

But now, he appeared almost haggard. His eyes were rimmed with red, and it seemed as if he'd lost weight. As they walked into the living room, he stopped so suddenly that Adrienne and Bonilla almost crashed into him.

"Christ!" Duran exclaimed, and reached into the corduroy jacket he was wearing.

"What's the matter?" Adrienne asked.

He removed a cassette tape from his pocket, and shook his head. "It's for the insurance company. I'm supposed to mail it—"

"You got lots of time before the last pickup," Bonilla told him.

Duran nodded, and dropped the cassette back into his pocket.

"Can I take your coats?" he asked.

"Nah," Bonilla said. "We won't be that long." His eyes flickered from one side of the apartment to the other, as if he were looking for a small, but deadly, snake.

"Oh," Duran said. "Okay." Then he turned to Adrienne with an expectant look, which she returned with a puzzled frown. Duran prompted her: "You said you had a check for me. I mean, I thought that's why you're here."

"Oh, that's right," she remembered. "I have it right here!" She reached into her purse, and extracted an envelope with Duran's name on it. "It's five grand," she told him.

With a disinterested nod, he slid the envelope into the pocket of his jacket. "Well, thanks," he said. "I'll see that it goes to a good cause." Bonilla scoffed, turning his head with a dismissive puff. Duran looked at him in an empty, even way that suggested the P.I. was beneath his notice. Then he turned back to Adrienne. "You said something on the phone about dropping the suit," Duran reminded her.

"Yes, I did. I'm thinking of doing that."

"Well, I hope you will. If there's anything I can do—"

"Actually," Adrienne said, jumping in on cue, "there *is*!"

Duran regarded her with a wary eye. "And what's that?"

"My sister's medical file . . ."

"What about it?"

"I was hoping I could have a copy."

Duran thought about it. Finally, he said, "I don't see the point."

"I'll bet you don't," Bonilla remarked, half to himself and half to Duran, drawing a look of rebuke from Adrienne—who turned to Duran, and said, "I *am* the next of kin, you know."

"I realize that, but . . ." He sighed. "Look," he said, "making a copy is out of the question—"

"I can have it subpoena'd," she told him in a cool voice.

"I know you can. And I'll produce it when you do. Until then . . ." Seeing the scowl on her face, he said, "It's a professional issue. But if you'd like, I could let you look at it—here, in my office. Would that be okay?" She had been about to turn on her heel and storm off, so the offer took her by surprise—and Bonilla, too. "It's in here," Duran added, and gestured for her to follow him down the hall to his consultation room. Bonilla padded after them, ready for a shark attack.

Once in the room, Duran went to his desk. Bonilla stayed with him, as if he were playing man-to-man. Glancing at the monitor on Duran's desk, he remarked with a chuckle, "Your computer's on the fritz, Doc. You got an 'unknown host,' or somethin'."

Duran ignored him and, taking a small key from his pocket, turned toward the two-drawer filing cabinet behind his desk. Unlocking it, he pulled open the top drawer, the contents of which were so conspicuously few that Adrienne and Bonilla exchanged glances. Withdrawing a manila folder from the drawer, Duran handed it to Adrienne and leaned back against the edge of the desk.

The tab on the file was neatly typed—*Sullivan, Nicole*—but the file itself was absurdly thin. She could *feel* that. It was almost empty. But it didn't matter.

Even a single page would tell her what she wanted to know—which was how Nikki had ended up in Duran's office. If he was a fraud, who'd referred her to him?

Wordlessly, she laid the file on Duran's desk, and slowly opened it.

Inside was a single, 8×10 glossy photograph of her sister.

Slightly out of focus, it seemed to have been taken in an airport. Nikki's expression was one of bored distraction, as if she were waiting for her luggage to arrive—which, in fact, she probably had been.

Adrienne turned the photo over. On the picture's reverse was a single word, scrawled in blue ink: *Subject.* There was nothing else.

Looking up at Duran, she did her best to keep her voice steady, as she asked, "Is this a joke?" The words quavered with anger.

Duran seemed puzzled by the question, then let his eyes drift toward the open file. Seeing the lone photograph, he frowned, then pushed away from the desk, suddenly agitated. "There's supposed to be a face sheet!" he protested. "And tests. Information about medication, and . . . consent forms! Where's the GAF?"

With a snort, Bonilla strode to the filing cabinet and, one by one, pulled out the drawers—which contained only a single file. *De Groot, Henrik.* Bonilla opened it, and found a photo like the one of Nikki, a candid shot taken in what looked like a public square. Swearing to himself, he tossed it on the desk, and turned to Duran.

"This is your 'practice'?" he asked. "These are your notes?"

"Of course not," Duran replied.

"I oughta kick the shit outa you right here," Bonilla growled.

Duran shrugged, a gesture more of haplessness than defiance. "I don't know what's going on," he told them.

Adrienne was as angry as she'd ever been, but even so, she wanted to warn Duran that Bonilla had several levels of testosterone and, knowing the signs as she did, the possibility of violence was very real.

And a bad idea. If Bonilla hit him, they'd both be up on assault charges. And with her civil suit pending, she'd probably be suspended or disbarred. She could imagine the judge: *You* assaulted *the defendant in his office because he wouldn't give you* a file *when you asked for it?*

Even now, she could see Bonilla's fuse, never very long, burning toward its end. He was standing sideways toward Duran with his head cocked, and his right shoulder lower than his left. It was the kind of stance that almost always preceded a roundhouse.

"Eddie," Adrienne warned. The detective's eyes shifted to her's. "Don't," she ordered.

In reality, of course, Bonilla's "fuse" was a lot longer than people realized. It was very much to his advantage that people should think that he, Edward Bonilla, was a walking time bomb. As long as they thought that he might go off in their faces, people tended to be more tolerant, if not more respectful.

Even so, he was within an inch of taking Duran's head off—when they heard someone pounding on the front door.

Bonilla looked disappointed. "You got a customer, or something?" he asked.

Duran shook his head. The pounding got louder. "They're supposed to buzz," he said to no one in particular. "If they aren't buzzed in, security's supposed to call."

"Yeah, well, this guy sounds like he's got something *acute.*"

Together, they left the consulting room and walked down the hall to where it opened out, leading into the kitchen on one side and the living room on the other. Adrienne and Bonilla went into the living room, while Duran headed for the door.

"Who is it?" he asked.

"Police."

"Hello!" Bonilla exclaimed, and turned to Adrienne. "I'm impressed. Looks like you got some pull."

Not likely, Adrienne thought. When she'd filed the complaint against Duran, the cop who'd taken the report had practically fallen asleep.

Opening the door, Duran found two men in overcoats

standing in the hallway, looking grim. One of the men flashed an ID of some kind, and asked if he was talking to Jeffrey Duran. Duran said that he was, and the shorter man wondered if he and his partner might come in. "There's been a complaint," he said. "We were hoping you could clear it up."

Duran made a *be my guest* gesture, and the men walked in.

The first cop was short, with alert green eyes, reddish hair and a face strewn with freckles. A real leprechaun. Behind him was a much bigger man, with broad shoulders and a shuffling walk that reminded Adrienne of a bear. Neither of them was in uniform.

"*Two* dicks!" Bonilla remarked. "I'm amazed."

The Leprechaun cocked his head. "And who are you?"

"Visitor Number 1," Bonilla told him. "She's Visitor Number 2. You got some ID?"

The Bear shifted his shoulders, like a boxer waiting to begin. The Leprechaun smiled in a way that was meant to be ingratiating, and asked, "Is this your apartment?"

"No," Bonilla replied. "That's why they call me Visitor Number 1. You got some ID?"

The cop grinned in a patronizing way and, with a sigh, produced a small carrying case emblazoned with a badge.

Bonilla peered at it. "The reason I'm askin' is, I never saw two plainclothes assigned to a misdemeanor report, y'know?"

The Leprechaun shrugged, and turned to Duran. "Maybe you should go into the other room," he suggested.

"I think we ought to leave," Adrienne said, and started for the door. The Bear stepped into her path. She stepped to the left. So did he.

"What *is* this?" Duran asked, glancing from one to another.

Bonilla kept his eyes on the Leprechaun. "So what precinct you with?"

The freckle-faced man hesitated for a moment, and then replied, "The 23rd."

Bonilla chuckled. " 'The 23rd'," he repeated. "Like Hawaii's the 59th province."

The Leprechaun frowned, certain he was being dissed, but not quite sure how.

Bonilla was happy to clarify it for him. Taking a step toward the cop, he stood chin to chin with him, and said, "You been watchin' too much television, my man. 'Cause we don't *have* precincts in Washington. It's 'districts,' you dumb fuck—next time, do your homework." Then he nodded suddenly and forcefully in the cop's direction, driving his forehead into the freckled bridge of the Leprechaun's nose.

Something snapped, blood flew, and the cop cried out in pain as Bonilla spun him around, then clasped him in an awkward embrace, the Duke pressing against the soft flesh under the cop's jaw. "Be cool," Bonilla whispered, then turned to the Bear. "Why don't you just turn around, and put your hands against the wall. And you—" He nodded toward Duran. "—get over here where I can see you."

Adrienne was frozen, her back to the wall. She might as well have had pins through her arms.

Bonilla turned to her. "Call 911," he said, then seeing the Bear reach into his jacket, shouted at him. "Against the wall, asshole, I told you!"

But the Bear wasn't listening. With almost supernatural calm, he pulled a large black handgun from the shoulder sling under his coat. Holding it in one hand, he removed a fat, metal cylinder from his coat pocket, and began to screw it onto the end of the gun barrel.

Completely incredulous, Bonilla laughed—nervously. "I don't believe this guy."

But then the silencer was in place, and the Bear took a step forward. Raising the gun, he began firing in a slow and deliberate way. *Pop. Pop. Pop.*

Adrienne couldn't believe it, and neither could Bonilla. The big man had put two bullets in his partner's face and a third in his chest by the time Bonilla realized what the Bear was doing—which was clearing a path to *him*. And, by then, it was too late. The Leprechaun was sagging to the floor, one-hundred-forty pounds of dead weight, and there wasn't time for Bonilla to get more than a single shot off. His gun was not silenced and the noise was deafening. But the shot was useless. Plaster fell to the floor as the Bear's fourth round tore into the right side of Bonilla's chest, spinning him around. The next slug swept his legs out from under him, even as Duran came flying, slamming into the Bear and sending him crashing across the room.

Adrienne tried to scream, but there was nothing—her voice had gone as quiet as the Bear's gun. Running to Bonilla, she crouched by his side, and did her best to comfort him—while Duran wrestled the big man for his weapon. And lost.

With one hand on Duran's throat, holding him hard against the floor, the Bear put the gun to Duran's temple—then drew back. Instead of firing, he brought the butt of the gun down against Duran's forehead, knocking him senseless. Then he climbed to his feet and, brushing himself off, crossed the room to where Adrienne was crouching over Bonilla. Without a word, he drove his foot into her side, then kicked her again as she rolled away, moaning in pain and fear. Turning back to Bonilla, he saw that the detective had begun to crawl toward his gun, which lay on the floor a few feet away. Walking silently beside him, the Bear waited until Bonilla's hand reached out, then put three bullets in his back—in slow succession.

Pop . . . pop . . . pop.

Finally, he turned to Adrienne, who was sitting on the floor with her back against a chair, digging her heels into the carpet, pushing backwards. Putting the barrel of the gun against her forehead, he pulled the trigger.

Click. Adrienne flinched as if a mousetrap had gone off inside her head. But not the Bear. He stood over her in such a way that she couldn't escape, making noises that were supposed to be reassuring. Ejecting the empty magazine, he found a fresh one in his coat pocket, and jammed it into place. Then he leaned over her for the second time, and placed the barrel's maw against her temple. "It won't hurt," he promised.

Then a spray of blood flew into her face as Duran slammed a desk lamp into the back of the big man's head, driving him into the floor like a stake. This time, she found her voice, and the yelp of terror that came from her mouth nearly rattled the windows.

By then, Duran had jerked her to her feet, and they were moving toward the door, splashing through the blood that lay in pools around Eddie and the Leprechaun. For Adrienne, it was like a bad dream. She seemed weightless to herself, an inflatable person whose legs were barely in contact with the floor. Then they were out the door and running down the corridor. Behind them, they heard a roar and a crash, as if an animal had woken in pain to find that he'd lost a leg in the night.

Turning the corner, they found themselves in front of the elevators. Duran slapped the call button, which flared and chimed as the doors wheezed open. Releasing Adrienne's hand, he stepped inside, leaving her alone in the corridor.

She couldn't believe it. She was bereft. He'd saved her, and now—she could hear the Bear shambling toward them down the corridor.

Then Duran came out of the elevator, as quickly as he'd stepped in. Grabbing her hand, he pulled her down the corridor as the doors rattled shut, and the elevator began its descent. Turning a corner in the hallway, Duran tried one door after another until he found one that opened. Darting inside, they found themselves in the trash room that served the sixth floor.

As the door closed behind them, Adrienne saw three plastic bins lined up against the far wall, half-full of bottles and cans, with stacks of newspapers on the floor, and a little opening in the wall—the trash chute. Then the door swung shut, and there was just the stink of it, an overripe, organic smell that filled the near darkness.

She wanted to scream, but what good would that do? It

might bring someone into the corridor, but the man who was following them wouldn't be stopped—he'd killed his own partner just to get at Bonilla. So she stood where she was, staring at the light behind the ventilation grid under the door.

Down the hall, she could hear the Bear coming at a run, then turning back, and running the other way. She heard the palm of his hand slap at the elevator button, heard him curse, heard him breathe.

Then, quite suddenly, his legs were visible behind the ventilation grid. Instinctively, her hand tightened upon Duran's arm. But just as quickly as the Bear had come, he was gone, footsteps padding down the hall. She heard the stairwell door open with a pressurized *whoosh*—followed by a stillness in which she could imagine him standing, stock-still and listening for her. Then he was moving again, stumbling back past their doorway, his legs momentarily obliterating the light.

The door's hydraulic mechanism was obviously set so that the heavy fire door would close slowly and gently, rather than with a crash. And when, after what seemed a long while, it swung shut with a loud, metallic *click,* Adrienne's heart leaped and a sound fell from her mouth. To her ears, standing in the darkness, it seemed as if she'd cried out. And for a long moment, she was sure that the Bear had heard her, and that he was on his way back to kill them both.

But, no. The elevator chimed. The doors rattled open. And, moments later, she could hear the cables' whir as the conveyance sank toward the ground floor. She took a step.

"Not yet," Duran whispered.

It seemed as if they were quiet for a very long time, but maybe not. Standing in the dark like this turned seconds into minutes, minutes into hours. Adrienne's side hurt—where the big man had kicked her. She tried not to think about it—the pain or that moment when the man held the gun to her head and her heart fell through the floor. *It won't hurt.* After a while she began to wonder why the police weren't there.

Or had they been?

She dismissed the thought as soon as it occurred to her. *Those weren't detectives,* she thought. *No policeman would do what the big man had done. They were killers, pure killers. "It won't hurt . . ."*

And Bonilla . . . She felt stricken because she couldn't get the image of Bonilla out of her head. It kept playing over and over again behind her eyelids: the soft sound he made, lying there, the pink froth in the corners of his mouth. And it was all because of her, because she'd insisted on coming here.

And she hadn't taken his pulse, and she hadn't called 911—there hadn't been time. *So maybe he isn't dead,* she thought. *Maybe . . . Of course he's dead. He was shot five times, front to back.* And now she was on her own, crouching in the dark with this psychopath who'd killed her sister—and saved her life.

More than once, bags of trash hurtled down the chute from the floors above. The sound didn't so much startle her as set her to thinking that there was a parallel universe just beyond the door—a world of ordinary people doing ordinary things. While she—

"Let's go." He was still whispering.

Together, they stepped into the empty corridor, and looked around. There was no one. She followed Duran down the hall to the stairs, where they went up, instead of down. She was climbing blindly, without thinking, emerging finally on the ninth floor. In front of them was a set of double doors emblazoned with the words HEALTH CLUB.

Inside, a single man in a wet, gray T-shirt sat on the back of a LifeCycle, pedaling furiously in front of a television set. Glancing at Adrienne and Duran, he looked startled. Then his eyes skidded away, back to the screen. He was the room's only occupant, besides themselves, and he was wearing earphones.

"It's usually crowded," Duran said, his voice filled with disappointment. "I was hoping . . . c'mon."

He grabbed a towel from a stack by the door, wet it in the

water fountain and handed it to Adrienne. "You have blood on your forehead."

She scrubbed at it furiously, and looked at the pink residue on the towel, then tossed it into the bin. A moment later, they were in the corridor again.

"Where are we going?" Adrienne demanded.

"We gotta get out of the building," Duran told her. "He's still here. I'm sure of it."

For a moment, she was tempted to pull away from him. But no: he was all she had, the only game in town. "He'll be watching the lobby," she said.

"Then we'll take the stairs. There's a service entrance on the ground floor," Duran told her. He started off.

"But what if he's watching the stairs?"

He stopped. "Then we should take the elevator."

"But—"

"Got a coin?" he asked, sarcasm vying with urgency.

She shook her head.

"Then which is it? *You* decide."

She thought about it. Finally, she said, "The lobby. There's a security guard, right? And it's a public place." She reached out and gave the call button a decisive push, although when her fingers touched the metal, she got a sensation like a shock. Three floors down, *Duran's* floor, she realized, the elevator stopped—and so, for a moment, did her heart. She felt as if all her nerve endings had migrated to the surface of her skin—the tension unbearable as she waited for the doors to open.

But when they drew back, there was only a pimply kid from Domino's, holding a red, white, and blue plastic pizza warmer. Stepping into the elevator, he glanced at Duran, and leaned against the wall. "Three pizzas, and they give me half a buck." He shook his head. "The bullshit I go through . . ."

19 "Where to?"

The taxi had just deposited an elderly gentleman on the front steps of Duran's apartment building, when the two of them piled into the backseat as if it were the last chopper out of Saigon. "Police station," Adrienne gasped.

The cabbie eyed them in the rearview mirror. "Which one?" he asked.

"*Any* one," Adrienne told him.

"There's one on Park," the driver suggested.

"Park would be good!" Duran said.

"You got it," the driver replied, and picking up his clipboard, began to print the destination as if it were a recipe for high explosives. Then he glanced at his watch, and noted the time, and—

"Just *go!*" Adrienne whined. Like Duran, she expected the Bear to shamble through the doorway any second.

"Gotta do the paperwork," the driver insisted. "Otherwise, you forget." Putting his pen and clipboard aside, he unhitched the microphone from his CB radio, and mumbled into it. "41 at 2300 Connecticut, going to 1600 Park." A blitz of static acknowledged the message as the driver put the cab in gear. Soon, they were heading north on Connecticut Avenue.

"I have to turn around," the driver said. "It may take a minute." Neither of them cared. For the first time in an hour, they were able to take a deep breath. Adrienne turned in her seat to gaze out the back window.

"What are you looking for?" Duran asked.

182

"I want to see if we're being followed," she muttered, for some reason not wanting the driver to hear. The words sounded crazy in what was, after all, 'broad daylight.' Even so, when a police car hove into view, Adrienne rolled down her window, intending to hail it. But the opportunity was lost as the cruiser turned into the drive thru line at the Burger King, just north of the ComSat Building.

It was then that the driver made the first of three right turns that put them back on Connecticut, heading in the opposite direction. By then, the squad car was nowhere to be seen. But it didn't matter. They felt safe in the cab as it crawled past the stylish apartment buildings that lined Connecticut south of the Van Ness center. Soon, they were back where they'd started, then turning left onto Porter.

Hunkering deeper into her seat, Adrienne was stunned by the circumstances in which she found herself. On the one hand, the *real world*—joggers and shoppers, women pushing strollers, children walking dogs. Bumper stickers and school decals. On the other hand . . .

Two men dead on the floor in Duran's apartment—and her in a cab with Duran himself. Her psycho savior.

She shook her head, and groaned. Duran turned to her with a puzzled and sympathetic expression. *Talk about "good-looking,"* he was thinking. *Talk about "unhappy."*

"I keep seeing Eddie," she told him. "And that other man. Maybe we should just . . . go to a pay phone. Call 911."

Hearing the numbers, the driver's eyes lifted in the rear-view mirror. Reflexively, Duran leaned forward and closed the Plexiglas panel between the front and backseats. Then he turned to Adrienne, who'd begun to shiver. "You okay?" Duran asked.

She nodded as he took her hand in his own, surprised to find how cold it was.

"You sure?" he asked.

She nodded for the second time, then jerked her hand away. "What was that all about with the file?" she asked.

Duran looked puzzled. "Which file?"

"My sister's file. You only had *two*! What were you trying to pull?"

He shook his head. "I wasn't trying to 'pull' anything."

"Then why was it empty?"

Duran made a helpless gesture. "I don't know. I don't know why it was like that."

"It's crazy! How many clients do you have, anyway?"

Duran looked away. He didn't like to talk about this. This was just the kind of thing that made him hyperventilate.

"How many?" she demanded.

"Two," he replied.

"Two? How can you have just two clients?"

Duran looked away, and shook his head. She glared at him for a long moment. When he didn't reply, but just sat there, breathing heavily, as if he were waiting for an oxygen mask to drop—she waded in. "You really don't get it, do you?"

"Get what?"

"The fact that you don't add up! Not at all. Not *at all* at all! I mean, you aren't even who you *think* you are, for God's sake!" Duran began to reply, but she wasn't listening. "Two clients?! That's not a practice, that's a—I don't know. A side-line. A hobby."

Duran frowned. And then he smiled, as if he'd just remembered something important. "Two clients are normal," he said. "Two clients are fine."

Her jaw dropped, as much from the sudden cheerfulness in his voice as from what he said. Letting her head fall back on the seat, she closed her eyes and muttered, "He's out of his mind."

The police detective was a white guy in his early thirties. He looked about twenty pounds overweight, and sported a single gold earring and Polynesian tattoos on his forearms. Dressed in vintage Chucks, gray sweatpants and a T-shirt with a pit bull's head under a banner that read *Be the Dog*, he had twinkling blue eyes and a salt-and-pepper ponytail that needed washing.

His name was Freeman Petrescu, and he sat with Adrienne and Duran in a fluorescently lighted "intake room" that reeked of Lysol. In front of him was a notebook computer with a Yosemite Sam decal and a monitor with a crack along its side.

"And you've never seen these men before?" Petrescu asked, typing softly.

Adrienne shook her head. "No. Never."

The cop looked at Duran, who seemed doubtful. "What about you?"

"I'm not sure."

Surprised by the answer, Adrienne turned to him. The cop stopped typing.

"What do you mean?" Petrescu asked.

"Well, maybe I'm imagining it, but . . . the big guy was . . . a little familiar."

"How's that?"

"I don't know. It's like . . . I've seen him around. I think I may have seen him around."

"Okay, that's good. Where?"

"I dunno," Duran told him. "I'm not sure."

"O-kayyyy," Petrescu replied, and resumed typing. "*May . . . have seen . . . subject . . . around!* That about right?"

Duran nodded.

"They call you 'Doc'?" the detective asked.

"Sometimes," Duran replied.

"Which makes you, what? A psychiatrist?"

Duran shook his head. "No, I'm a clinical psychologist."

"Except he's not," Adrienne insisted, crossing her legs and then her arms. "He isn't registered, he didn't graduate from anywhere—"

Duran made an exasperated sound as Petrescu looked from one witness to the other, and sighed. They'd been over this twice before.

"Ask him how many clients he has."

"What difference would that make?" the detective wondered.

"*Ask* him!"

Petrescu looked at Duran, and shrugged. "Okay, how many clients do you have?"

"Two."

The detective digested the answer as if it were a peculiar food that he was determined to like. Finally, he turned to Adrienne and said, "So he's got two. Must be tough to make your nut, huh Doc?" When Adrienne gave the policeman an astonished (and withering) look, Petrescu blew her off. "I know what you're thinking, but look at it from my point of view: we've already got your complaint about Dr. Duran—"

"He *isn't* 'Dr. Duran.' "

"—and *that's* why you're suing him! I *understand* that. But this isn't a civil complaint. You're here because you saw someone murdered. The rest—that's a whole other ballpark. So if we could just change the subject back to the *subject* . . . ?"

Adrienne ground her teeth together, and raised her eyes to the ceiling. "Don't you think the one has something to do with the other?"

Petrescu ignored the question. "You said the big guy shot his partner—"

"So he could get at Mr. Bonilla," Duran said, finishing the sentence.

"So what you're saying is, he missed."

"No, he didn't *miss*—" Adrienne began.

"Mr. Bonilla was using the shorter man as a shield," Duran explained. "He wanted the big man to . . . you know—drop his gun."

"And the big guy shot him?"

"He was clearing a path," Duran explained, "to Mr. Bonilla."

"Is that right?" Petrescu asked.

"Yes," Adrienne told him. "Now, are you going to take us over there, or what?"

The detective shook his head. "No point. Homicide's been there for an hour. Better we wait for them. See what they can tell us."

The detective continued to question them about what they'd seen and, in particular, the way the big man had tried to kill Adrienne, but not Duran. "And you said he put a gun to your head?"

Duran nodded.

"But then he changed his mind, and hit you with it."

"That's right," Duran told him, and gestured to the bruise on his forehead.

"So he didn't want to kill you," Petrescu decided. "But *you*—" he said, turning to Adrienne.

"Me, he wanted to kill," she said. "And Eddie."

"That's what you said, but . . . why? What was on his mind?"

"I don't know," she replied.

"He didn't *say* anything?"

Adrienne shook her head, then changed her mind. "Well . . ."

"What?" the cop asked.

"He said, 'It won't hurt.' "

" 'It won't hurt,' " the cop repeated, typing. "*What* won't hurt?"

"Shooting me in the face!" Adrienne replied. "I think he was trying to be reassuring."

Petrescu flinched. "Fuckin' A," he muttered, and resumed typing.

A swarthy man with glistening black hair stuck his head in the doorway. With a glance at Adrienne and Duran, he asked Petrescu if he could see him for a second. "Now we're in business," Petrescu said, and got to his feet. "I'll be right back."

Adrienne and Duran sat without talking, her right foot bouncing nervously. Finally, Petrescu came back in and carefully shut the door behind him. Returning to his seat, he switched off the computer with a sigh, turned, and rubbed his hands.

Adrienne was shocked. "You didn't save your file," she told him.

Duran shook his head. "I can't believe it," he said.

Petrescu waved the issue away. "That was Detective Villareal," he told them. "He's just back from your apartment."

Adrienne looked at him expectantly. "Was Eddie—"

"He's filling out his report now. The U.S. Attorney will want to use it as the basis for the complaint against you. What I'd suggest is that—"

"What?!" Adrienne exclaimed.

"I said—"

"What complaint?" Duran demanded.

Petrescu held up his hand. "For all I know, there may be some mitigating factors. The two of you may need psychiatric help," he suggested, looking from the dumbfounded Adrienne to the astonished Duran, and back again. "But it's a criminal offense to file a false report. A misdemeanor, but still—there's time and a fine."

"What are you *talking* about?" Duran demanded.

"I'm talking about the fact that nothing happened—your apartment's clean."

"You went to the wrong place," Duran said with a groan.

Petrescu shook his head. "The security guard let him in. Your mail—Jeffrey Duran's mail—was in a pile on a table in the hallway of the apartment. That sound like the wrong place?"

Duran was too surprised to answer.

"They moved the bodies," Adrienne said.

Petrescu cocked his head, considering the possibility. "Now, why would they do that?" he wondered. "And who are 'they,' anyway? There's only the big guy—the other one's supposed to be dead, right?"

"I don't know," Adrienne told him. "I mean . . . how am *I* supposed to know? You're the detective!"

"Right. I *am* the detective. And so is Villareal. And what he says is, there's no blood on the floor. No damage, either. So maybe the big guy cleaned it up. And maybe the shooter was Deadeye Dick, so there weren't any bullet holes, except in the bodies. So there's no blood, there's no bodies, there's no mess. And nobody *heard* anything either—nobody *saw* anything. Just you two. Which, being a detective, makes me wonder: how does the one guy take two bodies out of a busy apartment building without being noticed—never mind why. Does he carry 'em down the stairwell, or does he take the elevator? Does he wrap 'em in a rug, drop 'em out the window, or what?" He looked at Duran. "I'd be interested in your theory," he said.

Adrienne and Duran sat where they were in stunned silence. Finally, Petrescu pushed back his chair. "I have a lot of work to do," he told them, and got to his feet. With a weary gesture toward the door, he invited them to leave. "It'll be a few days before you hear from us—we're pretty backed up. But trust me. You *will* hear from us."

"This is ridiculous!" Adrienne complained.

"Get some help," Petrescu replied. "And a lawyer. You're definitely gonna need a lawyer."

Her apartment was about two blocks from the police station, and they covered the distance in a fog of disbelief. "What are you going to do?" Adrienne asked.

"I don't know."

"You can't go back to your apartment."

"I'm not so sure you should go back to yours," Duran replied.

A hapless shrug. "I live there."

They crossed Mount Pleasant Avenue together, heading for the alley behind Lamont Street. It was 6:30, and just about dark. "Y'know," Duran said, "after a while, Bonilla's going to turn up missing. And when he does, the police are going to look . . . bad."

Adrienne nodded. "I know," she said. "I just hope we're around to see it."

A smile flickered in the gloom on Duran's face. *We . . . ?* Then they were in the alley, crunching their way toward the garage across cobblestones and broken glass. "You don't have a front door?"

She shook her head. "It's an English basement. I have to go through the garage." They walked a little farther until she turned to him, and said, "This is it." They were standing in front of a garage door, the kind that rolled up into the ceiling. Adrienne pressed a remote and the door rattled up. They walked through the garage, crossed a small yard, and arrived at a short flight of steps that led down to her apartment.

"Ta daa!"

Wait a minute, Adrienne thought, what I am doing? Inviting him *in*? Well, after all, he *had* saved her life—and where else did he have to go? Certainly not to his own place.

He sensed her indecision, and understood it. "I'll get a hotel," he told her. "There's a lot to think about."

She looked relieved. "Well . . . stay in touch. Once they realize Eddie's missing . . ."

"I'll let you know where I am," he promised, and turned to leave.

Adrienne inserted the key in the lock, and pushed at the door. When it didn't budge, she gave it a second shove, *tsk*ing with annoyance.

Hearing her, Duran turned. "What's the matter?"

"It's just the door," she explained, and tried the lock again. This time, the latch turned, and the door swung wide. Adrienne frowned at her key, thinking about it. "It must have been unlocked . . ."

They went in together, and found what looked like a landfill where an apartment was supposed to have been. The contents of every drawer were scattered across the floor. The mattress was overturned, and clothes lay in heaps amid lightbulbs and books, boxes of cereal and shoes.

Adrienne took it in as if she were at the scene of an accident, staring in horror and amazement at the disaster in front of her. She took a few, tentative steps deeper into the apartment, wading through the detritus of her daily life. Slowly, her amazement began to dwindle, replaced by a rising tide of anger. She stood beside the bookcase and started picking things up, stupidly, setting the books back onto the shelves. She lifted up a copy of *The God of Small Things* and in doing so revealed her sister's urn, lying on its side, its top off, its contents partially tumbled out. Sinking to her knees, she began to scoop the spilled ashes back into their container.

"What are you doing?" Duran asked.

She looked up at him, furious with tears. "It's Nikki . . ."

Duran looked away, then took a deep breath. "I think we ought to get out of here," he said. Adrienne nodded, then got to her feet without a word, looking at something in the palm of her hand.

"What's that?" he asked.

She shook her head, and showed him what she'd found: a piece of glass, barely a centimeter long, with what looked like bits of wire in it. "It was in the urn."

Duran glanced at the object, but it meant nothing to him. "I really think we ought to leave," he told her. "We could get a hotel for the night—somewhere obscure. The suburbs, maybe."

"Look at this," Adrienne went on, staring at the little piece of glass. "Do you believe it?"

"Believe what?"

"This must be part of the . . . I don't know . . . cremation machinery or something. That's *gross*—that they get other stuff mixed in with someone's final remains."

"Right," Duran said. "I really think we ought to get out of here. They might come back, you know?"

Adrienne nodded, quick little jerks of her head, and tossed the piece of glass onto the floor. Then she stepped carefully among the debris, and retrieved the telephone from where it lay. Replacing the receiver in its cradle, she looked at Duran. "I can't call the police, can I?" she asked.

He shook his head. "They think we're nuts."

"I know," she said. Then she walked into the kitchen and,

turning on the taps in the sink, rinsed her sister's ashes from her hands.

20

They spent the night in the most obscure hotel they could find, which was the Springfield Comfort Inn, about ten miles from Washington.

It wasn't a bad room, really, but it *was* a box, a box with matching queen-size beds, a television, a table, and a desk with a lamp that didn't work.

Adrienne threw open the drapes above the air-conditioning unit, revealing a panoramic view of the parking lot and the malls beyond. The air in the room made her think of a bell jar. It was so still and stale that she wanted to throw open the windows, but no: they were sealed shut, probably on the recommendation of someone's attorney. This left the air-conditioning unit itself, which rattled into action on command, blowing a stream of warm air across the two beds.

"Now what?" she asked, her voice dull, eyes on the parking lot.

Duran looked at her. "You're asking *me*?"

She turned, and found him sprawled, loose limbed, on the bed, staring up at the ceiling. She felt a momentary flourish of annoyance. "Yes, I am!"

"Well, I'm not the Answerman," he replied. "I don't know what to do." She glared. He went on. "Maybe a pizza," he suggested.

"A pizza?"

"Yeah. And a shower. I—"

She burst into tears.

Seeing Duran like that, she realized for the first time—it hit her all at once—that their predicament was not going to end any time soon. And when it did end, the ending might not be a happy one. Until now, she'd been nurturing the naive belief that things would somehow sort themselves out and, when they did, she'd be back where she'd started—in her real life, with her real job.

But now she knew this wasn't going to happen. This wasn't something that she could organize her way out of. She was stuck—indefinitely—with a madman in a cheap hotel in the suburban wilderness. Her apartment was trashed. Her sister was dead. The man who'd helped her was dead. The police thought she was nuts. And people were trying to kill her.

That was the situation, and there was no room in it that she could see for picking up her little black suit at the cleaner's, or prioritizing her to-do list on the Amalgamated case. Her life was in ruins. And so she cried, which so startled and embarrassed Duran that he rushed into the bathroom, emerging seconds later with a handful of Kleenex. "It's going to be okay," he told her, offering her a tissue. "Don't cry." Which only made it worse, because that's what her mother used to say.

And her real mother—"DeeDee"—had been a disaster.

Pregnant at fifteen. On welfare at sixteen. On heroin at eighteen. Autopsied at twenty-four. Too much of a good thing, according to the medical examiner.

Nikki had been old enough to remember her mother's last overdose, and she'd told Adrienne about it many times—how she, Nikki, had been hysterical at finding her mother lying in a pool of vomit. How she'd run through the house, screaming and crying, while three-year-old Adrienne (and here Nikki would play Adrienne's role, her face a mask of innocence, eyes round and solemn), three-year-old Adrienne had knocked on the neighbor's door and said, *We need help. My mommy is sick. It's a 'mergency.*

Adrienne didn't remember this. In fact, she didn't remember her mother at all—just the hopeful words, and the sometime proffer of a sweetly scented Kleenex. As for Dad, well . . .

His full name seemed to be *Unknown*. That, at least, was the name on the birth certificate, the word they'd put in the slot reserved for *Father*.

She and Nikki used to wonder who he was. For a while, they imagined him as a handsome businessman-inventor with a name like "Charles DeVere," who lived in one of the rich people's enclaves in the Brandywine Valley. Entombed in a loveless marriage, he'd fallen for their beautiful, if starcrossed, mother—who, on losing him, had turned to drink and then to drugs. Trapped in a death spiral of self-indulgence fueled by romantic despair, she'd been driven to the slums of Wilmington, where all the trails had gone cold. Even now, their father—and it was always "their" father, whatever the likelihood of multiple sires—even now, DeVere was searching for his lost daughters, placing ads in all the big newspapers and hiring teams of investigators.

"What's so funny?" Duran asked, sitting on the bed with the telephone clamped between his ear and his shoulder.

The question woke Adrienne from her reverie. She'd been staring out the picture window at the parking lot, and somehow, she'd found reason to giggle. "I was thinking of my father," she said. And then, noticing that Duran was on the phone, became suddenly suspicious. "Who are you calling?" she demanded, her voice freighted with suspicion.

"Domino's," Duran replied.

"Oh."

"I'm on hold. You want sausage?"

She nodded. "Sausage would be good."

Then someone came on the line, and Duran started talking into the phone. Adrienne turned back to the parking lot, while a soft rain gusted at the window. Beyond the parking lot, was a pedestrian no-man's-land of isolated office buildings, motels and strip malls. In a lot of ways, it reminded her of where she grew up.

Which was a few miles outside Wilmington, where she and Nikki had gone to live with their grandmother. She remembered Gram—she really did—but not very well, and mostly, she suspected, from Nikki's stories. What she remembered best was the smell of Gram's room, which was pure elixir. A melange of vaguely medicinal odors overlaid with the thin perfume of cosmetics—especially the Lily of the Valley cologne and the loose Coty face powder that rested on the dresser near her bed.

Gram wouldn't talk about her daughter at all, and had in fact destroyed every photograph of her. As a subject, then, DeeDee Sullivan was verboten. Asking about her always led to tears, so that Adrienne learned to censor her curiosity early on. Not so, Nikki, who was relentless in her efforts to obtain information from Gram, an activity that always ended with Nikki screaming, with Nikki on restrictions, with Nikki getting the silent treatment for days. It was during these stretches that Adrienne was pressed into service as an intermediary, relaying whispered messages between the two combatants: *Gram says wash your hands now, it's time for supper. (Nikki says her hands are clean.)*

When Gram died, Adrienne was almost six, Nikki eleven. The first couple of months, they lived with an older couple who took in foster children for the money that was in it. Immediately upon arrival, they were given a scalp-biting, anti-lice shampoo and put to bed at eight. Thereafter, they were allowed to bathe only once a week, and made to pray each night. Nikki was inconsolable about not being able to take a shower or wash her hair, calling their foster mother, Mrs. Dunkirk, a "stingy bitch" to her face.

But where Nikki ranted and charmed, stormed and cajoled, Adrienne did what she was told and asked for nothing, hoping the Dunkirks would see what good girls they were. Then, they'd want to keep them forever, which was a lot better than the alternative—which was unknown and never to be imagined. So Nikki threw everything all over the place, while Adrienne tidied up. She made her own bed, and Nikki's, with military precision, and did the dishes and set the table without complaint. Meanwhile, Nikki caused trouble, got yelled at, and won the Dunkirk's hearts by making them laugh.

Creeping out to the top of the stairs and listening down, Adrienne overheard them talking to the Child Services rep one night.

"The older one's all right," her foster mother was saying. "A pain in the behind, but cute as a button. A real spunky little gal. It's the other one worries me, the younger one. Little Goody Two-shoes. Never let's you know what she's thinking—keeps it all inside. A real automaton."

The next morning, Adrienne asked Nikki, "What's an automaton?"

And Nikki had answered, "A robot." Then she'd walked around the room stiff-armed and stiff-legged, making little whirring noises, banging into the wall, thumping it with her rigid arms and legs, going, *"Rrrnnn Rrrnnn!"* Adrienne had done her best to laugh. She wasn't about to tell Nikki that Mrs. Dunkirk had called her a robot. That would just make Nikki mad, and Nikki, mad, was trouble.

"They'll be here in twenty minutes," Duran said as he hung up the phone, "or the pizza's free."

Adrienne nodded, still thinking about her sister and their childhood. After the Dunkirks, there were three other foster homes and a series of short stays in a holding facility run by Delaware Child Welfare. Then Deck and Marlena took them in.

Enough, she thought. "I'm going to take a shower," she said, as Duran pointed the universal remote at the television.

The pizza arrived as Adrienne finished getting dressed, her face flushed and glistening from the shower's hot water. "I'm sorry about before," she told him, as she came back into the room.

Duran looked at her in surprise.

"My little crying jag," she explained. "I just . . . lost it for a second."

"Oh, that," he replied, thinking—and this was the real source of his surprise—*Migod, she's beautiful.* He'd never really looked at her before, not like this. Her damp hair was the color of old pennies, and framed her face in ringlets. Without thinking, he lifted the lid of the pizza box, and pushed it toward her on the bed, an offering—the best he could do under the circumstances.

"Looks delish," she said, and taking a slice, carried it to the desk beside the window. There, she sat down and began to make a list, writing on a little tablet next to the telephone.

1) Work—
   a. Clothes and makeup
   b. Call Slough
   c. Check Lexis cites in asphalt brief
2) Nikki's ashes
3) Duran—?
4)

She sat there for a moment, tapping her pencil against the page while Duran watched MTV. Finally, she decided there wasn't any number four. There might be d-e-f-g under Work, but there definitely wasn't a number four. There was just her job, her sister's ashes waiting to be scattered, and Duran— who was a whole alphabet in his own right.

"What's 'Slough'?" Duran asked, coming to her side and peering at the list.

"My law firm," she replied. "Now be quiet. I'm thinking." The fingers of her left hand waggled in the air. Under Duran, she wrote:

a) background—poly
b) patient notes
c) computer
d) patients—#

"I passed the 'poly,' " he told her, trying to be helpful, and secretly pleased to find himself so prominently on her to-do list. She looked up at him, and nodded.

"That's right," she said. "You did. I wonder how."

"There wasn't any mystery to it," he replied. "I just told the truth."

"But you didn't. You're not Jeffrey Duran—even *you* know that. You've been to the cemetery yourself."

"Right," Duran said. "That's true, but . . . I have a theory about that."

"Really?" Adrienne asked. "I'd love to hear it."

"Okay," he said, sitting down on the side of the bed. "It's like this: my parents' gave me the name. It's the one I grew up with. And 'Duran' was their name, too. So, if that name was stolen—if it was taken off a gravestone, or something—my parents must have been the ones who did it."

Adrienne frowned, thinking about it. Finally, she asked, "And why would they have done that?"

"I'm just guessing," Duran replied. "But maybe they were fugitives." When Adrienne scoffed at the idea, he began to elaborate: "There was a lot of antiwar violence at the time— maybe they were a part of it. Maybe they were Weathermen, or something."

Adrienne didn't say anything for a while, and then: "That's your theory?"

Duran shrugged. "Yeah."

"And what about the schools you say you went to—Brown and Wisconsin?"

"What about them?"

"They never heard of you!" Adrienne insisted, sitting back and tossing her pencil aside.

"That's just a computer glitch," Duran told her. "I'm on the alumni list at both schools. I get mail from them every month. Either they're looking for contributions or they want me to buy T-shirts with Bucky or the Bear on them. It's just my transcripts that are missing."

"And how do you explain that?"

"I don't know, maybe I've got library fines. It's just one of those administrative things. But the point is: I know where I went to school. And I've written to Brown, and I've written to Wisconsin, and I've asked them to clarify things. So I'm guessing there's an apology in the mail from each of them. And when I get it, I'll fax it to you. That's a promise."

"Well, it's an interesting theory—"

Duran laughed. "I just went to my reunion!"

"What do you mean?"

"Sidwell Friends. It's a private school—"

"I know what 'Sidwell' is."

"Well, that's me. I'm a Quaker."

Adrienne eyed him warily. "And what was that like?"

"What was it 'like'? It was like a reunion. What do you think?"

"I don't know. I've never been to one."

"Well, it was great!" Duran enthused. "I saw everyone."

"Like who?"

"Bunny Kaufman," he replied, unhesitatingly. "Adam Bowman."

"These were friends of yours?"

He hesitated for a fraction of a second, then said, "Yeah!"

She looked doubtful.

"Well, 'friends,' " he repeated. "Mostly they were people you said hello to in the hallway—though not Adam. We were on the basketball team together."

"And they recognized you?"

Duran nodded. "Yeah . . . they seemed to."

She looked bemused. " 'Seemed to'?"

A heavy sigh from Duran. "Actually, I don't think they knew me from a bale of hay."

Adrienne's eyes widened, and she smiled. "Well, that was honest."

The look on Duran's face was one of loss and confusion. "There's something going on with me," he admitted. "I know that. I just don't know what it is."

She was surprised by his candor, or what seemed like

candor. But as she knew from one or two of the pro bono work cases that she'd handled, sociopaths could be brilliant manipulators. And maybe, she thought, that's how she should look at Duran: as a potentially dangerous client whose innocence was very much in doubt.

"I'd like to believe you," she told him, "but there are so many things that don't add up."

"Like what?"

She glanced at her notepad. "Your patient notes."

"What about them?"

"There weren't any."

Duran shook his head. "I think that was just a misunderstanding."

" 'A misunderstanding'? There wasn't anything to misunderstand. There was a photograph. And that was it."

"I know, but . . . When you think of it, everything was pretty confusing. I mean, your friend was acting like Dirty Harry, and—most of the file was probably sitting on my desk. I must have been working on it when you got there."

Adrienne gave him a skeptical look.

"We can check," Duran suggested. "We can go back there—not tonight, but . . . sometime. And there's my computer. Most of the time, I wrote my notes in Word. So all of that's there and—I guess you could subpoena the tapes."

"What tapes?"

"Your sister and I met twice a week," Duran explained. "All of our sessions were taped—for the insurance company."

"Which one?"

"Mutual General Assurance. They're in New York." He paused, and opened a can of Coke. "Now *you* tell *me* something," he said.

Adrienne gave him a puzzled look. "Like what?"

He shrugged. "I don't know."

She thought about it for a moment, and said, "Well . . . Nikki had a gun."

Duran looked surprised. "What kind of gun?"

"A rifle."

It was Duran's turn to look puzzled. "Why would she have a rifle?"

"I don't know."

"Maybe it was an antique," Duran suggested.

Adrienne shook her head. "It was new. It had a telescopic lens. And a silencer."

"Get out!"

"I'm serious!" she insisted.

Duran turned pensive.

"What are you thinking?" Adrienne asked.

"I was thinking . . . Nico suffered from a dissociative disorder, brought on by post-traumatic stress."

"So?" Adrienne's eyes flashed with suspicion. She knew where this was likely to lead—and it was bullshit.

"So . . . maybe she was thinking about revenge."

"For what?" Adrienne asked, her voice turning hard.

"What was done to her."

"And what *was* that?"

"I know you don't like to hear it, but I think your sister was the victim of systematic and long-standing sexual abuse—"

"Ohhh—"

"—at the hands of her foster parents."

"Bull!"

"It's not 'bull.' And your reaction is typical. One sibling is ready to confront the abuse, the other insists that everything's fine. One accuses; the other defends."

"It didn't happen. I mean, think about it—it's ridiculous. People with hoods!"

Duran shrugged. "Your sister presented a *lot* of detail and although it went on for years—you were a lot *younger*. Sometimes, the younger victims don't understand that what happened to them was sexual abuse. Or even sexual in nature. So you could remember it, and not have the *vocabulary* to understand it in the same way Nico did."

Adrienne just shook her head. "You're in Candyland, Doc!"

"There was *a lot* of detail. You lived with Deck and Marlena in Beaumont, South Carolina," Duran recited, "in a house called Edgemont. It was white. The paint was peeling. And there were live oaks in the front yard." He cocked his head, and looked at her. "How am I doing?"

She smiled. "You're wrong about everything. Just for openers, I can tell you that we never lived in South Carolina—or in a house with a name, *any* name. We lived in a little brick rancher in Denton, Delaware. And there weren't any live oaks—just a couple of Catalpa trees with flat tops from the electric company."

"And your sister Rosanna?"

"There wasn't any 'Rosanna,' " Adrienne insisted. "It was just the two of us. Just Nikki and me—there was never anyone else."

With a sigh, Duran got up and walked to the window. Looked out at the parking lot. Finally, he turned to her and said, "Well, I'm not your therapist . . . and maybe it doesn't matter, anyway."

"What do you mean?"

"I mean, maybe it doesn't matter whether it's true or not—it's what your sister believed. And that might explain the gun."

Adrienne thought about it. "I suppose it might," she said. "Except . . ."

"What?" Duran asked.

"Who were the men in your apartment, and why did they want to kill me?"

Duran shook his head. "I don't know. But if Nikki was telling the truth—you'd be a witness."

"Except it was years ago, and I don't 'remember' anything—"

"Maybe not now—"

"Maybe not ever! Because it didn't happen!"

"Memories can be recovered," Duran suggested.

She just looked at him for a long while. Then she shook her head, and said, half to herself and half to Duran: "I can't believe I'm arguing with you about this . . ." And then, in a louder voice: "This is crazy!"

"What is?"

"Everything! You!"

"Why do you say that?" Duran asked.

"Well, this practice of yours . . ."

"What about it?"

"You said you had two clients."

Duran groaned.

"And yet," she continued, pressing the point, "you live in a big apartment in one of the nicest parts of Washington."

"So?"

"So, how do you pay for it?" Adrienne asked.

"Well, for one thing, I charge eighty-five dollars an hour."

"And you see—what? Two patients—how often?"

"Twice a week—each," Duran told her.

"So how much is that? Fifteen hundred a month?"

Duran frowned. He was beginning to have trouble getting his breath. After a moment, he nodded, not quite trusting his voice.

"Well, your apartment costs more than that! How do you *eat*?"

Duran rolled his eyes and got to his feet. Crossing the room, he picked up the remote, and pointed it at the television. While Adrienne watched, he flipped from one channel to another. A cop show. A movie. A talk show. Dan Rather.

Finally, she jerked the remote from his hands, and switched off the television. "You can't live on two clients, Doc—you just can't!"

"Two clients are normal," Duran assured her. "Two clients are fine."

She stared at him. It was exactly what he'd said before, when they'd been riding in the cab to the police station. She leaned closer to him.

"You can't live on two clients!" she whispered.

"Sure you can," Duran replied. "Two clients are normal—they're fine." But he looked troubled by her words. He frowned, as if trying to prise something out of his memory. Then he brightened, the distress easing from his features. "Besides, I have some money of my own. My parents, you know—there was insurance."

She sat down beside him on the bed. "Right," she said. "Your parents."

After a moment, he looked at her. *"What?!"*

"Even if that's true," she said, "two clients isn't exactly a *practice*, is it? I mean—what do you do with the rest of your time?"

With an exasperated groan, Duran got to his feet, and crossed the room to the window overlooking the parking lot. For a long while, he stood there, lost in thought, expressionless, while Adrienne stared. Finally, he closed his eyes and rested his forehead against the cool glass. He stayed there like that for ten or fifteen seconds, then turned to her, and with a regretful smile, explained, "Two clients are normal. Two clients are fine."

21

She couldn't sleep with Duran in the room. Though he'd saved her life, there was obviously something very wrong with him. The panic attacks and robotic replies, the imposture and false identity . . . he was way off the deep end. And knowing that, it was easy to imagine this otherwise handsome and easygoing guy going through some dark chrysalis in the middle of the night. Without wanting to, she could imagine him morphing into Anthony Hopkins, while muttering his weird little mantra about two clients being normal . . .

But it wasn't as if there was anywhere else for her to go. Her apartment wasn't her own anymore, not after what had been done to it. Whoever had been there before could go there again, whenever he liked. The police weren't going to stop him.

So she sat in the chair next to the window, reading and dozing, waking with a start, then falling off again. Eventually, dawn seeped across the highway behind the hotel, turning the parking lot into a table of gloom.

Getting to her feet, she clapped her hands, and gave a tug to the blanket that covered Duran. "Let's go!"

"Wha'?" Duran pushed up on an elbow, blinking in her direction. "What time is it?"

"Six-thirty!"

"Jesus," He groaned, and rolled over, pulling the covers over his head.

"C'mon," Adrienne said. "I want to go to your apartment."

Drugged with sleep, Duran sat up and rubbed his eyes. "You sure that's a good idea?" he asked.

Adrienne shrugged. "The police were just there. I thought we should look at your computer."

Duran nodded, still half-asleep. Finally, he swung his feet from the bed. Patted down his hair, and said, "Lemme get dressed."

"I was thinking about what happened," Adrienne explained. "About how they knew Bonilla and I were there."

Duran grunted, and began pulling on his socks. "Yeah . . . and what did you decide?"

"That your phone's tapped. Either that, or . . . *you* told them we were coming."

Duran frowned. "I didn't tell anybody anything." He yawned, and shook his head, and blinked away the sleep.

"You said one of the men looked familiar," Adrienne reminded him.

"Yeah, but—that was just in passing. Like I'd seen him on the street, or something."

"But—"

"Why would anyone tap my telephone?" Duran asked.

Adrienne looked him in the eye. "You want an honest answer?"

Duran nodded, surprised by her question. "Yeah."

"Because there's something going on with you."

His brow plunged. "Like what?"

"I don't know," Adrienne replied.

He thought about that for a moment. Finally, he said, "Maybe you're right." He paused. "Then again, maybe you're wrong."

"What do you mean?" she asked.

"I mean: *you're* the one they tried to kill. *You're* the one whose apartment was torn apart. Maybe it's *your* phone they bugged."

She thought about it for a moment. What he said made sense. (Then again: *Two clients are normal, two clients are—*) "Trust me," she said. "It's you."

They took the Metro from Springfield to the Cleveland Park station, emerging a few steps from Whatsa Bagel and Starbucks. From there to the Towers was only a five minute walk.

Duran used his Medeco key to enter the lobby. This was a large and marbled space beneath a huge chandelier, whose lights shone down on an array of tasteful couches and framed black-and-white photographs of old Washington. There were no doormen, as such, just a security desk that, at the moment, was unmanned.

Neither Adrienne nor Duran said a word as the elevator took them to the sixth floor, shaking a little from side to side. Finally, it shuddered to a halt with a loud *dinggg,* and the doors rattled open on the hallway.

" 'Jack be nimble,' " Adrienne whispered. Duran nodded his understanding.

Inserting the key, he turned the lock and pushed the door

open, half expecting the Bear to fill the space with the fury of a sudden storm. But there was nothing—no movement, and no sound but the distant hum of a refrigerator. Stepping inside, Duran was surprised to feel the tension within him dissolve. He remembered thinking, when he'd arrived back after the polygraph, how anonymous and generic the place was. But now he felt different. *There's something about this place,* he thought. *I just like being here.* "C'mon in," he said, speaking almost boisterously.

Adrienne shushed him, seeing at a single glance that someone had gone to considerable lengths to hide the violence that had taken place the day before. No bodies, no blood. Just a whiff of pine scented cleanser. Moving slowly through the room, looking for any sign of a disturbance, she'd almost given up when she found it: an indentation in the wall outside Duran's consultation room. And a gouge in the wooden baseboard. You had to know where to look, though. "You see?" she said. "Those are from bullets."

Duran nodded. "I'm a believer," he told her. "I was there." He looked at the damage. "They took the slugs, of course."

She sighed. "I can see why the police didn't buy it," she said. "I mean if someone tells you that there's a murder, that there are *bodies,* blood—and when they go to take a look, they don't find anything . . ." Her voice trailed away. "I mean, who's going to check for gouges in the woodwork. Who's going to look any further? I wouldn't."

Going to the spot where Bonilla had fallen, Adrienne stared at the floor. Finally, she said, "I don't get it."

"What?" Duran asked.

"Any of it. I can see where they might have been able to clean things up in the time it took for the police to get here, but . . . what did they do with Eddie? And the other man? How did they get them out of the building?"

Duran shook his head, as baffled as she. "Through the garage?" Then he pointed to an end table next to the couch. "Look at that," he said.

Adrienne frowned. "What?"

"The lamp," Duran said. "It's gone. I must have broken it when I hit the guy with it."

Adrienne shivered. "Where's your computer?"

"In here." He led her into the consultation room.

"You drive," Adrienne said, swiveling the desk chair in his direction.

"What are we looking for?" he asked, sitting down in front of the computer.

"Patient notes. Address books. Whatever we can find."

He pushed the *Power* button on the CPU, and the computer began to whir and tick, going through its incomprehensible boot up routine. It took a minute for the wallpaper to shimmer into view, then the icons, and finally they heard a fanfare of trumpets. "So—where do you want to go today?" he asked, resting his fingertips on the keyboard.

"Patient notes. Do you have a folder for Nikki?"

Duran nodded. Typing rapidly, he clicked successively on *Start, Find (files and folders)*, and instructed the computer to list everything in the *Sullivan* folder. A moment later, the names of fifty-six files appeared in a little window. Most of them were denominated *Nico*, with a number after her name. Adrienne watched over his shoulder.

"What are the numbers?" she asked.

"First session, second session, third—like that."

"Go to *Intake*," she suggested.

Duran double-clicked on the file, then opened it in Word. The Microsoft splash screen appeared on the monitor and, soon afterward, a page consisting entirely of row upon row of numeral ones. Thousands of them. Disbelieving, Duran scrolled down the first page to the second in the file, and then to the third. They were all the same. Finally, he turned to Adrienne. "I don't understand," he said.

"Let me take a look."

"You sure?"

She nodded as she took his seat, and began typing. "When I was in school, I had a part-time job at Dial-a-Geek," she told him, fingers flying over the keys. "My junior year. I only got

Tier One questions, but . . ." She stopped typing and looked up at him. "We've got a problem, Houston."

"I can see that, but—what is it?"

She pointed at the screen in front of her. He saw that it was a list of the files in the *Sullivan* folder. Scrolling horizontally, she pointed to the last column on the right. It was headed with the word, *Modified,* and under it was a series of dates and times corresponding to each file. The dates were all the same, the times within a minute of one another. *November 14, 3:02* AM.

"Son of a bitch," Adrienne muttered.

"What?"

She shook him off. "What's your other patient's name?"

"De Groot." He spelled it for her.

"Is there a de Groot folder?"

"Yeah."

She typed for a moment, and then sat back as the monitor flickered, and Windows listed the files in the de Groot folder. At a glance, they could see that all of the files had been modified on November 14 at about three o'clock in the morning. Hoping against hope, Adrienne called up *deGroot 13*—only to see that, like the *intake* file in the *Sullivan* directory, it consisted entirely of the numeral 1, repeated thousands of times.

She sighed. "Someone wiped your text files last night," she explained. "And only your text files."

Duran couldn't believe it. "How?"

Adrienne shrugged. "It's not complicated. I bet if you went into *Programs*, you'd see a little file with a cute name like . . . 'Wipeout' or 'Textburn.' "

"You're kidding."

"I'm not."

"Someone wrote a program—"

She shook her head. "You can download it from hackers dot com." She pushed her chair back from the computer, as Duran swore under his breath.

"But the information's still there," he insisted. "It doesn't actually go away."

"No?" she asked, arching an eyebrow.

"No," he told her. "It's like real memory. Even with amnesia, it's just a question of retrieval. The data's on 'the disk,' somewhere. All that's changed is that someone's erased the addresses."

Adrienne shook her head. "They didn't erase the addresses. They changed the 'data' in them to a lot of ones. That's their content. That's what they *say*." She glanced at the screen. "Unless you made backups?" She gave him a hopeful look.

"In here," Duran told her, pulling open the drawer on the left side of his desk. Only to find pens, pencils, scissors, and highlighters. A staple remover and paperclips. "I mean, they *were*."

Adrienne looked around, then reached into the wastepaper basket beside the desk. "Is this it?" she asked, showing him a zip disk that someone had crumpled like an empty beer can.

Duran looked at the label, and swore.

"You said you made tapes," Adrienne reminded him.

Duran nodded.

"So where do you keep them?"

"I don't," he said. "I mail them to the—" Suddenly, he winced and groaned. "—ohhh, jeez . . ."

"What?" Adrienne asked.

Shaking his head, Duran reached into the pocket of his jacket, and produced a cassette tape labeled *De Groot-34*. "I was supposed to mail it, but . . . everything went haywire."

"That's the only one you have?"

Duran nodded.

"What about *that*?" Adrienne asked, with a glance at the answering machine.

He looked at it. "There's only one message," he said, tapping the *Rewind* button with his forefinger. Slowly, at first, and then faster, the tape began to rewind, emitting a high and empty whine that reminded Adrienne of Nikki's robot impersonation: *Rrr-rrr-rrr.* Finally, it snapped to a stop with loud *cli-ick*.

"Whoever it is, he's got a lot to say," Duran remarked, and hit the *Play* button.

There was a crackling silence, followed by a man's voice, soft and confidential. *Hello, Jeff . . . I have a message for you—so it's important to pay attention, okay? This is for you. Put everything down, and listen carefully . . .* There was a second silence, and then a low, reverberating sound rose up from the machine, as if a tuning fork had been struck. The signal rose and fell, weakened and pulsed, so that it seemed to come closer and closer, only to withdraw—only to return again.

Puzzled by the noise from the machine, Adrienne listened hard to it, trying to make sense of the sound. But it was impossible—a machine noise that made no sense and gave no hint about its origins. After a while, she gave up on it and turned to Duran in irritation.

Only to find him transfixed.

"Jeff?" She'd never called him that before, and it seemed strange to do so now. Not that he noticed. He remained where he was, entrained by the signal that poured from the answering machine. Taking him by the sleeve, Adrienne spoke again, and again there was no reaction. "It's a fax, or something," she explained, tugging gently at his jacket. "Let's get out of here."

And still no reaction from Duran—who, she saw, had begun to tremble. Looking closer, she noticed a thin line of foam curling between his lips.

"Hey!" she said, stepping back involuntarily, her voice an urgent whisper. Frightened now, she tried to pull him away from the desk, but it was useless. He was immobile, immovable, a six foot column of quavering stone. "C'mon," she begged. "Let's go!" But he couldn't see or hear her—that much was obvious. His eyes were dilated, the irises gone and the pupils black, as if it were midnight in the darkest cellar, rather than midmorning in his own consultation room.

The tremors were stronger now, a real shaking. And then, to Adrienne's shock, she saw that he was beginning to bleed, a steady drip that fell from his nostrils to the front of his shirt. She knew what to do—the answering machine was in easy reach—but there was something wrong with her arms and legs. It was almost as if she were in a waking nightmare, paralyzed by the specter of something that, even then, was slouching toward her from the cellar.

And the blood was coming faster now, a steady drip that fell to the floor and spattered her shoes—so that, instinctively, she jumped back. And by that movement, broke whatever spell had been upon her. With a gasp, she slapped the buttons on the answering machine until the sound stopped.

"Jesus," Duran said in a dazed voice. "Look at that." He was swaying slightly, and staring at the blood on his shirtfront. "I got a nosebleed," he told her.

Now it was Adrienne's turn to shake as she took the telephone from him, and hung it up. Pulling a tissue from the Kleenex box on the desk, she gave it to Duran. "From now on," she said, "if there are any phone calls or messages—let me handle them."

Duran gave her a puzzled look, then turned his face to the ceiling. "Whatever . . ." he mumbled, keeping his head back. "Who was that, anyway?"

"You don't remember?"

He shook his head, still facing the ceiling. "No."

An idea occurred to her. "Well . . . let's just see." Lifting the handset on the telephone, she dialed *69. Then she grabbed a pen, and began to write on a Post-it, as an electronic voice revealed that: "The last number to call your telephone was 202-234-8484." Hanging up, she showed the number to Duran, but it didn't mean anything to him.

"We can still use your computer," she told him, sitting down in front of the monitor.

"What for?" he asked, watching as she double-clicked on the AOL icon.

"There's a reverse telephone lookup at anywho dot com. You give them the number, they give you the address." Duran watched over her shoulder as she filled in the appropriate windows, providing the telephone number and area code that *69 had given her. Together, they watched and waited as the hourglass floated in the center of the monitor.

Waiting for reply Transferring document 1% 2% 3% 26% 49% Query result The words Residential listing appeared, and under them the following information:

> *Barbera, Hector*
> *2306 Connecticut Ave.*
> *Apt. 6-F*
> *Washington, D.C. 20010*

Adrienne frowned. "Who's Hector Barbera?" she asked.

Duran stared at the information for a long moment, then held up a hand, and whispered, "We're in 6-E."

It only took a moment for Adrienne's eyes to widen. Then Duran picked up the phone and, shaking off her silent objection, dialed the number listed for Barbera. Soon, they could hear it ringing next door—a long, slow trill that came and went. After the sixth ring, Duran replaced the handset in its cradle.

"No one's home," he told her.

She nodded, suddenly relieved.

"You know how to pick a lock?" he asked.

She grimaced in reply.

"Doesn't matter," Duran told her. "Wait here."

"Where are you going?"

"Health Club."

"What?" She was about to ask him if he was out of his mind, but then, it occurred to her that she already knew the answer to that question. Of course he was: that was the whole point. *"Why?"*

But he was gone and, for the moment, she was alone in the apartment. Alone with the refrigerator's hum, and with the changing light as clouds drifted across the sun. And not just that—there was another sound that she couldn't quite place, and could barely hear, a low tone. Room noise, she decided. Or something.

Then Duran was back, carrying a twenty-five-pound dumbbell in his right hand. "Stay with me," he said.

"But—"

He glanced down the hall to make certain it was empty, then strode to the doorway of Apartment 6-F. Standing about three feet from the door, he drew the dumbbell back, then came around like a discus thrower, slamming twenty-five pounds of chromed steel into the door just above the lock, splintering the jamb.

As the door flew open on its hinges, Duran stepped inside—and what he saw took his breath away. The wall between his apartment and Barbera's was covered with a gray, wire mesh. In front of the mesh was a long table stacked with electronics equipment: there were oscillators, amplifiers, and receivers, and a cumbersome looking device that reminded Duran of a dental X ray. This last machine was pointed directly at the wall, and was warm to the touch, with a green diode that glowed brightly.

Glancing around, Duran saw that the apartment was not for living. The wooden floor was bare of rugs, the walls empty. The only furniture was a matte-black Aeron chair and a cantilevered desk lamp with a Halogen bulb. A telephone. And that was it.

Except for the objects that Adrienne was staring at: two padlocked steamer trunks, side by side in the far corner of the room. Feeling Duran's gaze, she turned to him, and shivered. "It's freezing in here." And so it was.

"He's got the air-conditioning on," Duran told her, crossing the room to her side, dumbbell in hand.

For a moment, they stood next to one another, gazing at the steamer trunks.

"I want to go," Adrienne announced. "I want to go right now." She tugged at his sleeve, but Duran was unmoving. And then, without a word, he stepped back and swung the dumbbell in an arc, smashing it into the lock on one of the trunks. Adrienne's knees buckled as he threw open the lid. Reflexively, she laid a hand against the wall for support, and looked away. Silence hung in the air between them. Finally, she asked, "Is it . . . Eddie?"

Duran didn't answer at first, just shook his head from side to side, more in wonderment than reply. "I don't know," he told her. "But it's somebody."

They left the Towers at a racewalk, uncertain what to do or where to go. Adrienne was convinced they should go to the police, but Duran was skeptical.

"All right," he said, playing the devil's advocate, "so what if we go there? What do we tell them?"

"About the trunks."

"Okay. And then what?"

"What do you mean?" she asked.

"I mean, what do you think they'll do? Do you think they'll go to the apartment and search it?"

Adrienne thought about it for a long moment. Finally, she sighed. "No. They'd probably just charge us with breaking and entering."

"Right," Duran told her. "That's what *I* think."

"Then let's go to my place," she said. "At least we can get my car."

Once again, he shook his head. "You might as well shoot yourself," he told her. "There isn't a chance in the world they aren't watching it."

"But I need stuff," she said. "I need clothes. Makeup. *Things!*"

"Then you'll have to buy them," he told her. "Until the police start looking for Bonilla . . . I don't think you want to go home."

So they took the Metro to National Airport and rented a car, then drove to the Pentagon City mall, where Adrienne bought an overnight bag, some makeup and lingerie, and two dresses from Nordstrom's. As they left the mall, Duran made a call to 911, saying, "I want to get something on the record—whether you do anything about it or not is up to you . . ." Then he told them, succinctly, exactly what he'd seen in Barbera's apartment, gave them the address and rang off.

On the way back to the Comfort Inn, it began to rain, just a few slanting specks against the windshield and then—before Duran could figure out how the wipers worked—an obliterating downpour that had him frantically pushing buttons and moving levers as he peered through the pearlized windshield.

When he finally located the knob that activated the windshield wipers, he turned to Adrienne and said, "I was thinking . . ."

Adrienne kept her eyes on the road. He was a more aggressive driver than she was used to. "About what?"

"All that electronics stuff."

"Unh-huh . . ." He didn't say anything, so she prodded him. *"And?"*

"Well, I was thinking—maybe it had something to do with me."

She just looked at him.

While Duran lay on the bed, lost in thought, Adrienne stood in the shower, relishing the hot water pounding down against the back of her neck and shoulders. She was thinking about Bill Fellowes, the intern from Howard University.

Like most interns, Fellowes spent a lot of his time doing shit work, but he was clearly going places. She'd gotten to know him when he'd been assigned to the Amalgamated case, helping her compile a database for the documents and work product. She remembered feeling guilty. Here was a guy who was law review and all that—and she was spending day in and day out, handing him papers to number and date-stamp. Then she remembered that *she* was law review, and what she was doing wasn't any more interesting than what he'd been assigned. On the contrary, they were doing it together.

But the thing about Fellowes was, he'd assisted on a case in the spring that was actually pretty interesting (compared to the Amalgamated matter). Adrienne didn't remember the details, but it had something to do with "recovered memory"—at least, she thought it had. In any case, there was an expert witness who'd testified on behalf of the firm's client. She was certain of that because Bill was a gifted mimic, and she could remember the look on his sunny brown face as he reenacted parts of the trial over tequilas at Chief Ike's Mambo Room. The doctor had been impressive—very cool and basso profundo.

She lathered her hair, squeezed her eyes shut and turned her face to the showerhead. She'd get the doctor's name from Bill. Maybe the doctor would look at Duran and, even if he wouldn't, he might be able to point her in the right direction—a colleague, or *something*.

After a minute or two, she rinsed the soap from her hair, stepped from the shower and wrapped herself in a towel. The bathroom was small and steamy, the mirror a gray cloud. Using a hand towel, she cleared enough of its surface to see herself, then yanked the hotel's plastic comb through the tangles in her hair. It didn't do much good. But it was the weekend—and it was all she had.

Finally, she pulled on her new panty hose and stepped into the navy-blue dress she'd bought. With her earrings in place, she emerged from the bathroom, transformed.

Duran looked up from the TV, and did a double take. "Hey," he said, "you look . . . nice."

"Thanks," she replied, stepping into her shoes. "I'll be back late, so don't wait up. On the other hand—don't get lost, either."

"But . . . where are you going?" he asked, as suspicious as he was concerned.

"To work."

" 'Work'? Are you crazy? We're in *hiding*, for Christ's sake! And it's Sunday—you can't go to work."

"Got to."

Duran snapped off the TV, sat up and looked directly into her eyes. "People are trying to kill you! Whenever that happens, you're supposed to take a day off."

"I can't."

"You have to."

"I won't."

"And what if they follow you?" he demanded.

"From *here*?"

He shook his head. "*To* here. From your office."

"They won't do that. They'd have to watch the office all day, just to see if I show up—and my apartment, too—because, when you think about it, I'm more likely to go there than to the office. Especially on Sunday, so . . . I'll be *okay*. It isn't like the KGB is after us."

Duran fell back on the bed. "How do you know?"

She smiled. "Very funny."

"You won't change your mind?" he asked.

She shook her head.

"Then I want you to call me," Duran told her, "when you get there, and when you leave. Okay?"

She agreed.

The rental car was a metallic-green Dodge Stratus. It had that new car smell in spades, and kept fogging up as Adrienne headed north on Shirley Highway past the Army-Navy Country Club. The rain was lighter now, but the humidity was terrific and there wasn't anything in the car to clear the windshield. So every half mile or so, she brushed the fingertips of her right hand back and forth across the glass, smearing it.

Not that it mattered. Her mind was elsewhere. She was thinking that Duran was right about going to work. The safest thing to do would be to stay away for a few days, and call in sick. But she couldn't do that. Slough wouldn't understand. And if she tried to explain it—if she told him what had happened—well, that would be even worse. Lawyers at Slough, Hawley did not get shot at. Or, if they did, they did not make partner.

And, anyway, she wasn't afraid. On the contrary, she was all tapped out on the fear front, and had been for a very long time.

The thing about fear was that it was exhausting. She'd known that ever since she was a child. For years she'd lived in a state of almost constant anxiety. After Gram died, there was the fear that there would be no one to take care of her. Then, after a series of foster homes, and interim periods in "care," there was the fear of getting hit, yelled at, humiliated, ignored, or bullied. Even the social workers scared her, the creepy way they held her hand and asked loaded questions whose significance and consequences she couldn't guess. That she didn't know the right answers was clear from the little twitches of disappointment in their eyes, the reflexive smiles, the rephrased questions. Once, she'd overheard them talking about a family's interest in adopting "the younger child"—her—and she'd been scared to death. For weeks she wouldn't let Nikki out of her sight, terrified that they'd be separated.

But those were the acute fears, the ones that rose and fell on an almost daily basis, like the tides. There was another fear, though, that was chronic and unchanging, an adrenal drain fueled by the worry that whatever sanctuary she and Nikki had found, it would soon disappear.

Not surprising then, that after a while, her capacity for being afraid dwindled toward zero—so that by the time she and Nikki were placed with Deck and Marlena, Adrienne's demeanor had changed from a condition of alert vigilance to a kind of numbed docility. (The famous "automaton" of Mrs. Dunkirk's pronouncement.) Years later, while a second-year law student, she'd obtained her files under the Freedom of Information Act. There, she'd read a raft of speculation about what was "wrong with her": attachment disorder, borderline personality, lack of affect. The diagnosis changed from caseworker to caseworker. But the truth was, she was none of those things: what was "wrong" with her was simple. She had combat fatigue.

Turning off M Street, she headed downhill toward the river, and swung left in the direction of Harbor Place. Georgetown had an abandoned, rainy day feeling to it. Cruising slowly along K Street, she studied the parked cars that she passed. But there was nothing unusual about any of them. So she parked on the street, avoiding the underground garage, which charged twelve dollars for the first three hours.

It was only a block to the office but, even so, she was wet when she got there. Stopping in the ladies' room, she blotted her dripping hair with paper towels. Her dress was more than damp, as well, but there was nothing she could do about it—and, anyway, the color hid the rain.

She passed Bette's cubicle, and saw that she was hard at work, clacking away at the keyboard, printer humming, talking on the phone. Adrienne tapped the door as she walked by and Bette turned and raised a hand in greeting, eyebrows up and mouthing a silent "Hi!"

Adrienne hung up her jacket, then sat down at the desk, and pressed the space bar on her keyboard. While she waited for the icons to appear on her monitor, she pulled open the top file drawer—where she kept an electric kettle and a jar of instant coffee for emergencies. Going to the water fountain to fill the kettle, she found Bette waiting for her when she got back.

"Where *were* you, Scout?"

"What do you mean?" Adrienne asked, plugging in the kettle.

"Yesterday! Dream team's here, poring over the wonders of asphalt curing times and you were—what? You took off for lunch, and . . . now it's Sunday? What *happened*?"

She thought about what to say, and what not to say. It was tricky and awful, all at once, because she couldn't really tell Bette about Bonilla and Duran—or she'd seem like a lunatic. But she couldn't lie about it, either, because the truth would eventually come out. It had to. She *wanted* it to. Until then . . . "Things are real complicated, right now."

Bette's jaw dropped.

"You want some coffee?" Adrienne asked.

Bette blinked, milking the moment. Finally, she said, "Okaaaaay . . . so, when did Slough get you?"

Adrienne levered two paper cups off the stack, separated

them, and spooned out the shiny crystals of coffee. " 'Get me'?"

Bette blanched. "You mean—you haven't *talked* to him yet? Oh my God. You haven't been home?"

Adrienne frowned. "Not exactly."

"Well, I hope he was worth it," Bette said, "whoever he was, because . . . you didn't even check your messages?"

Adrienne shook her head for the second time.

Bette raised her eyes to the ceiling, and sighed. "Well, he left, *we* left—a lot of messages for you."

Shit. Adrienne's heart stalled for a moment, and she didn't know quite what to say. Finally, she blurted, "So . . . what's going on?"

Bette giggled—nervously—at what she thought was Adrienne's indifference. "Well, there's been some kind of meltdown in San Diego. Slough was flaps up hours ago. And, basically—you-the-man!"

"What do you mean, I'm the man."

"You're deposing McEligot."

"What?! When?"

"Tomorrow."

"But—" Adrienne began, "I've never deposed *anybody*. I'm not *prepared*. I don't know—Jesus, Bette!"

"Well, some of us are actually jealous. I mean—"

A quiet, high-pitched moan from Adrienne. The kettle shrilled. She picked it up and poured water into the cups, then stirred each one.

"He said he was sending you his prep work," Bette told her in a reassuring voice. "So you should check your e-mail. On the other hand, he was really in a hurry, so . . . who knows?" She sipped her coffee and headed for the door. "Delicious. Anyway . . . lucky you!"

"Wait a second," Adrienne asked, groaning inwardly at the prospect of another all-nighter. "Have you seen Bill around?"

"Bill who? You mean Fellowes?"

"Unh-huh."

"Not for a couple of days. He's in Detroit. I don't think he's back until Tuesday."

When Bette had gone, Adrienne called Bill Fellowes's number at home, and left a message on his machine, asking him to call her.

That done, she logged onto the Internet and checked her e-mail. There were eight messages: two jokes, forwarded by friends; a couple of come-ons from AOL and E*Trade; and four bulletins from Slough, which boiled down to: 1) Call me. 2) Where *are* you? 3) You're deposing McEligot. And 4) Here's my prep work. (You'll have to flesh it out a little.) Go get 'em!

This last message included an attachment that, once she downloaded it, caused her to put her head in her hands. *Flesh it out?* With the exception of two or three sentences that she didn't recognize, what Slough had sent her—his prep work on McEligot—was nothing more than the memo that *she'd* worked up for *him*. Which is to say that it included everything she already knew—and nothing more.

She called Slough's number in San Diego, and left a message, saying that she'd received what he'd sent and that she was at the office if he wanted to talk. Then she put her head down, and got to work.

Time did not fly.

The McEligot deposition was a minefield, with each question posing a different set of problems and opportunities—so that, by the time Adrienne looked at her watch, three hours had passed—and she'd forgotten to call Duran.

"I was *worried* about you," he said, when she finally got him on the phone.

"It's been really busy," she explained. "And it's going to be a couple of more hours. I'm not done."

"I don't like you being there," he told her. "I don't think it's safe."

His concern touched her. "I'm not alone!" she replied. "Everyone's beavering away. As soon as I can, I'll come back and finish up on the laptop. I'll bring food."

"Great, but—"

"Don't worry, I'll be careful."

"Good idea," he said, "but what I was going to ask is, why don't you get some beer?"

It was ten o'clock when her tiredness finally gave way to hunger, and she decided to return to the motel. By then, she was the only lawyer still at work, though not the only person on the floor. From the corridor came the dull roar of vacuum cleaners, the squeak of polish on brass, the chatter of Spanish.

She could refine her notes at the Comfort Inn, working on Nikki's laptop. She copied her work to a floppy, slung the laptop over her shoulder and flicked off the light.

Then she rode down in the elevator with a pretty girl in an Orioles sweatshirt who piloted her rolling bucket and mops through the doors when they stopped at the second floor. Alone in the elevator, the world seemed suddenly, eerily silent—until the doors slid open, and a wave of techno pop washed over her from a boombox in the lobby.

The rain had stopped, but a damp wind nipped at her cheeks as she hurried toward the car. *If anything's going to happen,* she thought, *now's the time, this is the place.* But there was no one that she could see. An old lady, walking a small dog. A young schizophrenic, shuffling down the sidewalk, dressed in what looked like half a dozen overcoats. Some musicians, sitting outside a club under the Whitehurst Freeway, sharing a joint. Parked cars and vans, but—not her own. A sizzle of fear zipped through her chest, then fizzled out when she remembered that she wasn't looking for her own aging Subaru, but a new Dodge.

And there it was.

Peering through the glass to be sure the backseat was empty, she got behind the wheel and tried the ignition. A sluggish sound rose up from under the hood. And again. And again. Just as she was beginning to panic, the engine turned over with a roar. Relieved, she pulled out into the street, heading for Rock Creek Parkway.

She was creeping past the Kennedy Center—Yo-Yo Ma was opening that night—when she noticed a shiny black car in her rearview mirror. She didn't know what kind of car it was, but it was low-slung and predatory looking. It seemed to her she'd seen it on the street outside her office, when she'd been looking for her own car—but maybe not. Then the traffic opened up and, suddenly, she was past the Ken-Cen, gathering speed on her way to the bridge. With a glance at her rearview mirror, she saw that the car behind her was now a van.

And so she relaxed, her mind turning to Duran as she crossed the Potomac, heading toward Springfield.

She couldn't believe that she was going to spend another night in a motel with this guy—or what was worse, that he was now her only confidant. *That,* more than anything else, really got to her. It boggled the mind.

Her eyes rose to the rearview mirror, and stayed there for several seconds before they returned to the road. Still no shiny black car, but in all this traffic, who could tell?

At the brightly lighted Sultan Kebob in Springfield, she ordered takeout for herself and Duran, then sat down to wait with the magazine section of the *Post.* There was a terrific recipe for preserved lemons and, reading it, she wished with all her heart that she might someday have time to do things like that—instead of spending her Sundays immersed in asphalt. Finally, the proprietor emerged from the kitchen with a pair of self-enclosed, Styrofoam trays containing rice, kebobs, and salad.

The motel was only a couple of minutes away, which was good—because, as she emerged from the Sultan Kebob, she saw the shiny black car, or thought she did. It was parked about a hundred feet away in a rank of other cars, facing in the opposite direction. What caught her attention was not so much the car itself, as the fact that its brake lights were on. Noticing that, she then saw a thin column of vapor rising from the car's exhaust, even as a hand reached out from the front seat to adjust the mirror on the passenger's side.

She saw this as she walked, and in her peripheral vision, she noticed that there were two men in the car. She could feel their eyes upon her in the side view mirrors. Or so she imagined.

Then she was at her own car, the rented Dodge. Fumbling for the key, she unlocked the door, got in and tried the engine. For the second time that night, it was slow to start. But start it did and, when it did, she took off like a teenaged psycho, accelerating through the parking lot, eyes on the mirror. For a second, she thought she saw the headlights flash on the shiny black car, but then she turned, and there was no one behind her.

At least, she didn't *think* there was anyone behind her.

The Springfield mixing bowl was a tangle of converging highways, half of which were under construction, and it would have been death to take her eyes off the road.

Then, again . . .

If she was being followed, Adrienne thought, they must have had a change of mind. About Duran, that is. Because the only reason they would follow *her*—when they could have grabbed her outside work—would be to find *him*. Which was strange, because Duran wasn't their target. At least, he hadn't *been* their target the day before. Then, the big man—the Bear—had gone out of his way *not* to kill him, turning the gun on Adrienne. So something had changed . . . but why? Was it the break-in? the 911 call? Maybe. Or maybe she wasn't being followed at all.

Soon, she pulled into the parking lot of the Comfort Inn, a vast expanse of concrete that glowed pinkly from the mercury street lamps overhead. Hurrying into the motel, she went straight to the elevator and up to the room, where Duran greeted her from his chair behind the desk.

"You're right on time," he told her, looking up from the *Post*. "I'm starving." Brushing by him without a word, she put the boxes of kebabs on the desk, flicked off the lights, and crossed to the windows—where she pulled the curtains shut, and peeped outside.

"I think I was followed," she told him.

"What!?"

She nodded. "I wasn't sure, but . . . yeah."

He went to her side, and peered out through the parted curtain. "What am I looking for?"

"The car behind mine. Next to the Jeep. Shiny black car."

He looked, and saw a Mercury Cougar parked in a space about fifteen feet behind the Dodge. The car was empty, or seemed to be, until he saw the lighted end of a cigarette flare in the darkness of the front seat. Duran took a deep breath.

"Now what?" Adrienne asked.

He shook his head. "I don't know." He paused. "How many people were in the car?"

She thought about it. "Two . . . I think."

He sighed. "Give me the keys."

She handed them over with a frown. "They don't know which room we're in—or even that we're together."

He stood beside the curtain, looking out. Finally, he told her, "Here's what I think: *that* guy's friend is at the front desk, right now, asking about us. And if it's the same guy we met yesterday—the big guy?—I think the clerk will tell him what he wants to know."

"So what do we do?"

"That's the really hard part," he replied. "I have no fucking idea."

Adrienne groaned.

"Get your things together," he suggested. "If we get outta here, you'll need something to wear."

" 'If'!?"

His look was incredulous, but what he actually said was: "Yeah—'if.' "

She pulled the shopping bag out of the wastepaper basket, and went into the bathroom, where she cleared the counter of everything it held. Then she tossed her clothes on top of that, and stood beside the door, waiting for Duran to give the word. Or have an idea. Or whatever it was he was waiting for.

Finally, Duran said, "There he is."

"Who?"

"The big guy," he replied, eyes on the parking lot. "He just came out the door."

"What's he doing?" she asked.

"He's getting the other guy." Suddenly, he turned to her. "We have to go."

"Why?"

"Because they're on the way up."

Lunging from the room, Adrienne turned instinctively toward the elevator, but Duran caught her by the sleeve and pulled her toward the emergency exit at the end of the corridor. Yanking open the door to the stairs, they heard the elevator ping and dove into the stairwell, taking the concrete steps two at a time.

Until Adrienne crashed with a yelp into someone a lot bigger, someone who was coming up the stairs as fast as they were going down.

"Bitch!" The Big Guy grabbed her by the collar with both hands, brought her close, then made a sort of no look pass, tossing her into the wall. She hit the cinderblock flat and square, the back of her head smacking against the rock. A gasp fell from her mouth as she sank to the floor—even as Duran came down the stairs, throwing a roundhouse that caught the Big Guy behind the ear. No *ooof* this time, but a bellow of pain and rage as the Big Man bounced off the wall and, with a feral growl, plowed into the therapist as if he were a tackling dummy, slamming him into the iron balustrade. The impact sent a shock wave up and down his spine, but the real agony was in his mouth, where Duran's teeth slammed shut on his tongue. He could taste the blood—but only for a moment, as the Big Guy hit him flush in the forehead, setting off a series of clicks and pops inside his head.

Rolling to the left, Duran counterpunched reflexively, but not to much use. In an instant, his adversary was behind him, looping his meathook arms under Duran's own, then clasping his hands at the back of his neck, pushing him down. Duran was in shape, but it felt as if his arms were going to snap like twigs—and there was nothing that he could do about it. The man he was fighting was fifty pounds heavier, a lot stronger, and just as quick.

Then something strange happened. Without thinking about it, Duran jackknifed, plunging his head toward his knees so quickly that the Big Man sommersaulted over his shoulders. It was a wrestling move, and its fluency surprised Duran almost as much as it did its victim. *Where did that come from?* he wondered, as the Big Man's tailbone smacked into the rock hard floor.

He lay there for a moment, stunned, as Duran glanced frantically around for something to hit him with—something to put him *out*. But there was nothing. Then the Big Guy was on his hands and knees, struggling to his feet. Terrified, Duran took a step back, then drove his instep into the other man's chin as if he were kicking an extra point, snapping his neck with a crack so loud it could have been a gunshot.

Then the night was still, and the only noise was Duran gasping for air—he was still lit up with adrenaline, still in pain—and a soft, whimpering sound from where Adrienne lay in the corner of the stairwell.

Kneeling by her side, Duran coaxed her to wakefulness. Putting his hand behind her head, he could feel the blood from an open wound, matting her hair. "C'mon," he said, lifting her gently into a sitting position. "We've got to go."

Reluctantly, she let him drag her to her feet, where she stood, swaying, holding his arm as if it were a life preserver.

"Where are the keys?" he asked.

She nodded to the shopping bag, which held her purse and other things.

He reached in, opened the purse, and fumbled through it until he found the keys. Then he took her by the arm, and led her down the stairs to the mezzanine, just off the lobby. There was no one at the front desk, and no security guard.

Seeing the open, empty expanse, Adrienne balked. "What about the other man?"

"He's looking for his friend," Duran said. "C'mon."

Together, they ran to a side door that gave way to the parking lot. Bursting into the night air, they sprinted for the car, jerked open the doors and dove in. Duran jammed the key in the ignition, revved the engine and said, "Put on your seat belt."

"What?!" Adrienne stared at him in disbelief. "Go!"

He shook his head, and revved the engine even louder. "Put it on!" he shouted. Then he reached over his left shoulder, and drew his own seat belt across his chest, fastening the strap in the receptacle by his side.

"But—"

Duran wasn't listening. His arm was on the back of the seat, and he was half-turned, looking out the back window.

Sputtering with exasperation and fear, Adrienne did as she was told and buckled up. Then she folded her arms across her chest, and sat stock-still, looking straight ahead in rapt frustration.

"There he is," Duran told her, as a wild-eyed man burst out the side door of the motel, looking left and right.

"Are we going to sit here forever?" Adrienne asked.

In reply, Duran shoved the gearshift into reverse. The tires squealed, caught, and shot the Dodge backwards into the front end of the Mercury Cougar, ten yards behind them. There was a crash of glass, and a geyser of antifreeze as the Mercury's hood jackknifed, its engine compacting and right wheel well folding in upon itself.

Adrienne screamed, and the man in the doorway roared—haplessly, if that's possible. Easing the gearshift into *Drive*, Duran reversed direction, pulling away from the scene with the comment that "Seat belts aren't just a good idea, y'know. They're *the law*."

22 They were out of the parking lot, and almost to the highway before Duran noticed that the rain had turned to mist. Pools of water glowed in the indelible twilight that passed for night in the city. Up ahead, a dull roar rose from the interstate like heat shimmering over a desert highway.

Adrienne groaned. Duran glanced at her.

She was acting as if she had a concussion, fading in and out like a weak radio signal. No sooner were they on the highway, heading north, than she asked him to pull over onto the shoulder so she could throw up. After that, she seemed a little better. More alert.

But they didn't talk. Using the controls on the armrest, he rolled down the car windows, so the cold air could help them focus. Driving past Capitol Hill, he turned to her, and asked, "You mind if I say something?"

She shook her head. "What?"

"I told you so."

She blinked. Frowned. "What do you mean?"

"Just what I said: I *told* you so."

Her frown deepened. "And what was it you told me?"

"Not to go to work."

Her lips parted in reply, then closed in a pout. It was disgraceful of him to throw that in her face—even if he was right. *Especially* if he was right. And if he didn't know that, well . . . After a while, she asked, "Where are we going?"

"Bethany Beach."

She looked at him in disbelief, and he could see that she was feeling better. "Are you out of your mind? I can't go there! I have to work!"

Duran rolled his eyes toward the roof.

"Turn around," she demanded.

Duran laughed.

"I mean it!" she said. "Get off at the exit."

"No."

"What do you mean, *'no'*? Stop the fucking car! I'm the one who *rented* it. It's my—*oooh!*" Her hand went to the contusion at the back of her head. When he glanced at her again, she was staring at the blood on her fingers.

"It isn't safe," she complained, almost in a mumble.

"What isn't?"

"Being with you."

A huge truck rolled past, rocking the car with its turbulence, kicking up clouds of mist. Neither of them said anything for what seemed a long time. They passed the exits for Annapolis and Duran noted the first sign with the seagull logo, pointing the way to the Bay Bridge.

After a while, she asked, "Why Bethany?"

Duran shrugged. "I spent the summers there as a kid. We had a beach cottage."

She gave him a skeptical look. "You sure?"

"Yeah—of course I'm sure."

"Because your record's not so great on this kind of thing. I mean, who you are, where you're from and all that."

Up ahead, a green sign cautioned them against drinking while driving: *Reach the Beach,* it told them. A second sign offered a radio frequency for traffic advice. Then they passed over a series of rumble-strips on the way to a line of tollbooths. Braking gently, Duran handed the attendant a five-dollar bill, and thanked him for the change before continuing on his way. The clock on the dashboard read 2:49.

Halfway across the Bay Bridge, he turned to her and said, "I remember the cottage, *exactly.*"

"Then tell me about it," she said.

Duran shrugged. "Well, it's got a name. They *all* have names, all the cottages in the old part of Bethany."

"What else?" Adrienne asked.

"The town used to be a church camp." He looked at her. "Our house was called 'Beach Haven.' It was written—in script—on a wooden plaque. Next to the front door. Screen door."

"How original . . . what else do you remember?"

"The sound the screen door made when it slapped shut, the way the paint was peeling on the ceiling over the porch swing." He paused. "I remember the garden—not that it was a garden, really. I remember the *plants*: a couple of hydrangeas, some irises, a stand of black-eyed Susans. I remember the outdoor shower, the way you could see the ground through the slats."

"Hunh," she said, impressed in spite of herself. "So who owned this cottage?"

They were crossing Kent Island, with its commercial strip of outlet stores and fast-food franchises. It was all very familiar. "My parents," he replied.

"The *Durans*?"

"I *know* what you're thinking," he said, "but—yes. The Durans. That was their name."

"The Durans weren't your parents."

"These 'Durans' were."

She looked away in frustration.

Somehow, even though it was long before dawn and there was no way to see beyond the stores, Duran could feel the nearness of the ocean. Maybe it was the sense that there was nothing *behind* the stores, no backdrop, no forms or shapes, no distant points of light.

"I remember so much," he said, talking as much to himself as to Adrienne. "I remember where we kept a key, under the third white rock in a series of rocks arranged along the walkway. I remember the battered Monopoly game that we kept at the beach. One year the shoe piece went missing, and my mother went crazy looking for it. It was her favorite piece." He smiled. "She used to say: 'I guess I'll have to settle for the iron.' Like it was a big disappointment."

They were rolling through the flat farmland of the Delmarva peninsula, the horizon an invisible line between the black earth and even darker sky. An occasional silo rose from the ground, where metal skeletons of irrigation equipment stood idle in fields of stubble corn. Every few miles, they passed produce stands that were boarded up for winter, hand painted signs leaning against the ramshackle buildings:

WE HAVE! CUKES, LOPES,
SILVER QUEEN CORN!!!

Arriving at an intersection, where signs pointed north to Rehoboth and south to Ocean City, Duran hesitated, unsure of which way to go.

"Take 113," Adrienne told him.

"But—"

"Trust me," she said. "I used to live around here, remember?"

Duran frowned. "No."

"Oh, that's right," she remarked in a sarcastic voice. "You had us down south. Where was it? Alabama?"

"South Carolina," Duran told her.

"Turn left."

About forty-five minutes later, they drove through Denton, Delaware, detouring past the house that Adrienne said she and Nikki had lived in. It was a tidy brick rancher, with a vinyl carport, and a mailbox painted with morning glory vines. In the front yard were a pair of trees whose rounded crowns had been gutted to accommodate a power line.

Half an hour later, they were on the outskirts of Bethany Beach, the horizon pink with dawn. Duran could feel the excitement mounting within him. Once he saw the beach house—once he actually stood before it—the past would be his again. And undeniably so. He could show it to Adrienne—the white rocks and outdoor shower, the little garden. Even if the place had changed, it would still be the same. He was sure of it.

Soon, he was announcing their arrival. "Coming up—the Bethany Beach totem pole!" A minute later, they rounded a curve and there it was, the towering kitsch emblem that marked the intersection of Main St. and Highway 1-A. As they drove closer, he could make out the elongated face of the Indian carved into the wood. It was like seeing an old friend. He remembered, with sharp nostalgia, arriving at this intersection as a boy, how he and his father shared a ritual, filling the car with war whoops.

"When's the last time you were here?" Adrienne asked.

He thought about this, but . . . "I don't know. I was just a kid."

When the street dead-ended at the steps to the boardwalk, he turned left onto a road that ran parallel to the beach.

"Were you thinking we could *stay* here?" Adrienne asked. "I mean, if you can't remember the last time you went to the cottage, it's not like it's still in your family, is it?"

She was right, of course, but he didn't know what to say—and that was strange, even to him. He'd never given a thought to the cottage. Was it still his? Was it *ever* his? It ought to be, but he couldn't say for sure. The question had never come up. But now that he thought about it: no, he hadn't been here since his parents died. His only memories of the place were childhood memories. Yahtzee and Boggle, Monopoly, and playing in the waves.

But all that would resolve itself, Duran thought, as soon as he saw the place.

Some of the houses they passed were modern and built on stilts to protect them from hurricanes. These tended to be much bigger than the old cottages, with elaborate multilevel decks. Fabric flags—lighthouses, crabs, sunflowers, ghosts—snapped in the breeze. The new houses were unfamiliar to him but everything else was just as he remembered it, right down to the realtors' signs beside every other driveway. *For Rent: Anna Liotta, Hickman Realtors. For Rent: Connor Re-*

alty Co. Same old firms. They would rent out the beach houses on a weekly basis all summer long—when the families who owned them were not in residence. He tried to remember if his own family had stayed at the beach all through the summer, but he couldn't.

"Well?" Adrienne asked.

"What?"

"I asked you—"

"I don't know," he told her in a distracted voice. "I don't know what happened to Beach Haven after my parents died."

"But you should—"

"I just want to *see* it," he insisted. "And anyway—it's right around the corner." Turning left onto Third Avenue, he recited the numbers: "One-thirteen. One-eleven. It's the fifth house, on the left. Right . . . *there*."

It was an old cottage, a little shabby. The sign that hung from the post beside the walkway trembled in the wind.

Gill's Nest

He stepped from the car, and stared. Adrienne got out, and came around to his side. The air was fresh with the smell of the sea, and they could hear the ocean's susurrating boom, just a block away. "They changed the name," Adrienne observed. "So that answers one question. Someone named Gill bought the place."

Duran shook his head. "This isn't it."

"What?"

He put his hand on his forehead, and closed his eyes, recalling the things that just weren't there: the wraparound porch and wide wooden steps to the front door, the dormered windows on the second floor. He tried to understand how the house in his head could have been changed—remodeled—to resemble the one in front of him: a narrow frame structure with two steps up to the door, no porch, no dormers. No hydrangeas, either, and no white rocks to hide a key.

"This isn't it," he repeated.

* * *

At Adrienne's suggestion, they drove up and down the streets of Old Bethany for nearly an hour. Maybe he'd gotten the address wrong. Maybe it had been torn down. Maybe. But try as he did to superimpose the house in his memory on the landscape before him, it didn't work. Beach Haven was a figment.

"God," Adrienne said when they stopped for coffee and she took a good look at the crumpled mess that was the rear of the Stratus. "I'm in for it with Budget." A little laugh escaped her. "Of course, at fifteen bucks a day, I waived the collision coverage."

"I'll pay you back."

She shook her head. "Forget it. My credit card will cover it. It's just—there's going to be a ton of paperwork."

Going inside the Dream Cafe, they found themselves the target of half a dozen stares. "My God, what happened to you?" the waitress asked, seeing the matted blood behind Adrienne's ear.

"I hit my head," she replied, and got up to go to the ladies' room.

While she was away, Duran sat, brooding over his latte. He knew, now, that something was terribly out of whack—that he wasn't who he seemed to be, that his memories weren't his own. Not the long-term memories, at least.

But last night was real—of that he was sure. He was sure because he hurt in so many places. His ribs ached, and his tongue was cut in a way that made it painful to speak. And not only that: his imagination wasn't up to inventing the sound he kept hearing, the crack of his assailant's neck as Duran drove his foot into the man's chin.

The noise was eidetic, like the pain that he felt, and like the pain, it wouldn't go away. So that was real.

But Sidwell? Had he gone to Sidwell—or just to the reunion? Because he'd certainly been to the reunion—he could hear the polite hellos, see Adam Bowman peering at his name tag. He'd remembered the school, but had the school remembered him? Not really.

"I used every, single paper towel," Adrienne told him as she sat down, hair wet, but free from gore.

"You ought to see a doctor," Duran told her. "You took a bad knock."

She shook her head. "I'm okay. I just need a scarf."

At Hickman Realtors—this was another of Adrienne's ideas—they asked about a house called Beach Haven, owned by a family named Duran. The agent, Trish, said she'd grown up in Bethany, and thought she knew everyone—but she didn't remember the Durans, and she was certain there wasn't a house called Beach Haven.

"I don't think so," she told them. "But I'm not infallible." She offered to look in the computer. "Even if Connor or one of the other firms handled the place, it'll be in here," she said, tapping the keys.

But it wasn't.

"What about another place?" she asked. "Pretty good pickings this time of year. Low rates. Get you a deal!?"

Duran began to stand up, when Adrienne surprised him. "Sure," she said, tossing a glance at Duran. "Nothing too big or expensive—so long as it's got a working phone."

Trish tapped the keyboard, manipulated the mouse, and studied the possibilities. "I can put you a block from the beach . . . two bedrooms with cable."

"How much?" Adrienne asked.

"Three-fifty a week."

Duran sat in his chair, barely listening, as Adrienne finalized the arrangements. Though his face was impassive, and his body still, he might as well have been hanging from a cliff. It seemed to him that the more he found out about himself, the less he knew. The more he looked, the less there was. And now, seated in a real estate office in the imaginary playground of his fictional childhood, it seemed to him as if his whole perspective—his stance toward the world and himself—was sliding toward a vanishing point from which there was no return, or no return that he could imagine.

I'm disappearing, he thought. *Whoever I am . . .*

23 SeaSpray was a powder-blue Cape Cod on 4th Street, just around the corner from the beach.

Sparsely decorated, and slightly forlorn, it was a beach cottage with mismatched furniture and amateur seascapes on the walls. A faint, but pervasive smell of mildew hung in the air as Duran lay down on the rattan couch in the living room, and gazed at the ceiling in a funk.

In the kitchen, Adrienne sat down to make a list.

1. Slough—she wrote, then sat back with a sigh. She had to call in. She *should have* called in—long ago—from the real estate office or a pay phone on the road. It was 10:30 already, which made her more than late: she was missing in action. So she really had to call in, only . . . what could she say? What could she possibly say without sounding like a lunatic?

She imagined the scene at work. When you counted the paralegals, the interns, and the court reporter, at least a dozen people would have assembled for the McEligot deposition. First, there would have been a grace period. Maybe fifteen minutes of chitchat, ending in a certain amount of frowning. Nervous glances at the clock, followed by expressions of bewilderment and concern. *Where could Adrienne be? I hope she's all right!* People would begin to make calls, go out for coffee, read the paper, look over their notes. Half an hour later (if that), counsel for the plaintiff would put away her notes and get to her feet—even as Bette placed calls to Adrienne at home, and to Slough in San Diego. *What? What do you mean she's not there?*

She heard Duran get up and turn on the television. Canned laughter floated toward her through the doorway to the kitchen.

2. Call Bill Fellowes—name/phone of memory witness
3. Insurance co.—re Duran's tapes of Nikki
4. Shopping: food, clothes, hairbrush
5.

There wasn't any 5. And, truth to tell, there wasn't any point in adding to her list until she'd crossed off the first entry. Everything else was stalling. So she gritted her teeth, gave herself a Nike pep talk—*Just do it!*—and dialed Bette's number at Slough, Hawley. Then she listened as it rang—or almost rang—and hung up.

It wasn't so much that she was afraid. She just didn't know what to say. Curtis Slough was not what you'd call a stand-up guy. On the contrary, his reaction to the news that she'd grown up an orphan had been a kind of embarrassed alarm—as if she'd confessed to having an unpleasant, and possibly contagious, disease. How, then, might he react to the news that she was sharing a beach cottage with a maniac, while running from a killer who'd murdered two people—including one of the firm's own investigators? And if to that she added the information that all this had something to do with her sister's recent electrocution, itself brought on by false memories of Satanic abuse . . .

Slough, Hawley was an old and respected Washington firm. Most of its lawyers were graduates of Ivy League schools, William & Mary and Stanford. They were ambitious and tightly-wrapped people who were bright, bland, and dependable. They did not stay in Comfort Inns. They were not orphans. And they never, ever "went on the run." So . . .

This isn't going to get any easier, Adrienne told herself, and began dialing.

Bette answered on the first ring.

"Bette. It's me—Adrienne."

"Oh my God! *Scout!* What *happened* to you?"

"It's hard to explain."

A nervous laugh. "It *better* be hard to explain. D'you realize what a *meltdown* we have here? We are talking fifteen people, including two partners just . . . *standing* there . . . looking at one another for almost an hour and—the Old Man's ballistic. Tell me you were hit by a car! Tell me you were killed! Were you?" This last, hopefully.

"No."

"Then—*what?*"

"There was a . . . an emergency."

"What *kind* of 'emergency'?"

"A *sudden* emergency." Before Bette could question her any further, Adrienne hurried on, explaining where to find the file on the McEligot depo. "It's not the final draft," she said. "I was going to work on it at the motel—"

"What motel?"

Ignoring the question, Adrienne plowed on. "It's in the *asphalt* folder on my computer. I think I called it—"

"Wait a second—you mean you're not coming *back*? What am I gonna tell Curtis?"

"*I'll* call him."

"And tell him what? That you had 'an emergency'?"

To Adrienne's ear, her friend sounded more excited than worried. "Exactly."

"But he'll want to know what *kind* of emergency—other than 'sudden.' 'Sudden' won't cut it."

"Then I'll tell him it was 'a female emergency.' "

"A what?"

"You heard me."

"But I don't even know what that is," Bette protested. "I mean, what's that supposed to *mean*?"

"I don't know—but I do know Slough and, trust me, he won't ask."

As soon as she hung up, she gritted her teeth and called Slough in San Diego—where, to her delight, she found he wasn't in. So she left a message:

Curtis? Adrienne Cope. I'm really sorry about this morning, but . . . there was an emergency, a sort of a . . . female thing and, well . . . everything's back to normal, now. I'll reschedule the depo as soon as I get in. And I'll try to reach you later. Bye!

Then she called Bill Fellowes who, to her surprise, was unaware of the morning's fiasco. "I just got in myself," he said. "What's up?"

"Remember that divorce case you worked on when you were interning with Nelson?"

He thought about it for a moment, then said, "No."

"I think it was a divorce case. The guy worked for the SEC—"

"Oh, you mean the Brewster case!"

"Right!"

"That was a lot more than 'a divorce case.' But, what about it?"

"You had an expert witness—a shrink or something. Knew a lot about memory."

"Yeah, sure."

"Well," Adrienne said, "I was wondering if I could get his name—"

"Ray Shaw!" Fellowes boomed. "Neuropsychiatrist to the stars!"

"You know where I could find him?"

"Last I looked—Columbia Medical School."

"And he's good?" she asked. "On memory?"

"Bulletproof. He wrote the Encarta entry."

She laughed. "Okay, but . . . is he in court a lot?"

It was Fellowes's turn to chuckle. "You mean, is he a professional witness?"

"Yeah."

"No. I think Brewster was his first time out. And he only testified *then* because he went to school with the guy."

"So he's the real deal," Adrienne said.

"Absolutely. Hang on. I'll get you his numbers."

She did and he did, and then she thanked him and they said good-bye. Canned laughter rose and fell just past the door. What would she say to Shaw? And what did she expect from him?

I'm with this man, Doctor, who thinks he's a psychologist— but he's not. He was treating my sister when she committed suicide and, since then, someone's been trying to kill me—or maybe us, I'm not sure. Anyway, he isn't who he thinks he is— that person's dead, too—and I was hoping you could help him recover his memory—so we can figure out what's going on—and maybe I can get my life back together.

Hmmmnn. Maybe not. He gets that call, and the first call *he* makes is to Bellevue. *There's a madwoman on the phone . . .*

She turned to a new page in the pad, and wrote *Shaw* at the very top. Then she tapped her pen against the page a few times, and added: *Lawyer—Fellowes—Brewster case*

She sighed. If she knew a little more about the Brewster business, that would be good. It wouldn't seem as if she were coming out of left field. The easy thing to do would be to look it up on Nexis.

Nikki's laptop was in the car. All she needed to access the Web site—which archived the full text of more than five thousand newspapers and journals, going back twenty years—was the law firm's user-ID and password. Which she knew by heart. Everyone did. The user-ID was *1SLOUGH1*, the same as Curtis's license plate. And the password was *torts*—one of the boss man's little jokes.

Leaving the kitchen to get the laptop, she passed through the living room, where Duran was lying on the couch. She paused to see what he was watching. Jenny Jones. "You watch this stuff a lot?"

He thought about it for a moment, and shrugged. "I guess."

He was completely affectless, as if he'd been tranquilized to the point of sleep. It was weird. Weird enough to make her think of Gertrude Stein's remark about America (or was it just Berkeley?), saying there was no *there*, there. That's the way Duran was in front of the TV. There wasn't any *him*, in him.

Removing her sister's laptop from its pink carrying case, she set it down on the kitchen counter and waited for the machine to boot up. The first thing she'd do was send the McEligot memo to Bette and Slough, attaching it to an e-mail—that way, at least they'd know she hadn't been slacking.

Searching in the carrying case for the external modem, she found a pack of Orbit gum, two pink hair clips and a little bottle of pills. Although the bottle resembled the kind you'd get from CVS or RiteAid, there wasn't any refill number or physician's name. All it said was:

#1
Nicole Sullivan
Take as Directed

And under that, in Nikki's bold hand: *Placebo 1*. What? She opened the bottle. The pills inside—she spilled them into her open palm—were capsules, filled with a dusky brown powder. They bore no pharmaceutical imprints or identifying marks. What were they? Vitamins? Maybe. But it didn't look like a vitamin bottle. It looked like a medicine bottle. And *Placebo 1*? Was that supposed to be a joke?

She put the bottle on the counter, thinking she'd ask Duran later. But first: Nexis.

She found the modem in the carrying case, hooked it up and rebooted. Then she logged on to Nexis-Lexis, using her firm's password and ID. The Web was slow, and it took her half an hour to download the stories she was looking for: a *New York Times* profile of Doctor Shaw, a handful of articles about memory, and a couple of shorter pieces about the Brewster divorce.

Shaw was fifty-seven years old, a graduate of Erasmus Hall High School, Brooklyn College, and Yale Medical School, where he'd studied neurobiology and psychiatry. A photograph showed a genial man with unruly eyebrows, wearing a turtleneck sweater under a tweed sports jacket. According to the profile, Shaw was "the dean of research biologists" at Columbia University's Center for the Neurobiology of Learning and Memory, as well as a popular lecturer in the medical school's Department of Psychiatry. A frequent contributor to *The New England Journal of Medicine*, he'd written as well for general interest magazines like Harper's and the *Atlantic*.

All his articles were available from Nexis, and she downloaded them to a floppy. That done, she spent an hour reading about explicit and implicit memory, cognitive displacement, hypnosis, and the role of the hippocampus in long- and short-term memory.

None of it stuck.

So she turned her attention to the Brewster case, which was discussed at length in an old issue of *The American Lawyer*.

Shaw was a witness for the defense. At issue was Mrs. Brewster's "assisted" recollection of her husband's allegedly violent behavior, behavior that was otherwise undocumented.

Under questioning by Socrates Nelson, Shaw undertook to explain the relationship between learning and memory. According to the neurobiologist, memories were dynamic, rather than static, and had a physiological basis. In other words, they changed, and the changes took place on a physical and cellular level.

"If this didn't happen," he told the court, "we couldn't learn." By way of example, Shaw discussed the complex task of learning to hit a baseball. This task involved at least three different kinds of memory—motor memory, visual memory, sequential memory—each of which took place in a different part of the brain.

Most people never got very good at hitting a baseball. But even the most limited competence at the task required repeated trials, efforts in which the most recent attempt was compared to its predecessor. This was what physical learning was all about—the refinement of technique by feedback. And what made it possible was the fact that each attempt to hit the ball *changed* the neurological framework of the memory itself. When the novice finally made contact, the relevant neurons encoded the information as a successful attempt. Whereupon, the encrypted data became a kind of template for all future at-bats.

"It's just common sense, really. Memories are transformed by new experiences. We understand this on a gut level," Shaw testified, "but what we may not understand is that the same mechanism which allows us to learn—that is to say, which allows us to modify memory—makes it possible for us to remember the past in a defective manner.

"When my wife and I recall a shared incident—a concert, an argument, a trip—we seldom remember *the same* incident. Through a process called 'chunking,' our memory of the concert is affected by memories of other concerts, including concerts we've seen on television and in the movies, even concerts we've only *heard* about. And all of these memories exchange details with one another—so that our recollection of an afternoon at Lincoln Center is changed by the documentary that we saw about Woodstock, and also by what we've read of Wagner—not to mention the dream we had of porpoises swimming through La Scala.

"It works like this: every memory is connected by neuronal highways to every other. But inasmuch as no two people have had the same experiences, each of us has a unique matrix of memories and neuronal connections. So when my wife and I attend a concert, we have similar, but different, experiences—and similar, but different, recollections of that same event. And not only that: since these memories are themselves subject to constant and further evolution, my wife's recollection of the concert may one day be entirely unrecognizable—at least, to me."

Over the objections of plaintiff's counsel, Shaw had then gone on to review various experiments concerning eyewitness testimony—citing the work of Elizabeth Loftus and others. The studies revealed that although most people—"the general public, doctors, lawyers, even psychiatrists"—tend to hold the belief that "memory" represents a procedure of *review*, the reality is quite different. In fact, "memory" represents the *reconstruction* of an event in the mind. It sounded like "splitting hairs" Shaw said, but the "difference could not be more profound."

The key point was that such reconstructions were unreliable. "Memory is a novelist, not a photographer," Shaw told the court.

To illustrate his point, Shaw described a series of experiments in which short films were shown to students, who were then asked misleading questions about what they'd seen. When the students were questioned a second time, about a week later, it was found that most of them had integrated the misleading data into their own recollections. They now "remembered" things that they'd been asked about—but hadn't seen. "In other words," Shaw said, "they formed pseudomemories."

Adrienne's eyes were beginning to strain—despite the overcast day, the cottage was flooded with light, and Nikki's laptop screen wasn't an active matrix. Was she ready to call this guy? Maybe yes, maybe no.

Getting to her feet, she stretched, and went to the front door. Stepping outside, she took in the damp air and the smell of the ocean.

It's all about memory, she told herself. About Nikki's confabulations, and Duran's. Doctor Shaw was the Memory King, and if he couldn't help her, no one could. But would he?

She took in another lungful of salt air, and returned to the kitchen, passing Duran on the way. "You want some coffee?" she asked. He shook his head, caught up in the histrionics of a soap opera.

In the kitchen, she made a cup of instant coffee, and sat down in front of the laptop. Logging onto the Web, she ran a search in Dogpile, telling it to fetch *pseudomemory*. A minute later, she had dozens of hits, most of which revolved around the use of hypnosis to "recover" memories of alleged sexual abuse—precisely what had happened with Nikki. The phenomenon appeared to be epidemic, the debate intense. There were even dueling nonprofits: the False Memory Foundation, which set out to debunk such accounts, and Believe the Children (Inc.), which sought to shore them up. Nikki, she remembered, had left some money in her will to the latter.

By now, the "recovery" of memories had become so commonplace—and so controversial—that The National Association of Psychology had instituted guidelines. First, therapists should be on guard against unconsciously guiding their clients toward the "discovery" of long-repressed incidents of abuse—which, in fact, may never have occurred.

A second guideline suggested that therapists should be aware that memories recovered through the use of guided imagery or hypnosis were likely to be challenged in court— should any litigation occur. Since these "memory enhancing" techniques had been shown to increase "suggestibility" and the formation of pseudomemories, most insurance companies now required that sessions of this kind be taped for the protection of the therapist.

And, in fact, it was this very practice that won the Brewster case. According to *The American Lawyer*:

> Shaw's commentary on the therapist's tape recordings of his sessions with Mrs. Brewster was particularly trenchant.
> "He's cajoling her," the professor told the court. "If we listen to the questions he asks, it becomes clear that he's proposing scenarios by implication—scenarios which she then adopts. The process becomes a true collaboration, a kind of pseudotherapeutic conspiracy, when she amends the scenarios in idiosyncratic ways that he then embraces, rewarding her with well-timed bursts of sympathy and congratulations.

Adrienne shut down the laptop, got up and stretched. The pounding of the surf was beginning to get on her nerves.

"Hey," she called to Duran. "You awake?"

He appeared in the doorway to the kitchen, looking rumpled and sleepy. "More or less."

"You know those tapes you made?" she asked.

"For the insurance company?"

Adrienne nodded. "I was wondering if you could call about them. Maybe you could get copies."

Duran gave her a quizzical look. "You mean . . . now?"

She looked him up and down. "Well . . . yeah, *now*. Unless you're too busy—"

He glanced at his watch, gave her a lazy smile. "I guess I've got a little window here." Going into the living room, he picked up the remote and turned off the TV. Then he went to the phone, and called Information. Five minutes later, she heard him say, "Just don't turn me over to the machine, okay? Because I already made this call once. I want you to check Mutual General Assurance, all right? M-G-A. Mutual General Assurance *anything*. Limited. Inc. Company. Whatever." He listened in silence for a while, and then hung up.

"What's the matter?" she asked.

"I can't get a number for the company. Which doesn't make sense, because I know the address. I mean, I sent tapes out two or three times a week. In fact—" he patted the pockets of his sports jacket. "I've still got one." He removed a cassette from his inside jacket pocket, and laid it down on the counter. "I never got a chance to mail it, but . . . I *know* the address: 1752 Avenue of the Americas. Suite 1119. It's . . . Manhattan."

"Let me look it up," she suggested, and turned to the laptop. "*Anywho*'ll have it."

"Mutual General Assurance," he said. "Not *In*surance. A—"

"I know," she said. "I heard you." As the modem dialed into the Web, she picked up the pill bottle she'd found in the computer's case, and held it out between her forefinger and thumb. "You know anything about this?" she asked.

He took the bottle from her and examined it while she searched the Web for Mutual General Assurance. Finally, he put the bottle back down on the counter, and shook his head.

"Maybe it's some kind of clinical trial," he suggested. "Though . . . 'Placebo 1'? I don't think so."

"Maybe she went to an herbalist," Adrienne supposed.

"You think?"

She put the vial in her pocket and shrugged. She was thinking, *Maybe I'll get the pills analyzed* . . . The blue bar completed its slow crawl across the bottom of the screen, and a list of insurance companies snapped onto the page in front of her. All in all, there were nine listings for companies whose names contained some combination of the words *Mutual*, *General* and *Assurance*. But there was no Mutual General Assurance Company, or anything like it, in New York State.

"Take a look," she said, as Duran leaned over her shoulder and studied the screen. She scrolled down. "Worth calling them?"

He shook his head. "No. Different name, different address. There's no point. If we had to, we could go to New York, but . . ."

"What's on this tape, anyway?" she asked, tapping it with her fingernail.

"A client. Dutch guy." As soon as he said it, his face turned ashen. "Oh, Jesus! What's today?"

"Monday."

He looked stricken. Turned on his heel. Turned back again. Ran his hand through his hair. "This is not good," he told her.

"What isn't?"

"I missed my appointment!" Duran glanced at the ceiling, and sighed.

"No kidding."

He didn't hear the sarcasm in her voice. He was beyond it. "Disappearing like this—I don't know what he'll do. The relationship between a client and his therapist . . . sometimes it's the only relationship they *trust*! You break that trust and—"

"Earth to Duran?" Her fingers enclosed "Duran" in quotes. "You're not a therapist, remember? In fact, you're not even Duran. We don't know *who* you are. You're a—a 'disturbed person' with bogus credentials. This Dutch guy? Trust me: he'll be okay without you!"

He looked at her for a long moment, seemingly confused, then flopped down on the couch in front of the television. "Y'know something?" he asked. "You can be a real bitch when you want to."

The remark took her by surprise, and she started to laugh. He was right, of course.

Then he reactivated the sound on the TV, and disappeared behind a wall of chitchat. It was a talk show of some kind—Jenny Jones or Ricki Lake or Sally Jessy—Adrienne didn't know the players. And she didn't care. But it was interesting in its own way. A couple of dirt bags were sitting together on chairs, sharing a smirk of guilty pleasure. Their eyes shone as the women in the audience swayed and bounced, faces contorted, shouting, hooting, and rolling their eyes.

What had he called it? Adrienne wondered. What was the term Shaw used? *A pseudotherapeutic conspiracy* . . . Live, in your own living room.

24

She hated calling people she didn't know. It wasn't a phobia, exactly, but it made her uncomfortable enough that she procrastinated whenever she had to do it. And procrastination almost always backfired. Like this afternoon: if she'd called Shaw earlier, she wouldn't have to do it now. She wouldn't have to be doing it at night. And she wouldn't be calling him at home—which was worse, somehow. Instead, she and Duran had gone to an outlet mall to buy some things they needed (which was basically everything) and here it was, a quarter to eight.

Reluctantly, she lifted the receiver and punched out the numbers, thinking *I'll hang up if he doesn't answer by the second ring. If he doesn't answer by the second ring, he's probably busy, he's probably—*

"Ray Shaw." The voice was low and sonorous.

She hesitated, then recovered. "Hello?"

"Yes?" He sounded dubious, as if he suspected she was a telemarketer.

So she took a deep breath, and dove in. "Doctor Shaw— this is Adrienne Cope at Slough, Hawley. Bill Fellowes gave me your name."

"Oh? And how's Bill?"

"He's fine! Doing great. Said, 'When you call Doctor Shaw, say hello.' "

Shaw chuckled. "Well, Bill's a terrific kid."

"He is!"

"So!" Shaw boomed, the niceties done. "What can I do for you?"

"Well, actually . . . I was hoping I could bring someone to see you."

Silence at the other end.

"It's a very unusual case," Adrienne continued, "and—"

"I don't know if Bill told you," Shaw interrupted, "but . . . testifying in court isn't something I have time for. I did it once, as a favor to an Old Blue—but that's it. You know what they say: 'Once a philosopher, twice a pervert.' "

She laughed politely. "I understand completely, and Bill *did* tell me that the Brewster case was a one-off proposition. But this isn't one of those."

"Oh?"

"No. As I said, I was hoping you could see someone—"

"Whoa, whoa, whoa! You mean—a *patient*?" He pronounced the word as if she'd promised to produce a platypus.

"Yes."

Rueful chuckle. "Well, I don't think I can be of much help,

then. Between teaching and research, I don't really have a lot of time for patients. It's a terrible thing to say, but—"

"I'm not asking you to take on a new patient, Doctor—I was just hoping we could get a sort of . . . 'preliminary evaluation.' It's a very unusual case."

His grunt was skeptical. "How so?"

Careful, she thought. *Don't tell him too much, or the men with the butterfly nets will come through the door.* "Well, it's a little awkward on the phone, but . . . the man we're talking about is completely delusional."

"Is he functioning?"

"Yes."

"How highly?"

"He thinks he's a therapist."

"Really!" Shaw's bemusement was as palpable as his earlier skepticism.

"Yes. And that wouldn't be so bad, except: he treats people."

"Oh." Shaw's tone went from sharp to flat in the space of a second. "Bring him in on Thursday," he told her. "I can see him at ten." Then he gave her the address, and she rang off, feeling virtuous.

Joining Duran in the living room, where he was finishing a beer, she told him "I've made an appointment for Thursday morning—"

"With who?"

"A neuropsychiatrist. In New York."

Duran gave her a skeptical look. "And what's that supposed to accomplish?"

Adrienne shrugged. "I thought a professional opinion might be useful."

"An opinion of what?"

"Of you."

"Me?" he asked.

She nodded, bracing for the objections she knew would be coming. *There's nothing wrong with me—I'm fine! In fact—*

"Good idea," he said.

* * *

The next morning, she got up early and drove to a little strip mall, south of town, where she bought a cheap tape recorder. On the way back to SeaSpray, she stopped at the Dream Cafe and picked up coffee and croissants for the two of them.

As she came into the house, Duran wandered out of the kitchen, running a hand through his hair, and yawning—as if he'd just gotten up. "I thought we could listen to the tape," she suggested.

"Which tape?"

"The one you didn't mail."

"Oh," he said, and frowned. "That one."

"What's the matter?"

He shook his head. "It's complicated."

"What is?"

"Well, for one thing, there are ethical issues. Henrik's a client, and when he talks to me, it's in confidence. It's as if I were a priest."

"You mean, it's as if you were a therapist."

He ignored the sarcasm. "And the other thing is: you're suing me, so . . . I'm not sure this is such a good idea."

"I'm not suing you."

"Why not? You were."

"But I'm not anymore. I'll have the complaint dismissed as soon . . . as soon as things get back to normal."

"How come?"

"Because it's a mess. I can't sue you one day, and check into a motel with you the next. It doesn't look good. And, anyway, things aren't as simple as I thought."

He considered that for a moment. Finally, he said, "Okay, but—you don't need to know the client's identity."

She inclined her head in agreement. "I just want to hear you work."

The man's voice was deep and tremulous, his English perfect, but with a Benelux lilt. Duran was sprawled in an armchair across from the couch, looking at the ceiling as the tape rolled. "You actually met him," he said.

"I did?"

He nodded. "When you came to my office the first time."

She tried to remember.

"We were having a session," Duran reminded her. "Big guy. Blond hair."

Adrienne leaned over to the tape recorder, and adjusted the volume. She frowned, unable to recall Duran's client.

"You yelled at him—remember? Said he should wake up."

"Ohhhh . . . right."

"And you called me a—"

She nodded. "I was upset. Now, shhhh—I want to listen." She rewound the tape for a bit, then turned up the volume.

> *Duran: Concentrate on your breath. Thaaaaat's it. I want you to breathe with me . . . good! That's really good. Can you feel the peace, Henrik? It spreads all the way through us, all the way to the edge of our skin. And when we exhale—it just increases the feeling. Like that. Yes, just like that. I want you to feel the air, coming and going. Do you know where we are, Henrik?*
>
> *Henrik: In the safe place.*
>
> *Duran: Right. We're in the safe place. On the rock. I can hear the little waves lapping, just below us. And there's a breeze on the water. Can you feel it in your hair?*
>
> *Henrik: And a seagull. Overhead.*
>
> *Duran: Right. There's a seagull, turning in the sky above our heads, riding the wind.*
>
> *Henrik: It's nice.*
>
> *Duran: Now, I want you to remember the night when you were driving . . . you were driving in your car . . . and you were on your way to Watkins Glen. Do you remember that, Henrik?*

The reels of the microcassette unwound slowly.

Henrik: It was late in the afternoon—a clear day. I was walking past the sweet shop—

Duran: No, I don't think so. I don't think you were walking. Perhaps you were riding in a car. Do you remember being in a car? At night?

Henrik: Yes.

Adrienne glanced at Duran, who unfolded his legs, and sat forward, listening harder now.

Duran: And whose car was it?

Henrik: . . . I . . . I don't remember.

Duran: Perhaps it was your parents' car?

Henrik: Yes. It was.

Duran: Excellent. And then what happened?

Henrik: There were lights.

Duran: What kind of lights?

Henrik: I'm thinking: these are headlights, but—

Duran: No. I've told you before, Henrik: that's what your father thought. You were seven. You didn't know what to think. And then the light was everywhere. You were bathed in it, remember?

Henrik: Yes. Yes, of course.

Duran: It was like—can you tell me what it was like, Henrik?

Henrik: I don't know.

Duran: It was like a searchlight, wasn't it?

Henrik: Yes! In my chest. 'It was like . . . a searchlight in my chest!'

Adrienne shut off the tape recorder, and stared at Duran, who was himself on the edge of his chair, looking shocked. "You're making it up," she told him.

He nodded.

"It's like a script," she said.

"I know."

"That's supposed to be 'therapy'?"

He shook his head. "No. It's . . . something else. I don't know what it is."

"And this guy thinks . . . what? What's his problem?"

Duran cleared his throat. "He's completely delusional. He thinks he was abducted by a flying saucer. He thinks there's a worm in his heart that gives him orders."

Adrienne's laughter came in a short, angry burst, then stopped as suddenly as it began. "What are you doing to this man?"

Duran was speechless for a moment. Then he cleared his throat for a second time, and said, "Well, it *sounds* like I'm driving him crazy."

"Like Nico, only with a different story."

He didn't know what to say.

Leaning over, she pressed the *Play* button, and listened as Duran led his client deeper and deeper into madness. Half an hour later, when the session had come to an end, she hit *Stop* and looked at him. "I don't get it," she told him. "Why are you putting all this . . . *crap* in people's heads?"

"I don't know."

"It's like you're training them for the Jerry Springer Show! I mean, my sister thought the Devil was screwing her when she was ten, and *this* guy—Henry—"

"Henrik."

"Whatever! *This* guy thinks he's got a tapeworm in his head—"

"Heart."

"Don't! I'm not one of your patients!"

"I know that, but—"

"What's *up*, Doc?"

He shook his head, searching for the words. Finally, he said, "I'm not sure. I mean, it's not me—that's not me."

"What?!"

"Well, it *is*, but . . . I wouldn't talk to a client like that."

"You can *hear* yourself."

"I know, but—"

"What? It's you? It's not you? Which is it? *What?"*

He was silent for a moment. Finally, he said, "Yeah. Like that. Just like that."

That evening, Duran went out for dinner, returning half an hour later with a rotisserie chicken, plastic tubs of potato salad—and a chilled bottle of Chardonnay. They ate in the kitchen, in silence, at a gray formica table whose metallic edge reminded Adrienne of the kitchen table in Deck and Marlena's house.

Finally, she stood up, the chair scraping loudly against the floor. "I'm going out for a while," she told him.

"You want company?" Duran asked.

"No. I need to think."

The night was cool, the air fresh. But she was having a hard time dealing with the thought of Duran coaxing Nikki into madness, just as he'd cajoled the German (or whatever he was).

And then, just as she was starting to *like* him (he had a nice sense of humor, after all, and the good habit of rescuing her from harm) . . . Just as she was starting to like him (he was really quite good-looking, when you got down to it—tall and lean, with even features and cobalt-blue eyes) . . . Just as she was starting to like him, it was becoming more and more apparent that he was like . . . *Rasputin*.

She walked to the end of the boardwalk and thought about turning back, but instead took the wooden steps down to the beach. She'd get sand in her shoes, but she didn't care. It was a gorgeous night, the stars so luminous they looked wet, the moon a cold clean sphere beaming a path of pure silver onto the black water. The tide was out. The surf rolled in with a soft roar, and receded with a chatter of pebbles.

Duran, she thought. *What was he doing?* He was as fragile, in his own way, as Nikki had been—or, at least, as disconnected. Taking off her shoes, she carried them in her hand as she walked along the waterline, flirting with the little waves. *Why such crazy ideas?* she wondered. They weren't even original, or particularly interesting. Aliens and Satanic abuse.

It was ridiculous. No one took that sort of thing seriously—not anymore, not if they ever did.

And a worm? In the heart? *Pleeeze.*

It would be absurd if it weren't murderous—and it *was* murderous. Bonilla was dead, and so was the partner of the man who'd killed him. And the guy in the Comfort Inn stairwell, as well. And her, too, if it wasn't for . . . Duran.

She muttered to herself, and shook her head. It didn't make sense. Why did Nikki have a gun—and *that* gun? What was that . . . *stuff* in the apartment next to Duran's? And what were they looking for in *her* apartment?

She couldn't figure it. Pretty much the only thing in her apartment that had anything to do with Nikki was: her ashes. If they were after the gun, well, she didn't have that. It was still at Nikki's place, sitting in her closet. The only other thing was . . . the laptop.

But she'd already looked through its folders and files, and there was nothing in it. The address book contained a dozen names beside Duran's and her own, and none of them was of much interest: Ramon and the bank, a couple of takeouts. Jack's vet. There were some other names that she didn't remember, but all of them were transparent. A nail salon. Merry Maids. That kind of thing. There were no boyfriends who might be blamed for her suicide, or any listings to suggest membership in the Georgetown Militia or the Lady Snipers Association.

Still . . .

When she got back to the house, she saw that Duran had done the dishes and cleaned up the kitchen. She heard the television in the other room—a bright voice delivering a line of dialogue, a responding surge of laughter—but when she went in, she found Duran asleep on the couch.

Carrying the laptop into the kitchen, she set it on the table, raised its screen and toggled the *On-Off* switch. Then she sat back, and waited for the machine to boot up.

It took a minute to go through its routine, and when it was done, she logged onto Nikki's AOL account, letting the automated password routine do its work. Soon, she was in the "Mail Center," looking at *New Mail, Old Mail, Sent Mail* . . . and, of course, there was nothing of interest. A couple of bulletins from Travelocity; some newsletters from the Jack Russell Terrier Society; come-ons from E*trade and a couple of e-tailers selling vitamins, makeup and nutritional supplements. But that was it.

Signing off, she returned to the Windows Desktop and clicked on the icon for Nikki's accounting program, Quicken. She had the vague intention of "following the money," but the program must have been bundled with Windows when Nikki bought it, because it had never been used.

There was a calendar in the Microsoft Outlook program, and if Nikki's life had been anything like Adrienne's, it would have been quite revealing. Her own calendar was crammed with appointments and reminders of every kind. It tracked her weight, and logged the distances she ran. It reminded her of birthdays, deadlines, and a lot more. But Nikki's calendar was as stripped-down as her life. There were appointments— with Duran, the nail salon, the hairdresser, the vet. And every two weeks, the simple legend: *A—here at 7,* or *A—her place at 8*—reminders of the alternating venues for their dinners together (half of which, Adrienne realized, she had weaseled out of). But that was it. The calendar did not reveal Nikki to be a secret churchgoer, devil-worshiper, or art student. She had not attended a support group for the ritually abused. Neither had she taken marksmanship lessons.

All in all, the laptop's files were a disappointment, but they were not a surprise. After Europe, Nikki's life had been remarkably self-contained. She'd gone blading, walked Jack, and kept almost entirely to herself. Other than that, and her sessions with Duran, she hadn't done much of anything except, perhaps, watch television. So the blandness of her calendar did not come as a shock.

But it did raise an obvious question: why did Nikki need a computer at all? She could have done as much with a pad of Post-its. So maybe it wasn't the computer they were looking for when they turned her apartment upside down. Maybe it was something else. (Then again, maybe she'd overlooked something.)

Suppressing a yawn, Adrienne went through the calendar, month by month, looking for something—anything—that might be unusual. But there was nothing. A dental appointment in July, a trip to the kennel in October, a reminder to see Little Feat at Wolftrap.

Adrienne frowned. *Kennel?*

Returning to the October entries, she clicked on the 19th, and brought up a screen:

> *Subject: Jack to kennel.*
> *Location: Arlington*
> *Start time: Sun 10/07*
> *End time: Fri 10/12*

Adrienne sat back in her chair, and eyed the screen with a look of puzzlement. Nikki never *went* anywhere—so why would she put Jack in a kennel? She thought back to the month before. There were a couple of days—she remembered, now—when she'd tried to get in touch with Nikki, but couldn't reach her by phone. What was *that* all about?

She remembered being concerned, concerned enough, at least, to send an e-mail—which Nikki ignored, just as she'd ignored the messages on her answering machine. Adrienne had been about to go over there, to see if she was all right, when Nikki finally got in touch, acting as if nothing had happened.

Where have you been?

Nowhere.

'Nowhere'?

I was busy. I forgot to call you back.

Adrienne thought about the date. *October. Beginning of October. Right about then.* A surge of guilty pleasure ran through her, riding the realization that her sister had lied to her. It was right there on the computer, and in her own words: *Jack to kennel / Where have you been? / Nowhere.*

She shut off the computer, got to her feet, stretched and yawned. Nikki had had a secret life. Somewhere.

In the morning, she woke to the sound of rain—a lot of rain—and the muted roar of surf, the unfamiliar feel of a bare mattress under her skin, and a scratchy blanket.

The cottage didn't come with linens and this had slipped her mind when she and Duran went to the outlet mall. There were a couple of tattered beach towels, though, so at least a shower would be possible. Her head hurt and she put her hand to its side, gingerly exploring the swelling above her ear, a swelling that seemed, if anything, more tender than it had the day before. Swinging her feet out of bed, she glanced at her watch and blinked with surprise: it was almost noon!

She dressed quickly, pulling on a T-shirt and running shorts, although her plans for a morning run seemed overruled by the rain. Duran had been up for hours. He sat on the couch, showered and shaven, the remote in his hand. When she entered the room, he pressed the *Mute* button.

"Hi," he said.

"You watch a lot of television, don't you?"

It was a rhetorical question, but the irony went right past him. He thought about it. Finally, he said, "Yeah. I do."

Like it was a realization.

He snapped the TV off, and tossed the remote aside.

"You should have woken me," she told him.

He shrugged. "Why? It's pouring outside."

"There are things to do—before we go to New York."

"Like what?"

"Coffee first," she replied and, turning, went into the kitchen to put the teakettle on the stove. There was a plastic Melitta cone and a box of filters on the counter. Putting a filter into the cone, she placed it atop a blue cup, and spooned a couple of tablespoons of coffee into it.

"Did Nikki ever go away that you know of?" she asked.

"What do you mean?" Duran replied, joining her in the kitchen.

"I mean, did she ever go out of town—as far as you know?"

Duran frowned.

"It would have been in the beginning of October," Adrienne continued. "About ten days before . . ." The teakettle began to scream, and she let the sentence die as she poured the boiling water over the coffee grounds.

"She missed an appointment," Duran told her. "Around that time."

"Did she do that often?" Adrienne asked.

He shook his head. "No. Hardly ever."

"Do you know where she went?"

Duran shrugged. "No, but . . . when she came back, she was tan. I remember kidding her about it. I asked her where she'd been."

"And?"

"She said she'd gone to the beach."

"Which one?" Adrienne asked.

"She didn't say. And I didn't press it."

"Why not?"

"She didn't want to get into it. And, I guess I wasn't that curious."

The wind had begun to kick up, the rain turning into a storm of interesting proportions. Lightning flared behind the windows, which rattled to the thunder. For a moment, it seemed as if the sky was coming apart.

"Nikki was terrified of lightning," Adrienne remarked.

"She never said."

"Really? She used to put on tennis shoes when she was a kid—for the rubber soles. Then she'd hide in the basement."

A shutter tore loose outside and the wind bashed it against the house, smacking the wall over and over again. Duran headed outside to fix it, but Adrienne stopped him at the door, tugging at his arm. "Are you *crazy*?" she asked, and they laughed like kids, giddy with excitement.

Her hand was still on his arm, and for a second it seemed as if a kiss might happen. But then the air exploded like a bomb outside the windows—the lights blew, Adrienne jumped, and the house was plunged into a dark and sudden twilight.

When she caught her breath, Adrienne gulped and said, "Well, there goes the power."

Duran grinned. "For a second, I thought it was the Rapture."

So they played chess, which seemed safe enough, and didn't require a lot of light. Duran improvised some missing pieces, using bottle caps as pawns and saltshakers for rooks. Adrienne wasn't much good at the game, and Duran beat her in just a few minutes, playing in an effortless and distracted way.

"I think you've played this game before," she remarked.

Duran shrugged. "Seems like it."

"Take it from me," she said, setting the pieces back in their squares. "I'm not much of a player, but Gabe . . ." She stopped herself. "I had a *friend* once who was pretty serious about it—I mean, he was in a club or something. Anyway, he tried to teach me, so . . . it's not like I'm an idiot at it." She thought for a moment, then swivelled the board around and replaced the pieces she'd lost. "This time," she said, "you play black. And don't be so polite. See if you can really kill me."

He did. And it didn't take long. In fact, the only time it took was the time that Adrienne took to think through her moves. Duran's moves were almost automatic, as if he knew every situation by heart—whereas she had to think her way through every pitfall and trap that he'd set for her. After her ninth move, he looked at her and said, "Mate."

She stared at the board, then shook her head. "I don't see it."

He shrugged. "It's there."

She looked at the board and frowned. "Where?"

"Coming right at you."

Her eyes darted from piece to piece. Finally, she looked up, suspicion dawning in her eyes. "What are we talking about?" she asked.

Duran gave her a look of puzzled innocence. "Chess," he told her. "What else?" Then he took her pawn, en passant, and in so doing, placed her king in check. Two moves later, and the game was over.

It was in the middle of the fourth game that the shutter blew off. Torrents of water gusted against the glass, surging with the wind. "Do me a favor," Adrienne asked, sitting back in her chair. "Close your eyes, and tell me what comes into your mind when you think about chess."

Duran humored her. Closed his eyes, and thought.

"Well?" she asked.

"The board," he said. "And the pieces."

"Right, but—"

"Black and white. Red and black."

"What else?"

He thought some more. Said, "Rum."

She blinked with surprise. "Rum?"

"Yeah. The way it tastes. Sharp. And the . . . the bouquet, like cognac, the way it fills your lungs."

She didn't know what to say.

For a moment, he could feel the heavy glass in his hand, see the dark surface of the drink, a single small ice cube floating in it, melting to oblivion.

"What else?" It was as if her voice were being piped in from far away.

"Heat. I remember playing where it was hot, somewhere hot—my shirt sticking to my back."

"Where?"

"I don't know. It's not really a memory. It's more like a . . . like a memory—*of* a memory."

"What else?"

"Music." He even cocked his head, as if somehow this would allow him to hear it, but the motion broke his concentration and he opened his eyes and looked at her.

"Stay with it," she told him.

He tried, but it was gone and, finally, he said so.

By now, the rain had slackened, and the sky was brightening to a jaundiced gray. "That was strange," Duran said. "Like being at a seance."

She leaned back in her chair and regarded him, tumbling a rook in the fingers of her left hand. "And that was all you got? Rum, heat, and music?"

He shook his head. "I was free-associating, and it was more a sensation than anything else. But, yeah: that's what I got."

Adrienne frowned and, in her lawyer's voice, asked, "Don't you think it's weird that Nikki had this prolonged amnesia—and all these phony memories—and you do, too?"

Duran looked confused, as if he wanted to answer her, but couldn't. Finally, he said, "We have different points of view."

"You listened to yourself on tape, didn't you?"

"Yeah, but—"

"Well?"

He sighed. "You think I have amnesia?"

"I *hope* you do."

Duran's brows dipped. "Why do you say that?"

"Because it's the lesser of two evils," she replied.

As the afternoon headed toward evening, Adrienne sat with her sister's laptop. After an hour or so, the battery light began to flicker, and she switched it off.

"What about her credit card statements, and her checking account?" Duran asked. "If she went out of town in October . . ."

Just before five, Adrienne called her sister's bank, and requested copies of the last six months of statements and checks. The clerk was reluctant to comply, but her supervisor finally agreed to mail the documents to the client's "address of record." It was the best they could do.

Listening to the conversation, Duran was impressed by the way Adrienne refused to take no for an answer.

"You're tough," he told her, as she hung up the phone.

"Like you said: I can be a bitch." Then she smiled, and added, "Let's go out."

Leaves were everywhere—and branches and limbs of trees, strewn across the streets and lawns. Raw gouges of bright blond wood on the dark trunks of trees marked the places from which they'd been ripped. Sirens howled in the distance. And the air fizzed with the rinsed feel that some-times follows a downpour.

They took their shoes off and walked along the beach, the sand littered with debris tossed up by the thunderous surf: horseshoe crab skeletons, strands of rope and fishing line, ragged hunks of Styrofoam, driftwood, fish.

When they returned to the cottage, Adrienne went out for a run. Duran had neglected to buy running shoes so he stayed by himself, sitting in the kitchen, trying to come to grips with the sense of loss he'd felt when they'd turned the corner and come to a stop in front of Beach Haven—and it was not there. He couldn't articulate the way he felt, but it was as if he'd stepped onto the landing of a flight of stairs, only to find that there were no stairs—and that he himself was suddenly in free fall, plummeting through space. The only thing he could trust, really trust, was the here and now. The world in front of him—not as it had been or would be, but as it was.

The kitchen. This moment. Even the memory of playing chess with Adrienne, as rich in detail as it had been—as *recent* as it had been—was unreliable. His memories of "Beach Haven" had also been rich with detail. And yet, Beach Haven was a figment—as imaginary as "Jeffrey Duran." Which left him with the possibility that Adrienne might also be an illusion. As might yesterday, and the day before. Nico. De Groot. And the Towers. All of it: a figment of his own imagination. Or God's.

Maybe—

"That was great!" Adrienne exclaimed, coming through the door, glistening with vitality.

He watched as this very real woman drew a glass of water from the tap, and turning her eyes toward the ceiling, drank in long, slow gulps. His eyes washed over her, lingering here and there, then moving on, as if she were a banquet.

The glass drained, she set it down on the counter and cast a questioning look in Duran's direction. "Penny for your thoughts," she told him.

He opened his mouth to answer. Thought better of it. "No way," he said.

She'd just come out of the shower when the telephone rang, and she picked it up.

"Oh, right," she said. "Of course . . . yes. Yes it is. It went out three, four hours ago." Because Duran was looking at her in a puzzled way, she put her hand over the receiver and whispered, "Trish."

The real estate agent.

Then back to the phone. "Sure . . . no. No, it's no problem. I keep a little penlight in my purse." She rubbed at her hair with a towel, and laughed. "Yes I *am* one of those people. My nickname is Scout." She leaned over, wrote something down. "Okay, if we have any trouble, we'll give you a buzz." Hung up the phone.

"What was that?" Duran asked.

"There's a sump pump in the basement," she told him. "And when the electricity goes out, it doesn't work—and the basement floods. Which causes problems with the furnace. There's some kind of generator that's supposed to kick in, but half the time it doesn't. So she asked if we'd go down and flick on the emergency switch." Adrienne disappeared into the bedroom and returned with the tiny, plastic penlight that she carried in her purse. And, together, they went down.

It wasn't a basement, really. It was a cellar with a dirt and gravel floor. The entrance was outside, behind the house, where a pair of angled metal doors opened onto a short flight of concrete steps. Adrienne led the way.

"Kinda spooky," she muttered, as her flashlight cut through the darkness, a dim orange beam.

"The sump pump's over there," Duran told her, pointing to

a contraption beside the south wall. Adrienne went over to it and, reaching down, flipped a switch. The pump clattered, and roared into action.

It was a little after nine when the electricity came back on. They were eating a pizza by candlelight, and drinking beer, when half the lights in the house flared. For a moment, it was as if they were caught in a photographer's flash. They froze as the television revived with an accelerating growl of sound, followed by a spurt of canned laughter.

Duran began to chuckle, then fell silent when he saw the look of desolation on Adrienne's face. Her eyes surged with tears.

"What's the matter?" he asked.

She shook her head, and looked away, hiding the tears.

"What *is* it?"

Finally, she said, "When I was looking for Nikki, in her apartment . . . the lights were off . . . because there'd been a short circuit. From the heater. And then Ramon threw the breaker and . . . suddenly, there she was. In the tub." Tears rolled. She looked away.

"I'm sorry," Duran told her.

He washed up—not that there was much—while Adrienne got back on the computer. She logged in their start and finish points on a mapping site, which then provided directions to Dr. Shaw's office in New York. Finally, she searched for a hotel, grumbling about how expensive they were.

The thought of money made Duran frown because it was obviously an issue with Adrienne and, so far, she was paying more than her share. He didn't have his checkbook with him and he didn't *have* a bankcard. Adrienne found this unbelievable. "*Everyone* has an ATM card."

"There was a bank in the basement of the Towers," Duran told her. "I just went there when I needed cash."

Adrienne tapped and clicked on the computer, as Duran drifted toward the living room. He'd been resisting the impulse to watch television because he knew that she disapproved of it, but he was exhausted by the uncertainties that, taken together, seemed to be his only real identity. He needed to *not* think. And television was good for that.

"I can't see paying that kind of money just for a place to *sleep*," Adrienne remarked as he walked past her. "I'll take some numbers along. Maybe we won't need to stay there."

"Whatever," Duran replied and, dropping onto the couch, picked up the remote. Ghosting from one channel to another, he finally settled on *Dharma & Greg*. Sat back. And disappeared into himself.

25

They left in the dark like thieves in the night, with Duran riding shotgun.

Adrienne drove the entire way using cruise control, the speedometer frozen to sixty-five. The trip was pleasantly tedious, thankfully uneventful—and mostly silent. They could have been anyone. As they followed the shafts of their headlights north, Adrienne worried about her absence from work, while Duran sat beside her in a carefree mood, gazing into the darkness. If he closed his eyes, it was easy to imagine that he was leaving town with his girlfriend, heading off on a long vacation. Even when dawn overtook them, and the rising gray light revealed the bleak landscape of exurban New Jersey, Duran's buoyant mood dimmed only a little.

Eventually, the Dodge carried them through the Lincoln Tunnel to Midtown, where they turned north, heading for the Upper West Side. When they found the address that Doctor Shaw had given her, Adrienne circled the neighborhood for fifteen minutes, waiting for a parking space to open up. Finally, one did.

"I hate to pay for parking," she explained.

"I'm not surprised," Duran replied. "After all the gas you've wasted, we probably can't afford it."

Shaw's office was on the twenty-third floor of a smoked glass skyscraper that had probably seemed the height of modernity when it was built, circa 1965. Now, it had a forlorn and grimy look, as if the future had passed it by.

The office itself was more cozy than tidy, its walls hung with paintings, diplomas, and memorabilia, most of which were slightly askew. Books and papers stood in stacks on every horizontal surface but the floor—which lay beneath one of the most exquisite Oriental rugs that Adrienne had ever seen.

Shaw had the comfortable look of a Dutch uncle. A heavyset man with watery brown eyes under unruly brows, he wore a soft, almost regretful, smile. Greeting them with a firm handshake, he led the way to an overstuffed sofa and bade them to sit.

He wore a corduroy jacket, khakis, and running shoes, and sported a bright red, plastic Swatch that he'd buckled over the cuff of his shirt. The watch had such a large face that Duran could read it halfway across the room. Adrienne guessed the doctor was in his midfifties, though his face was as unlined as a baby's—and somehow radiant.

"Coffee?"

They agreed to some, then got down to business.

"I'm intrigued by what you told me on the phone," Shaw began. "I suppose you might say, I *collect* case histories of unusual memory loss. So I think the best way for us to start would be for you to go back over what you said on the telephone. You might start," he continued, focusing his brown eyes on Adrienne, "by telling me when the man next to you first crossed your radar. And then," he said, inclining his head in Duran's direction, "we'll get to you."

Shaw propped an ankle on one knee and sat back in his chair, fingers interlaced behind his head, elbows out, as if he had all day.

They broke at noon, with Shaw signaling an end to the session by stretching, massively, in his chair.

"Well, it's a remarkable story," he told them, "but even psychiatrists have to eat. What I'd suggest is this: I have a luncheon engagement with my daughter, and a 1:30 appointment after that. If you'll come back at three, I'll do an intake interview, and we can go on from there."

"What's in an 'intake interview'?" Adrienne asked.

"Oh, well—" Shaw rolled his hand through the air.

"It's a basic medical history," Duran explained. "Operations, dizzy spells, allergies—"

"And a bit of testing," Shaw added. "Routine stuff: the TAT, the MMSE—"

"Which are what?" Adrienne asked.

Shaw shrugged. "Well, the names don't tell you a lot more than the acronyms. But they're tools we use to ascertain the patient's psychopathological status, identify cognitive impairment and thematic perception curves—that sort of thing."

Adrienne nodded, even as Duran frowned. What was he actually agreeing to by coming here? Was he going to be this man's guinea pig?

Shaw winked at him. "I'm sure Mr. Duran knows as much about the tests as I do—not so?"

Duran shrugged. "I know what they are," he said, "but I've never really had much use for them in my own practice."

"Well, I'm a great believer in testing," Shaw told them, "and if we have time, I think we'll take a shot at the Beck Depression Inventory." He saw the wariness in Duran's eye, and rushed to reassure him. "Just to get a take on things."

"I understand," Duran said, "but . . . what we're talking about is memory—not my sanity. My memory."

Shaw rolled his head from side to side, as if the distinction was unimportant. "Well," he said, "if everything you've been telling me is true, there's clearly a dysfunction of *some* kind. The tests are just investigative tools. And the first thing we need to find out is whether your amnesia is organic or adaptive, the result of trauma or . . . something else." He clapped his hands together. "We need to get some idea of the *kind* of thing we're dealing with."

"Which is what?" Adrienne asked.

Shaw turned his palms toward the ceiling. "There's no way to say, at this point. Amnesia can have any number of causes, from a knock on the head to epilepsy, extreme stress or—I don't want to frighten you, but—a brain tumor. It could be a form of hysteria."

" 'Hysteria'?"

Shaw winced. "It's an outdated term. Basically, we're talking about adaptive amnesia, the kind of amnesia that results from psychological—as opposed to physiological—causes." Shaw steepled his hands and peered over his fingertips: "Of course, the lines can be blurred. But, generally speaking, hysterical amnesia is amenable to talk therapies. These days, we tend to classify it as a dissociative disorder." He glanced at his watch, then bounced to his feet. "In any case, the tests will give us a leg up on things."

He shook hands, then shepherded them toward the door. "See you at three."

They checked the car (no ticket), fed the meter, and found a deli a few blocks from Shaw's office, where they ate pastrami sandwiches with a side of half-sour pickles and cans of Dr. Brown's Cel-Ray soda. Duran was in a funk, uncomfortable with being someone else's patient, Shaw's litany ringing in his head: *cognitive impairment, dysfunction, hysteria.*

"What's the matter?" Adrienne asked, as she speared a slice of pickle on her fork.

Duran shook his head. "If he tries to throw me in the bin," he said, "I'm outta here."

" 'The bin'?"

"It's a clinical term," he explained.

With more than an hour to kill, they decided to check out the offices of Mutual General Assurance. "They'll probably give us copies of Nikki's tapes, if you're the one to ask for them," she said. "I mean, you're their client, right?"

A subway ride and a five block walk got them where they were going, though it was anything but obvious when they arrived.

The address on Avenue of the Americas turned out to be a branch of *Box 'n Mail*, one of those places that sell bubble-wrap and cardboard boxes, while packaging and sending items via UPS, FedEx and the postal service. As a sideline, this particular *Box 'n Mail* was also a mail drop, renting boxes to people who found it problematic to receive mail at home.

Mutual General Assurance's offices in "Suite 1119" was in fact a 4- by 6- by- 12-inch tray. A pressed metal door obscured whatever contents it might have held.

Adrienne and Duran waited in line behind a woman sending a care package to her son at Cornell. When it became their turn, Adrienne asked how she could get in touch with Mutual General Assurance.

The clerk was an energetic slob with long blond hair. "Only one way," he said. "You write them a letter."

"But there's a list, right? I mean, there must be some kind of contract—between you and them."

The clerk shook his head, turned his attention back to the package on the counter in front of him, expertly affixing a length of sealing tape to a seam.

"Couldn't you just give me a phone number?" Adrienne cajoled. "It's important—I mean, I *really* need to *talk* to these people."

"Lady," said the clerk, "why do you think people rent these things?" He swept a hand toward the ranks of cubbyholes. It was a rhetorical question but Adrienne answered anyway.

"As a place to receive mail."

The clerk looked at her, then flipped the package in his

hands, examining every side. Finally, he dropped it into a white plastic crate on which someone had scrawled UPS.

"They rent them because it's a *discreet* way to receive mail. Discreet," he repeated. "You want a phone number for one of these outfits, you can call 411."

"This place is unlisted," Adrienne told him. "I already tried that."

The man gave her a regretful grin. "Yeah, well, that's why I say you oughta write 'em a letter. They want to talk to somebody, they're probably not gonna rent a box from us."

They stopped at the car to feed coins into the meter and when they returned to Dr. Shaw's office, Adrienne was given the option of cooling her heels in the reception or—"I think I'll go for a run," she said. "The park's only a few blocks away." Retrieving her running clothes from the car, she changed in the ladies' room outside Shaw's office, then took the elevator down to the first floor, leaving the psychiatrist and Duran to themselves.

She loved running in Central Park. The distance around was almost perfect, about six miles, and there was something wonderful about jogging beneath a canopy of skyscrapers and trees.

She ran for an hour and, once or twice, got turned around, emerging from the park on the wrong side. Each time, she went back the way she came, crossing the park, thinking, *You idiot. What if you'd sprained your ankle? You should have brought money—enough, at least, to make a phone call. And anyway, you should have been paying attention.*

The receptionist—a punky young woman with blue fingernails and henna colored hair—left at six. When she'd gone, Adrienne went to her desk and used the telephone to make a reservation at one of the hotels whose numbers she'd taken off the computer the night before. Then she changed back into her regular clothes, and began to read *Newsweek*. By 7:30, she'd read *New York*, *People,* and was halfway through the *New Yorker*, and beginning to worry that something was wrong. Twice, she got up from the couch and stood, listening, outside the door to Shaw's office. But the door was solid, and all she could hear was a low mumble.

It was 8:45 when they finally emerged, and the sound of their voices startled her so that she jumped up, as anxious and eager as a relative in a hospital's waiting area.

Shaw smiled at her and she could see that he was excited. For his part, Duran was exhausted, looking pale and tired, a shadow of stubble covering his jaw.

"It's a pain in the ass," Shaw was saying, "but nothing that *hurts*." Turning to Adrienne, he lifted his palms toward the ceiling, and apologized for keeping her waiting so long. "I'm completely *baffled*," he told her, "but more intrigued than ever. I've never seen anything like it! And as I was saying to Jeff, I'd like to run some tests in the morning. Nothing too strenuous—"

Adrienne frowned. "But, surely you have some idea. I mean, you've been in there for *hours*."

Shaw sighed, entwined his hands and stretched his arms above his head. He closed his eyes, and rolled his head in a circle. Then he lowered his arms and rotated his shoulders. Finally, he said, "Why don't we sit down?"

They did.

"It's a very odd business," Shaw began. "What interested me at first was the duration of what I was led to believe was an amnesic fugue, but—"

"You changed your mind," Adrienne suggested.

Shaw nodded.

"And now what do you think?"

"I think—that I don't *know* what I think. I can honestly say I've never encountered anything *like* Jeffrey's mind. He knows almost nothing about his past and what he does know is less remembered than learned. It's as if he read about himself, and memorized the details."

Adrienne looked at Duran.

"I'm a fascinating case," Duran told her, his voice thick

with sarcasm. "Ray's gonna name a disease after me. Call it Duran's Syndrome."

Shaw smiled. "If I ask Jeffrey about an incident in his past, one that he recalls, he'll relate the story in the same way each time, bringing up the *same* details in the same sequence."

"So?"

"They're anecdotes—remembered stories, rather than memories *per se*. It's not uncommon, really. All of us do it to some extent, embellishing our recollections to conform to one agenda or another, making ourselves look more attractive, our parents more loving—whatever it may be. But in Jeffrey's case, his memories aren't just polished, they're set in stone." Seeing Adrienne frown, Shaw went on to explain that "I asked Jeff to recall certain incidents from his past—the kinds of things no one would embellish."

"Like what?" Adrienne asked.

"Ohhhh . . ." He rolled his hand in the air. "The time you lost your first tooth." He paused, and nodded encouragingly. "How was that handled in *your* family?"

Adrienne blushed. "I don't know—"

"Of course you do. Think about it. When you lost your baby teeth—was it handled matter-of-factly? Or was it a big deal?" The psychiatrist pressed his hands together and put them in front of his face, so that his fingertips touched his lips.

Adrienne thought about it. "Well," she said, a little nervously, "in *my* family—that's kind of a loose construct, just for openers. I did a lot of moving around between 'families' when I was a kid."

"That's not what we're talking about," he objected, impatient for an answer. "*Wherever* you were, whoever you were with, you lost your first baby tooth. Take it from there. What happened?"

She shut her eyes, squeezed her face tight, made a show of having to remember although why she was doing this she didn't know—because she *did* remember, she remembered quite clearly. Finally, she said, "I lived with my grandmother, and she made a big deal about it—which wasn't really like her."

"Go on."

"Well, she had a little ceramic case. A special case that was shaped like a tooth."

Duran laughed.

"Really! And it had a hinge that you opened, and 'Tooth Fairy' was engraved on the top. I thought it was wonderful," Adrienne told them, "though now that I think about it . . . well . . . it seems a little strange." She giggled nervously.

"Go on."

"Well, the tooth went in the box and the box went under my pillow and, when I woke up in the morning, there was always a dollar bill—all folded up in a tiny little wad—instead of the tooth. Gram didn't understand how mercenary I was—I was ready to pull out the rest of them."

"You see," Shaw said, gesturing toward Adrienne with an open palm, "you recall it perfectly. As you should. Losing a tooth is a rite of passage—and almost everyone has some recollection of it. But not Jeffrey. Jeffrey doesn't remember anything about it at all."

He glanced at Duran, who shrugged.

"Anyway, as I was telling Jeff—I have a catalog of unimportant incidents of that kind. Things we all did—like eating lunch in elementary school, going out for a haircut, going to the dentist. I could give you dozens of examples of what amount to collective memories, memories that you might say are common to the human condition—or at least to the American condition. But—" Shaw turned to Duran with an apologetic smile. "Our friend, here, might as well be from Mars. Of all the events I suggested—and there were a dozen of them—Jeffrey responded to exactly two." He held up his fingers, like a peace sign. "He remembers going to the beach—Bethany Beach—with his parents. And he remembers blowing out the candles on a birthday cake. Everything else is a blank—and that's *not* what I expected."

Adrienne looked puzzled. "Why not? We know he has amnesia."

Shaw tilted his head from side to side. "Yes, but we also know he's a confabulator. And that's what makes the case so interesting: he's a twofer. And not just any twofer. Mr. Duran is convinced that his recollections are true—that's why he passed the lie detector test that you mentioned, and that's why he naively took you to a beach cottage that didn't exist. All of which is consistent with what I learned this afternoon. When I asked Jeff about these insignificant events that we've been talking about, he made no effort whatsoever at invention. Either he remembered them, or he didn't. Mostly, he didn't."

"But what does that mean?" Adrienne asked.

"That he's not a con man."

"And?"

"That he's delusional as well as amnesic." Shaw turned to Duran. "Are you sure you're comfortable with me discussing you in this way?"

Duran rolled his eyes. "Yeah. Adrienne and I are old friends. Ever since she stopped suing me."

Shaw looked surprised. "You're suing him?"

Adrienne shook her head. "No. I *was*. But I'm not."

The psychiatrist took this in stride. "At any rate, we went through some of the clinical tests I mentioned earlier."

"And?"

"Everything's normal—except the patient." He smiled. "So I hypnotized him."

Adrienne frowned. "But . . . I thought you were opposed to hypnosis."

"On the contrary. It's a useful tool—and I thought it might relax him. Loosen his inhibitions."

"And did it?" Adrienne asked.

"No—even under hypnosis, he was still drawing blanks. But the incidents he *did* recall—going to the beach, his first birthday cake (and first birthday party)—well that was even more interesting."

"How so?"

"He told me the same stories. And I mean, *exactly* the same stories. Almost word for word. As if he were reciting a poem, or a speech."

"Which means what?" Adrienne asked.

Doctor Shaw shook his head. "Too soon to say. But there are a couple of tests I'd like him to take—just so we can rule a few things out."

"Like what?"

"Hippocampal damage."

"And these tests . . . what are they?" Adrienne asked.

"CAT scan. PET scan. MRI."

It was Adrienne's turn to roll her eyes. "I don't think Mr. Duran has the money—"

"He's insured," Shaw told her. "We checked."

"Is he?" she asked. "With Mutual General?"

"No," Duran told her. "I've got Traveler's. The other was malpractice insurance—for the tapes."

Shaw got to his feet, and went to the receptionist's desk. Opening one drawer after another, he finally produced a map and some papers, which he handed to Duran.

"What's that?" Adrienne said, looking over Duran's shoulder.

"A map of the hospital, shows you where the lab is. Consent forms." Shaw glanced at his watch, and made a helpless gesture. "Oh, Jesus," he said, "I'm going to catch hell."

"Sorry," Adrienne told him, pulling together her little bundle of shoes and sweaty running clothes.

The psychiatrist waved away her concern. "Won't be the first time." He led them out the door to the elevator. "You the nervous type, Jeffrey? Claustrophobic?"

Duran shrugged. "How would *I* know?"

Shaw chuckled. "Well, if you think you'll have a problem with the MRI, tell the technician. He'll give you something that will help you chill out."

The car had a ticket tucked under its windshield. "God damn it!" Adrienne wailed. She rushed to pluck it free, as if it might replicate if she didn't remove it in a hurry. "It's a hundred bucks!" She looked at it and saw that the ticket had been written hours ago, during the time she'd been running. Getting lost in Central Park—she'd been worried about getting back late to Shaw's office and had forgotten about the meter. It wasn't fair but she turned toward Duran as if it was his fault: "Why did you have to take so long?"

He could sense her frustration, and knew better than to test it. So rather than making a wisecrack, or replying that the trip was her idea, he said, "I don't know. I'm sorry you had to wait."

Two minutes later, they were in the car, heading toward lower Manhattan, and she was apologizing. "It's my fault," she said, her tone emphatic and remorseful. "*I* parked there. I forgot to feed the meter. I don't know why I'm yelling at you." She sighed. "Sometimes, when I get stressed out—"

"Forget it."

"No, that was bad. I know it wasn't your idea to spend all that time in his office, being grilled from A to Z. I'm just a jerk." She seemed so disconsolate that he wanted to put his arm around her.

Instead, he said, "I know you're worried about money. You didn't even want to spend the night here."

"Yeah, but don't try to talk me out of it," she told him, beginning to laugh. "I like to wallow." She let out an exaggerated moan. "A hundred dollars . . . shit!" The windshield fogged up and she rubbed at it with the heel of her hand.

"Where are we going?"

"I made a reservation at a hotel on Washington Square."

"Great."

She laughed. "I doubt it. It's going for seventy bucks a night."

"Ah . . . and what does Lonely Planet say about it?"

"That it's 'reasonably clean. Safe. A budget alternative.' "

"There you go!" Duran exclaimed. "That's the trifecta."

"Well . . ." she said, her voice doubtful.

"What's not to like?" he asked.

She thought about it for a moment, and said, " 'Reasonably.' "

26

The hotel was a dive.

Their room—a "kitchenette"—was "clinically depressing," according to Duran. It had the tired and dingy look of a place that had been slept in too often by people who'd only recently been "released." Lumpy twin beds were covered with suspect chenille bedspreads which looked (from the evidence of a few dark streaks) as if they had once been orange, but were now a played-out blond. In the corner, a low table stood on an expanse of wall-to-wall carpeting, mottled with stains. Peppered with cigarette burns, a mustard-colored chair waited beside the window, itself opaque with grime. Nearby, a twenty-seven-inch Sony Trinitron rested on a built-in cabinet.

In the kitchen area, behind a formica counter, was a sink in desperate need of reenameling, a small refrigerator with a very big hum, and a wall of Sears cabinetry that held a stack of Melamine plates and cups.

Adrienne opened the refrigerator, and glanced inside. Happily, there was nothing to be seen but an ice cube tray that looked as if it had been handmade of compacted aluminum foil.

"I hate it here," she said.

Duran wedged a chair under the doorknob.

In the morning, they took the subway uptown to the Pashten Medical Center, where the staffers in the neuro-imaging suite greeted them in high spirits. The Asian receptionist slid open a translucent window and gave Duran a big smile. "Oh yes," she said. "Duran. You're here for the works, right? Let me call Victor."

Moments later, a sharp-featured Latino emerged through the door. He wore aqua scrubs and had a face that looked as if it had come from an Aztec frieze. "If you'll give Melissa your consent forms," he said, "we can get started." Then he turned to Adrienne. "You Mrs. Duran?"

She felt her face begin to burn. "No," she said, a little too hurriedly. "Just a friend."

"Well, I don't think you're gonna want to wait around," he told her. " 'Cause it's gonna be a while. Maybe you could come back at four?"

When Adrienne had left, they took Duran's vital signs and led him into an examination room, where he waited to be summoned. The room was decorated with a pastel, geometric border at the junction of the ceiling and wall. A single Norman Rockwell print hung on one wall. It showed a white-coated doctor with a kindly smile and a stethoscope, approaching a quaking boy, his bare bottom exposed beneath a too short surgical gown.

The syrupy image of the kindly pediatrican harkened back to a time that had little in common with the world in which Duran found himself. The neuro-imaging center was a technophile's dream, a forest of computers and diodes, oscilloscopes, and putty-colored machines that seemed, at once, modern and prehistoric.

The CAT scan came first.

For this, Duran was asked to lie down in a prone position with his head braced upon his chin. A rubber device was put in his mouth, and he was told to bite down upon it, the better to keep his head still. Movement, he was told, is the enemy. And so he lay there like a fallen log, suddenly aware of every itch and tingle, determined not to move and inspired by the unending patter of his nurse-technician-cheerleader.

All the while, she operated a device that rolled along the armature around his head, taking a series of forty-eight cross sections of his skull. The device moved with a dense whir, and it was difficult not to react when it locked into place, and clanked and snapped to register an image.

Listening to his cheerleader-nurse, it occurred to Duran that her tone was precisely the one that people use to address dogs and babies.

After the CAT scan, an Indian woman grabbed his color-coded chart and ushered him into a room whose door bore a sign that read:

ECHO-PLANAL MAGNETIC
IMAGING RESONANCE

This time, things didn't go so well.

The MRI machine was a long table that rolled into a large, but coffinlike, drum—"the magnet," as the technicians called it. Lying down on the table, Duran was fitted with a kind of football helmet—the head coil—which was itself attached to a plastic grid that covered his face. The nurse handed him a device that was meant to serve as an alarm, and told him to push the panic button if he became claustrophobic. Then he was asked to lie still, and ignore the pumping sound that the machine was about to make.

So far, so good. So far, no problem.

Then the nurse touched a button, and the table rolled into the drum, swallowing him. Peering through the plastic grid, his eyes were about eight inches from the bottom of the drum—until the table rose, lifting him to within an inch or two of the surface above his face.

He took a deep breath. *You're in your safe-place,* he told himself—and hit the panic button—hard. An alarm went off. The nurse came running. The table subsided, and rolled back.

Whispered conferences ensued, and eventually, Duran was returned to the examination room. There, a young man with a shaven head and a gold ring through his septum gave him a shot that he said would help him relax. And, indeed, it did. The remainder of the morning and much of the afternoon passed—not like a dream, but a documentary. Handheld. Black and white. No narration.

Duran couldn't remember how many tests were taken, or how often his veins had been "palpated."

But the last test was the PET scan. Aztec Charlie—which is how he was known at the clinic—explained to Duran that PET stood for Positron Emission Tomography. "Basically," he said, "we're gonna light you up with this." He lifted a syringe out of a brushed aluminum tray. "It's a radioactive isotope," he explained. "Lights up your brain, so the doc can see what's happening." He tapped the syringe with his fingernail, and asked Duran to lie down on a paper-covered table.

He did, and barely felt the needle.

Two hours later, he joined Adrienne and Doctor Shaw in a small conference room at the clinic.

A dozen images—cross sections of Duran's brain—were clipped to a bank of backlit viewing screens. Holding a pointer, Shaw went from one image to another, tapping the pointer's tip against a small, bright spot in a sea of gray.

"Right here," he said. "And here. And here. And you can see it on this one, too!"

"It's like a piece of rice," Adrienne said.

"What is it?" Duran asked.

Shaw thought about it for a moment, frowned and said: "I don't know." Then he thought some more, and shrugged. "I can tell you what it's *not*," he assured them. "It's not *tissue*. It's not a bone, or a nerve. It's not flesh. It's not blood. Which is to say, it's 'a foreign object'—which is what we call things when we've exhausted every way of looking at them, and still don't know what they are." The physician frowned and paused. One of the fluorescent light fixtures on the ceiling fizzed. "You don't recall suffering a head injury?" he asked Duran in a hopeful tone. "Maybe a car accident? Ever been in the army? Or a plane crash?"

Duran made a wry face. "Not that I can recall."

Shaw smiled. "Very funny."

"Wait a minute," Adrienne asked, looking at Shaw. "That's what you think? That—"

"A physical injury might be responsible for his condition?" Shaw's arms flew up, and his face contorted in an exaggerated expression of perplexity. "Let's just say . . . it's a working hypothesis." He gestured toward the display of images. "The history of psychology and neurobiology is full of examples of the ways physical trauma can affect memory. In fact, some of our best information *about* memory comes from accidents—crazy accidents in which brains were maimed. Which isn't surprising, really. I mean, these aren't experiments you can carry out in a hospital." Shaw beat out a little rhythm on the surface of the counter then let it fade.

"Is it possible," Adrienne asked, "that that *thing* . . . is interfering with Jeff's memory?"

Shaw shrugged. "Absolutely," he said. "It's quite possible."

"But you can't say for sure," Duran suggested.

"Not without examining it." Seeing Adrienne deflate, Shaw gave her a sympathetic smile. "Memory is a very strange thing," he told her. "People like to think that we store memories in the brain the way librarians store books—side by side, in categories of one kind or another. But it's not true. We know it's not true because we've done experiments—lots of experiments. And what we've learned is that memories aren't localized, but *distributed*. Like smoke, they're *diffused* through the brain. So if you teach a rat to run a maze—then mutilate its brain to the point where the rat can barely walk— it will still remember how to get from A to Z. Not as quickly, perhaps, but it will remember.

"What's particularly interesting about your case," Shaw continued, "is that we're not seeing any of the usual profiles of memory loss. Your short-term memory is undamaged. And you seem to retain the *ability* to form long-term memories."

"So what's your theory?" Duran asked.

"I don't have a theory," Shaw replied. "All I have is an object." He tapped one of the images on the light panel. "*That* object."

Duran stared at the image on the wall, and felt a surge of elation. The psychiatrist might be right. The object could explain a lot. Not everything, of course—not the murder of Eddie Bonilla. But . . . a lot.

"So where do we go from here?" Duran asked.

Shaw hesitated. "Well," he said, "that's up to you."

"How so?"

"We could go in," the psychiatrist answered. "Take it out. See what it's made of. See what it is."

"Is that dangerous?" Adrienne said.

Shaw's pointer beat out a rhythm on the table, then faded to a slow, monotonous tapping. The shrink seesawed his head back and forth. "Not *especially*. It's in an area that's relatively easy to access. You'd be in a semi-sitting position, and we'd enter the sphenoid sinus cavity through the anterior nasal septum."

"My nose."

Shaw stopped tapping the table and slapped the pointer into his open palm. "Right. You'd need broad spectrum antibiotics, but otherwise—I should think it would be a piece of cake."

"But there are risks," Adrienne suggested.

Shaw nodded. "There are always risks."

"Like what?" Duran asked.

"Damage to the optic nerve."

"He could go *blind*?"

"It's very, *very* unlikely. I'd be more concerned about leakage."

"Of what?" Adrienne asked.

"CSF. The brain's floating in a pool of cerebrospinal fluid. In surgery of this kind . . . ?" He ended the sentence with a shrug.

"Christ," Duran muttered.

"The mortality rate is less than one percent."

No one said anything.

"Of course," the psychiatrist went on, "there might be consequences to leaving it in place, too. It could be the cause of some localized infection or swelling—the PET scans show a sort of odd . . . *excitation* . . . around the object." He shuffled through a sheaf of large colored prints of Duran's brain. The colors were intense—cerise, magenta, sapphire—so that Duran's brain had a psychedelic look, as if it might be the model for a line of retro T-shirts.

The doctor placed a photographer's loupe over one of the images. "Here. You can see the excitation quite clearly. Take a look."

They did, in turn. Duran saw a tiny yellow blip surrounded by a halo of purple.

"So what do you want to do?" Duran asked.

"An exploratory—see if we can get in and out without a lot of ancillary damage. If we can, we'll remove it. See what it is."

"And you'd be doing the surgery?" Adrienne asked.

Shaw shook his head. "I'll find someone with better hands." He whirled to a bank of files behind him, pulled open a drawer, extracted a folder, selected some papers. He tapped them into a neat stack, then clipped them together. "Here," he said, handing the papers to Duran. "Consent forms. You'll want to read them carefully. Get a good night's rest and . . . call me in the morning."

They found a Cuban-Chinese takeout a block from the hotel, and returned to their room with cartons of rice and beans, and a six-pack of Tsing Tsao.

Duran glanced through the consent forms as Adrienne brought their plates to the little table in the corner.

"I could go blind," he told her. "Or go through a personality change. Then, there's my favorite: 'loss of cognitive function.' "

She handed him a beer, and asked, "What's that supposed to mean?"

"It means I could be an idiot."

"Jesus!" she said. "I don't know . . ." She threw him a glance.

"What?"

She shook her head. "I don't want to *say* anything. I mean, I don't want the responsibility."

The food was terrific.

"Chinese-Cuban," Adrienne said. "Not a combination I would have come up with. I wonder how that came about."

Duran shrugged. "There are lots of Chinese all over the West Indies," he said. "At least in Jamaica and Haiti there are. So it stands to reason they'd be in Cuba, too."

She paused, chopsticks suspended on the way to her mouth. "How do you know?"

"What do you mean, how do I—"

"I mean really," she said. "Think about it. Have you been there? To Jamaica? The Caribbean."

He thought about it. "I think so," he said. "To Haiti, anyway."

"Well, let's think about it! See what you can remember."

He savored another spoonful of rice and beans, then closed his eyes, and sipped his beer. Finally, he said, "Big, white house. Verandah. Palm trees." He stopped for a moment. He could hear the traffic in the street, the dull roar of white noise. "When the wind came up and blew the palms around," Duran said, "it wasn't a soft sound, like wind moving through the leaves. It was a thrashing sound." He paused, and then went on. "There was a gardener who used to climb the trees when a storm was coming . . ." He fell silent.

"Why?" Adrienne prompted.

"To cut the coconuts—so they wouldn't damage the verandah."

"Keep going," Adrienne encouraged. She put the chopsticks down. "It's like when we were playing chess. Remember? The rum, the heat, I think—"

Across from her, Duran's face had been relaxed, with just a tiny frown of concentration pinching at his eyes. Suddenly, he was on his feet, eyes wide.

"What's the matter?"

He shook his head, looked away, then took a couple of deep

breaths. Finally, he turned to her. "Sometimes . . . when I start to remember things . . . I see this room—and it scares the shit out of me."

"What room?"

He shook his head, and walked to the window. Looked out. "I don't want to talk about it."

"You *have* to."

He kept looking out the window, as if he was searching for something. A minute passed, and then he said: "I've been trying to figure out the color."

"What color?"

"Of the room. It's not yellow, but . . . ochre. And there's blood everywhere." He heaved a sigh. "I really don't want to think about this."

"But you should, that's exactly what you should do—you should think about it. *Keep going*. Maybe—"

"No!"

"Fine," she said, picking up her chopsticks again. She ran them through the reddish sauce, then concentrated on capturing a single black bean.

"I'm sorry," Duran told her. "I just can't do it. It's . . . I don't know. I can't explain it."

"No problem," Adrienne replied in a dismissive tone. "Whatever."

"Look—"

"I just think, you know, you've got some kind of memory trace there, something important happened—I'd think you'd want to go with it."

He didn't say anything for a while. A lock of his dark hair, which he kept combed back, had fallen down onto his forehead and he pushed at it with his fingers. "I'm not explaining this very well, but it's like—I *can't* go with it. I can't *stand* it."

She sighed.

"I see that room and . . . it's like I'm going to pass out," he told her. "It's like I *want* to pass out."

She shook her head, as if it were a way to change the subject. "I guess you've got enough on your mind," she told him.

He looked puzzled. "I do?"

"Well, brain surgery." She placed the pointed end of one chopstick atop a single black bean, punctured it, then tried to obscure what seemed like an unfortunate metaphorical action by messing around with the rest of the food on her plate.

"Do you always do that?" he said after a while, his tone light.

"What?"

He indicated the little mounds of rice and vegetables she'd constructed. "Because Dr. Freud has some pretty interesting opinions about that kind of thing."

She laughed. "Playing with my food," she said, pushing the food into a single mound, then squaring it off. "My detractors would say it's the only kind of play I'm capable of."

"You have detractors?"

She drew diagonal paths through the square of food, separating it into four triangles. "Ummmm. 'I'm not much fun. I'm a worker bee. I'm all business.' "

He laughed. "I think your detractors are jealous."

She smiled. Said, "Thanks." Thought, *Uh-oh.*

She was starting to get attached to this guy. In fact, she was starting to like him—and maybe *more* than like him (which would be a *real* disaster). *Probably the Stockholm Syndrome,* she thought. While Duran wasn't her captor, they were captive together in this weird situation, and it was natural, she supposed, that she would begin to feel that they were some kind of . . . *team.* She ran her thumb down the side of the Tsing Tsao bottle, leaving a clear path through the condensation. Then she picked it up and drained it.

An hour later, she was standing in the kitchen, washing up, when she heard him make a call. Turning off the water, she set the plate in the drainer, and listened.

"Yeah, Doc," he said, "It's Jeff Duran . . . right. Fine, thanks. Listen, I just wanted to say—I've thought it over, and . . . I'm in."

27 Shaw telephoned at eight in the morning, waking Adrienne even as Duran pulled a pillow over his head.

"We can do it on Tuesday," he told her. "I've got Nick Allalin on board—he's the neurosurgeon—and I'm lining up the O/R. I may have to do a bit of camel-trading, but . . . we're there."

Adrienne swung her legs out of the bed, and sat up. "Tuesday?"

Shaw could hear the disappointment in her voice. "Best I could do," he said. "Even that—"

"Tuesday's fine," she decided. "It's just that . . . I was wondering what we'd do in the meantime. New York's so expensive, and—another three days . . ."

"Why not go home? Tell Jeff to put his feet up for a while, and—I'm sure you're missed at Slough, Hawley."

"Mmmnnn . . ."

They rolled into Bethany at dusk, and stopped at the supermarket, first thing.

"I wish I could cook something fabulous," Adrienne said, as she requested a rotisserie chicken from the clerk—who expertly plucked it free of its metal prongs and slipped it into a bag lined in aluminum foil. They continued down the aisle, stopping to get a prepackaged salad. "But the truth is," she continued, "the kind of things we ate at home, well, I'm not sure you'd be too happy."

"What," Duran said. "You mean, like meatloaf? I happen to like meatloaf."

"Meatloaf—that would be haute cuisine. My personal specialty was tater-tot casserole," Adrienne said. "And Hamburger Helper was pretty big. Tuna wiggle. Chicken à la king. And you know that thing with marshmallows and coconut that someone always brings to potluck dinners? I used to *love* that."

"What's a tuna-wiggle?" Duran wondered. "Sounds like—"

"Don't ask. You need noodles, and cream of mushroom soup. And lots of Ritz crackers."

Returning to the cottage, parking behind it, hearing and feeling the familiar crunch of the pea gravel under their tires—all this gave Adrienne a brief flush of pleasure, a spurious (she reminded herself) sense of coming home.

When they'd eaten, she changed into jeans and a sweater and, accompanied by Duran, went for a walk on the beach, braving the cold. She loved the smell of the sea, the thump of the surf, and the clatter of pebbles dragged by the undertow. But the air was freezing. She could see her breath, and it made her shiver. Noticing this, Duran put his arm around her shoulders, even as he lowered his head against the onshore wind. For a moment, Adrienne stiffened—then, warming, relaxed, sagging into him ever so slightly.

After a while, she asked, "Are you worried about the surgery?"

Duran shrugged.

"You'd be crazy not to be."

He chuckled. "Well, that's the point, isn't it?"

After a couple of hundred yards, they returned to the house, invigorated. "I want to take another look at this," Adrienne said, sitting down at the dining room table with Nikki's computer. "I'm sure there's something on it that I missed." She waited for the machine to boot up. "You any good with these things?"

Duran shrugged. "I could take a look." He leaned over her shoulder.

"I've been through everything I could think of: calendar,

address book, e-mail, accounting programs. I've called up every file I can find, and there's nothing."

"You look at the temporary Internet files?"

She rolled her eyes. "No."

Duran sat down beside her. "Go to *Start*," he said. "Then *Settings*. Then *Control Panel*." She moved the pointer as he directed. "Now hit the Internet icon and . . . you see where it says, 'Temporary Internet Files' . . . click on the *Settings* button, and—"

" 'View Files'?"

He nodded. She clicked, and a window appeared with scores of Internet addresses, listed by *Name*, *Address*, and *Last Access*.

The two of them scanned the addresses together, scrolling down the page. Besides the usual assortment of cookies, banner and GIF files, there were lots of URLs, though most of them had been accessed only once or twice:

> *cookie:jacko@jcrew.com*
> *cookie:jacko@washingtonpost.com*
> *http://www.travelocity.com*
> *http://www.mothernature.com*
> *http://www.theprogram.org*
> *http://www.jcrew.com*
> *http://www.victoriassecret.com*
> *http://www.theprogram.org*

"What's that one?" Duran asked, stabbing his finger at an entry that came up, time and again:

> *cookie:jacko@theprogram.org*

Adrienne shook her head. "It's like she went there every day."

Duran nodded. "And who's Jacko?" he asked.

"Her dog," Adrienne explained. "I guess she named her computer after her dog." She continued scrolling.

cookie:jacko@theprogram.org
cookie:jacko@ceoexpress.com
http://www.theprogram.org
http://www.theprogram.org
http://www.theprogram.org
http://www.mothernature.com
http://www.jcrew.com
http://www.theprogram.org

"It's every day," Adrienne said. "Sometimes, a couple of times a day." She looked at Duran. "Shall we?"

He nodded.

She closed the Control Panel windows, clicked on the AOL icon, and waited as it went through its routine. Finally, there was a rush of white noise, some honks and beeps—and she was on.

"You want a beer?" Duran asked, getting to his feet.

"Sure," she replied. Moving the cursor to the window at the top of the screen, she typed *theprogram.org*, and hit *Return*. A moment later, Duran was back with a couple of bottles of Hop Pocket Ale, which he set on the table beside her as he took a seat. Her foot was tapping impatiently on the floor. "I hate how long this takes," she muttered.

Transferring document: 1% 5% 33%

And then:

Unknown Host
Description:
Could not resolve the host:
"www.theprogram.org" in the URL
"http://www.theprogram.org/".
Traffic Server 1.1.7

With a groan, she cleared the screen and tried again, typing the address exactly as it was in the Temporary Internet file.

Hit *Search*. Once again, the site started loading. Sipping her beer, she watched the little blue bar filling up at the bottom of the screen: 24% 25% 32% Finally, the screen flipped, and the same message popped into view:

> *Unknown Host*
> *Description:*
> *Could not resolve the host . . .*

She swore to herself, and sighed. Took a long sip of beer. "Why don't you try?" she asked. "I'll be right back." Then she got to her feet, stretched, yawned, and wandered off.

Returning to the dining room, Adrienne sat down beside Duran, and asked, "Did I leave out a hyphen, or . . ."

He was tapping away at the keyboard, and didn't answer. Annoyed, she peered over his shoulder at the laptop's screen—and what she saw made her feel as if she'd been given an injection of ice water at the base of her spine. There was a cascade of images and text, scrolling and flipping so fast that she could not focus. No one could. It was moving at warp speed to a strange, electronic beat—a kind of nonmusic.

"What the . . . what *is* that?" she asked, but Duran still didn't answer.

Then the screen shimmied, steadied, stopped. Against an emerald green background, a message began to blink:

> *Hello, Jeffrey.*

Duran typed something, and hit *Return*.

> *Where are you?*

Once again, Duran typed a brief message, and tapped the *Return* key.

"What is this?" Adrienne asked. "What are you doing?"

> *Thank you, Jeffrey.*

" 'Thank you, Jeffrey'? Who are you talking to?" Adrienne demanded.

Duran maneuvered the cursor to the AOL logo and double-clicked. The computer emitted its usual *Good-bye*.

"Is this the Web site?"

But Duran still didn't answer. Instead he shut the computer off, and picked up something from the counter—something she hadn't noticed before. This was a transparent plastic sheet imprinted with little squares.

"What's that?" she asked, reaching for the sheet, which Duran held on to in the dogged and determined way of a tod-dler. Silent and unsmiling, he tried to pull it away from her.

"What *is* it? Give it to me!" she insisted, tugging at the sheet to no avail. After a few seconds of wordless struggle, Duran put an end to the contest by closing his free hand around her wrist with such force that she gasped.

"Hey!"

He ignored her complaint, squeezing harder and harder until her knees began to buckle. As she sank toward the floor, he pried open her fingers one by one. Then extracted the piece of plastic from her grasp, and placed it carefully inside the in-struction book for Nikki's computer, making sure that its edges did not protrude. This done, he replaced the instruction book in one of the side compartments of the computer's car-rying case, and zipped the case shut.

Setting it down on the floor he looked at her with a smile that made her take a step back. It was a jack-o'-lantern smile with nothing behind it, a smile as big and empty as the desert.

Jesus, she thought. *What's the matter with him?* His grip had been *ferocious*. What if he'd wanted more than a piece of plastic? What if . . . For the first time, she was afraid of him, and the fear arrived like a sucker punch, unexpected and sick-ening. She felt a weakness in her legs, as if she were melting from the ankles up. *One minute, he's so caring and kind . . .* She thought of the arm he had put around her shoulders on the beach. *And the next . . . It's so easy to forget: he's insane. A psychopath.*

A sharp little sound fell from her mouth and, hearing it, Duran turned to her on his way to the living room. "You okay?" he asked.

He still had a lights-out look in his eyes, and there was something funny about the way that he moved, as if he were gliding on well-oiled tracks. And his voice—his voice was perfectly normal, which was chilling, because his smile was so airless and cold, his eyes so distant and unfocused that it seemed to her that he was gazing toward the horizon.

Adrienne nodded. "Yeah, fine," she managed, leaning back against the dining room table.

With a shrug, Duran continued into the living room. Sat down on the couch. Turned on the TV.

Call Shaw. Now. She took a sip of beer, and searched through her purse for the scrap of paper on which she'd written the psychiatrist's home and office numbers. Finding it crumpled in the bottom of the bag, she flattened it out and began dialing. Then she leaned to her left to see if Duran had noticed what she was doing, but no, he was sitting on the couch in the living room, encapsulated in the soft glow and relentless good humor of the television.

Shaw answered on the fourth ring and, as soon as the psychiatrist said hello, she said, "We've got a problem."

"What's up?"

"Duran," she told him. "He scared me." She related what had happened, feeling a little silly because it didn't sound like much when you said it out loud. But Shaw was understanding.

"Have you ever seen this . . . lack of *affect* before?"

"No," she replied.

"And what's he doing now? You're whispering, so I assume he doesn't know that you're talking to me. Is he alert? Is he cognizant?"

"Sort of. He's watching television. But he's really blitzed, Doc. I mean, I could be a lamp, for all he cares. It's like I'm not even here." Shaw was quiet for what seemed a long time—long enough, at least, for her to prompt him. "So . . . what do you think it is?"

"I don't know," Shaw replied. "Sounds like a trance state. And you say he was sitting in front of the computer when—"

"Right."

"Well, I suppose . . . it could be some kind of entrainment—"

" 'Entrainment'?"

"—caused by flicker."

"I don't know what you're talking about."

"I'm talking about the rhythm of a flashing light— flicker—synchronized to the electrical rhythms of the brain. That's 'entrainment.' "

"Okay, but—we're not in a disco, Doc!"

"I understand that. But you said he was using the computer."

"Right."

"Well . . . most monitors are in a constant state of flicker— because they're 'refreshing' the video signal." He paused, and asked, "Was there any sound on this Web site, or was it just—"

"There was some kind of sound," she told him. "Electronic music, or . . . maybe it was just noise—whatever, it was *something*."

Shaw grunted.

"What!?" Adrienne asked.

"Well, it could be a problem with the monitor, but . . . it could be *the Web site*. I mean, it's a classic recipe . . ."

"What is?"

"What we're talking about—combining rhythmic pulses of light with certain frequencies of sound."

"To do what?"

"Induce a trance state. Shamans have been doing it for thousands of years, playing drums around a bonfire. Though I'd hate to think there's a Web site—"

"But—"

"Let me talk to him," Shaw suggested.

"Really?"

"Ummm. Can't hurt to try."

Adrienne took a deep breath, turned, and called out to Duran in as "natural" a voice as she could manage: "Jeff— Dr. Shaw wants to talk to you for a second."

When he didn't reply, she went into the living room, where he was sitting on the couch, watching television. Seeing her, he pressed the *Mute* button, and looked up. His face had an expressionless and somehow out-of-focus look, as if he were wearing a mask of himself.

"Phone call," she told him.

They were on the phone for a long time, maybe twenty minutes, with Shaw doing almost all the talking. Duran sat with his eyes closed and every once in a while, said, "Ummm-hmmm," or "Yessss," his voice low and indistinct. Finally, he put the phone down, and heaved a huge yawn.

"Adrienne? I think Dr. Shaw would like to talk to you now." His voice sounded normal, if sleepy. "I'm really tapped out," he explained, handing her the phone. "I think I'm gonna crash." With a yawn, he turned, and made his way to the bedroom.

Adrienne was astounded, watching him as he disappeared down the hall. "What did you do?" she asked, her voice in an urgent whisper.

"I hypnotized him," Shaw replied.

"Over the phone?"

"Yes. It wasn't that hard. He was already in a trance."

"And—"

"I gave him a couple of posthypnotic suggestions—did he go to bed?"

"Yes."

"Well, he'll be fine in the morning. Refreshed, and feeling pretty good about himself."

"Thanks, Doc."

"If he gives you any more trouble—and I don't think he will, but *if*—the best thing to do is just: walk out. Play it safe. Give me a call, and I'll take it from there."

When they'd said good-bye, Adrienne went into the

kitchen for a glass of water, then wandered back to the dining room to take another look at the plastic sheet that she and Duran had been struggling over.

Removing the sheet from the computer handbook, she saw that it was embossed with a grid, almost like graph paper, although the spaces were rectangles rather than squares. There were two- or three-hundred of them, she guessed, and judging by its size, it was obviously meant to fit over the screen of Nikki's computer.

Which it did. Perfectly. Indeed, there were small holes in each corner of the sheet that corresponded to markings on the monitor's frame. Placing the sheet over the markings, she saw that it created a precise, transparent overlay.

With the sheet in place, she turned on the computer, signed onto AOL and went to the Web site.

Unknown Host

Just like before. But the grid revealed nothing at all, it spidery lines crisscrossing the error message. She sighed. Duran must have gone to another Web site, while she'd been in the bathroom, brushing her hair. Then she remembered the trick Duran had shown her earlier and, with a little experimenting, she found the icon for the "Temporary Internet Files." What she wanted, of course, was to identify the site Duran had visited—the interactive one with the *Hello, Jeffrey* message. It should have been the second site on the list, but, no: the first and second sites were the same.

http://theprogram.org
http://theprogram.org

Which was frustrating because that was the nonsense site, the one Nikki had gone to, the one with the error message. She stared for a while at the letters, wondering what they meant, thinking, *Maybe Duran erased the address . . .* But no, he hadn't. She'd watched him sign off AOL, and close the computer. Then they'd argued. So . . .

She needed a nerd. And she knew where to find one.

Carl Dobkin was famous for sleeping four hours a night, so if she could get him on the phone, he might be able to talk her down. It was unlikely that he'd be at work, but you never knew with Carl. So she tried Slough, Hawley, punching his name into the voice mail system—which then patched her through to his extension. He wasn't there and she didn't leave a message. She knew Carl lived in Potomac with Caroline Stanton, a partner in the firm. Bette had been there once for a cookout and (cattily) described the place as "E-*nor*-mous! Faux Tudor. No landscaping." Adrienne got the number from Information, and called it.

She hoped Caroline wouldn't answer. She didn't want to be grilled about where she was. And she got lucky.

"Hello, Hello."

Relief darted through her. "Carl! Hi, it's Adrienne Cope."

"Hey, Scout. What's up? I suppose you know: they're taking your name in vain down at work."

"I'm sure they are." There was a long pause that she made no attempt to fill.

Finally, Dobkin asked, "So what can I do for ya?"

"You could be a genius for me."

Carl laughed, his lazy chuckle. "No problem. It's what I do best."

She described her attempts to investigate Nikki's travels in cyberspace. "And I got to this one site that she seems to have visited almost every day—sometimes, several times a day— and it won't boot up."

"What do you mean, 'it won't boot up'?"

"I get an error-message. 'Unknown host.' "

He thought about it for a moment. "Were one of you using Unix? Maybe there's a compatibility problem."

"I'm using the same computer she was. And it's pure vanilla. She had an AOL account—nothing exotic."

"Tell you what—can you get online and talk to me at the same time?"

"No," she replied. "I've only got a single line."

"Lemme put you on hold. I'll go into my study." A little later, he came back on the phone. "You there?"

"Still here."

"Okay, now we're cruisin'." She heard the clack of the keyboard, Carl typing at warp speed. "Let me log on here . . . okay, give me this site's address."

She spelled it out for him. "The program—one word—dot org."

"Hang on. It's bootin'."

"It's always bootin'. Then it doesn't go anywhere."

"Hunh!" Dobkin exclaimed. "You're right. Look at that!" He was silent for a moment.

"Carl?"

"The weird thing is, it's loading that page."

"What do you mean?"

"It's not an error-message," Dobkin explained. "It's the actual Web site. You go there, and that's what you get."

The two of them sat on the phone for upwards of a minute, saying nothing, thinking about the problem.

Finally, Dobkin asked: "Was your sister into anything . . . ummm, *kinky?*"

Adrienne thought of the gun. And lied. "I don't know—why?"

"Well, there are some locked and hidden sites on the Web, sites you can't get into without a password or key."

"You mean, like—one of those porno sites?"

"No, because with those, you know what they are. I'm talking about sites that put up an innocuous front—"

"Like what?"

"Like a quote from the *Bible*—or an error-message. You just have to know how to get behind it."

Adrienne considered what Dobkin was telling her. "But . . . why would someone do that?" she asked.

"Could be a joke. Could be hackers, screwing around,

doing it because they can do it. Or it could be something illegal."

"Like what?"

"I don't know . . . child pornography." As Adrienne began to protest, he hurried on, "Hey, I'm just throwing things out. I don't know *what* it is."

She was quiet for a moment, then told him about the overlay. "Could that be something?" she asked.

"Yeah! Sure, it could. You play with it at all?"

"A little. But I didn't get anywhere."

"Well, you might want to give it another ride," he suggested. Then he thought for a moment, and asked: "Would it help to know whose Web site it is?"

"What?"

"The Web site," he repeated. "Would it help if you knew where it was, and who it's registered to?"

She couldn't believe he was asking that. What did he think? "Well, yeah!" she said. "I mean—that would really float my boat."

"Well, maybe I can help you with that," he told her. "We've been getting a lot of spam at work, and I've gotten pretty good at tracking them down. I've got a program that runs a high-speed graphical trace route, working backwards from one computer to another, pinging the nodes—"

"Uhhh, Carl—you're beginning to break up."

"I'm . . . what? Oh, I get it—very funny. Tell you what: how long are you going to be awake?"

"I don't know . . . an hour?" The truth was, she wasn't at all sleepy.

"Give me your number. I'll get back to you when I've pinged it."

When she'd hung up, she detached the flexible plastic sheet from the computer's screen and put it carefully back in its case. Then she thought about it, and decided to put the overlay somewhere that Duran couldn't get at it. Rolling it up, she stuck it in her purse—which she'd keep with her in her room.

Then she laid out what she'd need in the morning, and set it by the front door. Somehow, without consciously thinking about it, she'd reached a decision about her job: in the morning, she'd go to Washington. Not to work (after what had happened at the Comfort Inn, there was no way she could go to the office). But if she got up early enough—at six, say— she could catch Slough at home. He never got to work before 10:15, so if she got there by nine or nine-thirty, she might be able to explain things. And save her job.

That, at least, was the plan, and it was certainly better than sitting around in Bethany Beach, waiting for Duran to go off.

When she'd finished getting her things together, she scrubbed the kitchen sink and wiped down the counters, emptied all the trash into a garbage bag and carried it outside to the Dumpster. Then the telephone rang, and she ran back in to answer it.

"Scout?" It was Carl.

"Hi!"

"I got it for you. The site with the error message."

"Oooh! *What* a good boy! Tell me, tell me, tell me—"

"Believe me, this was *not* a piece of cake."

"I believe you."

"For some reason, there's a lot of insulation—"

"*Tell* me."

"It's in Switzerland. Something called the Prudhomme Clinic." He spelled it for her. "It's in a town called Spiez." He spelled that, too. "Any of this mean anything to you?"

"Not exactly. Although my sister—she had . . . well, she had a head injury in Europe, and part of the time—she *was* in Switzerland. But I'm not sure where."

"Well, I looked the place up. It's been in business since '52. Specializes in eating disorders. Your sister anorexic?"

"No. She was in a coma for a while. And when she woke up . . . she had amnesia."

Carl grunted his disappointment. "So it's probably not this place, then." His voice brightened. "Wait—did she have a drug problem? Because this place does drug rehab, too, what they call addiction services."

"Well . . . I don't think she was an addict, but . . . yes."

"Yeah? Well, there you go."

She thanked him for all the help he'd been, and hung up, thinking that she'd better get to bed if she was going to be up at six.

Going from room to room, she locked the doors, turned down the heat and shut off the lights. Then she set the alarm and climbed into bed, where she lay beneath the covers, thinking about the Prudhomme Clinic. Maybe the fact that the Web site had all that "insulation," as Carl put it, had to do with medical privacy. Could it be an aftercare protocol of some sort, where former patients checked in for support? She sighed. If so, Nikki had never mentioned it. And what about that weird stuff with Duran? What was his connection to the clinic? The Web site was interactive in some way, and in his case, it had induced a trance state. And what about those images, flipping and rolling like that?

It didn't make sense. None of it did.

28 She left a note for Duran in the morning, explaining that she'd gotten up early and gone to Washington to get Nikki's mail—the checks Nikki had written and her credit card records. She'd be back by five with a couple of steaks and a bag of hardwood charcoal for the grill. She remembered that he didn't have any cash, and left him a twenty.

> *Buy a bottle of cabernet, okay?*
> *A.*

What she didn't mention, because she knew that Duran wouldn't approve, was that she was going to see Curtis Slough, first. Not that she'd given much thought to what she'd say. But something had to be done. She couldn't just disappear. And neither could she go to the office—that much was for certain after what had happened at the Comfort Inn. At any rate, he wouldn't even *be* at the office today. It was Sunday, and she was going to catch him at home. At least she hoped so.

Driving through the flat Delmarva farmland, the sky brightening in her rearview mirror, Adrienne thought about what she might say—and rehearsed it as she drove, babbling at the windshield, making fun of herself.

In point of fact, Curtis, the most remarkable thing occurred the other night: as I slept on my cot at the hospice, where I've been caring for the elderly and infirm . . . No. Slough didn't give a damn about the elderly or infirm. But he *did* make a big deal about people in the office giving to Catholic charities, so how about: *Curtis, I've had a vision of the Blessed Virgin, and need a leave of absence to communicate her message.* No. That wouldn't do either.

It lifted her spirits to joke like this, but the truth was, a lot was riding on the meeting she was about to have—and whatever she said, it had better be good. *I need a lawyer,* she told herself. *And not just any lawyer, but a trial lawyer—Johnny Cochran, or Racehorse Haynes. A real advocate.* But she didn't have one. Which put her in the awkward position of having to fall back on the truth.

It wasn't her fault, after all. On the contrary, she'd risked her life to go to work last week, and it had almost gotten her killed. And it wasn't as if she'd taken a lot of time off before her sister died. On the contrary, she'd worked sixty-hour weeks for nearly a year, with no vacation or sick-days, coming in on weekends and holidays. *Admittedly,* she'd blown the deposition, but hey—depositions could be rescheduled. At most, she'd inconvenienced people—for which she was sorry, but it wasn't as if she'd had any choice.

So it went, from 7 to 8 and 8 to 9, rehearsing her spiel through farmland, suburbs and, finally, the Beltway and city traffic—by which time, she had her story down pat.

Curtis Slough's house was a million-dollar pile in Spring Valley, an Edenic woodland in the heart of the city, just off Rock Creek Park. Adrienne had only been there once before, and that was on an errand, bringing Slough his briefcase from the office. She didn't remember the number, but there weren't that many homes in this most expensive of Washington subdivisions—and Slough's house was an eyeful that one didn't forget.

According to Jiri Kovac, who worked in the firm's L.A. office and came to Washington once a month for meetings, the house was a dead ringer for Marshall Tito's villa at Lake Bled. Three stories tall, with stucco walls and Palladian windows, it sat on a low rise behind boxwood hedges and a circular drive with a small fountain at its center. Parking behind Slough's 700-series Bimmer, Adrienne got out and crossed the driveway to the front door, feeling like a kid at the top of the drop on the Rebel Yell at King's Dominion.

Yikes, she thought, as she knocked softly on the hard, wooden door. *Maybe this isn't such a good idea, maybe—*

"Adrienne!" Slough appeared in the doorway—in brown cords and an olive sweater—with a look of emphatic surprise. "*What the . . . ?* Come on in—it's freezing out there!" Holding the door open, he let her in and led her down the hall to the living room, where a pair of wing chairs faced each other across a sprawling Chinese rug in front of a limestone fireplace. "Is everything all right? Hang on a minute, and I'll have Amorita bring us some coffee . . ."

She waited nervously, studying Slough's collection of Russian icons, until a pretty Latina came in with a silver tray and a coffee service. Adrienne poured herself a cup, and was sipping it when Slough returned, fastening his huge Breitling wristwatch.

"Whut up?" he asked, in a crazed attempt to be one of the boys (or something).

"Well, it's complicated," she told him, "but I think I'm going to need a leave of absence."

Slough dropped into a wing chair, and frowned. " 'A leave of . . .' Isn't this something we could talk about at the office?"

"Well," Adrienne replied, "that's the point. We really can't."

Slough's face contorted into a kind of skeptical and puzzled grimace. "What!?"

"I can't go there. If you'll let me explain . . ."

And so she did. She told the story as economically as possible, reprising her childhood in thirty seconds, then segueing into her sister's illness in Europe. Slough listened thoughtfully beneath furrowed brows, sipping his coffee and wincing sympathetically as Adrienne recounted the discovery of her sister's body. He was clearly fascinated. But lest he jump to the conclusion that she wanted time off to grieve (which, she knew, would be "unlawyerly"), she went on to recount her sister's sinister relationship to Duran, Bonilla's retainer, his subsequent murder, the skepticism of the police and . . . well, the whole nine yards, including the incident at the Comfort Inn and Duran's impending surgery. When she was done, she set her cup down and said, "So you see: I really need to stay away from work for a while. Because—I know how melodramatic it sounds, but—someone's trying to kill me."

Slough sat back in his chair, nodding his head and looking thoughtful. Finally, he set his cup and saucer down, leaned forward, and said, "So . . . you're shacked up with this guy?"

Adrienne's jaw dropped.

"Is that what you're saying?" Slough asked.

"No," she protested, "that's not it at all. That's—"

The lawyer grunted. "Let me explain something: I don't think there's a law firm in this town that's more considerate of the people who work for it than Slough, Hawley. If someone's going through the grieving process, we don't take a backseat to anyone: we'll cut you all the slack you need. But *this* . . . this goes *way* beyond 'slack.' The police? The 'Comfort Inn'? My God, woman—what's next? A trailer park?" Slough shook his head in a regretful and disbelieving way, then got to his feet.

"But," Adrienne began, "you don't understand—"

"Oh, I think I do," Slough told her. "Details aside, you're 'accident-prone.' " He wagged a finger at her to emphasize a point. "Not a good trait in a lawyer." He paused. "I've got some thinking to do," he told her, and clapped his hands, signaling the conversation was at an end.

And not just the conversation, she sensed. Despite herself, she was afraid she was going to cry. Fighting back the tears, she followed her boss to the front door, where he turned to her as he opened it.

"Maybe a leave of absence *is* a good idea," he suggested. "Take a little time to sort things out. Get your ducks in a row. After that . . . we'll see where we stand."

Adrienne nodded, sinking her eyeteeth into her lower lip, suppressing a tidal wave of candor with a burst of well-timed pain. "Thanks," she said, bathing him in a bright smile.

"I'll have Bette take over the asphalt brief. She's not the sharpest pin in the cushion, but . . . she's there. And right now, I'll settle for that."

Adrienne's dry eyes and smile survived to the end of the driveway, at which point she burst into tears. She'd worked so hard, for so long. And now, she was . . . *what?* What had he called it? *Beyond slack.*

Like someone dangling at the end of a rope.

She followed Rock Creek Park down to P Street, and exited into Georgetown. Parking in the lot next to Dean & DeLuca's, she stopped for a latte, drinking it at one of the little tables in the long, glass room that runs beside the grocery. As depressed as she was from the meeting with Slough—she was obviously not going to be at the firm next year—she was relieved to have it over with, and out of the way. Relieved, too, not to have to think about asphalt anymore, or covering for Curtis Slough. In fact, when you thought about it, maybe she was better off. There were other jobs, she told herself.

When she'd finished her coffee, she went inside and bought a bag of hardwood charcoal and a couple of strip steaks, which the butcher packed in ice. She stowed the groceries in the back of her car, and walked to her sister's apartment, two blocks away.

Ramon was standing in the foyer in his doorman's uniform, hands behind his back, rocking on his heels. Seeing Adrienne, he broke into a broad smile and held open the door. "Heyyy," he exclaimed, "it's good to see you. You come for the mail?"

She shook off the cold with a shiver, stamped her feet for warmth, and said, "That, and to clean up a little. How's Jacko?"

"Never better! And guess what? I 'followed my bliss.' Like Nikki said."

"She did?"

"Yeah. We had a talk—just before . . . what happened. And I took the part."

"What part?"

"In the Scorsese movie. I'm 'Doorman #2—Ramon Castro de Vega.' How 'bout that?"

"Wow!"

"So now, I'm thinking: maybe I'll do some community theater, y'know?"

"Why not?"

"Anyway . . . the mail's on the kitchen counter in the apartment. I put it there for you. You need the key?"

"No," Adrienne told him. "I've got one."

Ramon guided her to the elevator, pressed the button, and touched the brim of his hat. "I'll tell Jacko you were askin' after him!"

"I'd like that," she said.

And then she was upstairs, moving toward her sister's

apartment, thinking, *I have to do something about her ashes. I have to—*

As she entered the apartment, she was hit by a gust of grief that was as strong as it was unexpected. Maybe it was all the stress she'd been under, or maybe it was the apartment, with its dead plants and listless air. Whatever the source, the sadness hit her like a truck. Tears shot into her eyes for the second time that morning. Walking out to the balcony, she stood in the freezing cold and wept for Nikki, the high-rises across the river fracturing behind her sadness.

After a few minutes, she couldn't stand the cold any longer. Returning inside, she got down to business. The apartment was depressing; its untidiness seemed in some way disrespectful to Nikki. She was going to have to clean this up some day and she thought it might make her feel better to do it now. The refrigerator was a mess, reeking of sour milk and some fishy remains in Chinese take-out cartons. There were orange peels with puckered skins, and yogurt containers bristling with a sort of fur. She swept it all into a green garbage bag, and carried it out to the trash compactor in the hall. Then she went from room to room with a spray bottle of Fantastik and a roll of paper towels, wiping the dust from tables and counters. That done, she gritted her teeth and went into the bathroom—which the police had left a mess. Fingerprint powder was everywhere because, as the police had explained, until her sister's death was ruled a suicide, the crime scene had to be treated as if a murder had occurred.

The plants on the balcony were dead but Adrienne didn't have the energy to drag them to the trash room. So she did the next best thing, compacting them into a corner of the terrace, where they looked neat, at least.

Which left the gun. She'd been thinking a lot about the gun. If Nikki herself had bought it, where and when? Maybe it could be traced. There must be a serial number or something. Crossing the room to her sister's closet, she opened the door and reached inside for the lime-green carrying case.

But it wasn't there.

At first she thought she'd forgotten where it had been. Lifting the bed skirt on her sister's bed, she looked on the floor and saw . . . a tangle of dust bunnies and a couple of paperbacks. Getting back to her feet, she went into the hall and looked through the closet there, then into the living room and under the couches, searching everywhere. But it was gone. It was big and green and you couldn't miss it . . . and now it was gone.

Or what was more to the point: it was stolen. As much as she hated the idea of dealing with the gun, the notion that someone had come into Nikki's apartment and taken it . . . *that* gave her the creeps. It was like what happened in Duran's apartment, when Bonilla's body disappeared.

It made everything seem precarious and insubstantial, a kind of existential first draft subject to constant, but invisible amendment. It made her queasy to think about it, as if her mind—her *world*—was a staging area for someone else's possibilities.

Ramon reminded her about the mail (which in fact, she'd left upstairs), and then, when she came back down, waved her on her way. She thought about going to her own apartment, if only to pick up Nikki's ashes, but decided it was just too dangerous. In the end, she got back to Bethany just after six.

Duran was in a good mood. She told him about cleaning Nikki's apartment and the rifle's disappearance, but not about her meeting with Slough. She sent him to the supermarket for a prepackaged salad and some Paul Newman dressing. They cooked the steaks out back on a Weber Grill, and opened the bottle of Glass Mountain Cabernet that he'd bought earlier in the day.

He was in an expansive mood, looking forward to the answers that the operation must certainly provide. And he'd had an insight: for as long as he could remember, he'd felt uncomfortable whenever he left his apartment. He told her about the panic attacks that he'd suffered, and the agoraphobia he sometimes felt. "It's gone, now," he said. "It hasn't been there for days—not since we went to the Comfort Inn."

"And what do you think that's all about?" she asked.

He shook his head. "I don't know. But you saw all that stuff in the apartment next door, right?"

She nodded.

"Well," he asked, "what if that was having . . . I don't know . . . some kind of *effect* on me?"

She looked puzzled. "What do you mean?"

He shrugged. "I'm not sure. I just know that I feel a lot different. Better. More myself."

She nodded thoughtfully, but couldn't resist: "And that would be . . . ?"

Duran smiled. "Whomever."

She was in bed when she heard it, and it was amazing that she did. If the sea had not been so calm and flat, the sound of the surf would have masked it. But the night was breathless, the sea inert, and she was restless and half-awake, her mind at the races.

The sound that woke her—a faint but distinct metallic squeak—seemed to rise through the floorboards. And for some reason, it alarmed her. *Someone's under the bed,* she thought. But, no, that was crazy. Lying there in the dark, unmoving, yet straining to hear, she realized that the sound had come from farther away. *Someone's in the basement.*

Then a long time passed—a minute or two—when nothing could be heard. She'd almost decided that she was imagining things when, suddenly, she realized that someone was standing outside her bedroom door. How she knew this, she couldn't have said. There wasn't any sound. There was nothing with the light. It was just . . . a fact.

And then the door was opening. She kept her eyes closed, but she could feel the other person watching her. Duran? Had to be. And yet, it didn't *feel* like Duran. She'd just had dinner with him, and whatever else you might say about the guy, this wasn't his style at all. It was someone else. But who?

What seemed like a long time passed—though she had no way of knowing if it was one minute or five. She thought she heard another sound—not from the door, but from the basement again. Was she hallucinating? Maybe. Maybe not. Whatever . . . It was driving her crazy to stay so still. And yet . . . it was her only advantage—the secret that she was awake.

After a while, she slotted her eyes in a glance, fluttering her lashes in a semblance of REM sleep. The look revealed a slash of light where the door met the jamb, and a backlit shoulder. Then the door eased shut with a whispered *snickkk* and the light was gone.

And that was it. She could hear the sea, the listless thudding of the surf. She could even hear the distant thrum of traffic from the A-1, six blocks away. She listened for footsteps in the house, for sounds from the basement, for the sound of the front door closing. But there was nothing, just the white noise of the surf and distant traffic. She might just as easily have been in a sealed vault.

So she lay there, watching the minutes tick by on the luminous dial of her bedside clock. Finally, when six minutes had passed, she heard the faintest crunch of gravel from outside the window. Getting to her feet, she ran to the window, inserted a finger between the flexible slats of the blinds, and peered out toward the sound that she'd heard.

It was coming from up the block. Footsteps on the gravelly walk. The thunk of a car door. And an engine, growling to life. Straining her eyes to peer through the watery moonlight, she saw the glint of metal as a car ghosted around the corner of the alley and disappeared.

"D'you hear something?"

She turned like a dervish, startled to see Duran standing in the doorway to her bedroom. He was barefoot and looked sleepy, although she noticed that he was dressed.

"There was someone here," she said.

"In the house?"

"In the basement," she told him. "And then in the house. I think he was after the computer."

Duran nodded.

"Well?"

"What?"

"Did he *get* it?" What was the matter with him?

"I don't know. I'll take a look."

Then he gave her a sort of loopy grin—*Oh for chrissake,* she thought, *I'm in my underwear*—and went into the living room. She pulled on a pair of jeans and a sweater, as Duran called out, "It's right where it was—on the table!"

Coming into the living room, she saw that the house was as she'd left it when she went to bed. Nothing had been moved, or touched, as far as she could tell. Going to the window, she saw that the car was in its parking place, just as it had been. "Maybe I was mistaken," she said.

"I don't think so," he told her. "I heard something, too."

"I thought it was in the basement, but . . . now, I'm not sure."

They looked in all the rooms again, but nothing seemed to be disturbed—or even touched. Finally, Duran slipped into his shoes and grabbed a coat. Together, they went outside and around the house to the metal doors that gave access to the basement. "We might as well take a look," he said, and lifted one of the doors.

"That was the noise!" she whispered, as the doors opened with a distinct creak. "That's what woke me up."

"Hnnnh," he said.

She followed him down the steps into the darkness. At the bottom of the stairs, he began walking forward, waving his arms in search of the light cord that hung from the ceiling. Finding it, he snapped on the lights, and glanced around.

It was more of a cellar than a basement, with a spooky-looking crawl space angling off under the front porch. Aluminum-tube deck chairs with webbed seats were folded and stacked against one wall. Ropes, and a few garden tools hung from another, along with a selection of mildewed life jackets and beach toys.

"I don't see anything," she said.

"Me either." They walked past the furnace, then the water heater. The ceiling was so low that Duran had to duck, swags of cobwebs catching his hair. Peering into the crawl space, Duran cocked his head, and reached out to put a hand on her arm.

"What?" she asked.

"Do you smell gas?"

"I'm kind of stuffed up," she told him. "All the dust at Nikki's."

Duran grunted. "I think it's gas," he said. And a few seconds later. "It *is* gas."

"Let's call the real estate agent," she suggested, turning toward the door. "Gas scares me. They should fix it."

Irritated, she pulled sharply on the light cord and started up the steps.

"Hey!" Duran called out. "Wait up! I can't see a thing."

She apologized with a giggle. "I thought you were right behind me." Turning, she swung her arm through the air, hoping to hit the light cord. It was amazing how elusive the damn things were. Then she found it, and yanked.

He was standing there with a thoughtful squint, as if he were about to sneeze. "Wait a second," he said, his voice low and urgent. "Turn it off."

"What?"

"Just turn it off!"

She did, this time taking care to keep the cord in her grasp.

"That's weird," Duran said, his voice loud in the darkness. "There's like a . . . *glow* . . . coming from the crawl space. Turn the light back on."

She did and crossed the cellar to the corner where he was standing. He was in a crouch, leaning on a concrete abutment, looking into the crawl space. Her eyes followed his gaze.

And then she saw what he saw: a votive candle, flickering in the darkness.

Neither of them knew what to say. So they stared, and watched as the candle's flame seemed to change and grow brighter, lengthening into an elongated blue pillar, the orange wick glowing within. And then the flame evaporated and it was just the glowing wick. Duran grabbed her by the arm and, straightening, yanked her toward the basement doors. The ferocity of his grip scared her and, for a moment, she remembered the night before, when he'd seized her wrist and wrestled the plastic overlay out of her hand. Only now, he was even more violent, pulling her toward the door.

"Hey," she said, "wait a minute!"

Her feet were scrabbling for purchase, more or less bouncing up the cement steps, her ankles and shins barking painfully on the edges. Then they were out in the air, and he was hustling her down the alley toward the ocean, moving so fast that she was barely in contact with the ground.

That's when the sound came—a rolling growl that exploded into a concussive *whummmmp*, followed by a pressure drop that made her ears pop. Then the air behind them dissolved into a cloud of fiery foam, ballooning outwards. Now, she was running on her own, the heat surging at her back. Not till they reached the beach did it seem safe to stop. Turning, they saw a column of fire roaring through the roof of the house.

"But . . . how did you know?" she asked.

"You saw the light . . . the candle . . . get brighter—right?" She nodded.

"Propane's heavier than air, so it lays on the floor, and it just sorta . . . builds up. They had the candle up in the elevated crawl space, so when the gas reached the flame, a lot of it had accumulated. You saw how the flame went out; that's because there was no oxygen left. It was all gas. We were lucky."

Duran's attention was reclaimed by the house. There were new sounds now, sharp cracks as the windows exploded, the shriek of metal coming apart in the heat. Every once in a while, a fresh roar told them that the fire had discovered new territory, new fuel. Then they heard an enormous siren wail, summoning the volunteer firefighters.

Adrienne started to shiver, from cold or shock, she couldn't be sure. *They tried to kill us both,* she thought. *They turned on the gas, and shut off the pilot light. Or something.* A column of sparks blasted into the air. *Then they lighted a candle, as if it were a mass. That's what I heard,* she thought, *the noise in the cellar. And then they checked—they checked to make sure I was there.*

"They tried to kill us," she said, her voice dull, her face flushed from the fire.

Duran nodded.

He put his arm around her and, together, they walked back toward the house. There were sirens all over town now, wailing closer. Suddenly, Duran tensed, stopped, and slapped his hips. Then he smiled with relief. "Car keys," he said.

It was getting hotter now. In the intervals between the houses, they could see the first fire truck roaring down the street, siren screaming, lights whirling. The sky fluttered with the wheeling lights—yellow, red, yellow, red. They walked past a man whose pajama bottoms were visible below the puffy parka he wore. He stood with his arm around a woman in a bathrobe and furry slippers. They were staring at the house as Adrienne and Duran walked by. "Like a torch," the man said, his voice hushed. Then a part of the roof collapsed, falling into the house with a soft thud that sent up geysers of fire and sparks.

Duran unlocked the door to the car, and flicked the button inside. Adrienne heard the snap of the locks as she stood there, staring at what was now an architectural skeleton, with flames dancing along its blackened ribs. The temperature must have been 130 degrees on one side of the street, and 35 on the other.

Duran got out and came around to open the door for her, his feet crunching in the gravel. As he reached for the door's handle, he cursed and yanked his hand away. "Slide in the driver's side," he told her. "The door's like an oven."

As they drove away, she turned in the seat, and said, "I think the police station's somewhere around the water tower."

"We're not going there," he told her.

She looked at him as if he were insane (which, of course, was a theory). "We have to," she insisted. "We can't just keep running around—"

"It's better we don't go there," he said, turning onto the highway out of town.

"Why?"

"Because we're better off dead."

She turned her head, and looked at his reflection in the window. "What do you mean?" she asked.

"I mean, if they think they killed us, that's good. We'll live longer that way."

29 "It won't work," she announced.

"What won't?"

"Playing dead."

Duran adjusted the rearview mirror, dimming the sunrise. "Why not?"

"Because the car's gone. Which suggests we weren't in the house. And the newspapers will say no one was killed."

Duran shrugged. "At least it gives us a day."

Another couple of miles rolled by, and Adrienne turned to Duran. "So let's go to Washington," she said.

"Why?"

"Because we have time, and because I want to go to my apartment. Get some things."

He gave her a skeptical look.

"You *said* it gave us a day."

"Yeah, but . . . what if I'm wrong? I mean, I don't even know how they found us in the first place."

"I do," Adrienne told him.

Duran gave her a suspicious look. "You do? How?"

"You told them."

"I what? Told who?"

"You told them where we were," she said. "You were on-line . . . in a chat room or something."

Duran glanced at her, to see if she was kidding. But she wasn't. She was dead serious. "What are you talking about?" he asked.

"The night before last. You scared the hell out of me."

"I *did*?"

"You were on some crazy Web site. All these images were flashing by, and then . . . it was like one of those instant messages on AOL."

"What!?"

"Trust me."

"So . . . what did it say?"

It was her turn to shrug. "I don't know: good morning, or something."

"That's *it*?"

She shook her head. "No. It said: 'Hello Jeffrey.' Then it asked where you were. And you typed something."

"What did I type?"

"I don't know. It didn't come up on the screen. But they asked, and you answered. You could have given them the zip code and parking directions, for all I know."

"Get out!"

"I'm serious," she insisted.

"Why didn't you stop me?"

"I tried! And it was like . . . I don't know. It was like you were gone. *Way* gone. I had to call Doctor Shaw."

"What?!"

"I was afraid of you! So he hypnotized you over the phone," she told him. "You don't remember this?"

Duran shook his head, thinking, *It didn't happen. Or I'd remember it. Because my short-term memory is fine. Shaw said so. Which means Adrienne's lying or . . . there's more than one me. Jekyll and Hyde. MPD. Christ—* The dashboard emitted a warning beep, and his eyes went to the gas gauge. "We have to stop," he told her.

They found a Gas 'N Stuff somewhere near Bridgeville but couldn't get the pump to accept Duran's MasterCard. Duran turned to Adrienne for help, which made her blanch because "My purse was in the house! I don't have a dime!"

He called the 800 number on the back of his credit card, punched in the account number, and hit the voice-mail option that was supposed to inform him of the card's "available credit." Instead, a recorded voice told him that his account had been "frozen," and that he should stay on the line for a "customer service" representative. He did, and was told that his card had been reported stolen. "We'll have a new one to you in . . . maybe two or three working days. It's in the pipeline."

Duran couldn't believe it. "Look," he said, "I have the card, right here. It's in *my hand*. I didn't report it stolen."

"Someone did."

"Ask me my mother's maiden name."

"That's not something—"

"You've got validating questions. Use them!"

"I'm sorry, Mr. Duran, but once a card is reported stolen, a new one has to be issued."

"Look. I've got like—" He glanced in his wallet. "Two bucks on me. I'm outta town. I'm outta gas. Isn't there any way—"

"No."

"What?"

"I'm sorry—there's nothing we can do. You'll just have to wait for the new one."

Returning to the car, Duran pumped $2.28 worth of gas,

and explained to Adrienne what had happened. "The bank fucked up," he told her.

She shook her head. "It doesn't sound like it. That's what they do when someone reports a stolen card."

"Yeah, but—"

"I wonder who did it . . ."

The way she said it, it almost sounded as if she thought he'd done it himself. And maybe he had.

They got as far as the Beltway before the dashboard beeped a second time, and the fuel light snapped on. Adrienne directed Duran along a complex route that took them past the Capitol, and up 16th St. They were less than a mile from her apartment when the car began to lurch, and the engine died. With the help of a couple of Latinos who were waiting for a bus, they pushed the Dodge into a loading zone on the edge of Meridian Hill Park.

"What happened to your car, man? You smash it up and then drive through a fire?"

The trunk, dented from the Comfort Inn parking lot collision, was something Adrienne was already obsessing about. She'd heard it could be a real hassle when you dented a rental car. She didn't like to lie, but she'd told Duran that under no circumstances should he admit that he was driving. That could really tangle things up.

Now she followed Duran around to the passenger side, where his new friends were shaking their heads over the paint job. Which was . . . puckered.

"Son of a bitch!" Duran muttered.

"You need some bodywork, my friend." The Latino began to fish through his pockets. "Let me give you my card—I give you a good price."

"It's a rental," Adrienne moaned.

"For real?" the first guy said, shaking his head. "Oh, man. They going to *bleed* you." Both men ran their fingers over the car door, and shook their heads sadly.

Adrienne was writing out a note, which she stuck under the

windshield wiper. Stood back. Repositioned it. Said: "They'll give me a ticket anyway."

The Latinos chuckled. "They gonna tow your ass."

Duran had to work to keep up with Adrienne's quick march to her apartment. Fearful of a ticket or, worse, a tow truck, she was almost jogging. In the end, they covered the mile in about twelve minutes.

Wearing a bibbed apron and a faint look of alarm, Mrs. Spears let them in. "Adrienne! Where have you been?" she asked.

"I lost my key. Can I get in through the laundry room?"

"Of course," the landlady replied, with a hopeful look at Duran.

"Oh, I'm sorry. Jeff—this is Mrs. Spears."

"Would you like a cup of tea?" she asked.

"No, thanks," Duran said.

"We're in a hurry," Adrienne confided, moving down the hall to a door that gave way to a flight of stairs leading down to the basement. With Adrienne in the lead, the two of them passed through a small storage room on their way to her apartment. Opening the door, she stopped so abruptly that Duran almost walked into her. "Jesus!"

She'd forgotten how bad it was. The room was a sea of detritus, with Adrienne's belongings scattered everywhere: books, videos, couch cushions, clothing and CDs, shoes, blankets, towels, vases. And on top of it all, like whitecaps, were hundreds of pieces of paper.

Muttering to herself, she picked her way past some broken dishware, pots and pans, moving toward a door on the other side of the room. It was stuck, at first, but she put her shoulder into it and squeezed through while Duran remained where he was, gazing around the room, curious about Adrienne's world.

Which, despite the mess, had so much more texture than his own. There were romantic posters of long ago places and faraway things (Biarritz and the Orient Express), and a series of TinTin covers, matted and framed. Stooping, he picked up a book, and was surprised by its subject: Lonely Planet's guide to *Sri Lanka*. He picked up another: *Trekking in Turkey*. And a third: *Mauritius, Reunion, and the Seychelles*.

"You travel a lot?" he asked.

"No," she replied, emerging from the other room. "I never go anywhere."

Duran pondered that as she stutter stepped through the debris of her living room. "Why not?" he asked.

"No money." She paused. "Do you see a music box?"

He glanced around, and shook his head.

"What about you?" she asked.

"What *about* me?" Duran replied.

"Do you travel a lot? Have you been a lot of places?"

He thought about it. "Yeah. I think so."

"Where?"

He shrugged. "I don't know."

She crossed the room to a small desk and, reaching beneath it, extracted an inlaid wooden box that had fallen to the floor. "Plaisir d'Amour" began to play as she opened its cover and removed two credit cards and a passport. "Voila!"

"Are we going somewhere?" he asked.

"It's the only ID I've got," she told him. "Everything else went up in smoke."

She surveyed the mess. She'd thought they might spend a couple of hours cleaning it up, but it was hopeless. Overwhelming. It was going to take a week. But she'd have plenty of time to get into it when all this was over, she reminded herself, because she no longer had a job. She unearthed a few wearable items from the heaps, and snagged her Mason Pearson brush from the bathroom.

She led Duran out the back door, avoiding Mrs. Spears. Together, they walked through the alley to Mount Pleasant Avenue, where they bought a gallon of gas at Motores Sabrosa—only to find a pink ticket waiting for them when they got back to the Dodge.

"Another hundred bucks," Adrienne wailed. "That's hor-

rible!" She stamped her foot, which made Duran laugh—
which made her even madder. "What does it mean," she demanded as she got into the car, "when the only thing this
fucking city's good at is parking enforcement?"

Duran shook his head. "It's probably the end of civilization
as we know it."

The operation was scheduled for eight A.M. the following
morning, so Duran spent the night at Columbia Presbyterian
Hospital, leaving Adrienne to cool her heels in the Mayflower
Hotel.

Arriving on the neurosurgery ward, Duran was turned over
to an admissions nurse, who fitted him out with hospital pa-
jamas and a robe. A plastic band was affixed to his wrist, and
he was taken to a semiprivate room at the end of the corridor.
Nurses bustled in and out, taking his vital signs on what
seemed like an hourly basis, while his roommate (a much-
intubated man) lay comatose and staring.

In the evening, Shaw stopped by with the neurosurgeon,
Nick Allalin, a rabbity man with a pinkish nose, large teeth,
and a high-pitched voice.

Shaw introduced the two of them, and Duran noticed that
Allalin's hands were amazingly white, as if, when not in use,
they were kept in a box. They were the long and muscular fingers of a pianist, immaculate, and perfectly manicured. Designer hands.

The procedure was explained to him for the second time.
"Doctor Shaw will make a small incision in your upper gum,
just under the nose. Then he'll tunnel back through the nasal
passages to the sphenoid cavity. At that point, he becomes an
observer. I'll be sitting in a special chair," Allalin said, "next
to the table, working a surgical microscope with my foot, so I
can see what I'm doing with my hands in close-up—on a
monitor. The object is embedded in the hippocampus, and
we'll take it out."

"How long will it take?" Duran asked.

"Thirty or forty minutes." He paused, and then went on.

"You'll be sitting up, with your head back, for most of the operation—and semiconscious."

Duran blanched, and Shaw smiled. "You won't feel anything," the psychiatrist assured him. "Some discomfort the day after, but that's about all."

"One thing I wanted to ask you about," Allalin remarked, "is your previous surgery. What can you tell us about it?"

"I'm not sure what you mean," Duran replied.

The neurosurgeon frowned. "This isn't your first time," he told him. "The scar's right there, under your lip." Leaning over, he took Duran's upper lip in his fingers, and rolled it back for Shaw to see. When Shaw nodded, he let go.

Duran worked his lips. Finally, he said, "I think if I'd had brain surgery, I'd remember it."

Shaw nodded. "Of course you would—unless you're suffering from amnesia—"

"Which I seem to be."

"Indeed."

Shaw gave him another consent form to sign, then left with Allalin when Adrienne called to see how things were going.

It wasn't much of a conversation. The Valium he'd been given kicked in right after the first hello. And yet, when he hung up, ten or twenty minutes later, it seemed to Duran that he'd heard something in her voice, something that sounded a lot like concern—concern for him. Could it be?

Nah.

In the morning, precisely at eight, a male nurse wheeled him down the corridor to the O/R, where he was intubated and given a series of injections that left him in a state of limp and indifferent paralysis. The operation began some ten minutes later, and proceeded, as nearly as Duran could tell, exactly as Allalin had described.

Most of the time, he kept his eyes closed, listening in a disinterested way to the underwater voices of the surgeons, the rhythmic symphony of the various machines. He couldn't feel anything, but sensed the movement of those around him, the change in the light as Allalin leaned in, or moved away.

He heard clinks and dinks, instruments being picked up and put down on metal trays. At times, their words seemed to turn into nonsense syllables and he couldn't understand what they were saying.

At one point, Shaw seemed to say, "Radashay at the semaphore," and Allalin replied, "Dirapsian snide."

Once or twice, he opened his eyes, and when he did, the lights in the O/R starred and shimmered. It was almost beautiful, the way it all pulsed in time with the blurred symphony of machine sound.

And then, quite clearly, Allalin announced, "Got it!"

Someone heaved a massive sigh.

And then he heard Shaw say, "Jesus! What the hell *is* that thing?"

Doctor Allalin's face swam slowly into focus, fell apart into bands of light, and regained its form. Duran could see his mouth moving in an exaggerated way, but it seemed as if the sound took a long time to arrive.

"Effff." Like the letter of the alphabet. Duran was tempted to continue with the exercise: "Geeee, Aitch, Eye." But his mouth was too dry. Then he realized what the doctor was saying: Jeff.

"Wha?" It was as if he had a mouth full of toothpaste.

"At least he's vocalizing," Allalin said with an air of relief. He leaned over Duran again, his rabbitlike face slightly foreshortened—he was so close.

"Tell me, Jeff. What is your last name?"

Duran thought about it. He remembered he was in a hospital, remembered he'd had surgery. The surgery must be over. And he was all right. Neither dead, nor blind—nor a vegetable.

"Jeff?" The voice was patient, high-pitched. "Tell me. Do you remember your last name?"

Duran nodded.

"What's your last name, Jeff?"

"D'ran."

Suddenly, Adrienne was by his side, saying, "Hey, guy . . ." He felt her hand take his, and give it a squeeze.

Doctor Shaw said, "I owe you one, Nick—that was damned good!"

Duran lay where he was, with Adrienne holding his hand, listening to the doctors chat. Allalin said, "Keep me posted. I'll be very interested to know what Materials has to say."

"Count on it," Shaw replied.

Duran tried to shift himself into a sitting position, but everything in his visual field swayed, then slewed off to the left. He closed his eyes, and grabbed the sides of the bed.

"Hey," Shaw said. "Take it easy. You had brain surgery this morning."

Duran felt for Adrienne's hand, found it, and closed his own around it. "What was it?" he asked.

"You mean, in your head?"

"Yeah."

"It's going to take a while," Shaw replied.

"What do you mean?"

"He means it's being analyzed," Adrienne told him. "They sent it out to have it studied."

"Studied?" Duran asked.

"Let me tell you what I *thought* we'd find," Shaw suggested.

"Okay."

"I was guessing a surgical staple—something like that. Especially after we saw you'd had the operation before— or something like it. And if it wasn't that, I thought it might have been a bullet fragment, or debris from an automobile accident. Something that was overlooked in the initial extraction."

"And?" Duran asked.

"It's something else," Adrienne said.

Duran glanced from Adrienne to the doctor. "What?" he asked.

Shaw pursed his lips in a moue. "We don't know." When

Duran began to protest, Shaw overrode him. "What we *do* know is that it didn't get there by accident."

Duran frowned, his eyes following Shaw as he walked over to the window. "What do you mean?"

"I mean, it's an implant."

"*What?* What for?" Once again, Duran struggled to sit up, but failed.

"Ahhh, now *that—that* is the question. When Nick took it out, I thought it was a piece of glass—because that's what it looks like. Then we looked at it under a microscope . . ."

"And? "

"It's something else," Shaw said. "It has some kind of wires in it. It's some kind of micro-device."

Duran moaned.

"We've sent it out to the Applied Materials Laboratory," Shaw told him. "They have a biomedical component—"

"Are you telling me you took something out of my head, and you don't have a clue what it is?"

Shaw smiled. "No, that's not what I'm saying. I know what it is: it's an intercerebral implant. The question is: what does it do? For the moment, at least, its purpose is obscure."

"When you say it's obscure," Adrienne asked, "what are we talking about? I mean, what are the possibilities?"

"To be honest?" Shaw replied. "Aside from some very pre-liminary animal work on Parkinson's, the only implants that *I'm* familiar with have been used to control seizures—severe seizures."

"And that's what you think I have?" Duran asked.

"On the contrary. I haven't seen any evidence of that at all."

They were silent for a moment. Then Duran asked: "How long before we hear back?"

"Three or four days," Shaw replied.

"Will I be walking by then?"

Shaw chuckled. "You'll be *out* by then."

"You're kidding," Adrienne said.

The psychiatrist shook his head. "Not at all."

"Well, that's good news," Duran told him.

"Don't thank me—thank managed-care." Shaw smiled. "And in the meantime, I'll be very interested to know if that . . . object . . . had anything to do with your amnesia. Given its location, it may well have." His eyes glowed. "What I'm hoping, obviously, is that you'll start remembering quite a lot. We'll have some sessions. If you're up to it, we can begin tomorrow."

After the operation, Duran realized that he was living with a sense of elation that was as real as it was difficult to describe. He was lighter, somehow, as if he'd been subject to a gravitational field that had only now begun to subside.

He slept for twelve hours the first day, tried to watch television, but didn't feel like it—then slept some more. Adrienne called from the Mayflower to ask how he was feeling, and to tell him that she'd found a cheap parking lot, way over on the West side, "only fifteen blocks from the hotel."

On the morning of the second day, one of the residents subjected him to a battery of tests and quizzes, calculated to measure various aspects of neural function—touch, taste, smell, and vision. His recall rate was assessed, as were his motor skills and sequential memories. He took the Bender gestalt test and, when he was done, the resident suggested that he walk the halls.

"No *jogging*," he joked, "just take it slow. If you get dizzy—sit down. Otherwise . . . keep moving—it's good for you."

After lunch, Shaw came to the hospital for "a little regression work," and to ask how he was doing.

Duran told him that he felt as if a weight had been lifted from his shoulders, but that he was disappointed that his memory hadn't returned.

"Doesn't work that way," Shaw told him. "Even with something more basic—blindness, for example—once the stimuli return, it often takes a while for the patient to resolve them in a meaningful way. Someone who's been blind from birth—restore his vision and, chances are, he'll be bumping into walls for the first time in years. Why? Because he's adjusted to being blind. He's found a reliable way to cope with it. So if you take his blindness away, what's left is a riot of light and color that means nothing to him. The point being that it takes a while to learn how to *process* things. In your case, though we haven't identified the trauma, you've obviously worked out a way of getting along in the world, substituting this 'Jeffrey Duran' identity for your own. Since we haven't tried to disturb this particular perceptual filter, it makes sense that it's going to persist until it's weakened."

"And how's that going to happen?"

"Well, we'll do some hypnosis work, try to regress you with guided imagery—see what we get. We know *a few* things about you. Adrienne says you like chess, and . . . I gather the Caribbean has some meaning to you, and . . . you seem to know how to sail a boat."

Duran smiled. "I've got a good idea," he suggested, "why don't we charter a sloop, and play a few games on our way down to Jamaica?"

Shaw chuckled. "Don't tempt me."

Two hours later, Shaw sat back in his chair in one of the consultation rooms at the end of the hall. It was a clean and pleasant space, not at all hospital-like, with track lights, museum posters, and upholstered furniture set around a chrome coffee table.

The psychiatrist crossed an ankle over his knee and found Duran's eyes. "I know you're disappointed," he told him, "but I think we made some progress."

"What? I remember sailing? I remembered that before."

Shaw swung his head to the side. "No you didn't. Not like this. You didn't remember sailing in a regatta. You didn't remember that you'd *raced*. Which means you were a competitive sailor, at some point. Probably—given your age—when you were a student. That gives us something to work with."

Duran frowned. "Like what?"

"It seems likely you lived near water, at one time or another. Maybe went to a school that had a sailing team."

" 'Maybe,' " Duran said. "Then, again . . ."

"Give it a chance," Shaw said. "With most amnesiacs, memories don't come back all at once. They surface in a piecemeal way and often, quite slowly. It's typical that the memory of the traumatic event—a car crash or whatever it was that triggered the amnesia—which you'd think would be particularly memorable, will be the last thing to come back. If it comes back at all."

"Sometimes it doesn't?"

"Quite often. Quite often that particular memory— since it has few associations and isn't chunked with other recollections—well, it's just gone."

"Really."

"So don't be discouraged. The truth is, you're suffering from as extreme a dissociative state as I have ever encountered. To cope with that, you've reinvented yourself. Now the task is to get you back to who you really are. This will bring you face-to-face with a lot of the trauma you've repressed. It's not going to be easy. I can tell that, already."

"What do you mean?" Duran asked.

"I'm getting a lot of resistance—deep resistance. Even in a trance, you're constantly dancing away from anything that might connect you to your real past. The resistance is profound."

"Why would that be?"

Shaw smiled, his eyes kind and reassuring. "Something happened to you. Something your mind can't accept. Maybe there was a sailing accident, and someone you loved drowned. Perhaps you felt responsible. Perhaps you *were* responsible." The psychiatrist paused. "It's just a possibility," he added. "Who knows?" He paused a second time. "We'll try another tack tomorrow."

After dinner, Duran walked the halls for a while, and talked to Adrienne by telephone. Then he sat down with a copy of *Sail* that Shaw had left for him. It was strange. The beauty of the boats was a delight, but occasionally, his eye would fall on something in the background—a swatch of landscape or the figure of a person hiking out—and it would be as if the sun were sliding behind a cloud. A low and anxious feeling would come over him, and . . .

He tossed the magazine aside, and snapped on the television.

Fresh from the shower after a long, cold run in the park, Adrienne toweled off and put on her underwear. Then she slipped into a skirt and sweater, and made herself a cup of coffee in the little kitchenette beside the door. Moving to the desk in front of the window, she looked out upon a construction site that was even deeper than it was wide. Finally, she sipped her coffee, and began to sort through her sister's mail.

She'd almost forgotten about it. Bound with a thick rubber band, it had been sitting in the backseat of the Dodge for days. Now, it was time to take a look.

The first envelope she opened was from the bank. There were shrunken photocopies of Nikki's bank statements and checks, which turned out to be less interesting than Adrienne had hoped. Nikki lived on about $4,500 bucks a month—give or take $500, one way or the other. Every once in a while, every few months, there was another deposit, also by wire transfer: three grand this September, for instance, and almost $8,000 back in February. The statement did not identify the source of the money, which led Adrienne to make a note on the Mayflower's stationery: *Transfer—$ from where?*

It was a minor mystery, at best, since Adrienne was pretty sure that she knew where the money came from: the settlement her sister had made with the Riedles. Bonilla had mentioned a bank in the Channel Islands. In fact, he was going to fax her the specifics about the bank sending funds to Nikki's account in the States. The European account might be nothing more than a convenience, or it might contain the bulk of Nikki's settlement with the Riedles. In either case, it was a clue to Nikki's past. Unfortunately, Bonilla never got the chance to follow through on his promise. Adrienne made a note: *Query Riggs.*

The checks were more or less transparent. Rent and utilities accounted for more than two grand. Duran's fees took another big bite. There was forty-seven dollars a month to the cable company, a couple of checks to the vet. Payments to Visa, and checks to Harlow's (Nikki's hair salon).

So much for the checks.

The next envelope was from Chevy Chase Bank, which was the issuer of Nikki's Visa card. Curious, she scanned the transactions, trying to make sense of them—which wasn't hard. Marvellous Market: $19.37. Safeway: $61.53. America Online: $19.95. Amtrak: $189.60. Blockbuster—

Huh?

The Amtrak entry didn't say where she'd gone, but subsequent charges made it obvious: Hertz (Orlando): $653.69. La Resort at Longboat Key: $1,084.06. Tommy Bahama's @ St. Armand's Circle: $72.91. Moe's Stone Crab: $18.94. She looked at the dates.

Conch House Eat Place	*10-08*	$ 21.03
Sarasota Sunglasses:	*10-09*	226.05

All of the Florida transactions, or what looked like Florida transactions, were in the same time period, October 7 and October 12. About a week or two before Nikki died.

Which made sense. This was when Nikki had taken Jacko to the kennel. Dimly, she remembered Duran telling her that her sister had missed an appointment about a week before her suicide, and that the last time he'd seen her, she had been tan. And not just tan, she said she'd been at the *beach*. Some beach. A beach whose name her sister didn't remember, or wouldn't say.

But there it was: Longboat Key. Which was—where?

Adrienne was excited now, but frustrated, too, because Nikki's laptop had gone up in smoke with the house in Bethany Beach. If she had a computer, she could look it up—and not just the place, but La Resort, too. Maybe the Mayflower rented laptops—but, no. A phone call to the front desk elicited an apology, and the information that the easiest thing to do would be to go to Kinko's. There was one just up the street, about two blocks away.

A moonlighting college kid took her credit card, and signed her on to AOL. She put *Longboat Key* into the Lycos search engine and hit *Return*. Seconds later, she was looking at an aerial photograph of an eleven-mile long barrier island off the coast of Florida. Switching to a map, she saw that the island was about an hour south of Tampa, and connected to Sarasota by a causeway.

Which raised the question: *what was Nikki doing there?* Did she have a boyfriend? Maybe, but if she did, you'd think that she'd have mentioned it. What, then? What was important enough to make Nikki put Jacko in a kennel—which Adrienne happened to know her sister thought of as a "dog jail"—and then take a train all the way to Florida. And why a train? She wasn't afraid to fly.

She tapped her foot. Thought about it.

Oprah. She'd go to Florida to audition for Oprah ("The Devil made me do it!"). But wouldn't Oprah buy the tickets, and wouldn't they be plane tickets? And wasn't Oprah in Chicago, anyway?

What, then?

The truth was there was only one thing that had interested Nikki in the past year, and that was Satanic Abuse. It was all she talked about. So . . . maybe there'd been a conference of some kind. A conference for "survivors."

She decided to try Nexis, recalling the Slough, Hawley's user-ID and password. When the search screen came up, she entered *Longboat Key*—and *satanic* and limited the search to the past year. The computer digested the information, and came back with . . . absolutely nothing. No stories. So she revised the search words, substituting *recovered and memory* for *satanic*.

This time, six documents were listed. But five of them turned out to be variations on a story about a conference on Marine Ecology. The conference had been held at the

Holiday Inn on Longboat Key over the weekend of October 9.
And at that conference, a great deal of time seemed to have
been spent discussing how well the manatee population had
recovered from its decimation by red tide, and how the
memory of that event was still fresh in the minds of marine biologists. The remaining article concerned stolen cars that the
Longboat Key police department had *recovered* with the help
of *memory* chips.

She tried a new search, this time deleting the words
memory and recovered. Maybe if she just found out what had
been going on at Longboat Key from October 7 to the 12th,
she could take it from there. Connect the dots.

Her new search yielded ninety-eight stories. She looked
through the KWIK cites, which listed the headline, the name
of the newspaper it appeared in, the date, and the byline.
Most of the pieces were useless—announcements of Wine
Fests, gallery openings, tennis tourneys and golf matches.
But there was one story that was different from all the
others, and it almost stopped her heart when she saw the
headlines:

RESORT SHOOTING
BAFFLES POLICE

   WHEELCHAIR MURDER
   SHOCKS VISITORS

      SNIPER VICTIM
      WAS PROMINENT,
      LONGTIME RESIDENT

Now she knew why her sister had taken the train. You can
pack a rifle on the train . . . She pulled down the text of a
story published October 11 in the Tampa paper.

 *Longtime resident Calvin F. Crane was shot to death
yesterday evening as he sat in his wheelchair on the
boardwalk at La Resort, watching the sunset.*
 According to police, Crane, 82, was killed by a high-

*powered—and apparently silenced—rifle. The shot, which
severed the elderly man's spine, is believed to have been
fired from one of the high-rises overlooking the beach.*

*Crane was pronounced dead on arrival at Sisters of
Mercy Memorial Hospital.*

*Sources close to the police called the crime a baffling
one. "The man was dying of cancer," the sources said.
"Doctors gave him a year to live at the outside."*

*Crane's Jamaican nurse, Leviticus Benn, was ques-
tioned by the police, and released.*

Adrienne read on, scanning the stories, galvanized by the
words "sniper" and "high-powered rifle." According to the
newspapers, the Jamaican caretaker had not realized that his
charge had been shot—until someone screamed, and he saw
the blood. "I didn't hear a thing," he told police, "or see anyone
with a gun." Neither, it seemed, had anyone else, which led the
police to suspect that the killer had used a "suppressor." Adrienne remembered the fat black tube in the lime-green case
under her sister's bed.

Complicating the investigation was the fact that the caretaker had wheeled Crane from the beach to the pool area before he realized that his charge had been shot. The fact that
the victim had been moved made establishing his location at
the time of the shooting difficult, which in turn made it impossible to reconstruct with any accuracy the trajectory of the
bullet. Because of this, determining the position from which
the sniper fired was "nothing but a guessing game," according to police.

Adrienne read the stories about the shooting, and searched
for follow-up articles, hoping against hope that the case had
been solved. But, of course, it hadn't. Two weeks after the
murder, the police had no motive, no suspects, no useful witnesses, and no weapon. They were mystified.

As was Adrienne. It seemed obvious that her sister was involved, maybe even responsible—but *why*?

Sitting back in the plastic chair that she'd been given, she looked up at the fluorescent lights, and stretched. She wasn't a cop. She didn't know how to run a murder investigation. But she knew that most investigations were as much about the victim as the perpetrator. Moreover, in this particular case, she had a distinct advantage over the police: that is, she had a good idea who the killer was.

But who was the victim? Who was he really? All she knew for certain was that her sister had traveled a thousand miles to kill him—and that he was, by all accounts, a dying old man with a fondness for sunsets. How had the headline described him? As "a prominent longtime resident."

Or . . . no. That wasn't it. Not quite.

She went back to the first story, and saw at a glance that the headline had a comma in it. "Sniper Victim Was Prominent, Longtime Resident." Which is to say, he was prominent, *and* a longtime resident. Not just some old guy that everyone knew.

Okay, she thought, turning back to the computer. How prominent? Why prominent?

30 Shaw and Duran sat across from one another in the staff cafeteria at Columbia Presbyterian, ignoring the clatter of trays and silverware, the to-and-fro of nurses and physicians all around them. Cutouts of cardboard turkeys decorated the walls. It was Thanksgiving.

Shaw wore a puzzled expression as he looked at Duran over a bowl of Pritikin noodle soup. Finally, the doctor crossed his arms in front of his chest, and confessed, "I'm not sure how to proceed." He paused. "What I'm getting is an *increased*, rather than a decreased, tendency toward dissociation."

"Really?" Duran asked. In the wake of the operation, he felt peculiarly alert—as if he'd been seeing the world through beige-tinted eyeglasses, and living under sedation.

Now, that feeling was gone. And while the thrill of well-being had begun to fade, his clarity of mind had not. Everything seemed bigger and brighter, the colors more intense, the sounds louder and more precise.

Shaw pressed his fingers together, as if in prayer. Then he leaned forward, and confided, "I'd like to try sodium pentathol."

Duran looked surprised. "Truth serum?"

Shaw shrugged. "A small dose. I don't know what else to do, though I suppose we could always just . . . wait. As it is, I'm not getting anywhere. You're blocking."

"What do you mean?"

"I can't get in. You're like a black box. Every time I try to explore your past, I come up against a *wall*. And I can't, for the life of me, figure out why."

"And you think sodium pentathol—"

"Will help? Yes, I do."

Duran thought about it. "How can you be sure that what you're seeing is 'resistance,' rather than organic damage?"

"Because we've done our homework," Shaw told him. "There's no evidence of brain damage—none at all. What we're dealing with is a pathological aversion."

"To . . . ?"

"Your *identity*."

Duran sipped his soup, and thought it over. Then he leaned forward, and said, "So what you're saying is, I've got the psychiatric equivalent of an autoimmune disease."

Shaw blinked. Laughed. "Exactly. But that's not the only thing that's bothering me." He paused. "You're becoming depressed." Before Duran could deny the diagnosis, the psychiatrist hurried on. "Now, depression isn't all that unusual after surgery, but in your case, it's a little deeper than I'd expect."

Duran shook his head. "I don't see it. On the contrary, I feel so *alive*."

"I know. I can see it in your face. But then it goes, and . . ." He hesitated. "You lose affect. I'll be honest with you," Shaw went on. "I'm worried that you may be manifesting a rapid-cycle, bipolar state."

Duran frowned. "And if I am?"

Shaw ran his hand back through his hair. "Well, we can back off, and wait for the lab report, but . . . I'm concerned about your treatment in the long run."

"Why?" Duran asked.

"Well, we haven't really talked about your living situation, but you can't go back to being a therapist—you're not qualified."

"As far as we know."

The psychiatrist smiled. "Touché! 'As far as we know.' But what, then? Are you independently wealthy?"

Duran thought about it. "My parents died suddenly. There was some insurance."

"These parents—you mean Mr. and Mrs. Duran?"

"I guess."

"Huh." Shaw frowned. "But you do have some money. You weren't relying on your two clients to keep body and soul together. Because if you were, your rates must have been even higher than mine."

Duran responded with a weak smile. "I don't remember worrying about money. I suppose I could call my bank. . . ."

Shaw nodded, and cleared his throat. "And, uhh . . . what about Adrienne?"

Duran was puzzled by the question. "What about her?"

"You obviously *like* each other. I was wondering about your relationship."

A frown from Duran. "She's the plaintiff. I'm the defendant."

Shaw smiled. "She says she's dropped the suit."

"I guess."

"Then . . . perhaps you could stay with her for a while?"

It was Duran's turn to smile. "I don't think so," he told him.

Shaw looked disappointed.

"There are some things . . . I don't think Adrienne has talked to you about them, but . . . the two of us are . . . kind of in transit . . ."

" 'In transit' . . . "

"Yeah. For the foreseeable future."

Shaw digested this for a moment, then excused himself, and went to the cafeteria line. Returning with a fresh pot of tea, he sat down, and said, "Why don't we try the pentathol this afternoon? Actually—no. It's Thanksgiving. My wife would kill me. We'll save it for tomorrow. Anyway, I've got some sailing tapes—"

"Some what?"

"Audio tapes—*Sounds of the Sea*. Very relaxing. Water lapping against hull, lines rattling, sails snapping, fog horns—the whole nine yards—except you'll be in a trance. So I guess you could call it 'the whole ten yards.' "

Shaw was attempting to be funny, but the idea made Duran uncomfortable. *Lines rattling. Sails snapping.* "Where'd you get something like that?" he asked.

"What?"

"The sounds."

"New Age Audio. Sixty-third and Lexington." The psychiatrist swung his head to the side, sipped his tea and grinned. "Am I resourceful, or what?"

It was the jackets that triggered the memories—which was strange, because they never wore the jackets when they sailed. As Shaw had promised, Duran was immersed in the sounds of the ocean, the splash, and rush of water. With his eyes closed and the tape playing, he'd been racing with his friends, adjusting the rudder, falling off a little, judging the optimum heel and reach as they headed for the marker buoy. They were all wearing their jackets and, yet, as everyone knew, they never wore their jackets aboard.

"What 'jackets' are you talking about?" Shaw asked.

"Team jackets ... not what you wear in competition. They're what you wear before and after. And around campus."

They'd already tried to see the campus through Duran's eyes, to get him to describe its physical layout, the students, buildings, and professors, the *names* of the buildings, landmarks and statues. But Duran continued to block these efforts, forcing Shaw to focus on the seemingly inconsequential. Insignia printed on pencils and notebooks, area codes, and zipcodes, athletic gear—

And jackets.

"What color are they?"

"Black and white."

"Black and white. That's unusual. Are you sure? Are you sure you're not recalling a photograph? Maybe they're dark blue."

"No they're black. Ink black. White lettering."

"Tell me about them."

But Duran was growing more and more uncomfortable. He wanted to shift position, but he couldn't. To say that his aversion to recalling his past made him freeze was not metaphorical. It was the way his fear manifested itself. He actually felt frozen, both cold and immobile, as if he were encased in ice, his metabolism slowing. Afraid to move, afraid to jar anything loose. But why? A logical sector of his mind was still weighing in on his reactions and it disapproved of his discomfort. How could he be afraid of thinking about jackets? How could jackets be threatening?

"Slow down," Shaw said. "Describe them some more. Do they button or zip? What is the fabric made of?"

"I can't think. There's no room to think." His sensations had narrowed to: pressure and cold. He had the panicked sensation that his head was being squeezed from all sides by plates of ice, his brain crystallizing.

"You *can* think. Do they button or zip?"

Nothing.

"Let's hang the jacket up in your room," Shaw suggested.

That was easier. The jacket was on a hook, not him. "They zip," he said.

"Excellent! Is there anything on the front of the jacket? Apart from the zipper?"

"Embroidery."

"What color?"

"White."

"What is it—the embroidered thing? Letters? A word?" He hesitated. "Your name?"

"It's a bear," Duran said, surprising himself as well as the doctor.

"Just the head? Or the whole thing?"

"It's a bear," Duran told him.

"A white bear?"

Duran nodded. Speaking seemed to take a huge effort and a long time. "A polar bear."

"A *polar* bear," Shaw said, almost in a whisper. But there was a sense of elation in his words. "Black and white. A polar bear," Shaw repeated, this time in a louder voice—one that carried a distinct if muted tone of triumph, a tone that filled Duran with dread.

The polar bear was on the front of the jacket. And on the back, which he could now imagine clearly, were the words *Bowdoin Sailing*. These were the varsity jackets the school provided to its athletes: Bowdoin Sailing, Bowdoin Hockey, Bowdoin Soccer.

"Bowdoin," Duran said. "Bowdoin College."

"Ah," said Shaw. "Of course. Admiral Peary. Polar bears."

That was where he'd gone to school as an undergraduate: Bowdoin, not Brown. And no wonder he'd gone unrecognized at the Sidwell reunion—because he was a Maine boy, all the way. He remembered now. He'd gone to school in Bethel at the Gould Academy, where his mother had been an English teacher.

And then big segments of his past snapped into focus in a way that made his heart stagger—as if he had been on a long voyage, and the ship's engine had suddenly cut out. His life passed before his eyes in an instant that unwound for what seemed like hours, and the result was like a near death experience. For a moment—*that* moment—he was sure he was having a heart attack. But then, the engine started again, and he realized he wasn't having a heart attack, it was just Lew McBride, coming home to himself after a long absence. For an instant, he was overcome with elation—until an image began to form behind his eyes. An ochre room, a sort of . . . abattoir, the walls running with blood, and a nonsense thought shrieking through his head: *My God, I've killed them all.*

And then it was gone. The image vanished as quickly as it had come. His eyes flew open, and he found himself where he'd always been, sitting in a comfortable chair across from Doctor Shaw, filled with a wintry mix of joy and desolation. *Glad to know who I am,* he thought. *Sorry it had to be me.*

They stayed at it. Now that McBride remembered his name, he was struck by how well it fit. He remembered his mother—his real mother, not the icon in the picture frame at his apartment—lifting him up, and singing, "Hello, *yewwwww!* Hello, *Lewwwww!*"

"Wait a second," Shaw ordered. "I want to flip the tape."

He'd been Lewis. He'd been Lew. For a while, he'd been Mac—and, as he recalled, there was even a semester when his friends had called him Bridey. But *Jeff*, which he had answered to just an hour earlier, was as foreign to him as Horatio or Etienne.

"All right, ready to go again," Shaw told him. "You said your father medalled in the Olympics. Was that *it*? I mean— that's fantastic, of course. But, did he ever compete again?"

"No, just the once. He was the first American after Bill Koch to medal in a Nordic event. But he was thirty-four when he took the silver. After that, he worked mostly as a ski instructor."

"Where?"

"Killington, for a while. Sugarloaf. Stowe. Sunday River would have been handier, but it didn't exist at the time."

"That's in Maine?" Shaw guessed.

"Right. That's where we lived. In Bethel. Anyway, he'd go off for three or four months—come home midweek, if things were slow. Later, when cross-country caught on, he gave lessons at the Bethel Inn—which is famous for it."

"Were they happy?"

"Who?"

"Your parents."

McBride didn't know what to say. At the moment, he was wondering why *he* wasn't happy—why, in point of fact, he was filled with a sense of trepidation. Finally, he shrugged. "We didn't have a lot of money," he said. "So there was *that*. My mother clipped coupons and hunted down bargains. Teachers in private school don't earn that much, and my father's income was . . . sporadic. And I'm not sure my mother really trusted him when he was away. He was a go-for-it kind of guy. Even during the run up for the Olympics, my mother wasn't behind him the way wives are on those segments you see on TV."

"Oh?"

"He stopped working to train and my mother didn't want him to. She was pregnant with me. And even after he made the team, it wasn't like *she* got to go to Sapporo. It would have cost too much."

"And after he won?"

"Well . . . he didn't win, and it wasn't the hundred meters. He finished second in the ten-kilometer biathlon—so there wasn't a Wheaties box in it, or anything else, for that matter. I think my mother thought he was a case of arrested development. I remember, one time, he blew out his ankle. Which was not so good, because he didn't have disability insurance, and he couldn't work. So things were tight. I remember my mother standing at the top of the stairs and tossing the bills down, then coming down to see which ones were face up, because those were the ones she'd pay." Duran paused. "Would it be okay if I had a glass of water?"

"Of course," Shaw said, and scurried to fetch him a cup from the cooler.

Not that McBride was actually thirsty. He was just buying time—because he could feel the panic rising inside him, hear the tremor in his voice as his concentration began to fly apart—and this, despite the drug he'd been given.

"Thanks," he said, and took a small sip.

"Keep going," the psychiatrist urged.

"Well—where was I?"

"Things were tight."

"Yeah," McBride said, "they were tight, but she was crazy about him all the same—they were still in love, I think, to the day they died."

Shaw gave him a sympathetic look. "They're not living?"

McBride shook his head. "No. A semi fell on them."

The psychiatrist was taken aback. " 'Fell' on them?"

"Cat-Mousam Road. Truck jackknifed, went over the rail, and landed on the Interstate. Landed on their Volvo. Complete freak."

"I'm sorry."

McBride shrugged. "It was a long time ago."

"Who took care of you? Aunts and uncles?"

"Never had any. But my mother had some life insurance. I was in college when it happened."

"And before that? Were *you* happy, as a child?"

"I don't know. I suppose so. Bethel was nice. I had friends. And I worked."

"Where?"

"Stocking shelves at the IGA, setting pins in the bowling alley. When I was older, I worked as a camp counselor. Lots of camps in Maine."

As the afternoon wore on, Shaw sent out for coffee, and later for pizza. Several times he asked if McBride was too fatigued to continue—but the strange lassitude that had gripped him for so long—the languor which had enabled him to kill entire days watching television—was gone. Except for the sense of dread that came at him in waves, he felt awake and anxious to remember all he could. The drug that he'd been given had worn off, and Shaw was eager to keep going.

They talked about his childhood and his college days, about Bowdoin and Stanford, where he'd earned a doctoral degree in psychology. "I was interested in research," he explained.

"So you didn't do clinical. I mean, like Jeffrey Duran?"

"No, I never had a client, never shrunk a head. Eventually, I might have but . . . I received a fellowship that, uh, went on for a while."

"Which fellowship was that?" Shaw asked.

"Institute of Global Studies." McBride stirred uncomfortably in his chair. Coughed, and crossed his legs.

"Tell me about it."

"It's a foundation that makes grants to researchers in various disciplines."

"So it doesn't just pay your tuition somewhere."

"No. They give you a stipend, and travel expenses. It's pretty generous—plus, you get a lot of exposure."

Shaw frowned. "What kind of exposure?"

Duran thought about it, then made a helpless gesture. "I'm sorry, I . . . I guess I'm uncomfortable. I mean, I'm trying to think how long . . . how long I've been *away*."

Shaw shook his head. "Now, this is what happens when you start blocking. So don't get fixated on trying to figure out where Lew McBride begins and Jeff Duran ends. Just . . ." His right hand rotated in the air between them. "*Roll with it.* You were talking about the fellowship."

McBride nodded. "Yeah, well, the way it worked: I wrote a sort of letter, a report, really, every month or so. I'd send it to the director of the Institute, and the Institute would send out copies to a slew of publications, the idea being that they could reprint it for free, so long as they gave the Institute credit.

Other copies went to interested academics, and an A-list of influential people in the States and elsewhere."

"Sounds wonderful. How do you apply?"

"You don't. What happens is, someone recommends you— they don't tell you who, but it's usually a professor, a former fellow—someone like that. Anyway, they take you to lunch a couple of times, and ask what you'd do if you had the time and the money to do what you want. After a while—unless you're an idiot—you find yourself pitching a study. They make some recommendations about how the study could be better, and the next thing you know, you're taking a lot of tests."

"What kind of tests?"

"Like the ones you gave me. MMPI, Myers-Briggs . . . it took all day. I remember that."

Shaw made a face. "Hunh! Why would they do that?"

"I asked the same question. They said it had to do with identifying candidates who could work on their own—there's very little supervision. Basically, they pat you on the back, and send you on your way. And I think they want to be sure they're getting people who are comfortable working abroad—because they're big on that."

"On what?"

"Working abroad."

"What was your area of study?" Shaw asked. "What did you pitch?"

McBride smiled, a little sheepishly. "The title was 'Animist Therapeutics and the Third World.' "

Shaw raised his eyebrows. "Interesting!"

"The idea was to study the psychological and therapeutic components of nativist religions. Which meant studying everything from Indian sweat lodges to the induction of trance states, the effect of eclipses and different ways cultures used hallucinogenic mushrooms."

"And did you?"

"Yes. I started in this hemisphere and . . ." McBride's voice trailed off.

"What?"

Suddenly, he felt as if a small bird was doing barrel rolls in his stomach. "I'm sorry," he said. "I get distracted."

Shaw's brow furrowed. "So what did you do?"

"I was in South America a lot, and the Caribbean. I wrote pieces on everything. Faith healing, Santería, one on ultra-marathoning as a form of flagellation and meditation. Two of the articles I wrote were reprinted in the *Times*."

"What were they about?" Shaw asked.

"One was about the spiritual aspects of video gaming—the quest, you know. The other was about communal drinking games as a way of relieving seasonal affective disorder."

"And how did *that* work?"

McBride laughed. "I went up to the Yukon in February, and got drunk with the Inuits."

"And then what?"

"I stopped caring about the weather."

Shaw chuckled. "You mentioned the Caribbean."

"Right. I was in Haiti for a while. Studying cadence and tempo cues in posthypnotic suggestions."

"Sounds fascinating."

"It was, actually," McBride said. He rapped out a rhythm on the table with his fingertips. *Tippety tip tip!* Five taps. "Something as abbreviated as that could do the trick."

"Really. Well, not so surprising, I guess. Aural memory tends to be sequential so that once you initiate a progression of sounds, the mind tends to complete the sequence. So, where else did you go?"

"I was supposed to go on to Jamaica."

Shaw waited for McBride to continue. When he did not, the psychiatrist broke the silence. "Yes?"

Suddenly, Duran couldn't speak. There was an ache in the back of his throat that had to do with flying back to San Francisco from Port-Au-Prince, bringing home his tapes and photographs and notes. It was expensive, flying back, but his apartment was a good place to write and, what was even more to the point, it gave him a chance to spend time with Judy and

Josh. They could be a family—if only for a few days each month.

The news of Judy's pregnancy had come hard on the heels of the news that he'd won the fellowship, and they'd agreed that he couldn't pass up the chance it represented—that they'd just make the best of it. He would come home, as often as possible, and that would be that.

And that's exactly the way it was. In the months before Josh was born, Judy had come to join him for a week here and a few days there—whenever she was able to take time off from her own career as a graphic designer. But that stopped when Josh arrived because . . . well, for one thing, they couldn't afford it and, even if they had been able to, the places he was going were no place for a baby.

"Lew?" Doctor Shaw leaned forward, his forehead wrinkling with concern.

McBride could hear a helicopter outside and, down the street, a siren moving closer, with its fluctuating wail. Sunlight poured through the slats of the venetian blinds, striping the bloodred, oriental carpet.

No place for a baby.

"Lew?"

He had the sensation that the pattern of light and shadow had risen up from the floor, and shone through his brain. And that the wail of the siren was the inconsolable bawl of an infant.

A baby.

He heard Shaw's voice, but it was very faint, and muffled, as if it were traveling a long distance, or moving through layers and layers of insulation.

"Jeff? What's going on? Are you all right?"

He didn't reply. He was in the ochre room. The nursery. The abattoir. He had the bat in his hand, the Louisville Slugger that Judy kept in the umbrella stand by the door. He could feel it cracking bone, then sinking into the soft melon-flesh of, first, his son, and then his wife. The blood was flying, misting the air. He was skating in it, slipping and swinging until there was nothing left of Joshua and Judy but pulp.

31 Finding out about Calvin Crane was about as easy as taking a cab to the New York Public Library. Walking past the magnificent stone lions that guard its entrance, Adrienne climbed the stairs to the third floor reading room, where she found a much-thumbed copy of *Who's Who* among a shelf of reference books. Taking the burgundy tome to a mahogany conference table, she sat down beside an elderly man with a nimbus of flyaway hair, and searched for Crane's entry. Finding it, she began to read:

> *Crane, Calvin Fletcher—*
> *Philanthropist, foundation head. B. July 23, 1917, Patchogue, N.Y. Yale, '38. Harvard Law, '41. Atty., Donovan, Leisure (New York), 1942, 1945. Office of Strategic Services (OSS), London, Basel, Maj., 1942–5. Central Intelligence Group (CIG–Washington, D.C.), 1946–7. Foreign Service Officer, Dept. of State (Zurich), 1947–9. Secretary-Treasurer, Institute of Global Studies (IGS), 1949–63 (Zurich). President and Treasurer, IGS, 1964–89; President Emeritus, IGS, 1989–. Legion d'Honneur, 1989. Member, Council on Foreign Relations, Bilderburger Society. Clubs: Yale, Century, Athenaeum. Residence: Longboat Key, Florida.*

Adrienne sat back in her chair, and drummed her fingertips on the open page. As she did, the old man to her right gave her a sidelong glance, then returned to the book he was reading: *Secrets of the Great Pyramid*.

The *Who's Who* entry required a certain amount of deconstruction, Adrienne thought. Harvard and Yale suggested money. Then a job at some law firm, interrupted by the war. OSS. That was spy stuff. Then back to the law firm. Then a spy again, and then a job with State—in Switzerland where, she noticed, he'd been before. After that, the foundation job. For forty years. Prestigious clubs and honors, capped by a Florida retirement.

Prematurely ended by her crazy sister.

There had to be more. Getting up from her chair, she went to the reference desk and asked directions to the periodicals reading room, which turned out to be just down the corridor. With a librarian's help, she selected microfiche spools from the *New York Times*, *Miami Daily News*, and the *Sarasota Star-Tribune*. Each of the spools covered the same period in October when Crane had been killed.

Sitting down at one of the readers, she went from obit to obit until she had a sense of the man—if not an understanding of her sister's relationship to him.

The references to the OSS were especially interesting. From what she read, the organization had been formed under the influence of British intelligence at the outset of World War II. Like its European counterpart, it had recruited from the country's upper classes, drawing as much as possible from the best schools and most prestigious firms on Wall Street. According to the *Times*, the OSS was "at once the principal precursor of the CIA, and a transatlantic Old Boys network *par excellence*."

As if to emphasize the point, there was a page of photographs—billed as "a visual tribute"—in the *Star-Tribune*, showing Crane at different ages. As a young man, he'd been almost movie-star handsome, with bold eyebrows, a strong chin, and a shock of thick dark hair that fell, Kennedyesque, over his forehead. He was shown shaking the hand of Franklin Roosevelt; posing on the slopes around Gstaad with Allen

Dulles; clinking champagne flutes with de Gaulle; and escorting Audrey Hepburn through the front doors of the Esplanade Hotel in Zagreb. Forty years in Switzerland, give or take a day. Lawyer, spy, foundation head. How do you make that transition, Adrienne wondered. And then Florida. Where he supported a slew of good causes, including the Sarasota Symphony Orchestra, the Conch-House Preservation Society, and Native Ground, an ecological group dedicated to combating the overthrow of native flora by invasive species. Before his confinement in a wheelchair, those causes and the game of golf seemed to constitute the major parameters of the old man's life.

It was all very interesting, Adrienne decided, but it didn't tell her anything about why her sister took a train to Florida and shot him. It occurred to her that Nikki might have imagined Crane to have been one of the men who'd "abused" her, but it seemed a stretch. In fact, if his *Who's Who* entry was accurate, Crane had been living in Switzerland all during the time that Nikki had been growing up.

Returning to her hotel, Adrienne found the red diode blinking on the telephone next to the bed. Retrieving the message—*Call ASAP, any hour—Ray Shaw*—she phoned him at his home.

"We've had a breakthrough," Shaw told her.

"Fantastic! So . . ." She cleared her throat. "So come on, who is he?"

"Well, he's a very troubled man."

"Doc . . ."

"His name is Lew McBride—Lewis with an 'e.' That's the good news. The bad news is: he beat his wife and son to death with a baseball bat."

"What!?"

"I think you heard me, though whether this is another fantasy of his—or something else—we can't be sure."

Adrienne let her head fall back against the wall behind the bed. "Where did this happen?" she asked.

"San Francisco." Shaw filled her in on McBride's background, from Bethel to Bowdoin to Stanford, including his parents' deaths. "Bright young man—no question. Magna cum laude. Doctorate in psychology, prestigious fellowships—it was all ahead of him. Until . . ."

"What?"

"He went off the deep end. Suffered a psychotic break, of some kind. Beat his family to death. Swears he wasn't on drugs, though you have to wonder if angel dust wasn't involved."

"He killed his wife?" Adrienne couldn't believe it. *Didn't* believe it.

"*And* his infant son. Three months old."

They fell silent for a moment. Then she asked: "Was he arrested, or . . . what?"

" 'Or what,' indeed!" the psychiatrist exclaimed. "According to the patient, everything slips into soft focus at that point. He remembers the murders, but that's it. The next thing he knows, he's in Washington, and he's Jeffrey Duran, therapist."

"So . . . where is he now?"

"In restraints. I have him on A-4. Security ward."

Adrienne couldn't imagine it. "You think he'll try to escape?"

"No. I think he'll try to kill himself. In fact, I'm sure of it."

"Then . . ." Adrienne was at a loss for words, and running short on ideas, as well. Finally, she asked, "What about . . . that thing?"

"The implant?"

"Yes."

"That could have been a part of the problem, but I really can't tell you anything. I'm having a helluva time finding out about it," Shaw complained. "I've called the lab three times and . . . nothing."

"So—"

"I'll deal with the lab," Shaw promised. "But, I have to say that if Mr. McBride's recollection of himself as a murderer is accurate, it would explain a lot—the dissociation he experienced, the hysterical amnesia—even the sublimation of his personality into an alternate identity."

" 'If' . . ."

"Pardon me?" the psychiatrist asked.

"You said, 'if' his memory is accurate."

"So I did."

Adrienne was quiet for a moment. Then she picked up the complimentary pen beside the telephone, and asked, "When is this supposed to have happened?"

"Five years ago—in San Francisco."

"Let me look into it," she suggested. "And if I find out it's true . . . ?"

"I don't think either of us would have any choice. We'd have to notify the police."

She knew he was right. But she also knew there was room for doubt—and that any call to the police at this time would be premature. Until the day before, the recently-confessed murderer had been someone else entirely. "I just can't believe it," she said.

"Neither can I," Shaw replied. "I really can't. But I'll tell you one thing."

"What?"

"*He* does."

The next morning, Ray Shaw sat behind the wheel of his Mercedes, going nowhere on his way to work. Unmoving, the car was stranded in the middle lane of the George Washington Bridge, immersed in a cacophony of horns. Irritated, Shaw removed the Star TAC from his briefcase, punched in a number that he knew as well as his own, and laid the cellphone against his right ear.

The thing was, Raymond C. Shaw was not a man who asked favors of other people. Not often, anyway, and on the rare occasions that he did, he expected the favors to be granted—especially when, as now, the prospective grantor was someone with whom he'd played squash, twice a week, for years.

Charley Dorgan was 1) his best friend and 2) the senior research physicist at Columbia University's Laboratory of Engineering and Applied Materials. Shaw had sent him the implant for analysis within an hour of removing it from Lew McBride's hippocampus, and only three hours after losing to Dorgan in straight sets at the Manhattan Sports Club.

That Dorgan had not yet gotten back to him was only mildly surprising: the physicist was a very busy man, juggling his teaching responsibilities while presiding over a department that had lucrative and complex relationships to a number of private firms and government agencies. So Shaw wasn't really shocked that Dorgan should need prodding. But he *was* surprised to find that his calls were not getting returned.

And it pissed him off.

Charley was an old friend. When he pulled the Dorgan string, he expected it to *hum*.

So he called him—again. This time, at home. At seven in the morning. "Guess who?"

Dorgan grunted.

"Charley, it's—"

"I know who it is."

"Well?" Shaw asked, his voice larded with as much irony as he could manage.

"Well, what?"

"I'm calling about . . . about the *object* I sent you."

Dorgan's reply consisted of a long silence.

"Hello?" This, from Shaw.

"I'm here," Dorgan replied.

"Good, because—"

"I really can't talk about it, Ray."

Shaw thought he'd misheard him. "You can't *what*?"

"I said I can't talk about it. Neither of us should."

"I don't believe I'm hearing this," Shaw replied. "What are you—"

"Look—I gotta go," Dorgan told him. "I'm late. I'll talk to you later." And with that, he hung up, leaving his squash partner sputtering into his Star TAC.

By now, Adrienne knew the lions' names: *Patience* and *Fortitude*. And she also knew where to go to find a computer that she could use to log onto Nexis. Sitting down at an open terminal in one of the library's computer rooms, she went to the Nexis Web site and entered Slough, Hawley's user-ID and password. When the appropriate page came up, she hit the *Search* button, and then *News*. Finally, she entered *McBride*'s name in the panel for search terms, then added, *San Francisco,* 1996 and—just to be certain—*1995* and *1997*.

Thirty seconds went by before a list of documents materialized on the screen. All in all, there were 204 that mentioned someone named McBride in the context of San Francisco during the relevant years. These included—indeed, were dominated by—trivial references that had nothing to do with anything. There were P/R releases announcing the promotions and retirements of executives who happened to be named McBride. Richard McBride. Fred McBride. Delano McBride. There were half a dozen stories about the Prep Football Top 25 (whose number included a wide receiver named Antwan McBride), as well as articles about a geriatric judge, a popular restauranteur, and a Bay area restaurant reviewer who—like the others—was named McBride. And more.

But there was nothing in any newspaper published in America in the last ten years that reported a murder, or a double murder, perpetrated by a man named Lew McBride—or Anything McBride—in San Francisco during the 1990s. Adrienne expanded her search, substituting California for San Francisco, and came up with half a dozen hits. Closer scrutiny, however, revealed that none of these were relevant. A man named McBride had killed a convenience store clerk with a shotgun in Fresno in 1996. Another McBride had been charged with vehicular homicide in a drunk driving incident that left two dead (the family wanted him charged with murder, but he wasn't). And so on.

And so forth.

She was tempted to return to the Mayflower, call Shaw and tell him that Duran's most recent identity, like his last, was an illusion. But because she was a lawyer—and prided herself on touching all the bases—on *being prepared*—she went through the original list.

Which wasn't so bad, really. The KWIK Search feature highlighted the words in which she was interested as they appeared in each of the stories. So it wasn't as if she had to read them all—just skim them.

And that's what she did, going backwards from 1997 until she came to Article No. 138, which appeared in the *San Francisco Examiner* on June 16, 1996:

LOCAL MAN FEARED
DEAD IN PLANE CRASH

Cap Haitien (Reuters)—San Francisco resident Lewis McBride, 26, was feared dead today when rescuers called off their search for his missing plane in the rugged mountains west of this city.

McBride was the only passenger in a chartered Cessna that disappeared in a storm Tuesday evening. Haitian air controllers in Port-au-Prince report that no urgent or emergency broadcasts were received from the plane.

The area in which the Cessna is believed to have gone down is uninhabited, mountainous jungle. Efforts to search for the plane have been inhibited by continuing bad weather.

A Stanford University graduate, with a doctoral degree in psychology, McBride had been traveling on a foundation grant for the last two years. Professor Ian Hartwig of Stanford expressed his shock and sadness at the "tragic loss of this fine young man."

McBride leaves no survivors.

Graphic: photo (McBride)

Adrienne sat back in her chair and thought about it. Was Duran really McBride? Or was this just another stolen identity? What if he had a whole series of identities, a nesting set like a matrioshka doll—and this one, Lew McBride, was still several shells away from the innermost one? What was this business about beating his family to death? There was nothing in the papers about it—and, clearly, the Reuter's article meant it never happened. If McBride had killed someone, the story would have mentioned it—and the Stanford professor would not have described him as a "fine young man."

Nexis generated text, not images, but if a photograph appeared with a story, that information was included in the printout. Graphic: photo (McBride). So that meant when she found the article on microfiche, there'd be a picture, too. A picture of McBride.

When Charlie Dorgan got to work, Ray Shaw was waiting for him on the couch in the reception area outside his office. Seeing his old pal, Dorgan lowered his head, nodded to his secretary—"Pearl"—and marched into his inner sanctum.

With Shaw hard on his heels, closing the door behind them.

"Charlie—"

"I don't want to hear it," Dorgan told him, raising a hand as if he were about to swear an oath. "I can't talk about this."

"What do you mean?"

"I mean we can't talk about it. I mean that you will *not* receive a report about the little item you sent—so stop asking me, or you're going to ruin a beautiful friendship." With that, the physicist collapsed into the chair behind his desk, swiveled around and turned his eyes toward the ceiling.

Shaw made a helpless gesture. "I don't get it."

"It's classified," Dorgan said.

"What is?"

"The device. It's a neurophonic prosthesis. Made of bioglass."

"So it's invisible to the body's immune system."

"Right."

It was Ray Shaw's turn to sit down. Settling onto the arm of a leather chair, he thought about what the physicist was saying.

"You should have told me how sensitive this was," Dorgan complained.

"I didn't know—"

"I was showing the Goddamn thing to anyone who'd look at it! And Fred—you know Fred—he goes way back—he takes a look, and *he* says, 'We used to play with these in grad school.' And I said, when was that—the Stone Age? And he laughs, and says, 'Yeah, it was—everyone in the lab had his own lava lamp.' Very funny. So I asked him: what is it? And he says, 'Well, Charlie, it's a neurophonic prosthesis—now I have to kill you.' Ha ha, I say. And he gives me a funny look. A funny look!"

"You're kidding."

"The hell I am: he gives me a funny look, and says, 'Seriously,'—*seriously*—'you shouldn't have that thing. It was a government program. Very hush-hush. One of those programs that never happened. An experimental program.' "

Shaw's face darkened. "This wasn't an experiment," he said.

"What do you mean?"

"I mean, I removed it from a patient."

Dorgan blinked several times. Got his breath back. And asked: "Is that supposed to be a joke?"

"No."

The physicist pursed his lips, and took a deep breath. "The next thing you know, I've got *visitors*." He paused for emphasis.

"Who?" Shaw asked.

" 'Who?' Who do ya think? The Smoking Man and his evil twin—the Other Smoking Man."

Shaw chuckled.

"I'm not kidding," Dorgan insisted. "These guys were straight out of Central Casting. Big trench coats, and no sense of irony."

"They say who they're with?"

"Yeah, as a matter of fact—it came up. They said they were with the Pentagon," Dorgan replied, "only I notice their business cards have a 301 area code."

"Which means . . . ?"

Dorgan shrugged. "NSA?"

Shaw frowned. "So what was the point of the visit?"

"They wanted to know how I'd 'come into possession of the device.' "

"And you *told* them?" Shaw asked, his face a mask of disappointment.

"Of course I told them! What was I supposed to do, Ray? They scared the shit out of me."

"So . . ."

Dorgan hesitated. Finally, he said, "I don't know. Maybe you should expect a visit."

32 She had been sitting in the reception area for nearly twenty minutes when the door to Shaw's office swung wide, and two men in black trench coats emerged, looking grim. Crossing the room to the hallway, they let themselves out without a word, while Shaw himself lingered in the doorway with a worried look on his face.

Tossing the *New Yorker* onto the table beside the couch, Adrienne got to her feet, and cleared her throat.

The psychiatrist turned to her with a distracted air. For a moment, it seemed as if he didn't recognize her. Then he did, and, waking suddenly, exclaimed, "Adrienne! Migod, come in."

She followed him into his office, and took a seat in front of his desk. "Is something wrong?" she asked.

The psychiatrist looked worried and confused at the same time. "I'm not supposed to mention their visit," he told her.

"Whose visit?"

"The men who were just here."

"Oh," she said, uncertain what he meant.

Shaw frowned. Looked her in the eyes. "You haven't told me everything, have you? About our friend."

She shifted uncomfortably in her chair. "No," she admitted. "Not everything."

"Because, now . . . well, now there's trouble."

She was stricken at the thought that she'd drawn this kind and generous man into the mixing bowl of her own problems. And Duran's. *McBride*'s. Nikki's. "I thought, the less you knew . . ."

"They asked me for his medical file. I refused to give it to them."

"Who?"

"The men who were here."

Adrienne thought about it. "And who are they?"

The psychiatrist shook his head. "They said they're with a government agency."

"What agency?"

"They didn't say."

Adrienne made a face. "Well, if they want his medical file, they can get a subpoena—"

Doctor Shaw shook his head, and smiled ruefully. "I don't think that's the way they work. They were very forceful."

"Oh."

The psychiatrist did his best to push the men out of his mind. "You were going to look into Mr. McBride's story. Did you find anything?"

Adrienne was relieved to change, if not the subject, the direction it was heading in. "Absolutely!" she exclaimed. "Beginning with the fact that he is who he says he is—except that he's supposed to be dead."

"What?"

"And he isn't married. No wife, no child. No indictments for murder or anything else. None of that happened." She removed a copy of the LOCAL MAN FEARED DEAD article from her purse, and pushed it across the desk. "He's got longer hair in the picture, but . . . you can see it's him."

Shaw put on his reading glasses, glanced at the photograph, nodded, and focused. After a while, the psychiatrist looked up. "How can you be sure—"

"I went through every article on Nexis that mentioned anyone named McBride and San Francisco—'95 through '97. There were hundreds of them, and there was nothing even remotely like the fairy tale he told you. And if I missed it, somehow—which I didn't—it would certainly have been in the story about the plane crash—*if* it ever happened."

Shaw leaned back in his chair, contemplating the ceiling. "And if he had a common-law wife? And a baby with a different last name? And if he was never a suspect in the murders . . . ?"

"Doc. Please. You're reaching."

The psychiatrist thought about it. "I suppose I am."

They agreed to meet at the hospital the next morning. In the meantime, Shaw said that he'd instruct the nursing staff to keep McBride under restraints, but desist from any further sedation.

Returning to the Mayflower, Adrienne changed into her running clothes, slipped a $10 bill into her right shoe, and took the elevator down to the lobby. Someone was taking down the Thanksgiving decorations. Rubbing his gloved hands together, the doorman shook his head in admiration as she stepped out into the freezing cold. "If I'm not back in an hour," she told him, "send a St. Bernard for me."

Overhead, the bare branches of ancient oaks and sycamores framed the sky. Mounds of dung lay on the powder-soft, equestrian trails. And then, a long hill, leading to a dark pond on the southern-most edge of Harlem. Clusters of private-school kids stood together, tieless and smoking—laughing, conspiring. The slur of Rollerblades on the pavement. *Thwockk* of tennis balls in the distance. Then the Reservoir, ringed with Cyclone fencing, the sun behind it, setting. Light flickering through the fence as Adrienne ran beside it, thinking about McBride.

How do you imagine a family, she asked herself, *imagine it so perfectly that you become suicidal in the belief that you've killed them? And why now—why would McBride recall an imaginary and toxic past after the implant had been removed?*

It didn't make sense. Unless, of course, that was the point: to make "Duran" commit suicide if and when the device should ever be removed, if and when he should ever recover his memory. His real *memory.*

And now the men in trenchcoats . . .

Adrienne arrived at the hospital the next morning, almost half an hour early, refreshed from a long and dreamless sleep. She was hoping to see McBride before Shaw arrived, but the nurse at the reception desk rebuffed her. "We don't allow visitors on A-4. I'm sorry, but there are no exceptions."

To the nurse's irritation, she insisted on waiting.

It was ten A.M. when Doctor Shaw stepped off the elevator, looking gloomy and determined. He barked at the supervising floor nurse, who objected to Adrienne following him through the heavy doors that gave entry to Ward A. Nearby, a bank of television monitors flickered with the images of a dozen, small, white rooms, each of which held a single person, none of whom were moving much.

"You know the regulations, Doctor—"

"You're right," Shaw told the nurse. "I do. And if we weren't in a hurry, I'd transfer the patient to another room—but we don't have time for that."

We don't? Adrienne thought.

"Well, if you're going to violate protocol," the nurse began, "I should think—"

"Why don't you just make a report?" Shaw asked, striding away. "I'll be releasing him in short order, anyway."

"Releasing him? Mr. McBride isn't in any condition—"

But Shaw wasn't listening. He was walking so fast that Adrienne had to move at double-time, just to keep up with him.

All the rooms on the ward had large windows facing out on the corridor. The windows were made of the kind of glass that was embedded with a kind of chicken wire.

Shaw opened one of the doors, and stepped inside.

The room contained a built-in console with drawers against one wall and a bed against the other. A television was mounted on the wall facing the bed, and there was a video camera affixed to the ceiling. A small toilet in the corner. And that was that.

McBride lay in the bed, his head propped up on a pair of pillows, staring at a soap opera. He hadn't moved when they entered the room, and now she saw that he couldn't: his wrists were belted to the bed.

Adrienne was shocked. "Take those off!" she demanded, moving quickly to McBride's side.

"Soon enough," Shaw promised, gently lifting her hand from one of the restraints. Stepping closer, he laid a hand on McBride's shoulder. "Lewis," he said, "I want you to pay close attention to what I'm about to say."

No reaction.

"It's important," the psychiatrist insisted, "and I'm worried that we don't have a lot of time."

Nothing from McBride—who looked as if he'd aged ten years since Adrienne had seen him, years in which he'd undergone some terrible ordeal. His face was drawn and his cheeks were covered with stubble. Hollow eyes that averted her own.

Frustrated, Adrienne reached up and snapped off the TV.

McBride turned his head toward her. "Thanks," he said. "I hate that fucking show."

Adrienne giggled, delighted to get a reaction—any reaction—from him.

"Listen to me, Lewis," Shaw demanded.

The patient shook his head, closed his eyes. "Let me alone, Doc." His voice had all the resonance of a stone.

"I'm going to release you," the psychiatrist announced.

It took a moment for the words to penetrate the insulation in which McBride had wrapped his understanding. Then his eyes blinked open, and he turned to Shaw with a sidelong glance.

"But you have to pay attention," Shaw told him.

He was.

The psychiatrist cleared his throat.

"You didn't do it!" Adrienne blurted. "You didn't kill anybody."

"Let me handle this," Shaw insisted.

Adrienne put a hand on McBride's cheek and, turning his head to her, looked him in the eyes. "No—I checked the papers. And it's all a lie. There was nothing! No murder, no police—"

McBride shook his head. "I know what happened, kiddo. I know what I did."

"But you're wrong. You weren't even married. There wasn't any baby!" She paused. Should she tell him he was supposed to be dead? "It's like Nikki," she said. "They've given you one of these memories—"

"*Who* has?"

His question took her aback.

"Who has?" he repeated.

She didn't know what to say. Looked to Shaw for help. Got none. Shrugged. "I don't know," she admitted. "Someone."

McBride looked away. "I can feel it," he told them. "I can feel the bat in my hands . . ."

"Lew," Shaw began—.

McBride turned back to Adrienne. "So, what you're saying is: I'm just a screen for someone else's projector."

Adrienne weighed the metaphor. Shrugged. "Right," she said.

McBride swung his eyes toward the psychiatrist. "Okay, let's say you're right. Then: *what's the point?* Why would anyone want to make me think I killed my wife and child?" When Shaw frowned, McBride turned angrily to Adrienne. "What's the point?" he repeated.

The question hung in the air, floating through the weird silence of that empty and sterile room. It was a good question, a tough question and, for a moment, Adrienne despaired of an answer. Then it came to her, and it was so simple. She cleared her throat. "So you'd kill yourself," she said. "Like Nikki."

Once the restraints had been removed, and McBride had seen the clipping from the *Examiner*, Shaw told him that "I want to put you in a trance."

"No, thanks, Doc. Been there—done that. If you don't mind . . ."

"There's no way that I'm going to release you," Shaw said, "until I'm certain you're free of posthypnotic suggestions— whatever the source."

McBride chewed on that, a defiant look in his eye.

"Let me be honest with you," Shaw continued. "After what you've been through, it's going to take a long time for you to get well. Under any other circumstances, I'd recommend counseling and therapy—and lots of it." He paused, and heaved a sigh. "But we don't have that luxury. As Adrienne can tell you, I've been contacted by a government agency. They say they have 'equities' in the matter. That may be so. I don't know. But what I do know is that they don't have *your* best interests at heart. In fact, I got the distinct impression that they don't care about you, at all."

McBride thought about it. Finally, he asked, "And you think I've been given posthypnotic suggestions—"

"Absolutely! That's why I was having such a helluva time getting through to you. Anytime you came close to your past—your real past—this brutal figment, this *syndrome*—

would begin to surface. And when it did, you'd sense it and, psychologically, you'd start to panic. Fight or flight. It's brilliant. They created a false memory so toxic that it gave you a built-in aversion to your real self."

Even with the restraints removed, McBride remained where he was, in a sink of depression. "Maybe you're right," he said in a skeptical voice. "Then again, isn't it more likely that I just got away with it?"

"No," Adrienne exclaimed, her voice trembling with anger. "It isn't more likely! You know somebody fucked with your head. Wake up! You didn't kill Eddie, you didn't blow up the house, you didn't trash my apartment—"

"Who's Eddie?" Shaw asked, his voice thick with alarm.

Adrienne ignored him. "And you aren't the one who's trying to kill me."

"Oh, Jesus—" Shaw muttered.

"So placing your bets on the 'more likely' explanation is kind of stupid, isn't it?" she asked. Then she wrapped her arms around her body, turned away, and walked toward the opposite side of the room.

"Who's Eddie?" Shaw asked.

"You don't want to know," Adrienne told him, her back to the psychiatrist. Suddenly, a thought occurred to her. "Wait a second," she said, turning toward him. "I thought hypnosis was benign. And it was impossible to make hypnotized people do something that would cause harm. I heard you couldn't make a person hurt anyone—let alone kill himself."

"That's a myth," Shaw said, dismissing the idea. "PR from the hypnotism industry." He gestured toward McBride. "Lewis can tell you all about it. He's in the field."

"What do you mean, it's a myth?" Adrienne asked.

Shaw glanced at his watch, then ran his hand through his hair. "It's all a question of context," he explained.

"What context?" Adrienne asked.

"Well, for example: if the patient believes he's in a war, and that the war is a just one, he could probably be made to kill someone that the hypnotist tells him is the enemy. Or if he's persuaded that someone is intent on killing *him*, and that he's acting in self-defense—"

"I get the point," Adrienne said, "but it's all theoretical."

"Hardly," Shaw replied. Turning to McBride, he asked: "What was that case? The one in Denmark?"

"Palle Hardrup," McBride answered. "Bank robbery—in the Fifties—a guard was killed." Adrienne noticed that McBride was alert now, the discussion having overcome his indifference.

"Right!" Shaw said, with a congratulatory smile. "You've got an excellent memory."

It took a second, but they all smiled. Then Adrienne looked from one man to the other. "His name was Hardup? And he robbed a bank? Is this some kind of shrink in-joke?"

McBride smiled. "Haar-*druup*," he corrected. "He was arrested after a bank robbery. Shot a guard, and killed him. Which puzzled the police because he didn't really need the money, and he wasn't a violent guy. He was pretty ordinary, in fact. A good citizen. So the question was, why did he do it?" McBride looked at Shaw, who nodded for him to continue. "It was totally out of character. But then they found out that he'd been hypnotized by his therapist—and that the therapist had ordered him to rob the bank and shoot the guard."

"And the judge bought this?" Adrienne asked, her voice larded with the skepticism of a good attorney.

"Yes, he did. Because the therapist confessed. Said he'd engineered the crime as a test of his powers."

"Huh," Adrienne remarked, uncertain if she believed the story.

"It's a famous case," Shaw told her. "It came up in the Manson trial."

"Why?" she asked.

"Because the therapist wasn't on the scene when the crime was committed—and yet, the gunman was obviously under his influence and control."

"So how did he do it?" Adrienne asked. "The therapist."

"Do you remember, Lew?" Shaw asked.

McBride nodded. "He created a persona, a supernatural persona, that he called 'X.' 'X' was like God. And it was X who told Hardrup what to do."

"And he did it?" Adrienne asked. "He shot the man?"

"Of course," Shaw replied. "He was a very religious man."

Adrienne thought about it. "And that's what you mean by 'context,' " she said.

"Right. As far as Hardrup was concerned, he was an instrument of divine will."

"And you think that would work for suicide?"

"Why not?" Shaw answered. "People commit suicide all the time. Under the right circumstances—in the proper context—it can seem an honorable, and even reasonable, thing to do." He glanced at his watch, and turned to McBride. "Are you up for it?"

McBride looked uncertain.

"We really don't have a lot of time."

McBride looked at Adrienne, and sighed. "Yeah, why not?"

Shaw smiled, and turned to Adrienne. "If you don't mind waiting for us in the cafeteria . . . I have an exorcism to do."

She was sitting at a square table in the cafeteria, working her way through the Business section of the *Times*, when Shaw strode in past the steam table, almost an hour after she'd left him. A little ripple of attention followed his progress across the room, with several nurses and doctors greeting him. He stopped to speak to a short, red-haired man in scrubs but otherwise just waved, smiled, mimed looking at his watch, and continued moving in her direction. She could tell from the response that Shaw was well liked.

"Where's Lew?" she asked.

He sat down across from her. "He'll be squared away in a few minutes. I signed the release, but . . . there's paperwork." He paused, and then went on. "Speaking of which: this is for you." He pushed a file across the table.

"What is it?" she asked.

"His medical file." Another pause, and then he explained: "If I don't have it, no one can take it from me."

Adrienne frowned. "I'm not so sure about releasing him," she said. "I mean, how do you know he's okay? What if—"

"Look," the psychiatrist told her, "here's the deal. I think he's going to be all right now. I really do." He tried a little smile that didn't make it. "There's no reason to keep him here. And as interesting as it has been . . . well—my involvement has to come to an end." He stared at his fingernails for a moment. "You haven't seen it, but I'm catching hell about 'proper channels' . . ." He shrugged. "I'm sure you understand: I'm not an independent operator. Not at all." He tried a smile. It wasn't successful.

What Shaw was saying was not unreasonable, but there was something wrong with *the way* he was saying it. He wanted her to say that she understood, but she wasn't in the mood.

"So you're bailing," she decided.

The psychiatrist winced. "No. Come on. I have other responsibilities, you must know that." He looked up at the ceiling, let the air seep from between his lips.

Adrienne managed a smile. "I know I'm not being fair," she told him. "You've been incredible. But . . . I'm just not sure . . . what to do now." She pushed her hair back from her forehead.

"I have a name for you," Shaw said, patting his pockets. Finding what he was looking for, he removed a yellow Post-it from his shirt, and handed it to her.

Adrienne saw that it was imprinted with the word Health-Source and, below that, Shaw had scribbled a name:

"Sidney Shapiro . . ." She looked up. "Who's he?"

Shaw thought about it. "He's a man who knows about these things."

"What? You mean—memory?"

A funny little look came over Shaw's face. "No. I mean about your sister—and Lewis."

She still didn't understand. "He knows what happened to them?"

Shaw shook his head, and got to his feet. "He knows about implants," he told her. "The ways they're used and misused. He knows more about that than anyone in the world." The psychiatrist hesitated for a moment, as something occurred to him. "Or maybe not."

Adrienne studied the name on the Post-it. "But who *is* he?"

Shaw thought about it. "He's . . . a retired civil servant." Then he chuckled. Ruefully.

"And you think he'll talk to us?"

Shaw shook his head. "I don't know. If you show him that file, he might."

"Okay, but . . . do you have a number for him?"

The psychiatrist shook his head for the second time. "He lives in West Virginia, near Harpers Ferry. I suspect he's in the book."

"All right," Adrienne said. "Sid Shapiro. We'll give it a shot." She got to her feet, and put out her hand to shake.

He took her hand in his own, then covered it with his other hand. "If he asks where you got his name . . ."

"What should I tell him?"

Tight little smile from the nice shrink. "Well, don't mention me. Just tell him you heard about him in a documentary on A&E."

"Which one?" she asked.

"I think it was about 'mind control.' "

McBride was waiting for them in the lobby, and it was obvious that the two men had already said their good-byes, because Shaw gave him a little salute, then hurried off down the corridor.

Maybe it was her imagination, but Lew McBride looked different somehow. He looked taller, his posture at once more athletic and relaxed. He smiled at her as she walked toward him and the smile seemed different too—less guarded. Happier. And there was something in his eyes. Maybe he is all right now, she thought.

"Can I buy you lunch?" he asked. "We can talk about our future."

They walked out into the cold and sunny day.

She had to ask: "Do you have any money? I'm getting low."

"As a matter of fact," he said, "I do. The hospital gave me some walking-around money. Officially, I'm part of a research project. Had to sign a bunch of releases. I think Ray Shaw suggested I was going to sue." The sidewalks were crowded, full of purposeful pedestrians. He took her arm as they approached the curb and held it as they crossed the intersection. "Especially," he continued, "since I'm known to hang around with my own legal advocate."

"Your unemployed advocate," she corrected.

"We're both unemployed," he told her. "It's something we share."

She looked at him. He *was* different. This conversation was different from any she'd had with him. Maybe you couldn't joke around, she thought, maybe irony didn't work—if you didn't know who you were.

"So where are we going?"

"There's a piña colada stand across the street from Needle Park. Seventy-second and Broadway."

"Sounds perfect," she said. "The hotel's only a few blocks away."

"They have hot dogs, too. The natural kind, with crunchy casings."

"Grilled, not boiled!"

"Right! And real mustard—not that yellow stuff."

"So, I take it, this means you know New York?"

He shrugged. "I know where to get a good hot dog."

They walked on, looking for a cab. After a while, she said, "You're right about one thing."

"What's that?"

"I don't know about the hospital being spooked, but Shaw was. Spooked, I mean."

"Yeah, I got that feeling, too. Probably just his department, leaning on him. He took a chance, doing what he did."

"I know. If you'd gone out the window . . ." Her voice trailed away and she felt like an idiot, talking about suicide. Just a little while earlier, the man next to her had been tied to his bed in a pysch ward.

"That's gone, by the way," he said. "Along with the base-ball bat and the blood. It's so gone, it's hard to believe I bought it. Bought it right down to knowing what it would feel like to . . ." He shook his head.

"But you did," she said.

"What?"

"Buy it."

They were at another intersection. He took her arm again, restrained her as a Step-Van hurtled through the red light. "Yeah I did," he admitted. "And one thing's for sure."

They stepped off the curb. He didn't release her arm. "What's that?" she asked.

"I'm going to find out who sold it to me."

33 She was looking for the name of the man in West Virginia, the name Shaw had written on a Post-it in McBride's medical file, when the snapshot fell to the floor. McBride was in the kitchen, emptying a can of lentil soup into a pan, when she stooped to pick up the picture—and hesitated.

It was a 3 by 5 Polaroid photograph of . . . what? She picked up the picture from the floor, set it down on the desk, and cocked her head. Some kind of . . . thing. Unfamiliar, and yet—she'd seen it before. Where? It took a moment—then it hit her. She'd seen it on the floor of her apartment, spilled by whoever it was who'd trashed the place. Lying there in Nikki's ashes, that tiny transparent *thing*. Which she thought was a contaminant of some kind, an artifact of the cremation process. And yet, Doctor Shaw had taken a picture of it. How?

She turned the photograph over, and found a notation scribbled on the back under the date stamp:

> *Object X, 6.4mm × .6mm,*
> *removed from hippocampus*
> *of J. Duran*
> *S/ Dr. N. Allalin*

Her chest began to tighten with the realization that this wasn't the artifact she'd found in her apartment. Or, rather, it was the same *kind* of thing—a translucent tube of glass shot through with gold and silver wires—about as long and thick as a grain of rice. Different, but the same.

An implant.

Which meant that what had been done to Lew McBride had also been done to her sister. The tightening in her chest fused, turned into anger, and gave way to despair.

"Oh, Jesus!" she cried.

McBride looked up from the soup that he was stirring. "What's the matter?"

She just shook her head, tears flying.

Seeing her unhappiness, he rushed to her side. And saw that she was looking at a photo of the implant. "Hey," he said, giving her shoulder a squeeze, "take it easy. It's gone. It's out."

"It's on the floor of my apartment!"

Her outburst caught him by surprise. "What?"

"One of those! In Nikki's ashes—just like that!"

He started to ask how it got there, but caught himself in time.

"It was in the urn from the funeral parlor," she said, dragging a sleeve across her eyes. Then she giggled through her tears. "All that . . . bullshit!"

"What bullshit?" (He was trying to be encouraging.)

"About the Riedles. And 'her overdose'! And the settlement they gave her. That's why Eddie's asset search went nowhere. None of it *happened*. It was all a lie—like what they did to you." Suddenly, she wanted to kill someone. Specifically, she wanted to kill the person who'd turned her sister into the robot she'd met in the Nine West store, the girl who'd fried herself in the bathtub. Forget *closure*. "I'm going to crucify the son of a bitch who did this," she swore.

McBride nodded, shrugged, went back to the kitchen. "Take a number," he told her.

As Doctor Shaw had guessed, Sidney Shapiro had a listed number in the Jefferson County white pages. Seated cross-legged on the bed, drinking Genesee Ale, Adrienne worked up the nerve to call him. Or tried to. Cold calls were not her forte. Never had been. "Maybe you should phone him," she called out.

"God . . . *damnit!*" The expletive slipped through McBride's gritted teeth as he reacted to burning himself on the handle of a cheap aluminum pan. Adrienne watched as he used his sleeve as a potholder, pulling it down over his hand. Then he maneuvered it over to the cold burner. "I don't think so," he replied.

Leaving the tiny kitchen, he carried the pan into their room, and poured the soup into the two white bowls on the table. Also on the table were a pair of square, plastic take-out salads, a sourdough baton and some foil wrapped patties of butter. The rose that he'd bought for her was standing on the table in an empty Coca-Cola can.

"I think we should doorstep the guy," he told her. He gestured toward the table. "Dinner's ready."

She hopped off the bed and padded over in her bare feet. "You mean just go there? Why not call ahead?"

"Well, I'm sure that would be more polite, but . . . what are you going to tell him? That we want to talk about *mind* control? I don't think so. I think we just go there."

She shrugged. "I guess."

He raised his bottle of beer. "To you," he told her. "Thanks for . . ." he squinted, smiled a slightly crooked smile, "I don't know. Just, thanks."

They touched bottles. "Anytime," she said and then flushed because it sounded so stupid. What did she mean—*anytime?* Anytime, what? She smiled back at him, and his eyes seemed to hold her there, so she kept on smiling. There was something different about him now—that lazy crooked smile, for instance, was really getting to her. She'd been attracted to him before in a vague, diffused way but now she could hardly look at him without feeling a . . . a buzz. It was the last thing she needed or wanted, a useless complication that could only be trouble. *Someone's trying to kill me,* she thought, *not to mention him. I'm out of a job. I'm almost out of money. And I'm thinking this guy and I should . . . what? Get it on? Good plan, Scout.*

She bent down, dipped her spoon into the soup, filling it with the front-to-back motion she'd learned from an etiquette book, then put it in her mouth. It was so hot that she almost had to spit it out. But she didn't, grabbing her beer instead, and gulping some down.

"You all right?" he asked.

"Hot," she said. "I burned the roof of my mouth." She guzzled her Genesee.

He leaned toward her. "I know a folk cure," he said and for a moment, she thought he was going to kiss her, that *that* was 'the folk cure.' She felt it again, a sharp twist of desire. But he was leaning forward, not to kiss her, but to get up from his chair. He went to the kitchenette and returned with a glass of milk. *Get a grip,* she told herself, and took a sip.

He was smiling at her.

It's the Stockholm Syndrome, she thought. *Please God—let it be the Stockholm Syndrome.*

* * *

In the morning, McBride did the driving.

On the way, Adrienne filled him in on Sidney Shapiro.

She'd gone out after dinner—right after dinner—the night before. McBride was tired, still suffering the lingering effects of his confinement at the hospital. And she hadn't trusted herself to be in the same room with him, and so she had walked from the Mayflower to the library, where she'd cooled her heels, sitting in front of a stack of books about the CIA.

None of the books had that much to say about Shapiro, who'd presided over a program so "sensitive"—Adrienne took this to mean "criminal"—that virtually all its records had been destroyed. This, in the face of Senate hearings on "alleged human rights abuses by the U.S. intelligence community."

Moving from index to index in each of the books, Adrienne had managed to put together a rough dossier, one that was filled with lacunae, but would have to suffice. "He studied at Cambridge," she told McBride, reading from her notes. "Research psychology, just like you. Then MIT. After that, he was in Korea for a while—no one knows what he was doing there, but he was supposed to be a civilian employee of the Army. (This was in '53.) Then he came back to the States and set up something called the Human Ecology Fund. That was in New York."

"Then what?" McBride asked.

"I'm not done. This Human Ecology thing was supposed to be private, but all its money came from the CIA. So he was an NOC."

"A what?"

"An NOC! It means Nonofficial Cover."

McBride glanced at her. "Where did you get this stuff?"

"At the library—when you were sleeping."

"Hunh!"

"So, anyway, this fund was a CIA front. And what it did was, it funded behavioral studies—*secret* studies—in mind control. They called it Mk Ultra. Artichoke. Bluebird. Things like that."

"And Shapiro was part of this?"

"He *ran* it for about ten years. Then they closed it down, and he took over as head of the Science & Technology Directorate at the CIA. But it was interesting what they did. They studied psychotropic drugs, hypnotism, telepathy, brainwashing, psychic driving—"

"I saw a documentary about it," McBride told her. "On A&E. About a year ago. They were experimenting, testing hallucinogenic drugs on people they considered 'fair game'—people in prisons and mental institutions, suspected communists, people who were breaking the law."

"So, what happened? They got stoned, right?"

"Right. Only they didn't know they were stoned. These weren't exactly clinical trials. So most of them—what they thought was that they were sick or crazy."

"Of course. That *is* what you'd think."

"People lost their minds. And at least one guy lost his life."

"Who?"

"A scientist named Olsen. His 'colleagues' slipped him a dose of LSD—and he lost it. Completely. Or so we're told. A few days later, he threw himself out the window of his hotel."

"Migod . . ."

"Or that's what they said. According to the documentary, he probably had some help."

" 'Help'?"

"There's reason to think he was pushed."

"Oh."

They were crossing the Delaware Memorial Bridge. Below, the water looked metallic and sullen. Ahead of them, brake lights flared ruby-red as the traffic congealed before a phalanx of tollbooths.

"So it looks like you were right," Adrienne said.

"About what?"

"Showing up on his doorstep. I don't think a phone call would work."

At the tollbooth, McBride pressed a bill into a woman's outstretched hand. The air outside was cold, the woman's hand warm, the moment they touched oddly precise, carved out of time. It struck him as a perfect microcosm of commerce, passage over a river in exchange for currency, a transaction that had taken place all over the world for centuries. The river below seemed huge, sinuous, alive and he could sense its moist, dank presence in the air despite the heavy aroma of diesel. Sounds welled up around him, the roar and rush of vehicles unfurling into the air as they accelerated away from the booth. McBride couldn't get over how he felt, connected to his perceptions in a way that seemed brand-new. Even the drive down the Interstate which he knew was supposed to be tedious, struck him as exciting, the play of motion and space, the constant patterning and repatterning of the traffic a kind of jazz.

They checked into the Hilltop House, an old hotel perched on the mountainside in Harpers Ferry, overlooking the famous mountain gap where the Potomac and Shenandoah rivers meet. The hotel was nearly empty—too late for fall color tours, too early for the holidays, and they had their pick of rooms. Once again, and for reasons of frugality, they took only one. Adrienne decided on a double with a view, and— she made a point of this—two beds.

An aging bellboy showed them to the room, and waited at the door until McBride pressed a bill into his papery hand. Once the old man was gone, the two of them stepped onto the balcony and looked out. From here, the rivers were visible only as occasional flashes of silver threaded between the dark mounded shapes of the wooded slopes.

The address they had for Shapiro was a P.O. box in the tiny, unincorporated town of Bakerton. They drove there—it was only a few miles from Harpers Ferry—figuring they'd ask around. How hard could it be to find someone who lived in a place whose population was sixty-three?

As it turned out, not hard at all.

Bakerton amounted to twenty or thirty houses scattered over a hundred acres of rolling woodland. Besides the houses, and a couple of trailers, there was a church, and a country store with a single gas pump in front of it.

They went inside, where a man with a bushy beard, a mustache, and a corona of red hair, was standing at the register. All around him were bowls of penny candy, boxes of shotgun shells, and jars filled with pickled pigs' feet and hard-boiled eggs.

The P.O. box was not, as they'd expected, a bid for privacy. The town didn't offer home delivery of mail, so every resident had a box at the post office.

"Right through there," the clerk said after he explained this, gesturing through a doorway where McBride could see ranks of cubicles, each with a tiny door and combination lock. Against the doorway leading into the post office, a trio of men stood drinking coffee from Styrofoam cups. What they shared, beyond coffee, was a lot of hair, a lot of wrinkles, and a taste for camouflage.

From the look of them, McBride would have guessed that they'd be talking about NASCAR or deer hunting, but what he overheard as he approached them was: "You're telling me the NASDAQ isn't overheated?"

It almost made him laugh. But he kept a straight face, asked, "You know where I can find a guy named Shapiro?"

"You mean, 'James Bond'?"

McBride chuckled. "Yeah."

"He lives up Quarry Road," said a wizened little man in green fatigues and a baseball cap with the name of a feed company on the front: *Rimbaud*.

"Which is where?"

"Go out t'front door, across the street you'll see a little road runs crosswise to the one you drove in on. That's Quarry Road. You head on up there about a mile, look for a red mailbox on the left. That's Sid."

"Thanks a lot."

" 'Course, you might find him praying," said the tiny man. "And if you do, you'll have to wait him out."

"Not 'praying,' " one of the other men said. "*Meditating.*

It's different. But Carson's right. You come up on him when he's meditating, he won't even look at you. Seems rude, but that's Sid for you."

"Is he . . . *religious?*" Adrienne asked. She frowned at the thought. It didn't seem likely.

"Buddhist," the tiny man piped in his country twang. "One of them Jewish Buddhists. Says he's got a heavy karmic burden." He paused. "You watch A&E?"

Adrienne smiled, nodded.

"Then you know what I'm talking about. That boy's got some *shit* to come to terms with." The other men laughed.

"Pardon my French," the man continued, "but I guess he's trying to square it—" He tapped himself on the temple. "—up here."

Quarry Road was gravel, puddled from a recent rain. It passed through terrain that was heavily wooded, the trunks of the slender, immature trees black with moisture. They jounced up an incline, the sharp winter sun flickering on and off through the thin tree trunks. McBride turned the Dodge into the drive and a moment later, drew the car to a halt next to a battered white pickup. In the clearing stood a simple log house. Beyond it at a distance of a hundred yards or so was a large structure that looked like a greenhouse. To the right, a fenced-in pasture held half a dozen llamas. They trotted toward Adrienne and McBride as the two of them walked from the car toward the house. And then beyond them, toward the center of the pasture, they saw Sidney Shapiro—engaged in the slow, graceful movements McBride recognized as Tai Chi.

Despite the cold, Shapiro was bare chested, wearing only a pair of grey sweat pants. He appeared to be barefoot. He moved with great concentration and composure. Adrienne looked at McBride and raised her eyebrows, but neither of them spoke. After a minute or two, the llamas lost interest in them and resumed grazing—some of them venturing quite close to Shapiro, who seemed oblivious. The old man was thin, but with a stringy muscularity, and a full, thick shock of black hair. He looked agile and strong for a man in his seventies, extending one leg out with excruciating slowness until it was straight and parallel to the ground, then gracefully lowering the limb while turning in a painstaking and unhurried spiral. It was like watching a ballet dancer in extreme slow motion and McBride felt hypnotized by the fluidity of Shapiro's movements. For a moment, the sun poked out from behind the clouds and lit up the pasture like a stage, and McBride saw with something of a shock that if the man's body belied his age, his face did not. It was all bone, skeletal beneath the thin, stretched skin.

Shapiro finished his exercise with head tilted back, legs astride, both hands outstretched and upraised to the sky. He held this position for about thirty seconds, then gracefully brought his arms down and began to walk toward them, picking his way carefully through the field, stopping to stroke the neck of each llama. He let himself out through the metal gate, refastened it, and only then looked at them.

"Hello."

"Hi . . . Doctor Shapiro?"

"Yes."

"My name is Lew McBride. This is Adrienne Cope."

"What can I do for you?" he asked, swinging his focus from McBride to Adrienne and then back again. He seemed very composed, McBride thought, for a man with a "heavy karmic burden."

"Well, uhhh . . . I was hoping we could talk to you."

"Oh?"

"Yeah. I was hoping we could talk about . . ." Duran wasn't sure how to put it.

"Your work," Adrienne said.

"My work?" Shapiro turned to her. His eyes were coal-black, and glittering. "I'm retired."

"The work you used to do. MkUltra."

Shapiro frowned, and his eyes took on an irritated glint. "Are you reporters?"

They shook their heads.

"Because I told the young man on the telephone that I'm

not interested in appearing in any other documentaries. I didn't find the first experience all that rewarding." He looked up at the sky, then back to McBride. "Although as a form of penance, few things could be more . . . fulfilling . . . than seeing one's life reduced to sound bites interspersed with ads for a liposuction clinic." He shook his head. "It's not an act of contrition I intend to repeat."

"That isn't why we're here," Adrienne said.

"Oh?" Shapiro looked from one to the other. "Then why *are* you here?"

"My sister and . . . Mr. McBride . . . were victims."

Shapiro gave her a skeptical look. "I don't think so," he told her. "That was a very long time ago." He gave an apologetic chuckle. "If you think you're a victim of mind control—"

"Not me," Adrienne said. "My sister—"

"Then I'd suggest that you tell her to turn off her television set—and the 'mind control' will go away. That's my advice."

"I can't tell her anything," Adrienne replied. "She's dead."

Shapiro blanched. "I'm sorry." He paused. "Look," he told her, "this is a wholly discredited field. The territory was abandoned decades ago."

"Was it really?" McBride asked.

Shapiro ignored the skepticism. "It was supposed to be the next frontier. And maybe it was. We thought the benefits of going into outer space, putting men on the moon, would be trivial compared to what we might find . . ." He tapped his head. ". . . in here." Then he looked at Adrienne, and shook his head ruefully. "We called it 'inner space.' " He sighed. "But that was a very long time ago and, while I don't know how old your sister was, *this* young man would have been a toddler." He smiled a smile that never quite rose to his eyes. "And contrary to what you may have heard, we didn't experiment on children. So . . ." He turned to leave.

"Can we show you something?" Adrienne asked.

Shapiro turned back to her.

"Then—if you want—we'll leave," Adrienne promised.

"Deal," Shapiro replied.

Adrienne dug into her purse until she found the Polaroid snapshot of the implant. Wordlessly, she handed it to Shapiro.

Who, farsighted, held it at arm's length, squinting with skepticism. But, soon, his face went slack, and he looked up. "Where did you get this?" he asked.

"A neurosurgeon took it out of me," McBride told him. "Less than a week ago."

Shapiro's eyes returned to the photograph, which he studied for a long while. Finally, he gave a little shake of his head and, handing the snapshot back to Adrienne, said, "Come on in."

34

At a gesture from Shapiro, they removed their shoes. The interior of his cabin was a minimalist masterpiece. Tatami mats on scrubbed pine floors, walls so white they seemed to have been whitewashed. A green enamel woodstove stood at one end of the room, which was furnished entirely by a low table made of pine and half a dozen cushions. An ikebana arrangement—consisting of a single white orchid and two arching blades of long, dried grass—rested on the table.

Shapiro placed the snapshot beside the flower arrangement. "Please," he said, gesturing to the cushions. A few minutes later, he emerged from behind a shoji screen with a tray that held a squat, gunmetal teapot and three tiny cups. Setting the tray on the table, he subsided into a sitting position, and poured the tea. McBride realized that since he and Adrienne had entered the house, neither of them had spoken a word.

Shapiro blew vigorously across the surface of his tea, took a sip, and set the cup aside. Then he picked up the photograph of the implant, held it in the light, and examined it. Finally, he shook his head and said, "My legacy . . ." His mouth spread in a grimace.

Adrienne inclined her head toward the snapshot. "What would this thing do to a person?" she asked. "Exactly."

Shapiro shrugged. " 'Exactly'? I don't know. I'd have to take it apart—in a lab—and even then . . . there's been a lot of water under the bridge."

"But—"

"If you want to learn what this does, or what it might do, you're going to have to do a lot of reading. Starting with Delgado."

"Who's 'Delgado'?" Adrienne asked.

"The *Times* ran a front-page story on him more than thirty years ago," Shapiro replied. "I think he was at Yale." He paused, and sipped his tea. "There was a picture of him— standing in the bull ring with a transmitter—the bull right in front of him, pawing the ground. Tremendous showmanship!"

"And what happened?" Adrienne asked.

"Well, he stopped the bull, cold—in midcharge. Very dramatic. Then he pushed a second button, and the creature turned and sauntered away."

"So it was like a shock collar," Adrienne suggested. "Or an electric fence."

"Oh, no—not at all," Shapiro corrected. "This was nothing so simple. In fact, it was actually a dual test—the first button activated an electrode that controlled the bull's motor cortex. The second button targeted the hippocampus, which turned the animal's anger into indifference."

McBride frowned. This wasn't anything new. He'd read all about Delgado as an undergraduate. Everyone had. "What about this?" he asked, tapping the photograph with his forefinger.

For the first time, Shapiro looked uncomfortable.

"Look," he said, "I'm a dinosaur. I've been out of the field for . . ." He caught himself, and smiled. ". . . a long time. But there are things I can't talk about. I signed a secrecy agreement. So . . ."

"Hypothetically," Adrienne cajoled.

Shapiro sighed. "I suppose it could be a miniaturized version of . . . certain devices . . . that might have been used experimentally . . . at one time or another."

McBride snorted at the old man's circumlocution, which brought a frown to Shapiro's face.

Turning his eyes to Adrienne, the old man shrugged. "There's a lot in the open literature. I don't suppose I'd be giving anything away if I told you what it *looks* like."

"Which is what?"

"A depth electrode."

"And what would *that* do?"

He shrugged again. "Depends . . ."

"On what?" Adrienne asked.

"The frequency to which it's tuned," McBride suggested.

Shapiro smiled. "Very good."

"And if you had to guess—" McBride began.

"Four to seven megahertz might be interesting," Shapiro told them.

"Why?" Adrienne asked.

"Because it's the hypnoidal EEG frequency—and, *hypothetically,* it would enable the reception of a sinewave that . . . ummm, could entrain the brain."

" 'Entrain'?" Adrienne repeated the word to make sure she had it right. It was the same word that Doctor Shaw had used when she'd told him about McBride's behavior at Bethany Beach—when he logged onto that Web site. The program, or whatever it was called.

"It's when the brain locks onto a particular signal," McBride explained. "A flashing light, a repetitive sound—especially one that's been established in a trance state. They say the brain's 'entrained' to the signal."

Shapiro was impressed. "You've done your homework."

"I'm a psychologist," McBride told him.

"But what would happen?" Adrienne asked. "What would the purpose be?"

"Well," the old man replied, "it would allow a trance state to be continually refreshed and reinforced without the necessity of rehypnotizing the subject."

"So if you had one of these in your head, you'd be . . . what? Hypnotized all the time?"

"More or less," Shapiro said. "Though there's no reason to believe that that's its only function."

"Why not?" McBride asked.

Shapiro refreshed their cups of tea, which Adrienne drank more from politeness than thirst. It tasted like burnt seaweed.

"Because everything's changed," Shapiro finally replied. "An implant like this would probably use nano technology. It would have computers embedded in it. And God knows what else."

"But what for?"

"Hypothetically? I suppose one could introduce certain 'scenarios' that, coupled with hypnosis, would go a long way toward establishing a sort of . . . 'virtual biography.' "

Adrienne and McBride chewed on the expression. " 'A virtual biography' . . ." Adrienne repeated.

"A phony past—but one that felt right. Up to a point."

"Christ," McBride muttered.

Shapiro smiled. "Memory's not much more than a slurry of chemicals and electrical potentials—which aren't that difficult to manipulate, if you know what you're doing. For instance—it's well-known—if you raise the level of acetylcholine in the brain—and you can do that by hitting the subject with radio waves at ultrasonic frequencies—the synapses begin to fire more and more slowly until . . . well, until they don't fire at all. And when that happens, remembering becomes impossible. The memories are there, but they're inaccessible."

"So you could impose amnesia," Adrienne suggested.

"Exactly. More tea?"

It was all so civilized, McBride thought. This charming

and matter-of-fact old man, serving tea in his ascetic little house. Under the circumstances, it was hard to hate him for the damage that he'd done, hard to conjure the horrors that he'd contrived. Hard, but not impossible. McBride could feel the anger rising, a primitive ruckus in the back of his mind. The bulls. The cats. The ochre room. The virtual Jeff Duran. He'd like to smack this syrupy son of a bitch—let him know what the sound of one-hand-clapping was really like. Instead, he said, "Let me ask you a question."

"Shoot."

Don't tempt me. "Hypothetically—how would you put someone together? The whole package?"

The old man shifted uncomfortably in his seat. After a moment, he asked: "Based on what I've read in the open literature?"

"Of course," McBride replied.

Shapiro thought about it for a moment. "Well," he said, "I suppose you'd give the subject an EEG—get a record of his brainwaves under different stumuli. With that, and a PET scan, you could put together a map of the subject's brain—its emotive and intellectual centers."

"Then what?" Adrienne asked.

"Well, once you had *that* information, you could encrypt a set of audiograms that would target those centers, delivering them on the back of ELF transmissions—"

"Elf?" Adrienne asked.

"It's an acronym for Extremely Low Frequency radio waves. That's what I was talking about before: the four to seven megahertz band."

"And so, if you did all that, what would happen?" Adrienne asked.

"Well," Shapiro replied, "you'd change the landscape of the brain."

"What does *that* mean?" McBride asked.

"Just what I said: you'd bring about some very specific— but temporary—changes in the physical structure of the brain."

"And that would accomplish . . . what?"

"Depends on the audiograms," Shapiro told them. "But amnesia might be one result."

"Total amnesia?" McBride asked.

Shapiro shrugged. "You might remember how to speak Italian, but you wouldn't remember how you'd learned it—or if you'd ever been to Italy."

"Would you remember who you were?" McBride asked.

Shapiro looked at McBride. "That would depend."

"On what?"

"On what the programmer was trying to achieve. Once the subject was prepped, and his memory blocked, he'd probably have a neurophonic prosthesis implanted."

"A 'prosthesis,' " Adrienne repeated.

Shapiro uncurled a forefinger in the direction of the snapshot that was lying on the table. "One of those. If you were to look at the object in that photograph under a microscope, my guess is you'd find it contains insulated electrodes that receive and process audiograms on particular frequencies. The prosthesis would allow the transmissions to bypass the inner ear—the cochlea and eighth cranial nerve—delivering the messages directly to the brain."

McBride thought about it. "So it would be like hearing voices," he suggested.

"It would be like hearing God," Shapiro corrected. "But the implant is just a part of the process. The programmer would have other tools . . ."

"Like what?"

"Hypnosis . . . sensory deprivation . . ."

"And how would *that* work?" Adrienne asked.

Shapiro pursed his lips, thought for a moment, and replied. "Well, the subject could be given hypnotic suggestions, preparing him for the experience he's about to have. Then we'd lower him into a blackout tank filled with saltwater that's been heated to the same temperature as his body—around 98 degrees. It's a very strange experience—like floating in space."

"You've tried it?"

"Of course," Shapiro replied. "I've tried everything." He paused, and then went on. "After an hour or so in the tank, it's impossible to say where your skin ends and the water begins. You just . . . dissolve." He nodded at the cup in front of Adrienne. "Like a sugar cube in a cup of hot tea. And when that happens, the subject becomes . . . malleable."

McBride listened in fascinated disbelief, while Adrienne stared at the former spook, imagining her sister floating in the blackout tank.

"After a protracted period—"

"What's 'protracted'?" McBride demanded.

"A day. A week. A month," Shapiro told him. "The point is that, after a while, the subject's identity begins to disintegrate. It's like a near death experience, with all the senses shutting down—or seeming to. You can imagine: once you're in the tank, there's nothing to see or hear, nothing to taste or smell, no sense of touch. No sense of time. If you think losing your mind is unsettling, try losing your body." Shapiro paused, and a thin smile curled above his chin. "Even so, some people find the experience . . . enlightening."

"And others?" Adrienne asked.

The old man shrugged. "Others don't."

McBride leaned forward: "*Then* what?"

Shapiro gave him a sidelong glance. "Then? Well, then you take it to the next level."

"Which is what?"

" 'Intensification.' Once the subject's identity is broken down, he's basically a tabula rasa. It's a relatively simple matter to imprint whatever 'memories' you like."

"How?" McBride asked.

"We'd create scenarios compatible with his psychological profile, and turn them into films. The subject would watch the films in tandem with a subliminal stream of audiograms."

"Like in a theater," Adrienne suggested.

Shapiro chuckled. "No," he said, "it's more engaging than that. He'd wear a special helmet, one that's fitted with speakers and jacks. Audio in, audio out—that sort of thing. Then we'd plug him in and . . ."

"What?"

"Well, from the subject's perspective, it's like sitting six feet away from a sixty-two-inch television screen, watching 3-D images in binaural sound. It's a very involving experience—and that's just the conscious part of it all. Add hypnosis and drugs and . . . it's a lot like shaping clay. Soft clay."

"Drugs," Adrienne said. She flashed on that little vial in Nikki's computer: *Placebo #1.* "What kind of drugs?"

Shapiro made a face. "Pyschedelics of every description. We had a great deal of success with a drug from Ecuador called burrandaga. And with Ketamine—more commonly used as an animal tranquilizer. Both of them cause a sort of dissociative amnesia."

"Ketamine," Adrienne said. "Isn't that one of the date rape drugs?"

"Precisely," Shapiro said. "It would be very effective for that purpose for the same reason it was effective for our purposes."

"What do you mean?"

"Well, if you wanted to 'take advantage of someone,' as we used to say, ketamine has the effect of disconnecting a person from her body. Whatever happens seems to be occurring in another dimension. And these events fail to take hold in the memory."

"There's a built-in amnesiac effect?"

"Precisely. Afterwards, the rape—or whatever—it's as if it never happened. Subjects never remembered being in the tank, or the helmet, or being bombarded with 'new memories.' "

"So you'd have this person in this helmet. And what would . . . what would the person be looking at?" McBride asked.

"Men in hoods," Adrienne muttered. "Satanists."

Shapiro gave her a peculiar look, then turned to answer McBride's question. "It would depend."

"On what?" McBride demanded.

"On what you wanted him to remember—and what you wanted him to forget."

McBride sipped his tea, and found that it was cold. "How long would this take?" he asked.

Shapiro shook his head. "Hard to say. If you're tweaking the subject's identity, that's one thing. If you're building someone from the ground up—that's quite another."

" 'Tweaking the identity,' " Adrienne repeated, her voice heavy with a mix of wonder and incredulity.

"Right." Shapiro rearranged his legs on the cushion. "I'm curious," he said, shifting gears in the conversation. "What was your relationship with—" he turned toward McBride "—with this young woman's sister?"

"I was her therapist," McBride said.

"And she came to your apartment?"

"Yes."

"And, as it turned out, both of you had a prosthesis . . . ?"

"Right."

Shapiro frowned. "How can you be sure of that? Did she have a CAT scan or—"

"My sister was cremated," Adrienne explained. "I found the implant in her ashes."

The scientist blanched. "Christ," he muttered. Then he changed the subject, or seemed to. "Tell me something," he said, turning to McBride. "Did you leave your apartment often?"

"What do you mean?"

"I mean, when you were practicing as a therapist—did you get out much? Or did you stay at home?"

McBride's shoulders rose and fell. "I guess I stayed pretty close to home."

"I'll bet," Shapiro told him.

"Why?"

"Because I think it's very likely that there was a monitoring site in your building. The apartment across the hall—"

"—or next door," Adrienne suggested.

"Upstairs, or on the floor below . . . the point is: they'd have wanted a way to reinforce the signal. And one of the consequences would be that once you were out of range, you'd begin to feel uncomfortable—unless you were on medication. Were you taking medication?"

"No," McBride said, his voice thick with sarcasm. "I just watched television." He cleared his throat. "But what you're telling me is that people can be turned into puppets and zombies—"

"Automatons," Adrienne interjected.

Shapiro nodded. "Colloquially speaking, yes."

Adrienne looked away, tears in her eyes.

"So you could do whatever you wanted with them," McBride continued. "Make them laugh or cry, walk in front of a car—"

"—or give them a childhood that wasn't their own," Adrienne suggested.

Shapiro heaved a sigh. Turned his palms toward the ceiling. "Yeah." He drew a sharp breath, reached out toward the flower arrangement and tapped his fingernail against the arching blade of grass. Exhaled. "Look," he said, "I'm full of remorse for my part in this research. And I'm sorry if what I did has touched your lives. But there's nothing I can do about it."

"You can help us understand," Adrienne said.

"Can I?"

"Yes," she replied.

"It was a long time ago."

"I want to know who did this," Adrienne told him.

Shapiro inclined his head. "Of course you do. But why? You say it's because you want to 'understand'—but I suspect it's because you want revenge."

"Look," McBride said, "you can call it whatever you like, but . . ." He paused. A low-pressure front was moving through his head—at least, that's what it felt like—and if he didn't wait for it to pass, he'd go off like a flashbulb in Shapiro's face. Because what he really wanted to do was take this born-again Buddhist, with his pared down life and his cute little cups of tea, and knock the hell out of him. Instead, he said, "I'm a wreck."

"What!?" Shapiro was startled by the remark, and Adrienne, too, seemed taken aback.

"I'm sitting here with you in this very nice house, drinking tea," McBride told him, "and I may seem fine. 'No blood, no foul!' Right? Wrong. I'm a walking *shipwreck*—no shit. Whoever did this . . . whoever did this took everything from me. My childhood. My parents. My *self*. I'll never be the same. They took every memory I ever had, subverted every dream, and wasted I don't know how many years of my life. Even now, when I try to think about it, it's a blank. It's all a blank until *she* came through the door, yelling about how she was going to sue me." He paused, and took a deep breath. "Which is just a way of saying: I've lost a couple of things . . . and I'm not talking about books and furniture and clothes."

Shapiro shook his head. "I wasn't suggesting—"

"What about my sister?" Adrienne asked. "What happened to her was worse than murder. They turned her inside out—made her kill someone—and drove her to suicide. What about *her*?"

Shapiro closed his eyes for several seconds, then opened them. "The point I was trying to make is that what you're doing—"

" 'Doing'?" Adrienne repeated. "We're not 'doing' anything—except asking questions."

"Exactly," Shapiro said. "And my point is: that could be a dangerous thing to do."

The three of them were quiet for a moment. Finally, McBride said, "I want to stop whoever did this to me from doing it to anyone else."

Shapiro nodded slowly. Turned to Adrienne. "You said your sister killed someone?"

Adrienne nodded. "An old man. In a wheelchair." She paused. "And then she killed herself."

Shapiro reached across the table for McBride's medical file and, opening it, began to leaf slowly through its pages. After a while, he looked up and said, "I'd like to talk to your doctor . . . this man, Shaw." Adrienne and McBride exchanged glances. "Is that a problem?" Shapiro asked.

"I'm not sure," Adrienne said, remembering Shaw's tight little smile and the suggestion that she tell Shapiro she'd learned about him from watching a documentary.

Shapiro smiled, almost sheepishly. "I want to be sure that you are who you say you are—and that what you say happened, happened."

"You've got the file," Adrienne told him.

" 'The file,' " Shapiro repeated with a soft chuckle. "The three of us are sitting here, talking about counterfeiting human beings—and you're surprised that I should want to verify the contents of a manila folder?"

In the end, Adrienne couldn't see how talking to Shapiro could harm Ray Shaw. And it would only take a minute. All Shapiro wanted was confirmation that they weren't making the whole thing up.

Shapiro made the call from a cell-phone in the kitchen. They could hear him talking softly, but not well enough to understand what was being said. After a minute or two, he returned to the living room, and sat down beside them.

"So?" McBride asked. "What did he say?"

Shapiro shook his head. "I wasn't able to reach him."

"But—"

"I spoke with his wife . . ."

Adrienne and McBride exchanged glances. Shapiro seemed strangely subdued. "And what did *she* say?" Adrienne asked.

"She was distraught. She said her husband was struck by a car outside the hospital last night. The police are looking for the driver."

Though the three of them were sitting on the floor,

McBride felt his stomach drop, as if he were in a plane, and the plane had flown into an air pocket. "Will he be all right?"

Shapiro looked at them. "No."

35 McBride replenished the wood stove and stacked wood outside as the old scientist cooked dinner for the three of them—a simple meal of Jasmine rice and home-grown vegetables, served up with a bottle of Old Vine Red. It was delicious. While they ate, Shapiro reprised the sordid history of the CIA's mind control program.

"Most people think it was a response to what the communists were doing in Central Europe and Korea. There was a show trial involving a priest named Mindzenty, and lots of talk of 'brainwashing.' But the truth is, the program began long before that."

" 'The program'?" Adrienne asked, recalling the Web site on her sister's computer.

Shapiro frowned. "That's what we called it among ourselves. But whatever the name—and it had a lot of names—it began in Europe during the Second World War, when the OSS was searching for a 'truth drug' they could use in interrogations."

Pouring himself a glass of wine, the scientist explained that the project expanded after the war, with funding from the newly created CIA. By 1955, more than 125 experiments were under way in some of the country's best universities and worst prisons. Still other research was carried out in mental institutions, and in "civilian settings" using "unwitting volunteers."

"What's *that* supposed to mean?" McBride asked.

"It means we set up cameras in whorehouses, and tested drugs on the johns—without their knowledge," Shapiro replied. "It means that we used drug addicts like Kleenex—and homosexuals, too. Communists. Perverts. Hoodlums." He paused, and added with a smile, "Liberals and Dodger fans." Then he turned serious again, and went on to explain that in the climate of the times—which is to say, amid the permafrost of the Cold War—America's cultural conservatism was such that "transgressive personalities" were regarded as "fair game." "We didn't need 'informed consent,'" Shapiro pointed out, "because our research was classified. It was in the 'national interest'—which made it, and us, exempt from normal constraints."

"So it was easy to hide," Adrienne suggested.

"We didn't 'hide' anything—it was *secret*. And while some of us had ethical concerns about testing drugs and medical procedures on unwitting subjects . . . well, those concerns became irrelevant when you realized you were dealing with the enemy."

"I thought the Soviet Union was the enemy," McBride remarked.

"Of course. But the Cold War was as much a domestic jihad as it was an international one. It was a war for the American Way—which, I can assure you, did not (at least not at that time) include gays, lunatics, junkies or . . . sinners, even. They were all fair game."

"What kind of research are we talking about?" McBride asked.

The old man hesitated, thought about it for a moment, and shrugged. "Well," he said, as much to himself as his guests, "it's hardly secret anymore. There were hearings twenty years ago. Books and lawsuits."

"Right. So what kind of research are we talking about?" McBride repeated.

"Drugs and hypnosis, telepathy and psychic driving. Remote viewing. Aversive conditioning—degradation and pain."

" 'Degradation and pain'?" Adrienne asked, her voice disbelieving.

"How to induce it, endure it, use it—how to measure it," Shapiro replied. "Not that the pain experiments were particularly productive."

"Why not?" McBride wondered.

The scientist sighed. "We had difficulty finding reputable psychologists to do the research. And those we did find weren't as objective as we'd have liked."

McBride looked puzzled. "How so?"

"The studies kept getting mixed up with sadism—just as the drug experiments got mixed up with sex. In fact, it *all* got mixed up with sex. And that colored the results."

"You mentioned 'psychic driving,' " Adrienne said.

Shapiro shifted uncomfortably on his cushion. "Yes."

"Well . . . ?"

The retired CIA man considered the question. Finally, he replied, " 'Psychic driving' refers to . . . how should I put it? Terminal experiments in which the subject is given relatively large doses of a psychedelic drug and placed in a dark and sealed environment . . . where he . . . or she . . . is exposed to a continuous loop of recorded messages."

" 'A sealed environment'?" Adrienne wondered.

"We used morgue drawers," Shapiro explained.

McBride gaped, even as he tried to formulate the question on his mind. "When you say 'terminal experiments'—"

"No one died," Shapiro assured him. "But the subjects weren't expected to recover. And most of them didn't."

"So we're talking about—"

"Six hundred micrograms of LSD—daily," Shapiro said. "For sixty to one-hundred-eight days. In darkness."

Adrienne and McBride were silent for a long time. Finally, Adrienne whispered, "How could you *do* that?"

Shapiro looked her in the eye, and deliberately misunderstood the question. "As I recall, we catheterized the subject, fed her intravenously, and gave her a colostomy to facilitate things."

"Jesus Christ," McBride muttered.

"Refill?" Shapiro asked.

Adrienne shivered, and looked away. McBride shook his head. Shapiro just closed his eyes and sat there, savoring the Old Vine Red, the fire, the company, and his own regrets. When, after a while, he opened his eyes and began to speak, the effect was unsettling—as if he'd been watching them all the time. Indeed, the transition was so fast, it made Adrienne think of a bird of prey, an eagle or hawk winking at her with its nictitating membrane. "I know what you're thinking," he said.

"You do?"

"Of course," Shapiro told them. "You're thinking I'm a war criminal."

Neither of them said a word.

"Well," Shapiro concluded, "I suppose you had to be there." He sipped his wine, and looked at them. "It's easy, now, to condemn what was done then. But the truth is, the program was built by people whose motives were as pure as the driven snow."

Adrienne couldn't help herself: she rolled her eyes.

"They knew what men like Hitler could do. And it made them ruthless in the defense of freedom. I know it sounds corny—'freedom' always sounds corny—but it's true." The scientist paused, placed his left hand on the floor and sprang to his feet with surprising agility. Crossing the room to the woodstove, he opened it up, stirred the coals with a poker and put in a fresh log. Then he turned to his guests. "From the very beginning, the idea was to find ways to identify and eliminate men like Hitler and Stalin—*before* they came to power."

"So it was an assassination program," McBride suggested. Shapiro shrugged. "In part. The idea was to develop behaviorally-controlled agents who would carry out an assignment, even if the outcome was counterinstinctive."

"And what's *that* supposed to mean?" McBride asked.

"It means they didn't care if they lived or died," Adrienne guessed.

Shapiro inclined his head in reluctant agreement. "The agent's survival wasn't a critical issue—except in the sense that deniability was paramount. If the agent survived, and the agent was caught—well, that was a problem. And people *will* get caught. Not the first time. Not the second time. But, eventually."

They looked at him.

"Guns misfire," he explained. "Policemen become unexpectedly, even irrationally, interested in the most innocuous-seeming things. That's how it starts. And the next thing you know, your man's hanging by the balls from a hook in the cellar of somebody's Ministry of Defense, entertaining questions from one and all. So quite a lot of research went into the issue of building an agent who was deniable from the get-go."

"Let me guess," McBride suggested. "You drove them nuts."

Shapiro thought about it as he walked back to the table, and sat down. "No. If we'd done that, they wouldn't have been able to function. We spent years—and quite a lot of money—studying differential amnesia and ways of engendering multiple personalities. In the end, we decided that screen memories were the optimal solution—though, even there, we had problems. They tended to destabilize the personality, so you needed a therapist figure to provide reinforcement."

Adrienne glanced at McBride, then turned a puzzled eye on Shapiro. "What's a screen memory?" she asked.

The scientist considered the question. Finally, he said, "It's a memory that's verifiably false and inherently ridiculous—so that anyone who claims that it's real is discredited, simply on the face of that assertion."

"Give me an example," McBride suggested.

" 'I was kidnapped by aliens and flown to an underground base in the Antarctic,' " the scientist replied.

" 'Satanists tortured me as a child,' " Adrienne suggested.

"Exactly," Shapiro said. "It pigeonholes the speaker—in this case, the assassin—as a 'lone nut.' Which, as you can imagine, is reassuring to everyone involved."

" 'Reassuring'?" Adrienne spat the word at him. "You're talking about people's lives. You're talking about my *sister's* life!"

The old man was startled by her sudden intensity. "I'm talking hypothetically," he told her. "And, anyway, it's as I said: unless your sister was a lot older than you, this program had nothing to do with her."

"How can you say that?" Adrienne demanded. "You've seen the implant—"

"We lost our funding thirty years ago—and, by then, most of the work had moved offshore. So, the handwriting was on the wall. I mean, it was the Sixties, for God's sake! Every idiot in the country was conducting his own mind control experiments!"

Despite himself, McBride smiled. "When you say the work moved offshore . . . ?"

"Most of the studies were carried out at universities and research institutes. The funding was laundered through foundations and institutions we knew we could trust. As the years went by, and the Agency came under scrutiny from Congress and the press, some of the more sensitive studies had to be moved overseas. By the time the Rockefeller Commission began its investigation, the activity had been shut down. I retired soon afterward."

None of them said anything for a while, but sat where they were, watching the firelight play across the ceiling and the floor. Eventually, McBride cleared his throat. "So what about me?" he asked. "Where did the implant come from?"

Shapiro shook his head.

"And my sister!" Adrienne insisted. "What about her?"

Shapiro turned his palms toward the ceiling. "You're

talking to the wrong person," he told them. "You're talking to a dinosaur."

"I think I'm talking to someone who won't face facts— even when they're staring him in the face," Adrienne replied. "You saw his file. You saw the implant."

"I saw a photograph."

"Do you think we made it up?" McBride asked.

"No," the scientist conceded.

"Then . . . what? Obviously, the program never ended," Adrienne insisted. "The CIA—"

"—had nothing to do with this." Shapiro shook his head slowly. "Trust me: if the Agency was involved, I'd know."

McBride was trying to understand. "Then—"

"It's a Frankenstein," Shapiro told them.

Adrienne and McBride looked at each other, uncertain if they'd heard him right. "A what?" McBride asked.

"A Frankenstein." The old scientist finished his second glass of wine, and sat back with a strange little smile on his lips. "An agent or operation you can't control. Something you create that takes on a life of its own."

"So . . . ?" Adrienne looked to Shapiro to finish the sentence.

"I'm guessing," Shapiro admitted. "But seeing that implant, I'd say the program was privatized."

" 'Privatized'?" McBride repeated.

"I mean it's been taken over by someone in the private sector—or someone who went *into* the private sector. In other words, it looks like someone's continued the research on his own—outside the Agency."

"Who are we talking about?" Adrienne asked.

Shapiro shrugged. "I haven't a clue."

"It would take a lot of money to do something like that," McBride mused.

Shapiro nodded. "It would take millions. Then again, what doesn't?"

"But how could they keep it secret?" Adrienne wondered.

Shapiro considered the question. Finally, he said, "Set it up offshore. Keep it small. Put it in a clinical setting where the patient's privacy would be paramount." The scientist pursed his lips, and thought for a moment. "You know," he said, "if they've been working on this for thirty years—my God!"

"You said they'd put it in 'a clinical setting'?" Adrienne asked.

"Yes."

She leaned forward. "Then, tell me something: have you ever heard of the Prudhomme Clinic?"

The scientist furrowed his brows, thought for a moment, and shook his head. "Not that I recall."

Adrienne turned to McBride, who was looking at her with a question mark in his eyes, wondering where she was going. "What about you?" she asked.

McBride was taken aback. "What-about-me-*what?* Have I *heard* of it?" The question was out of the blue—he hadn't a clue as to what she was up to, but sensing her seriousness, he searched his memory. After a bit, he said, "No. There's that chef in Louisiana, but . . . I don't think that's what you're driving at." He paused. "So what's the Prudhomme Clinic?"

She ignored the question, and turned back to Shapiro. "You keep referring to 'the program' and . . ." She stopped for a moment, took a deep breath, and organized her thoughts. "A few days ago," she said, "before Lew had the implant removed, I found him sitting in front of my sister's laptop. He was logged onto this very weird Web site: theprogram dot org. (Theprogram is one word.)"

"Yes?"

"He was in a trance state—completely out of it. I mean, he was totally unresponsive—but not to the Web site. Which was interactive. He was typing in answers to questions that appeared on the screen. One of them was, 'Where are you?' "

"Well, that's very interesting," Shapiro remarked, "but . . . what's the point?"

"The *point*," Adrienne replied, "is that someone tried to kill us the next night. They started a gas fire. No one knew where we were, so obviously, they got the address from Lew—when he was on that Web site."

"And this Web site was . . . ?"

"I asked a friend who's kind of a geek to check it out," Adrienne told him.

"And what did he find?" Shapiro asked.

"He said the site's on a computer in something called 'the Prudhomme Clinic.' It's in a little town in Switzerland."

Shapiro nodded, shrugged. "Never heard of it."

Adrienne cleared her throat. "And there's something else I haven't told you." She turned to McBride. "My sister killed someone."

"What?!"

"She killed a man in Florida. She assassinated him."

Shapiro's eyes swelled with skepticism and surprise. "Why do you use that word?" he asked.

"Because the victim was an old man, sitting in a wheel-chair, watching the sunset. She shot him with a sniper rifle—the kind with a silencer and telescopic sights. The newspapers said his spine was cut in half."

"And . . . how do you know this?" Shapiro asked.

She explained about finding the rifle in her sister's apartment.

"And you're just telling me about this *now*?" McBride exclaimed.

"I didn't know what the gun meant," she told him, "until I went through her credit card charges, and saw that she'd gone to Florida. Then I looked up where she was staying, and read about this man who'd been killed while she was there. You were in the hospital—and, after that, we came here. I wanted to think about it."

McBride finished his glass of wine. "So who was he?" he asked. "The man who was killed."

"The papers said his name was Calvin Crane."

Shapiro's hand jerked involuntarily, almost knocking over his wineglass. Adrienne saw that his black eyes were round with amazement. "Your sister killed Calvin Crane?" he asked.

Adrienne nodded. "Yeah. No question."

"Wait a second," McBride mumbled, talking as much to himself as to the others. "There was a Crane with the Institute."

"If we're talking about the same person, he ran the Institute of Global Affairs," Shapiro told them. "For decades."

"That's right!" McBride exclaimed. "It was before my time, but . . . his name was still on the stationery. Director Emeritus, or something like that." He paused. Finally, he said, "Jesus . . ."

Adrienne nodded. "You. And Nikki . . . Crane and the Institute. You and Duran, Duran and my sister, my sister and Crane . . . it's a loop!"

No one spoke for a moment. Adrienne was hunched down in her chair, arms wrapped around her chest, a frown of concentration on her face. "But *why*?" she said in a plaintive voice. She looked back and forth between the men. "Jeff Duran, the implants, Calvin Crane . . . my sister. . . ." She shook her head. "What's it all *for*?"

Shapiro cleared his throat, and began to get up. To McBride, it seemed like the old man was shaken. "Well," he told them, "I won't ask you who 'Duran' is. I think we've probably taken this conversation about as far as—"

"How do you know him?" Adrienne asked, her voice all business again.

"Who?"

"Calvin Crane."

The former CIA man was quiet for what seemed a long time. Adrienne was about to repeat the question, when he said, "Calvin Crane was a legend. One of the Knights Templar."

"The what?" McBride demanded.

"That's what they were called—the inner circle around Allen Dulles. Right after the war, when the CIA was created. Des Fitzgerald and Richard Helms, Cord Meyer and Calvin Crane."

"So . . . he was a CIA agent," Adrienne said.

Shapiro winced at the naive terminology, and shook his head. "No. He went to the opening, but left in the first act." He paused. "Look," he confided, "you're nice people. But now you're getting into something very dark. Maybe you should just walk away."

" 'Walk away'?" McBride said. "They're trying to kill us. How the fuck—"

"Who's 'trying to kill' you?"

McBride turned questioningly to Adrienne—who shrugged. "I'm not sure," McBride replied.

Shapiro sighed. "The Institute was one of our conduits," he told them. "Crane was a good friend to the Agency—and completely trusted."

"So he was a part of the program," Adrienne suggested.

"He was *an asset*—one of the men we knew we could count on. This was a rich and well-connected patriot—no cartoon—a smart and sensible man." Shapiro hesitated. Frowned. "That someone should kill him in the way you've described is tragic." He paused, then added, "And ironic."

" 'Ironic'?" Adrienne asked.

Shapiro nodded. "A case of the snake swallowing its tail. Crane wanted to establish an assassination utility deep inside the CIA. But the support wasn't there."

Adrienne shook her head—a quick left-right-left that was meant to convey disbelief. "What did you call it?"

" 'An assassination utility.' "

She rolled her eyes. "You make it sound like the electric company."

Shapiro smiled. Weakly. "The idea was to identify—and eliminate—people who posed a threat to world peace. Or maybe it was liberal democracy—or the American Way. I don't remember, and I'm not sure Crane was entirely certain himself. But he was lobbying to create an inner sanctum within the Agency, one that would have institutionalized murder as an instrument of state."

"So you're telling us the CIA never killed anyone?" McBride

asked. "What about all those 'behaviorally-controlled assassins' you were talking about?"

Shapiro shook his head. "It's two different things: when I was running it, the program was a research endeavor. A large and secret one that necessarily included operational activities—but it was not an assassination activity itself."

"What about Castro?" McBride demanded.

"I understand what you're saying," Shapiro admitted. "But those were *ad hoc* exercises—and not at all what Crane had in mind. What's more, they were failures—which is, also, *not* what Crane had in mind."

McBride cocked his head to the side. "Doesn't it strike you as strange that so many 'lone nuts' have succeeded in killing political leaders, while the CIA—with all its resources—has failed—in every case we know of?"

Shapiro glanced at his watch, and got to his feet, signaling that the conversation was at an end. He began to clear the dishes. "Well," he sighed, "this has been interesting, but—it's dark, and you have a long way to go."

McBride took the hint, stood, and helped Adrienne to her feet.

"Actually," she said, "we're staying at Hilltop House. It's not so far."

Shapiro shook his head. "That's not what I meant," he replied. "I meant *it's dark*, and you have a long way to go." Escorting them to the front door, he opened it and paused. "Put on your seat belts," he told them, then closed the door, and was gone.

36 The ride back to Hilltop House was beautiful, silent, and sad, with the Shenandoah River glittering in the moonlight and the two of them saying nothing, or next to nothing, while thinking the same thing: *Everyone around me dies. Nikki. Bonilla. Shaw.* It was a roll call of the dead.

McBride drove with one hand on the wheel, and his arm thrown casually along the back of the seat. It made Adrienne tense, worrying that he was about to put his arm around her or, worse, that he would not. Not that his arm around her would be a good idea. On the contrary . . .

The car rolled through the countryside, the mountains and forests black against the starry sky.

Watery headlights loomed in the rearview mirror, sending a chill down McBride's spine. But then the car swept past them, and they were alone again. "I've been thinking," McBride said. "Maybe you should go someplace."

"Like where?"

"The moon, if you can get tickets. Otherwise, anywhere you can lay low."

She thought about it. And the truth was: there was nowhere she could go. Her basement bunker on Lamont Street was out. She didn't have a job anymore. And after Bonilla and Shaw, she wasn't about to stay with friends. "I want to find out what happened to Nikki," she insisted. "And, anyway: you need me."

"I do?" McBride glanced at her. The world inside the car

was chiaroscuro, all black and white, noir. It was the moonlight. She looked good in it.

"Yeah," she said. "You need the car, and my name's on the paperwork."

He shrugged. "Okay, you can stay."

"That was easy."

McBride chuckled, but what he was thinking was: *it wouldn't take much for my arm to slip around her shoulder.* Then Hilltop House hove into view, and the moment was gone.

But not forgotten.

In their room, he asked her to tell him what she'd learned about Crane. She responded by pulling out a sheaf of papers from her suitcase, and handing them to him.

They consisted, mostly, of printouts from Nexis, including a couple of obits from the *Washington Post* and the *Sarasota Star-Tribune*. He read them carefully, noting the organizations that Crane had belonged to and the name of a surviving sister in Sarasota. As he went through the printouts, one at a time, he did his best to ignore Adrienne, who was sitting on the bed, cross-legged. The room was small and stuffy, and he kept to the couch, an uncomfortable wicker object near the balcony.

"We're going to Florida, aren't we?" she asked.

"Yeah, I think we have to." He was doing his best not to look at her, keeping his eyes on the landscape outside the window. In the distance, down by the river, he could see parallel strings of lights—one white, one red, pulsing along in opposite directions. They appeared and disappeared as the road wound in and out of sight in the folds of the mountains. "We can look up the sister, for starters," he suggested, "see what she can tell us. Go to the courthouse—see if there was any litigation. Check out his will . . ."

"Ummmm," she said, stretching her arms over her head. "So, basically, we'll go down there and beat the bushes."

"Unless you have a better idea," he agreed, pulling open

the door to the balcony so that a rush of cold air entered the room—which had suddenly become quite warm.

She caught his eyes, held them for just a little too long and then executed another languorous stretch, extending her legs and flexing her feet, while raising her interlaced hands overhead. She arched her back, displaying her body, opening it toward him.

McBride groaned inwardly. Getting to his feet, he stepped out onto the balcony.

The truth was that all day, he'd been constantly aware of her, in the moony obsessed manner of an adolescent. It was like high school. No—worse—junior high. At various points during the day—even in the austerity of Shapiro's cabin, even in the darkness cast by his terrifying anecdotes, even in the face of the horrible news about Ray Shaw—he had suffered the painful tumescence that had made seventh grade an agony.

Standing out on the balcony, he looked down at the lights of the cars and thought about it: how long had it been since he'd taken a woman to bed? He couldn't be sure—his memory was still coming back in bits and pieces, flashes. But it was before Jeffrey Duran—that much was certain.

"So whatcha gonna do, boy?"

It was a line from Meatloaf's *Bat Out of Hell* album, and it reminded him of all the good music he'd missed, as well, Jeff Duran having been, not merely celibate, but entrained by a different drummer. Or not even a drummer: Oprah.

"Whatcha gonna do!?"

Adrienne was a fox, and that was a fact. But it was also a fact that Lew McBride was the last thing she needed. She'd already lost her sister, her job, and very nearly her life—and he was responsible for all of it. It wouldn't be right to take advantage of her simply because they'd been thrown together in what were, after all, desperate circumstances. Still . . .

It was unnatural, sleeping in the same room like this and keeping your distance. *It's human nature,* he told himself, arguing with his conscience. They'd been through a lot together, and it wasn't just a question of sex—he really liked her. She was smart and attractive, funny and vulnerable. It was like what happened during wars and natural disasters. People reached out. So why fight it? Why not just . . . *make your move!*

But it was too late—or, if not too late, an interregnum. The cold had had its effect, and he reentered the room, diminished. Adrienne remained where she was, sitting on the bed, reading the hotel's potted guide to Harpers Ferry and environs. She looked up at him from under thick, dark lashes—a killer look, her eyes full of allure and invitation. She shifted position, a series of fluid adjustments that made it impossible not to think of other adjustments her body might make. Without the clothing.

"Looking at the stars?"

His eyes went to the ceiling. "No," he replied. "I was thinking . . ." He laughed. "You don't want to know what I was thinking."

She made a little sound in the back of her throat, and it took all his willpower not to launch himself at the bed. A flying dive into the depths of her.

Instead, he said, "I guess we'd better get some sleep."

She nodded. Pulled her knees up to her chest and wrapped her arms around them. All closed off now. The radiator ticked in the hot room. After what seemed like a long time, she heaved a sigh, and flashed a bright little smile. "Great," she said.

It was a long way, and they took turns at the wheel, driving all the next day, arriving late at night. They checked into a Super 8, requesting a room with twin beds. She was actually embarrassed by the way she felt. She would not have thought her body capable of this swoony teenage lust.

In the morning, they went to the sales office at La Resort on Longboat Key, where a tanned blonde told them that the contents of Calvin Crane's condo had been cleaned out weeks before. The unit itself—three bedrooms, oceanside, with every amenity—was for sale. Were they interested?

No.

They drove back by way of Armand's Circle, stopping for lunch at Tommy Bahama's, where they ate salads and conch chowder, discussing their next move. Which was the courthouse in Bradenton, where they all but struck out. Crane wasn't engaged in litigation with anyone, or not, at least, in Manatee County. And his will wasn't as interesting as they'd hoped. Half of his estate was bequeathed, in equal proportions, to Harvard University and the American Cancer Society. The remainder was earmarked for his "beloved sister, Theadora Wilkins," and his "lifelong friend, Marijke Winkelman."

Their next stop was a trailer park in Bradenton, where Crane's Jamaican caretaker, Leviticus Benn, lived with a pack of barking dogs. A tall black man with an easy smile, Benn was gracious, but spooked—and a little angry at the way he'd been treated. "First night—Mister Crane's dead—Five-Oh come through my house with one of them tooth combs. And what they find? A little ganja. Just a taste. I mean, *residue.* From my personal use, you understand. Next thing, I'm in the middle of heavy manners. Like this trailer park is Gestapo Gardens. And I got to ask—I ask the policeman: how's this gonna solve your bad crime? Tell me that!"

It took a while for Benn to get past his ire and, when he did, there wasn't much that he could tell them.

"I was his nurse, you know? The human part of the rich man's wheelchair. So we didn't talk much. In fact, we really didn't talk at all. Just, 'Good mawnin', Leviticus. Good mawnin', Mr. Crane.' Like that?"

"So he wasn't that friendly?"

"He be keepin' to his own self, you know?"

* * *

Crane's sister resided at The Parkington, an assisted living facility housed in a lavishly landscaped glass and stone building on one of Sarasota's wide, pleasant streets. There was a sort of covered terrace out front with a phalanx of white rocking chairs standing along its length. Only one of these was occupied, and that by a ramrod straight lady, her white hair cut into a kind of short pageboy. Her fringe of white bangs fell into a line so straight that Adrienne thought they must have been trimmed with a ruler. The face under the bangs might once have been pretty, but the small features were lost in a marsh of wrinkled flesh. To Adrienne, she gave the impression of an ancient baby. She wore a blue and white striped shirtwaist dress with a wide white belt and matching white shoes and purse.

The woman levered herself to her feet as they approached. "You must be Adrienne and Lew," she said in a low and pleasant voice. "I'm Thea—although I don't insist on that. Mrs. Wilkins will do if you're uncomfortable addressing someone *quite* so ancient by what used to be called, in the days before political correctness, one's 'Christian' name."

"Pleased to meet you, Thea," Adrienne said, extending her hand and introducing herself. She'd been fearful when they learned that Theodora Wilkins was closing in on ninety and living in a nursing home. It had seemed likely that Calvin Crane's only living relative would not be mentally acute enough to help them. Obviously, that was not the case. "This is Mr. McBride."

The old lady told them to take a seat, then went inside to see if she could "drum up some iced tea." After a while she came back, trailed by an Hispanic man with a tray, and lowered herself carefully into her chair. Once the iced tea was distributed, she smiled. "Now," she declared, "how can I be of help?"

"As I said on the phone," McBride explained, "Adrienne thinks her sister, Nico, was in correspondence with your brother before he died. Her sister passed away—"

"I'm so sorry," Thea interjected.

"I was hoping to get the letters back," Adrienne told her. "As mementos."

The old woman pushed her lips together and wrinkled her nose. "Oh dear," she said, "I'm afraid I'm not going to be a big help. Cal and I were never close, you see."

Adrienne tried to hide her disappointment. "Oh."

"You've got to wonder about that, don't you? Here we are, brother and sister, an old biddy and an old codger, living half an hour away from one another, and we saw each other about—" She extended her lower lip and sent up a jet of air that lifted her bangs, a gesture that must have survived from her teenage years. "—every six months. Thanksgiving and Easter. That was all we could take."

"So you didn't get along."

"Not a lick. Cal thought I was a lightweight—and he despised my husband. Called him a dilettante. (Which, I suppose, he was, God rest him.) Still . . ."

"And what did you think of *him*?" Adrienne asked.

"My little brother?" she said. "I thought he was the most . . ." She paused, thought about it, and said: "I thought he was the most arrogant man I ever met."

"Really."

"Oh yes. He was idealistic, of course, but so was Hitler. They both knew what was right for everyone else." She raised one elegantly tweezed brow. "It's terrible to say, but I don't miss him all that much."

"Were you shocked when—"

"Oh yes—I mean, it made quite a *splash* after all. Cal would have hated it. After all, it's so *gauche*—to be shot like that. He would have hated it."

"Do you have any idea who—"

"Killed him?" she suggested. "No. I'm sorry. A man like that can acquire any number of enemies, though I have to say I wouldn't have thought any of Cal's associates would have been such . . . cowboys." She hesitated. Leaned forward, and whispered. "Have you talked to Mamie?"

They looked at each other. Shook their heads. "Who's Mamie?" McBride asked.

The old lady laughed, a deep chuckle, then took a sip of iced tea. "Mamie was Cal's paramour."

"Really."

"Oh yes. And she's not a bit like Cal. In fact, I quite like her—though what she saw in Cal, I can't imagine. But they were lifelong friends. Met in London, during the war. He was OSS—she was some kind of liaison. The married kind, as it turned out." Thea chuckled. "I used to call her 'the little Dutch girl' because . . . well, that's what she was! Dutch, I mean. Her name is Marijke Winkelman. 'Mamie' is just what Cal *called* her."

"And her husband?" Adrienne asked.

"Oh, he died—I think it was twenty years ago, now. He was with the Red Cross in Geneva. They both were. Refugee relief."

"I see," McBride said, though he didn't, really.

"That's where it started," Thea added.

"What did?" Adrienne asked.

"Their affair. He was in Zurich. Geneva wasn't so far away—though why she didn't marry Cal after her husband passed, I can't imagine. Too much bother, I guess."

"Do you think she'd know about any papers he might have left?" McBride asked.

Thea Wilkins stirred her iced tea and took a dainty sip, patting her lips afterwards with the cocktail napkin. "Well, if anybody *would* know," she told them, "Mamie would, though . . . I'll give you her address, and you can see for yourself."

"They didn't live together?" Adrienne asked.

"Oh, goodness no. They always kept separate residences. Mamie has a splendid place, right on the beach. Villa Alegre."

Villa Alegre *was* splendid, a low-slung pink stucco house with a barrel roof of terra-cotta tiles. It sat amidst lush vegetation in what amounted to a forest of old palms and banyans.

And she was nothing like her near contemporary, Theodora Wilkins. She wore shorts and a T-Shirt and Birkenstock sandals. While her neck might have been crepey, and her skin netted with wrinkles, she was still quite beautiful. She had wide-set, pale blue eyes, blond hair gone silver, and a wide, generous mouth. She led them around to the back of the house, pausing at a small pond filled with koi. "My fêng shui consultant insisted that I have them. He said the house needs motion. Anyway, they *are* terrific looking, don't you think?"

McBride admired them. Adrienne smiled politely.

"You don't like them, do you, dear?" Mamie asked.

Adrienne shrugged. "Not much, I guess. I don't know why."

"It's probably the colors," Mamie guessed. "Do you mind if I ask: are you a big fan of Halloween?"

"No. I've never really liked it."

The old woman tossed out a high-voltage smile, pleased to have her theory confirmed by this sampling of one. "Well, there you are!" She took Adrienne's arm in a companionable way, and led her up the flagstone path toward the house. There was something about the way she talked, Adrienne thought, the cadence or pronunciation . . . Then she realized what it was: "half in the bag," as Deck used to say. Not drunk, but getting there.

She would not talk to them until they were all "settled down" out back. They sat down in white wicker chairs under a vine laden pergola and admired the waves lapping at the nearby beach. A dozen wind chimes trembled all around them as Mamie excused herself, returning a few minutes later with a decanter of martinis and a plate of cheese, fruit, and crackers.

Once she had poured the drinks into traditional stemmed glasses, added olives, and handed them out to her guests, she declared herself ready.

"So," she said, raising her glass. "Salut." The first sip almost knocked them over. "Now what is it about Cal you'd like to talk about?"

They stuck to the pretext about Adrienne's late sister having a correspondence with Crane. Mamie said she didn't know anything about that.

"He never mentioned a correspondence like that, but then," she added, "he probably wouldn't have."

With the wind chimes tinkling all around them, they talked about the kind of man Calvin Crane was—which paved the way for McBride to inquire about "enemies."

"Of course the police are asking me this same question," Mamie told them, "but I have the sense they are just going through the motions, not really interested in my answer. So I don't think about it. I mean, not seriously." She took a tiny bite of cheese, and washed it down with a generous sip from her martini. "But I know Gunnar was unhappy with him."

"Gunner?" Adrienne asked.

Mamie shook her head. "Gunnar Opdahl. He was Cal's protege at the Institute, but . . . are you all right, Mr. McBride?"

No, he wasn't. He felt blindsided by the mention of Opdahl's name. His heart leapt, and a bolt of panic shot through his chest. He must have flinched because Adrienne put a hand on his arm.

"You okay?" she asked.

A puff of air set the wind chimes clattering.

He nodded, and lied. "I got some dust in my eye." Adrienne gave him a funny look.

To himself, he thought: *What the fuck was that?* Gunnar Opdahl was . . . what? Smart and urbane, a pleasant man to have lunch with. And yet, even as he thought this, he knew there was something else, something deeply unpleasant waiting to be remembered. Finally, he cleared his throat, and looked at Mamie. "You were saying . . . ?"

"Yes, I was saying they had a falling out. Gunnar and Cal."

"Do you know what it was about?" Adrienne asked.

"Not really" Mamie replied. Despite her birdlike sips, she had downed most of her martini. "I left Switzerland before

Cal did. The weather gets to you when you reach a certain age."

"When did Cal retire?"

"In '93," Mamie replied. "But their disagreement was more recent than that. I think it started—oh—maybe a year ago. A little more, perhaps."

"Was it about the Institute?" Adrienne asked.

Mamie seesawed her head, frowned, and replenished her glass from the decanter. "I think it must have been. That was their only common ground, really. And, even retired, Cal was still active in certain things. As one of the founders, he still had a say."

"What kind of say?"

"About the fellows, the research—and the clinic, of course. They do such very good work with troubled young people." She paused, and then went on. "This *contretemps* with Gunnar might—" But then she shrugged, did not finish the sentence. "I shouldn't say, really. Because I don't know. I'm just guessing."

"Tell us. Please?" Adrienne pressed. "We know so little . . ."

"Well, I was going to say I thought it might have to do with the money, with Gunnar feeling *impeded* in some way. That's just the sense I got from some of the telephone conversations I overheard." She fished an olive out of her glass and popped it into her mouth.

McBride leaned toward her. "Is there someone at the Institute who might be able to tell us more about the falling out between them?"

Mamie frowned. "Oh, I don't think so. Cal was the last of the original group. And the new crowd . . . well, I don't even know who they are."

"Lew was a fellow," Adrienne volunteered, with a sidelong glance at McBride.

"Oh, really!" Mamie exclaimed, her face cracking into a wide smile. "How exciting!" She reached out, pressed a girlish hand against his arm, and patted it in a proprietary way. "You must be jush . . . an outstanding young man!"

McBride smiled. Mamie was beginning to look a bit cross-eyed, and her words were beginning to slur. Probably the woman had told them all that she knew.

Adrienne noticed it, too. Mamie was down to the olive in her second martini, which suggested the conversation was about to deteriorate. So it would be best to get to the point. She picked up her glass by the stem, swirled it, and watched the oily bands of liquid curl. Out on the water, a Jet Ski whined, dopplering across the bay, as irritating as a mosquito. McBride was telling Mamie about his fellowship.

What if this was a legal *case*? she asked herself. What would she ask?

"Did Mr. Crane leave any papers?"

The question took Mamie by surprise. "Excuse me?"

"I know his belongings were sold," Adrienne said, "but sometimes—"

"Well, you're not the first to ask," Mamie told her, covering a tiny hiccup. "After he died, a man from the government came, and asked the same thing. Awful little man!" She tossed her head like a teenager. "I told him Cal was always quoting some dead Legionnaire. *'Pas des cartes, pas des fotos, et pas des souvenirs.'* "

Adrienne gave her a hapless look. "I took Spanish."

McBride translated. " 'No letters, no pictures, and no souvenirs.' " He smiled regretfully. "Which is not so great for us. Anyway," he decided, "we've taken enough of your time."

"You've been very kind," Adrienne agreed and, standing, extended her hand to the old woman.

Mamie took the hand and held it for what seemed a long while, scrutinizing Adrienne as if she were a Vermeer. "You have such an aura," she told her. Then she laughed. "Maybe you'd better sit back down." Turning to McBride, she added, "Cal was such a bullshitter—*pas des cartes,* indeed!"

37 She returned a few minutes later, lipstick refreshed, hair newly combed, carrying a battered briefcase and a small photo album. Raising the briefcase, she said, "He liked to do his correspondence here." Glancing out to the window, she said, "I think we're going to have some weather. Maybe the Florida room would be a better choice." Beckoning, she led them down a long hall to a low-ceilinged room with large expanses of old-fashioned, jalousied windows, and a ceiling fan that turned, ever so slowly, overhead.

Beyond the windows, behind a stand of thrashing palms, the Gulf of Mexico trembled with whitecaps, its surface black-and-blue. McBride imagined he could feel the electricity in the air. Nearby, the crimson and green leaf of a croton bush skittered across the tiled floor, pushed by the wind.

The room itself was a comfortable one, furnished with a scattering of old rattan furniture and a profusion of plants: fiddleleaf figs, ferns, hibiscus. Citrus trees in huge glazed pots. Gardenias bloomed by the door, filling the air with their dense perfume.

Mamie sat down between them on a little couch, with the album resting on her lap. Opening the cover, she began to turn the pages, one at a time, never lingering for long on any one. "My parents' house," she said, "in Amstelveen."

"It's beautiful," Adrienne remarked, and so it was.

"They worked for the bank," Mamie confessed. "Mother, too. A real Dolle Mina!" She turned another page, and another, musing over the photos. "My brother, Roel." She sighed. "So handsome!"

"Is he . . . ?"

Mamie shook her head. "No. He died during the war."

"A soldier?" McBride asked.

She shook her head. "Tuberculosis." Another picture, this time of a young woman at a café table in a European city. "Can you guess who that is?" she asked coyly.

McBride smiled. "Of course," he replied, "it's Greta Garbo. I'd recognize her anywhere."

Mamie guffawed—a big, uncompromising *Ha*! "Such a darling man! And what a liar!"

"It's you, isn't it?" Adrienne asked. "But you're so beautiful!"

"And you're very kind," Mamie replied. Then she turned another page and stopped. Her forefinger stabbed at a 5 by 7 snapshot of half a dozen men posing for a photo on an elegant terrace in what could only be the Alps. "There!" she told them. "That's what I wanted to show you."

It was a sepia-toned picture, with the men in ranks—three, standing at the back; and the same number, kneeling in front. They wore old-fashioned hiking clothes—knickers, knee-socks, heavy boots, and patterned wool sweaters. Behind them were some of the world's most recognizable mountains.

"That's Cal in the front—at the very center of things, as always."

Adrienne peered at the picture, which showed Crane and his friends, back from a hike in the Alps. She could see at a glance that Crane had once been young and handsome, with dark eyes, broad shoulders, and an aquiline nose that pointed the way to a cleft chin. To his left was a big Scandinavian with a broad face, apple cheeks, and spiky blond hair. His pale eyes were slightly hooded and stared directly at the camera.

"Who's that," McBride asked, "next to Mr. Crane?" The man seemed strangely familiar.

"That's Ralf," Mamie told him. "He and Cal worked together."

"At the Institute?" Adrienne asked.

"Of course," the old woman replied. "Gunnar is his son."

She removed the photograph from the little slats that held each of its corners to the page, and turned it over. Written on the back in fading blue ink were the words:

Eiger Monch & Jungfrau
L—R: W. Colby, J. DeMenil, F. Nagy
Kneeling: T. Barnes, C. Crane, R. Opdahl
September 8, '52: Palace Hotel Eiger (Murren)
Back from the Schilthorn!!!

"And these other men?" McBride asked.

Mamie smiled. "Spies," she said.

"Did they hike together often?" Adrienne asked.

Mamie shook her head. "No, I think just that once. There was some business." She thought for a moment, then nodded decisively at the recollection. "I know! They'd just opened the clinic," she said.

"The Prudhomme Clinic," Adrienne suggested.

Mamie nodded. "Yes. So there was a little celebration."

"How did you get the picture?" McBride asked.

"Get it? I took it," she told him. "That's my handwriting, not Cal's. And there aren't many pictures of him in those days." She quickly turned a couple of pages in the album until she found what she was after. "This is the only other one that I know of—though maybe Thea has some."

The picture had been taken in the summer. It showed a mansion on a residential block in the suburbs of a European city. The building reminded Adrienne of one of the legations along Massachusetts Avenue in Washington. Huge stone urns, spilling over with luxuriant vegetation, flanked a massive front door. And at the door, posing with one hand on the lion's head knocker and the other held up in a wave toward the camera was Crane. On the page beside the picture, in the same spidery hand as its predecessor, was the inscription:

Herr Direktor Arrives!
The Institute (Kussnacht)
3 July, 1949

"Well," Mamie said, as she got slowly to her feet, "I'll leave you to it. Me—I think I'll have a little lie-down. If you need anything . . ."

"Oh, we'll be fine," Adrienne told her.

It was raining now, thick drops slapping at the slatted glass of the windows. Thunder rolling over the Gulf. Opening the briefcase, McBride removed some folders and envelopes, a yellow legal pad, two or three kraft-colored folders, an antique Hermés diary and a copy of the *AARP Bulletin*. There was also, he saw, a thick packet of letters, held together with a rubber band.

It was, in other words, a mess—but promising. Both of them reached for the diary first, but Adrienne was quicker. Leaning back against the couch, she began to read, while McBride went through the other material.

Before long, he realized there wasn't much there. It was mostly a collection of bank statements and bills, and correspondence with various brokerages. The Harvard Building Fund hoped to be remembered in his will, and Sprint wanted him as a customer.

McBride looked up. "Anything interesting?"

Adrienne shook her head, closed the diary, and set it down on the coffee table. "It's poetry," she told him. "He was writing poetry in his old age."

"You're kidding," McBride reacted, unable to hide his disappointment.

"Look for yourself," she said, and removing the rubber band from a packet of envelopes, began to go through them, one by one. Meanwhile, McBride scrutinized the old man's bills, looking for God knows what. The minutes dragged by.

After a while, Adrienne reported, "It's almost all receipts. He bought his shoes at Church's, his books on Main Street, and his slacks at Beecroft & Vane. Filled his prescriptions at Rite-Aid." She looked up. "I'm not getting anywhere."

McBride shrugged, and turned his attention to the photo album. Opening it to the picture of Crane arriving at the Institute, he stared at it for a long while, trying to remember.

Adrienne noticed. "Where's Kussnacht?" she asked.

"Just north of Zurich. It's the Institute's headquarters." He stopped talking, frowned.

"What?" she demanded.

McBride shook his head. "I've been trying to patch it together, you know? To figure out when—*exactly* when—I became Jeffrey Duran? And the last thing I remember, the last thing I *really* remember, is that I was at the Institute. I'd come to Switzerland to talk about something or other with Opdahl. I was supposed to have lunch with him."

"The guy who had the falling out with Crane?"

McBride nodded, then turned the page to the group photo on the terrace in Murren. "He looks like his father," he told her. "Opdahl, I mean." And staring at the broad face and hooded eyes, McBride suffered the same dark shudder that he'd felt only minutes before. It was the kind of sensation that brought to mind the saying about someone stepping on your grave. He shook it off. "We'd better keep rolling," he said.

"Mmmmmm." Rain began to thrum on the roof, falling beyond the windows in ropy shafts of silver. Adrienne opened an 8½ by 11 manila envelope—glanced inside, and returned it to the table. "What's that?" McBride asked.

"Newspaper clippings," she replied. "Obituaries and stuff."

McBride shrugged, and picked up the yellow legal pad—which looked as if it had never been used. As he riffled the pages, however, an envelope dropped to the table—and he saw that there was a letter, or the first draft of a letter, on the very last pages of the pad.

Leaving the envelope where it lay, he focused on the handwritten, crossed-out and much corrected scribble in the recesses of the pad. Gunnar—it began.

McBride paused. *No "Dear," there—so no love lost. And*

what was stranger: why would someone begin a letter on the inside of a legal pad—indeed, at the very end of the pad, writing from the last page toward the front? It was a trivial question, of course, and the answer occurred to him as soon as it was asked: *because Crane had been carrying the pad around with him, scribbling secretly in public places, and didn't want passersby to glimpse a word.*

The simple answer is:

McBride paused again. *"Gunnar—The simple answer is . . ."* *What's the question?* McBride wondered.

I'm aghast at what you propose. Jericho is beyond belief, and I cannot imagine what twisted rationalizations were employed to justify it. To this day, I find the memory of my earlier passivity impossible to bear. A single plane goes down in Africa, and a million people die?

Where was your research? What were you thinking? Did we even—ever—have a fellow *in Rwanda?*

Whatever you were thinking, I won't be party to another such disaster—which, make no mistake, Jericho must certainly become. Indeed, it promises to make its predecessor seem like a practice run. So you will not *have the signature you require. It will not be forthcoming. And if, somehow, you find a way to proceed, I promise you that I will do everything in my power to prevent Jericho from coming to pass.*

Let me remind you, Gunnar, of some first principles— which it would seem that you've forgotten. Our enterprise was established amid the ruins of World War II. In the aftermath of that catastrophe, the West dithered its way into a Cold War that promised to add yet another Roman numeral to the serialized slaughter of the previous world wars. To prevent that, some of us came together to establish the utility over which you now preside.

Your father was one of us. Indeed, he was one of the best of us.

But all of us were of a part, eight men from half as many countries who'd labored long and hard in the cause of freedom—men from the OSS, the SOE and other services, who shared the same perception: that some power, some third class of individuals, aside from the leaders and the scholars, must exist—and that this third class must take upon itself the task of thwarting civilization's mistakes . . .

No more Hitlers. No more Stalins. No more Maos.

Never again.

The risks that we've taken have been unimaginable, the more so for the fact that we have never enjoyed the sanctions and immunities that are the natural lot of those in government service.

If we go down, we go down for good—and hard—and it must all come out—not just Batista, but Papa as well, and all the rest. Are you prepared for that? I doubt it.

The truth is, the Institute has always been a parapolitical enterprise—a third force, not unlike the Triads and the Mafia. All such institutions begin life as secret combatants, embarked upon a political mission of noble dimensions. Often, perhaps inevitably, when they lose their raison d'être—which is to say, when their cause has been finally won or lost—they do not go away, but devolve into criminal organizations.

And that, I fear, is what has happened to the Institute under your direction: in the beginning we slew monsters— hard targets whose identities we all agreed upon. And now, with the Cold War a thing of the past, our targets have become softer and softer. The truth is, the Institute should have been shut down when Gorbachev asked for peace . . .

"Look at this," McBride said, handing the letter to Adrienne. "It's incredible."

He watched Adrienne read for a while, thinking about the way the Institute had used its fellows to explore obscure technologies and practices that could be used in mind control operations (his own study, involving "animist therapeutics" and the Third World was a classic example).

"Jesus," she whispered. Looked up, and asked, "What's this about 'Papa'? Is that his father or . . . Hemingway?"

"I don't know," McBride said. "Right now, I'm more worried about 'Jericho.' " His eye fell on the envelope that, earlier, had fallen from between the pages of the same legal pad. Addressed to *Calvin Crane, Florida,* it had no stamp or return address. *Hand delivered, then,* McBride thought.

Opening it, he found a single page of unsigned text:

My Dear Cal,

I confess I was shocked by the piety and recklessness of your recent letter, which arrived by mail only yesterday. What were you thinking, to put such things on paper?

Perhaps it is your age that's made you careless—but is it possible that it has also made you pious? No one needs to remind me of "the first principles" on which this enterprise was founded. I live with them every day, as did my father—as, once, did you.

Neither is it necessary (or desirable) for us to discuss the operation that you have so carelessly mentioned in your letter. Your role in these affairs has long been at an end. I will not discuss events in Africa—or any other activity—with you. On the contrary, it's apparent that my decision to keep you informed of operations, even after your retirement, was a mistake.

But you are making an even greater mistake when you withhold your signature, approving the annual disbursement of operational funds from the banking facility in Lichtenstein. That two signatures should be required for such disbursements is, as you well know, an anachronism dating back to when the Institute and Clinic were separate entities.

That you should now take advantage of this anomaly to press your own agenda is disgraceful. And not just disgraceful: it is an attack, not only upon the Institute, but on myself. I beg you to reconsider.

McBride turned to Adrienne, who was reading over his shoulder, having already finished the earlier letter, inspiring the one in his hand. "Mamie was right," he told her.

"About what?" She was still reading.

"The money. Crane had some kind of lock on it. And he was squeezing them." He let her continue to read until she looked up at him, signaling that she was done. McBride didn't say anything, but just sat there, looking distracted. "What are you thinking about?" she asked.

"My fellowship," he told her. "I'm thinking the whole thing was a sham."

"Tell me again what—"

"I was studying bush therapies. That's what it amounted to. Everything from dance frenzies to speaking in tongues."

"So? I don't see how any of that would help the program."

"I do. That's what it was all about: altered states of consciousness. Drugs, hypnosis, trance states. And not only that, I was encouraged to write about 'Third World Messiahs' and 'mass conversion.' And I did. I reported on a charismatic faith healer in Brazil, a defrocked priest in Salvador who was said to work miracles, and a Pentecostal politician in . . . I think it was Belize."

"So?"

"Someone whacked the faith healer. Shot him onstage when he was up to his elbows in cancer and chicken guts. The newspapers said his killer was nuts."

"And you think . . . ?"

"I don't know what to think," McBride replied. The two of them sat back on the couch, listening to the rain thrashing against the windows. After a while, he leaned forward and began to put Crane's papers back in the attaché case. Adrienne got up, and crossed the room to the windows. Looked out.

"It's letting up," she said.

McBride nodded, then lingered for a moment over a thick manila envelope—the one with the clippings. In the upper right-hand corner was a notation in what McBride recognized as Crane's hand: *First Reports.*

Opening the envelope, he dumped the contents on the table and began to sort through them. It went quickly, at first, then more slowly. Then quickly again. They were newspaper articles—a few of them quite long, some short, most brittle and yellowing with age. There were obituaries of obscure personalities in dozens of countries, and long dispatches about the violent deaths of prominent people throughout the world. *Dateline: Rwanda—*

HUTU LEADERS'
PLANE MISSING

Missing?

McBride went through the articles, one by one. Finally, he looked up at Adrienne and asked, "Did you read these?"

She looked over her shoulder at him. "What?"

"These clips."

There was something in his voice that got her complete attention. "No," she said, turning to face him. "They're newspaper clips is all. Why?"

He didn't answer, at first—just shook his head in disbelief. Then he raised his eyes to hers and said, "I think we just found the Institute's hit list."

They copied the names—and there were a lot of names—onto a page of the legal pad, then tore it off and said their good-byes to Mamie. She gave Adrienne a big hug, and asked, with a coy smile, "Did you find your letters, dear?"

Adrienne shook her head. "No," she told her, and struck with guilt at the woman's kindness, added, "You know, Mamie, there never were any letters, really. That was just—"

Mamie smiled. "I know," she said, and squeezed the

younger woman's hand. "But don't tell me any more. I know what Cal's friends were like. Just promise me that when you come this way again, you'll stay for lunch. Is that a deal?"

They shook on it.

Half an hour later, Adrienne and McBride were on Longboat Key, sitting on the veranda of a conch house restaurant that specialized in "Floribbean cuisine." The air was heavy with the aromas of charcoal steaks, olive oil, and old money. Ceiling fans turned overhead, but only barely. The sign on the door read CA D'EUSTACE.

They ate by candlelight—fresh pompano, washed down with a bottle of cold Sancerre. By then, the rain had stopped, and the air was clear, fresh, and cool. Nearby, they could hear the surf, murmuring in the darkness.

"I don't know half these names," Adrienne said, looking at the list. "I mean, who's this first one: Forrestal?"

"I think he was . . . what? The first Secretary of Defense. Had some kind of psychotic break—thought people were after him."

"And what happened to him?" Adrienne asked.

"Fell out a window at Bethesda Naval Hospital. Top floor. They named an aircraft carrier after him."

Adrienne grimaced. "And Lin Biao?"

"Chinese guy," McBride said.

"That would have been my guess, too," she told him.

He took the sarcasm in stride. "It's not a guess. I *know* this. He was Mao's second in command. Very bad man. Died in a plane crash."

She was impressed. "I know the next one," Adrienne said. "Faisal. He was a Saudi prince, or something."

"King," McBride corrected. "He organized the Arab oil embargo. Nephew shot him in a receiving line. I remember reading about it: the king was standing there, waiting to be kissed on the nose—"

"What!?"

"Local custom. Anyway, his nephew waits his turn and, when it comes, he passes up the kiss and shoots him in the head. Instead." McBride paused, remembering. "The kid was a student at San Francisco State and, after the murder, everyone said he was out of his mind—even the Saudis. Then they realized they couldn't execute him if he was crazy. So they changed their minds, decided he was fine, and cut off his head."

"How come you know so much?" she asked.

"Double major. Psych and modern history." Reaching for the bottle of wine, he refilled their glasses.

"There are sixty or seventy names here," she said.

McBride nodded. "One or two a year, all the way back to the beginning of the Cold War." He glanced at the list, and pointed to a name. "That's the guy I was telling you about. The faith healer."

She looked at the page, where his finger rested beside an unpronounceable name.

" 'Jew-ow doo Gwee-ma-rice,' " he said.

Adrienne tried her hand at a few of the other names. "Zia-ul-Haq. Park Chung Hee. Olaf Palme."

McBride took up the roll call. "Wasfi Tal. Solomon Bandaranaike."

She hesitated. "And they were all assassinated?"

"The ones I recognize—yeah! Park was the President of South Korea. His intel chief shot him at the dinner table. Palme was the Swedish prime minister. Someone blew him away as he walked out of a movie theater with his wife."

Adrienne's eyes moved down the list. "Some of the names are easy, but I've never heard of most of them," she observed. "William Tolbert."

"Liberia," McBride guessed.

"Who's this?" Adrienne asked.

McBride read the name. "Albino Luciani." It was familiar, somehow, but . . . no. Luciani was one of the names he didn't know. "We can look him up later," he told her, and fell back in his chair. Like Adrienne, he was bewildered by what they'd found, and appalled by its magnitude. A minute passed, then two. Every so often, McBride shook his head and swore under his breath, a bitter little smile on his lips.

"It's just a list," she said. "It doesn't really prove anything."

"Right."

"I mean, it's just a bunch of newspaper stories. Maybe Crane was doing some kind of research project."

McBride nodded. "Yeah, that's probably it. He was probably 'doing a research project.' " He paused. "Is that what you think?"

She shook her head. "No," she said. "I think it's a hit list. And I think it means we're dead."

He nodded thoughtfully, and took her hand in his. She looked scared—and why not? *He* was scared. Knowing the truth about any one of these murders would be enough to get you killed.

"Now I know what he meant," she told him.

"Who?"

"Shapiro. He said it was dark, but you know what? He was just guessing. He didn't know *how* dark it really is." She looked off, into space. "So what do we do?"

McBride shook his head. "I don't know. I think . . . I think I'll have another drink," he replied. "Anyway, you're the lawyer—what do *you* think we should do? I mean, what do we have that we can take to the police? Or Secret Service—*someone*."

Adrienne sat back. "We've got your medical file."

"Which shows . . . what?"

"That you had neurosurgery—and that the doctors found something."

"Okay, what else?" McBride asked.

"Bonilla. They'll have missed him by now."

"Go on."

She thought. "The rifle."

"Except . . . we don't *have* the rifle."

"But I can tell them about it! I saw it." She hesitated. Shrugged.

"What else?"

She shook her head. "I guess that's it. There are the letters we saw—but they wouldn't get us anywhere in court. They're more like leads than evidence."

McBride sighed. "That's what I think, too."

"And the list—"

"—isn't even a list. It's just a bunch of clips. Which we also don't have." He paused, and summed up. "So . . . what we've actually got—that we can take to the police—is a missing detective, a missing rifle, some interesting leads and a photograph of *something* that was in my head."

"And Crane," she added. "We have Crane, too. He was murdered, and we can prove that Nikki was here when he was killed."

McBride nodded. "Okay. Good. So, let's say we go to the police with our little shopping list. Then what? What happens?"

She thought about it for what seemed a long while. Finally, she said, "If we're lucky? They'll write it up . . . and then they'll file it."

"That's what I think," McBride told her. "And by the time they get around to it—if they ever get around to it—you and I will be sharing the same astral plane as Eddie Bonilla and Calvin Crane. Not to mention Mr. Luciani—whoever he is. I mean, *was*."

"And 'Jericho'?"

The name coasted through his mind like an ominous wind. *Jericho.* The words from Crane's letter to Opdahl came back to him. Jericho: a *disaster*. Jericho: *beyond belief.* McBride knew that Jericho—whatever it was—was what all this was about. It was the dark star that had swallowed up years of his life. It was the force that had killed Calvin Crane, electrocuted Nico, chopped down Bobby Bonilla and pulped Raymond Shaw. What was it? He didn't know but it filled him with dread. Still, Adrienne was looking at him and he managed to dredge up a sort of determined, upbeat look, a look that was light-years away from the helpless weariness he felt.

"I don't know," he said to her, "but we're going to find out."

38 Maybe it was the wine, or being under the gun the way they were. Maybe it was both. Or maybe it was just the right time.

They were standing outside the Super 8—the proverbial "cheap motel"—waiting for the car to stop running. For whatever reason, the Dodge had acquired the habit of continuing to run even after the ignition was shut off. And while there was nothing that either of them could do about it, whenever it happened, they tended to wait by its side until they heard the engine sputter out.

"I can't believe this," Adrienne told him, as they stood there. "That list, everything." The air was cool. Palms trembled in the wind. The asphalt, still damp from the rain, shone under the parking lot lights. "I mean—every once in a while I step back from it, and I think: *no*. And then I think of Nikki. In the bathtub. And Eddie." She was looking out, away from the motel. Traffic hissed down the damp street. A splash of blue from a neon sign zigzagged along the asphalt. "That candle," she said. "The house in Bethany exploding." He watched her push one hand up until her fingers were anchored in her hair. As if she had to hold her head there. He saw the glitter of tears in her eyes. "And then . . . all those murders."

The Stratus finally coughed its last. "I know," McBride said. "It's dark." He put his arm around her.

They were always stiff with each other, meticulous and careful during any incidental physical contact—but this time she sagged into him, tears rolling down her cheeks, her body trembling against his. After a few moments, he turned her head toward him and brushed the tears away. And then he leaned over and kissed her as tenderly as he'd ever kissed anyone. Her lips were cool, moist as the air; she tasted like mangoes. It was meant to be—and it *was*—a doting-uncle kiss, or something like that. Chaste. She drew back fractionally, made a little sound: "Oh."

And then their lips came together again and this time the kiss got away from them. It didn't take long—maybe ten seconds—and then they were up against the car, fumbling at each other's clothing, teetering on the edge of public indecency. They were saved by a couple emerging from one of the motel rooms: the woman, blond, her ringleted mane bouncing, tapped along in her spike heels. She said to her companion in a loud, accented voice: "You want a TicTac?"

Adrienne started to laugh, a whisper of a giggle that bubbled up from inside her and then took on a life of its own. Together, they staggered toward 18-B, engulfed in laughter and desire. They barely managed to get the door closed before they were on each other. Adrienne seemed almost incandescent and as for himself . . .

Clothing proved far too obstructive and difficult to remove under the circumstances, the circumstances being that he was beginning to lose contact with where his body stopped and hers began. They parted to remove it. "This is a mistake," Adrienne said in a sultry voice that dissolved into a giggle as she executed a kind of warp speed striptease.

"I know," he gasped, flinging a sock across the room.

"It's just going to complicate things," she continued, throwing herself onto the bed.

"We should wait," he told her, taking her in for about a nanosecond—the wonders of Adrienne—then falling on her as if there was no tomorrow.

And it was a free-for-all. Adrienne, so buttoned up and buttoned down, was inexperienced, but fearless, in bed. They did everything. At one point, when McBride—pinned to the sheets by sweet exhaustion—thought they might be done, Adrienne propped herself up on an elbow. And then she said— as if their making love required justification—"Well, you know, we're healthy young animals. What did we expect?"

"Well 'animals,'—I'll give you animals."

"Hey."

"And 'healthy,' " he continued, "I'll give you healthy. But—"

"You'll pay for that," she said, a gleam in her eyes. She rolled on top of him, pinned his elbows with her knees, crouched above him.

He atoned.

She felt guilty, she said afterwards, laughing, about extracting payment.

"We have a cure for guilt," he told her.

"Let me guess . . ." She took the cure.

Afterwards, they lazed in each other's presence, enjoying their newfound intimacy. McBride found a deck of cards in the desk where a *Gideon Bible* was supposed to be and, sitting on the bed, entertained her with them. He could cut the deck with one hand—which looked easy, until she tried it herself, and the cards exploded all over the room.

"You got a hat?"

"No," she replied with a little laugh. "Why?"

"Because if you had a hat, I could show you how to toss cards into it from the other side of the room."

"And why would I want to do that?"

"Because you could win a lot of bar bets with it—I mean, in case the law doesn't work out." Then he made her pick a card.

" 'Any card'?" she asked.

"What are you—psychic?"

"Unh-huh."

"Well, pick one anyway."

She did.

"Now, remember which card it is . . . got it? Okay, now put it back in the deck."

She did.

Holding the deck between them in his right hand, he cut the cards—again, and again. Then he shuffled them, and handed the deck back to her. "Now take your card out," he told her, "and press it against your forehead."

First, with a skeptical look, and then with a deepening frown, she looked through the deck, searching for the card she'd picked. Finally, she said, "It isn't there."

"You sure about that?"

"Yeah," she said, with a laugh. "How'd you do that?"

"Do *what*?"

"Find the card!"

"What card?" he asked.

"The card I picked!"

"You mean . . . the queen of hearts?"

"Whoaa!" she exclaimed. "How'd you *do* that?"

He shrugged. "I don't know. It's just a trick. And, anyway, I don't have it."

"Yes, you do," she insisted. "Give it to me! It's under your T-shirt, or something. It has to be!"

"But it's not!"

"Is!"

"Isn't!"

Getting to her feet, she patted him down—which wasn't hard, since the only article of clothing he was wearing was a T-shirt. "Then, where *is* it?" she demanded.

He thought about it for a few seconds, his face settling into a solemn mask. Finally, he said, "It's in the bathroom sink."

She gave him a skeptical look. "No, really!"

"It's in the bathroom sink," he repeated.

"No, it's *not*! It can't be!"

He turned the palms of his hands toward the ceiling and gazed at her with the po-faced innocence of charlatans everywhere. *What can I do with this woman?* his eyes seemed to ask. *Why won't she believe?*

"Okay," she said, getting up from the bed. "But stay where you are. Don't move!"

"I won't move."

"Don't get up!"

"I won't get up."

Keeping her eyes on him, she walked slowly backward toward the bathroom, opened the door, stepped inside and—screamed. A second later, she burst into the bedroom with the queen of hearts in her hand and her eyes as round as saucers. "How did you *do* that!?" she shouted.

McBride laughed. "You'd be amazed at what I can do."

"But where did you learn how to do that?"

"When I was a kid. I read every book anyone ever wrote about Houdini. You want to know the truth? If I hadn't discovered basketball and girls, I'd probably be a lounge act in Vegas. The Great McBride." He smiled. Sighed. "I'd forgotten all about it until . . . just recently."

Soon after, they ventured into the shower, where they laved each other with soap, an activity that each of them knew could only end in one way, which it did—with the two of them on the floor, exhausted by each other's enthusiasm and inventiveness. Finally, Adrienne struggled to her feet, and went to the sink, where she drank long and deep from the tap, cupping the water in her hands. By the time McBride went to join her in bed, she was sound asleep, with the covers pulled up to her chin and a childlike smile on her lips.

Adrienne was the first to wake up, and when she did, she decided she might as well let McBride sleep. She liked the way he looked in bed, with his right arm thrown up over his head—as if he were swimming through his dreams.

After she'd dressed and brushed her hair, she wrote a note.

> *Hey—I'm at the library checking*
> *names. Back in a bit.*
> *Love,*
> *A.*

No.

Not *love*. It was way too soon for that. She'd never loved anybody—not really, not that way. Maybe last night would be the first of many nights and then again, maybe it wouldn't. So she tore up the first note and wrote a second, which she left on the counter in the bathroom, next to his toothbrush:

> *Hey—*
> *I'm at the library,*
> *checking out names. Back by Noon.*
> *Worker Bee*

She asked at the front desk for directions to the library. The woman gaped at her as if the question were a joke. " '*Lie-berry*'!?" she winced. "Sorry, hon'—I got no idea."

Using a pay phone in the lobby, Adrienne got the number from 411, called and got directions. As it happened, the library was only three blocks away. Five minutes later, she was there. And an hour after that, she was done.

McBride was still in bed when she came back. Hearing her come in, he stretched luxuriantly and groaned with pleasure. "Mmmmm. *Mmmmmmm.* C'mere," he said.

Adrienne was tempted. It would be nice to crawl back into bed—and dissolve in sensation. But she stayed where she was, clutching her yellow legal pad.

He propped himself up on an elbow, suddenly serious, concerned. "What's-a-matter? Second thoughts?"

"No."

"Whew! Because—I might be in *love*. I think—I think I *am* in love. You sure you won't come here?" His voice slowed, became theatrically sleazy. "Show you a good time."

"Lew."

The somber note in her voice got through. "Okay," he said, sitting up. "What's going on? Where have you been?"

"The library."

"Oh. So what did you find out?" He rubbed the sleep from his eyes, and looked straight at her in a parody of alertness.

"Albino Luciani," she told him.

"Luciani," he repeated, then frowned, trying to remember. "Oh, yeah," he said. "The list. So who *was* he?"

She turned her notepad toward him, so he could see what she'd written. He squinted.

John Paul I.

"Oh, Jesus," he muttered. "That's who Crane was talking about. That's 'Papa.' There were stories about him being poisoned after Vatican II."

"They're going to kill us," she announced.

He was silent for a long moment. Finally, he said, "I know."

"What do you *mean* you know?" There was a little quaver in her voice, and she worked to control it.

"I mean, I know they're going to try. They've already tried. But they won't get away with it—I mean, they won't succeed."

"Why not?" she demanded, sitting down on the bed.

"Because we're going after them."

"What?!"

"We're going after them! I'm gonna kill the son of a bitch," McBride swore.

"Who?"

"Opdahl."

"What are you—crazy?"

"It's the last thing he'll expect," McBride told her.

"Of course it is—because it's the stupidest thing you could do!"

"No, it's not. The stupidest thing I could do is keep running from him. Because, eventually, you run out of room."

"And how is killing him going to help?" she asked. "I mean, assuming you could—which you can't!"

"I'll plead self-defense. You can be my lawyer. We'll have a big trial, and everything will come out." He paused. "What do you think?"

She looked at him wordlessly for ten or twenty seconds. Finally, she said, "You're insane."

His head fell back on the pillow. "I know," he admitted. "But, unless you have a better plan, I'm going after him—because I don't know of any other way to stop Jericho."

" 'Jericho'? You don't even know what Jericho is."

"Yes, I do—a little bit."

"Like what?"

"It's a bloodbath," he told her.

She nodded in agreement. "Right. What else?"

"It's time sensitive."

She gave him a puzzled look. "Why do you say that?" But even as the words emerged, the answer came to her: because they'd sent Nikki to kill a dying man.

Seeing her look, he knew she understood. "They couldn't wait," he told her.

She nodded.

"And we know something else," he said.

"We do?"

"Yeah. We know who the hit man is—the guy who gets it started."

Adrienne frowned, uncomprehending.

"De Groot," he explained. "My client. You met him. The one who . . ." His voice trailed off.

"What?"

"Son of a bitch," McBride whispered. He was thinking of de Groot. The spiky blond hair, the athletic roll of his walk—a predator, always up on the balls of his feet. His ingratiating grin. The dancing light in his eyes. Even with the medication, the Dutchman had too much energy. He was constantly tapping his foot, or rapping his fingers against a leg, always humming a tune. Sometimes whistling. Always the *same* tune. They'd joked about it a few times, that it was a funny kind of tune for a hip-hop Dutchman to latch onto. *It's like an audio virus,* de Groot had complained. *You think it's funny, but I can't get rid of it! And I don't even know the whole tune—just the hook: about Joshua.*"

"What!?" Adrienne repeated, unable to read his mind.

"He was always humming that song—the one about Joshua . . . and Jericho."

"What song?"

He looked at her: "The one where the walls come tumbling down."

Neither of them said anything for a long while. Finally, Adrienne got up and crossed the room to the window. Looked out. "Did he have a screen memory?"

McBride nodded. "Yeah. An abduction scenario." He paused, remembered. "And . . . you're gonna love this . . . he thought he had a tapeworm in his heart. And that it gave him orders."

"I remember," Adrienne said.

She went to her legal pad, and began riffling through it. From somewhere down the hall, Adrienne could hear the motel's cleaning women, rapping on doors: "Housekeeping! Housekeeping!" Finally, she found what she was looking for. "Look at this," she said, and gave him the pad with her notes.

Henrik Verwoerd. South African P.M.—
architect of apartheid. Gunned down in '66 by Dimi-
trio Tsafendas. Tsafendas lone nut, cultist ("The Follow-
ers of Jesus"). Had five false passports when arrested.
Blamed assassination on a tapeworm in his heart.

"Fuck." The word fell softly from his lips—as if he'd whispered *lavender* or *shadow play*. Looking up from the pad, he said, "Jericho. It's South Africa." He let his head fall back on the pillow, and fixed his gaze on the acoustical tiles overhead. The tapeworm was an in-joke, of sorts, a sick reference to one of the Program's earlier successes. *An homage.* McBride flashed back to his sessions with de Groot, and for the first time, he understood what the Dutchman had been muttering about. It had nothing to do with *mandalas*—the rigidly symmetrical patterns that haunted the visions of so many schizophrenics. It was Nelson Mandela he was talking about, *Mandela* he was after.

McBride pushed himself up in the bed, and swung his legs on to the floor. Reaching for his clothes, he began to get dressed. "He's going to kill Mandela," he told her. "He's a racist, and he's going to set South Africa on fire."

They took turns at the wheel and drove straight through to Washington, smashing along the Interstate at eighty miles an hour, radio blaring. The sun went down in Georgia and, by the time it came up again, they were nearing the Virginia border. Even going eighty, semis rolled past them in the fast lane, rocking slightly from side to side.

It was 11 A.M. when they crossed the Potomac, heading north on Rock Creek Parkway. De Groot's apartment was on a sidestreet near Chevy Chase Circle. McBride remembered the name: the Monroe. He and de Groot had joked about it, with the Dutchman insisting that its namesake was Marilyn rather than James.

McBride hoped against hope that de Groot was still there. He thought if he could find the Dutchman, he might be able to defuse the screen memory. And if that didn't work, he'd find a way to put him out of circulation—whatever it took to derail Jericho.

"Penny for your thoughts," Adrienne promised.

"It's on the house," he told her. "I wish I had a gun."

She blanched, then peered at him as if to decide whether or not he'd gone insane. "What for?" she asked.

He returned the look. "What do you think? De Groot's a big guy." Entering the tunnel near the National Zoo, he added, "I don't want a repeat of what happened in my apartment."

"Eddie had a gun," she reminded him. "It didn't do him any good."

McBride kept his peace. Kept driving.

When they came out of the tunnel, she asked, "Do you even know how to shoot?"

"Yeah," he told her. "I'm good at it."

"Right," she replied, her voice a casserole of skepticism and sarcasm.

"I am!"

She looked at him again. Was he serious? "How come?" she asked.

"My dad taught me." He said it without thinking, but as soon as the words were out of his mouth, he flashed on himself and his father. A crystal-clear, brick-cold winter morning in Maine. Breath pluming from their mouths. Fingerless gloves. His father adjusting the gun on his shoulder, teaching him how to sight it in. The paper target stapled to a tree at the foot of a low hill, maybe thirty yards away. "He won a medal in the biathlon—did I tell you that?"

"What? In the Olympics? Get out!"

"No—I'm serious. The '72 Olympics. In Sapporo."

"That's fantastic!" she gushed. Paused. And asked: "What's the biathlon?"

He laughed. "It's the one where you cross-country ski for ten kilometers, and then you do some target shooting. What's hard is: by the time you get to shoot, your body's exhausted. So you have to be in tremendous shape, just to keep your pulse rate slow and steady. Then, when you stop to shoot, you take aim, wait—and squeeze the trigger between the beats of your heart."

"You can do that?"

"No," he told her. "That was my dad's thing. But I can shoot. Or I could if I had a gun. Which, unfortunately, I don't." Heading up Beach Drive, he considered how he might buy one without having to suffer through the requisite waiting period. At a flea market, for instance, or at a gun show—or just on the street. There were lots of guns in the 'hood. But there weren't any flea markets or gun shows in progress at the moment, or none that he knew of, and the idea of he and Adrienne cruising through a black ghetto in their rented Dodge Stratus, looking to get strapped, was . . . well, a hoot.

Then they were there. They found a parking space a block

away and walked. The building was a ten-story, glass-and-brick box with a sign out front, advertising EXECUTIVE RENTALS. Seeing Adrienne and McBride, a uniformed doorman hopped up from his perch on a low wall to open the door. Inside, a weary-looking, middle-aged man sat behind a desk and halfheartedly asked if he could be of help.

"We're looking for a tenant—Henrik de Groot," McBride told him.

The man frowned for a moment, then looked up. "The blond guy—7-G!"

"Right!"

Then he shook his head. "I haven't seen him in a couple of weeks. I don't think he's around. Travels a lot." Reaching for the in-house phone, he dialed a number and listened to it ring. After a bit, he replaced the handset in its cradle, and shrugged.

Five minutes later, they were back in the car and on their way to McBride's apartment. Going there was a risk, of course—there was a possibility it was still being watched. But there wasn't any choice, really. Their only plan—and it wasn't so much a plan as a notion—was to fly to Switzerland, confront Opdahl and find de Groot before it was too late. How any of that was going to be accomplished, he had no idea. But one thing was certain: he was going to need his passport (Adrienne already had hers)—and his passport was in the refrigerator.

All of his ID was.

That was de Groot's idea. The Dutchman was in the fire suppression business, retrofitting halon systems with environmentally stable gases. At one of their first sessions, the Dutchman had clucked about the outmoded fire security system in place at the Capitol Towers. "Something gets started in here, I don't think they'll put it out. Maybe you should keep your backup discs and tapes in the freezer," he suggested. "Also any papers you don't want to lose. They'll be safe there. It's waterproof and fireproof."

"Jeffrey Duran" hadn't made any backup discs, and the

only tapes were those he sent to the insurance company the same day. But he did have a passport and a couple of unused credit cards, so he'd made a show of putting them in a Ziploc bag and burying them under a tray of ice cubes in the freezer. As McBride had hoped, the effort pleased de Groot and helped him build a relationship of trust with his client.

All of McBride's ID was in the name of Jeffrey Duran, and that was what he'd have to use in Europe. Reestablishing his real identity was going to be a bureaucratic nightmare.

Pulling into the circular drive in front of the Capitol Towers, he told Adrienne to wait in the car. She didn't want to, but he knew by now how to push at least a few of her buttons. "They'll tow the car," he warned, as he opened the door and got out.

The security guard at the reception desk was a young guy with Buddy Holly glasses, and he recognized McBride, which was good. "Hey, Mr. Duran—where have you been? We haven't seen you for a while."

"I went to Florida for a few days," McBride told him.

"Sweet!"

"Yeah, it was—nice to be in shorts, you know?"

"Lucky you."

"But now? It's like I never left." They laughed. "But, listen, you got a spare key I can use? I left mine in the apartment."

"No problem," the kid told him, then bent down, opened a locked cabinet, and removed a key from one of the hooks. "Just don't forget to bring it back, okay?"

"Ten minutes," McBride replied, taking the key and heading toward the elevator. While he waited for it to arrive, he looked back to see if the kid was busy on the phone, but no—he was just standing there at the desk, smiling.

A minute later, he stepped out of the elevator on the sixth floor, and walked slowly toward his apartment. He was worried about the man next door—Barbera, the guy in 6-G—but, as it turned out, there was no need to be concerned. The door to 6-G was half ajar, and a country and western tune— *"She's gone country, look at them boots!"*—emanated from inside.

The air was heavy with the smell of paint. Glancing through the doorway on the way to his own apartment, McBride saw a scrawny little guy with a ZZ Top beard, standing on a spattered drop cloth, rolling the ceiling with Shell White. Otherwise, the apartment was empty. The gray wire mesh was gone, and so were the table, the steamer trunks, the wall of electronics equipment, and the Aeron chair. Of Hector Barbera, there was nothing left—except, perhaps, the faint and sickly smell of rotting flesh, buried under the pungent odors of paint thinner and cleaning fluids.

Seeing the apartment's emptiness, a feeling of relief swept over him, even as he felt a twinge of disappointment. Barbera could have told him things. . . .

His own apartment was just the way he'd left it, or so at first it seemed. On closer inspection, though, he saw that, with the exception of a few books, there wasn't a scrap of paper anywhere. Every bill, note, grocery list, and take-out menu—anything on which something might have been written—was gone. So were the computer, and the pictures of his faux family. Anything, in other words, that might have linked him to the Program. It was all gone.

But not the passport and the credit cards, which remained in the freezer under the ice tray. He glanced around, sensing that whatever happened, this was a place he wasn't coming back to. Then he threw some things in an overnight bag, and let himself out.

At a cyber café off Dupont Circle, Adrienne found a couple of B-sale fares on Swissair that didn't require advance purchase. The tickets were $484 each, round-trip, including tax—a bargain, considering the cab fare out to Dulles was fifty-five dollars.

"What are you doing with a passport, anyway?" she asked, as the cab made its way north on the Beltway to the Dulles access road. "I thought you didn't go anywhere—just watched TV all the time."

"They had to get me back in the States—I mean, they had to get 'Duran' back in."

"From where?" she asked.

"Switzerland." He frowned. His memory of that time, when Lew McBride segued into Jeff Duran, was beginning to come back. There was an ambulance, he remembered, and whirling lights. He couldn't move, but he was *moving*, rolling somewhere on a gurney. And he could hear people talking, people with Swiss-German accents—then Gunnar Opdahl whispering *Sh-sh-sh-sh* while Lew McBride lay there, eyes on the ceiling, suffocating. Sometimes, when he thought of it . . . McBride's body lurched in a myoclonic jerk, as if he were falling asleep.

"You okay?" Adrienne asked.

"I was just thinking about something."

"What?"

He shook his head. She didn't press it.

39 The Hotel Florida was a clean, if somewhat down-at-the-heels, nouveau deco *établissement* that looked as if it hadn't been redecorated since the Seventies. Much of the furniture was composed of chipped black formica, and there was a free-form, salmon-colored ceramic lamp on the bedside table. A blond dresser stood a few feet away, perched on inverted, cone shaped legs. The traditional mammoth Swiss comforter lay like a cloud, on the mod bed.

"It grows on you," McBride promised, seeing Adrienne's hesitation.

"But . . . why is this place even here? Why is there a Hotel Florida in Zurich? Why not the Alpenhorn? Why not the Willem Tell?"

McBride shrugged and opened the door to the balcony, where a gaily painted window box held a tangle of dead vegetation. "Someone had a vision," he explained.

Their room on the third floor looked out over Seefeldstrasse toward the Limmat River and the Zurichsee. Two blocks away, their rental car was parked around the corner from the tram stop. Every few minutes, a sleek new trolley car bombed down the street, passing beneath their balcony, heading for busy Bellevueplatz. One squealed toward them even now, rocking around the angled corner, its single headlight fracturing in the mist. McBride closed the door to the balcony, reducing the noise.

Adrienne fell on the bed and yawned. "What time is it?"

"Just after nine."

"Which is what?"

"Three in the morning, real time."

She yawned again. "I'm wiped. I didn't sleep at all on the plane." This was actually an understatement. In terms of psychokinetic effort, Adrienne had expended a huge amount of energy getting the plane safely across the Atlantic. He knew, because his right arm had borne the brunt of her nervousness. "So, what's the plan?" she asked, closing her eyes as she subsided into the cool comforter.

" 'The plan'? Well, the plan is: first, we get some sleep—then we go shopping."

She rolled over on her stomach, and pulled the pillow under her cheek. "Mmmmmn," she murmured. "That's a good idea . . ."

She was sound asleep.

Undressing, he lay down beside her and closed his eyes. It wouldn't be smart to go hunting for Opdahl, jet-lagged and ragged. He needed a couple of hours . . .

Opdahl . . . He remembered being in an ambulance, but he didn't remember the injury—just the lights flashing across the ceiling. Then a gurney, and Opdahl saying, 'You're very brave.' But he wasn't brave—not really. And Opdahl wasn't being encouraging. He was playing with him. Enjoying himself.

"Lew. *Lew!*" Adrienne was shaking him. "You're dreaming. Wake up."

His eyes snapped open. Relief surged through him. He'd been dreaming of a man with a tube in his throat—not a real man, but a man without a face. Or a man whose face had been torn away. The man was on television, in close-up, and the image terrified him. Even now, he couldn't get away from it: the empty visage stuck with him, shimmering in front of his eyes, pixilated and slightly blue. The man's eyes, wide with horror, the venous pulp where his face should have been—

But no. That was a dream. And here he was in the Florida, looking at Adrienne looking at him with a worried look. Beyond the windows, a tram clattered and whined toward the train station.

"Let's go out," he suggested, "before the shops close for lunch."

"They close for lunch?" Adrienne asked.

"Yeah—for a couple of hours, usually."

"Think of that," she muttered, having never been to Europe before.

Downstairs, the woman at the desk seemed charmed by McBride's German. He was looking for a Jäger-store, he told her. *Ein Speicher für Jäger.*

"Of course," the woman replied and, taking out a small brochure, marked the way in ballpoint pen from the hotel to the *Speicher* in question.

"What's a spiker?" Adrienne asked, as they stepped out into the cold, and began walking in the direction of Zurich's Old Town.

"It's a store," McBride told her, wishing he'd brought a pair of gloves.

"What kind of store?" she wanted to know.

"A store for hunters—a Jäger store."

This confused her even more. "You mean, like—bows and arrows, fishing rods and—"

"Shotguns. Yeah, like that," he said.

They continued walking for a while, until Adrienne stopped and turned to him. "Shotguns?" she asked. McBride nodded, and they resumed their stroll, crossing the Quail Bridge into the city's historic quarter. Once again, and suddenly, Adrienne stopped. "The other day—when you said you were going to kill Opdahl so that everything could come out in court—and I'd be your lawyer—that was crazy, right? That was a joke. I mean, it's not the plan—not really!"

He leaned on the parapet overlooking the Zurichsee, where a flotilla of white swans glided on the glassine surface. His breath came and went in clouds. Finally, he said, "You're trying to tell me you didn't pass the Swiss bar?"

She shook her head. "Didn't come close. Never took the test. Don't speak the language. Don't know where I am."

He nodded thoughtfully, and shrugged. "Well, it wasn't much of a plan, anyway." Then he smiled. "Don't worry," he told her, "I'm not going to shoot anybody—unless they try to shoot me first."

Two minutes later, they were standing in front of an old-fashioned store, looking in the window at a diorama of the hunt, replete with baying hounds, plunging horses, and men with post horns. Going inside, they were greeted by a stuffed bear, rearing on its hind legs. A wild boar's head bristled from the wall behind the cash register, while a herd of dead stags stared forlornly from the wall.

Adrienne rolled her eyes. "You can't just buy a gun," she told him.

"You can in Switzerland," he replied, studying the hand-guns that lay beneath the glass counter. "The country's armed to the teeth. In fact, there's a law: every male between twenty and forty, or something like that, *has* to own a gun."

"Get out!"

"And not just a gun," he added. "An assault rifle. It's the

law." He paused. "Listen," he said, "there's a department store just up the block. Would you get me something?"

She nodded. "Sure. What?"

"Curtain rods."

She didn't think she'd heard right. Asked him to repeat it. He did. "What kind of curtain rods?"

"Any kind," he told her. "As long as they are in a box and aren't more than five feet long. And I'll probably need some packing tape, too."

Before she could ask if he wanted cafe curtains or doilies as well, an elderly clerk came to the counter and inquired, in perfect English, if he could be of help.

McBride returned the old man's smile. "I'm looking for a combat shotgun," he told him. "Something with a pump-action and a pistol grip. A riot gun. Got one?"

Adrienne reacted in much the same way as if he'd asked for a suitcase full of pornography. Turning on her heel, she went out in search of the department store.

On the way back to their hotel, half an hour later, they stopped to buy some warmer clothes. A light snow was falling, and the air was clammy and cold. Happily, Seefeld-strasse was lined with stylish consignment shops, including one where Adrienne found a calf length Jil Sander coat, dove-gray and hooded, a long chenille scarf and a pair of soft leather gloves. Everything was marked down to a tenth of its designer's expectations, which made the purchases a bargain, but the total was still higher than anything she'd ever bought before.

Then it was McBride's turn and, to Adrienne's surprise, he waited until they found a consignment shop that was markedly funkier than the rest. Going inside, he came out a few min-utes later wearing a black watchcap, a khaki-colored Army jacket and a pair of Doc Martens that had seen better days.

Adrienne winced. "Could you afford it?"

"It's a fashion statement," he told her.

Soon afterward, they plunged into the warmth of the

Florida's lobby, and stood there for a bit, slapping the snow from their clothes, relishing the central heat. Steam rose in a cloud from Adrienne's hair as they waited for the tiny elevator to arrive. It took the better part of a minute to rattle down from the floor above. When it finally did, McBride held the frosted glass door open for them, and they wedged their way in.

"Now I see why," Adrienne said.

"Why what?"

"Why they called it the Florida."

"And why is that?" McBride asked.

"For psychological warmth."

Back in the room, McBride unpacked the shotgun, pumped the slide two or three times, and tested the trigger's pull. Then he sat down on the bed with a box of 00 buckshot, and loaded eight shells into the gun's extended magazine. Finally, he dumped the curtain rods out of the box they were in, and replaced them with the loaded shotgun. Then he closed the box with the packing tape and, producing a penknife, made an incision about two-thirds of the way down the box and three-quarters of the way around it.

Adrienne didn't even want to look.

She skimmed the pages of the *Herald-Tribune*. There was trouble in Chechnya again, e-tailers were having a big holiday season, and the Redskins were in the hunt for a playoff spot. Turning to the financial pages, her eye was caught by a story with Switzerland in the headline. It was about the upcoming World Economic Summit in Davos, which sounded more like a very expensive party than the financial conference it was alleged to be. The tickets cost $160,000 each. Attendees would include everyone from Bill Gates to Prince Charles, Warren Beatty to Kofi Annan. Fearing demonstrations, organizers of the Summit were laying on extra security. Adrienne didn't think they had to worry. Switzerland seemed like a pretty orderly place, and, as McBride had pointed out— all the men were armed to the teeth.

Including him.

"So what's the plan?" she asked, setting the newspaper aside.

"The plan? The plan is: I go to the Institute. Find Opdahl. And talk to him."

She was silent for a long moment, as if waiting for McBride to continue. When he didn't, she asked, "That's *it*?"

"Well, no. First, I'll put the gun to his head—so it won't be like a general conversation. I'll be real focused."

She nodded. Thought about it. Said: "Seems kind of basic, doesn't it? I mean, it's not exactly a *plan*. It's more like—I don't know—the headline for a plan."

McBride shrugged. "Well, that's my plan."

She gave her head a little shake, as if to be certain she was hearing him right. "And what are you going to ask him?"

"What do you think? Who. What. Where. When. Why. How."

Crossing the room to the window, she looked out at the lightly falling snow. After a bit, she turned and, leaning her back against the windowsill, said, "Okay, that's what we'll do—but I'm going in first."

McBride shook his head. "Unh-unh."

"They don't know me," she insisted. "If you go in, and they recognize you, that's it. What if Opdahl's not there? They'll alert him. And then you'll never get close to him. But, me? I'm just a student passing through. At least I can find out if he's there or not."

" 'A student,' " he repeated.

"Right. I'll say I was in the neighborhood. Skiing. And one of the fellows—who I met in the States—said I should stop in. Get an application."

"They don't *have* applications," McBride told her. "You have to be recommended."

"Right! That's what I mean. He said while I was over here, I should stop in and say hello. Let Opdahl know who I am. Because, 'I don't want to promise anything, but:' I think there might be a recommendation in my future."

"And which fellow was this?" McBride asked. "I hope it wasn't Jeff Duran, because—"

"No! Of course not! I never heard of Jeff Duran. Who's Jeff Duran? This was someone else. This was . . . who was it?"

"Eric Branch."

"Right!" she exclaimed.

"He was studying sub-Saharan migration. I read a couple of his reports. Good stuff."

"Great! So, I'll ask to see Opdahl. And if he isn't there, I'll find out where he is."

"And if they say, 'I'm afraid you can't just "drop in" on Dr. Opdahl,' " McBride said in a snotty German accent. " 'You must have an appointment.' "

Adrienne's voice turned waiflike and pitiable: " 'But I'm only in Zurich for a couple of days.' "

"Don't wheedle," he told her. "It's their loss."

Again, her voice changed, plunging to throaty and lascivious depths: " 'But I'm only in Zurich for a couple of days.' "

The tone was silly and irresistible, all at once. Lunging across the bed, he pushed her down, rolling with her in the cloudlike folds of the comforter, giddy and making out, with Adrienne trying one variation after another of "I'm only in Zurich for a couple of days . . ." Then the kissing became more serious, until Adrienne finally pulled away, flushed, her dirty blond hair in disarray, one strand plastered to her cheek. She was one of those women, McBride thought, who looked better disheveled. You could see the wildness in her then, which at most times she kept so well hidden.

"We can't," she said. Breathless. "It will get too late."

Reluctantly, he agreed. Stood up, plucked a tiny feather from his pants leg. "Which fellow?"

"Eric Branch." Adrienne found a brush on the bedside table, and began to brush her hair. "One thing: what if—what *if*—they say, 'Fine—Mr. Opdahl will see you right away'? What then?"

"Get out."

"But—"

"Just don't go upstairs with him," he told her.

"Why not? Maybe—"

He shook his head. "Promise . . ."

The tram took them most of the way to the Institute, with McBride clutching the box of "curtain rods." Adrienne sat stiffly, holding the cylindrical metal post. At nearly every stop the tram's accordion doors wheezed open to admit a blast of arctic air and some rosy-faced commuters. At this time of day, these were an odd mixture of senior citizens, working men who smelled of nicotine and well-dressed women with plastic mesh shopping bags. At one stop, a high-spirited influx of uniformed school children clambered aboard.

The animation of the children seemed to exist in counterpoint to McBride's own mood, which was bleak and getting bleaker. The closer they got to their destination, the more he worried that he was on a fool's errand—that they'd get to the address, and it wouldn't be there. Instead of a townhouse with mullioned windows and gargoyles, and a massive front door—there would be an empty lot or a train station. That's what had happened in Bethany Beach, and the effect of that now-you-see-it-now-you-don't memory was to make him doubt the reality of his own past.

"What's the matter?" Adrienne asked, but he just shook his head and looked away.

He'd thought all this was behind him, these worries about his memory, about what was real and what was not. He'd thought they'd gotten down to bedrock. He was Lew McBride, and that was that. Only it wasn't. That would never be that. *That* was something Opdahl had taken from him.

The conductor announced their stop, and the tram began to slow. He could see the station ahead, the widening of the platform, the Plexiglas shelter with its benches, a few waiting passengers. Children were shouting farewells to each other, getting up, queuing in the aisle toward the front of the car. Looking out the window at the row of solid houses—there was something familiar about it, although he couldn't have said what. "This is it," he told her, standing up to press the rubber button that opened the tram's rear door. Then they were outside and he began to wonder if the whole trip wasn't a terrible mistake.

The houses on either side of the street were stolid and old, the mansions and near mansions of Swiss industrialists, bankers, lawyers, and tax exiles. In front of each, two or three plane trees stood their ground in the cold, awaiting the spring.

Adrienne and McBride lowered their heads against the wind, which was blowing off the lake, even as a light snow zipped through the air, snowflakes flying like sparks.

They'd traveled three blocks before they came to a dogleg in the street. With each step, McBride's chest seemed to tighten. He told himself to breathe, just breathe, but how could he? Like a weight lifter finishing his third set of reps, he wasn't breathing at all, just straining to get it over. Either the Institute would be there, or it wouldn't. His sanity seemed to hang in the balance.

And then, there it was—just as he'd remembered: a three-story granite structure with mullioned windows and window boxes, filled now with junipers and evergreens. The heavy door with its lion's head knocker. The leaded glass transom. The small brass plaque with the Institute's name on it, and the closed-circuit camera overhead. Instinctively, he hung back, across the street and out of range of the camera.

The sense of foreboding that he felt was overwhelming. Suddenly, the idea of sending Adrienne inside seemed insane. "Maybe this isn't such a good plan," he said. "Maybe we should rethink it."

She shook her head, and straightened her back. Put her Scout face on. Prepared. Determined. The lawyer. Then she glanced around. "I think I got the long straw," she told him. "At least I get to go inside."

"We could have called him on the phone. We still can."

"It's too easy to blow someone off on the phone. This way, I'm in their face."

"If you're not back in fifteen minutes," he promised, "I'm coming in. And it won't be just a box in my hand."

She nodded. "Eric Branch, Eric Branch, Eric Branch," she said and, turning, marched toward the door.

McBride checked his watch. It was 2:36.

He forced himself to look at the building. Watched Adrienne ring the bell, saw the door open, glimpsed a woman in the doorway, watched Adrienne walk inside.

He was cold. It was freezing. And time didn't just slow down, it turned as glacial as the weather. He was standing across the street from the Institute, a quarter of the way up the block, leaning against a sycamore tree. And he felt very conspicuous. There was no reason for him to be there, holding this unwieldy box. But there he was, eyes glued to the massive front door, muttering, "C'mon, c'mon, c'mon . . ."

Because, all of a sudden, he didn't want Opdahl to be there. There was something about the Institute, something about the building he was watching, that affected him in a primal way—like waking in the middle of the night to see a snake writhing across the bedroom floor. The fear he felt came from the deepest and most instinctive part of himself, a region of the brain that had nothing to do with rational thinking, and everything to do with survival.

And then he remembered. Watching the building from across the street, he remembered the dream he'd had that afternoon, the one Adrienne had interrupted. And, suddenly, he knew who the man without the face was.

He'd gone to the Institute to meet with Opdahl—and he'd been ambushed. By a man with an aerosol. He remembered a cloud of spray, and then the floor, smacking him in the face. He remembered the long ride in the ambulance, the drugs wearing off, the gurney crunching over gravel as they arrived.

Then the operating room, where Gunnar Opdahl shone a penlight in his eyes. The big Norwegian dressed in surgical scrubs, a cap on his head. And beside the operating table, the monitor. Which held an expressionless McBride in close-up as a nurse peeled his face up and back and back—until it wasn't there anymore. McBride could feel the scream rising in his throat, where the trache-tube siphoned it off, turning his terror into a soft, gurgling sound. Nearby, a machine wheezed in and out, breathing for him. He tried to close his eyes, but he couldn't. And somewhere in all this, Opdahl saying, "A paralytic, but . . . not an anesthetic. You're very brave."

Brave?

McBride shivered, and glanced at his watch. *2:48. Twelve minutes, and counting,* he thought, *though why it should take so long . . . she should be out by now!* Unless Opdahl had a picture of her—which he wouldn't—unless he did. McBride looked at his watch a second time. 2:49.

Fuck it, he muttered, and launched himself toward the Institute.

He was halfway up the walk when the door opened. Putting on the brakes, he drew himself up, tried to look casual. Adrienne was standing in the doorway, smiling, dipping her head toward a woman in green. The woman peered around Adrienne, stared at McBride. Adrienne dipped her head again, made an explanatory gesture. He could see the animation on her face, the flash of her eyes, the white gleam of her teeth. And then she was turning, her hand ascending in a little wave as she came down the steps. The door closed. "What's wrong?" Adrienne asked.

"Let's get out of here," McBride said.

He wanted to know whether Opdahl was in the Institute. Because he wanted to kill him. But not with Adrienne at his side. He hustled her off toward the tram stop.

When they reached its puny Plexiglas shelter, he finally asked her: "Was he there?"

She frowned at him, didn't answer. "You look really spooked," she told him.

"Was he there?"

"Lighten *up*. What's the matter with you?"

"I'm sorry," he said. "I've had a rough ten minutes."

She grimaced at the sarcasm. "No," she said. "He wasn't there."

"But he'll be back," McBride suggested, his voice hopeful.

"Not until Tuesday."

His disappointment was palpable.

"Not to worry," she told him, sounding a little smug. "I found out where he is: he's at the clinic in Spiez."

McBride nodded as a tram rumbled toward them through the lightly falling snow.

"So?" Adrienne asked.

"So . . . what?" McBride replied.

"How far is Spiez?"

40 Spiez was only seventy miles through the mountains, but there were a lot of mountains, and there was a lot of ice. The landscape was ferociously beautiful, with evergreen forests flocked with snow, and the Alps brooding under a leaden sky. It took their rented BMW nearly three hours to get there, so that it was well past dark when they arrived.

Even so, they could see that the town was a special one, with its own castle hard by the lake, an elegant marina, and a view toward the Jungfrau. The streets above the lake were narrow, winding, and hilly, and they had to stop twice to ask directions—once at a *Gasthaus*, and then at a restaurant that specialized in wild boar.

Their hotel, the Belvedere, was in a residential area over-looking the marina. They'd picked it out of a guidebook in the lobby of the Florida, ignoring the high rack rate in favor of its proximity to the Prudhomme Clinic. Unless the street numbers were very misleading, the hotel was only a block away from the clinic, and on the same street.

And, in fact, it was even closer than that. The buildings were side-by-side, the one a mansion in the Beaux Arts style, with cupolas and spires, the clinic a fortress of poured concrete—gray, severe, and minimalist. "Let's see what kind of security they have," McBride suggested, and turned into the clinic's courtyard, where the gravel crunched beneath the tires in a way that was both familiar and unpleasant. Suddenly, the night exploded in a flood of light, and a man appeared in the doorway. "Pretty good," McBride concluded, looping back to the street and into the parking lot next door.

"But they saw us!" Adrienne said.

McBride pulled into a parking slot, and shook his head. "They'll think we made a wrong turn."

And then they were in Room 252 with a view across the lake, and the mountains silhouetted against the night. Adrienne sat on the large and comfortable bed, and took in the plush surroundings, while McBride stood at the window, gazing at the lights across the lake.

"Let's get some dinner," he suggested, and Adrienne readily agreed. Going to the lobby, they stopped at the front desk to drop off the gigantic key that opened the door to their room. "I'm curious," McBride told the stylish woman behind the desk. "The building next door—is that a hospital, or . . . what?"

"The Prudhomme Clinic? Mostly, it is for young people."

"What's the matter with them?" Adrienne asked.

The woman shrugged. "I think they are having eating problems. So they are very skinny."

"You mean, they're anorexic," McBride suggested.

"Yes. And I think some drug problems, too—though I hope you don't worry—"

McBride shook his head. "No, no—I'm sure the security's excellent."

"Absolutely. The clinic is very discreet. A good neighbor—if you don't mind the architecture."

McBride reassured her that they didn't and, with Adrienne at his side, wandered into the hotel's four-star dining room. Though they felt underdressed, the hostess didn't give their clothes a second glance, but led them to a table overlooking the lake.

"You are staying in the house?" she asked, handing each of them a huge menu.

"Yes."

She smiled. "Well, enjoy your stay." Then she lighted the candle and stood back a moment, as if to admire the crisp white linen and gleaming silverware. "You would perhaps enjoy a complimentary glass of Swiss wine?"

They glanced at each other. "Delighted," McBride said.

She returned a moment later. "It's called Fendant," she told them, setting a glass before each of them. "I think you'll find it refreshing. Now, if I may recommend something? The lake fish is . . ." She bunched her fingers into a bouquet and kissed them. "The best."

Before long, their first dish came. It was a cream soup of some kind, smoky and delicious, with bits of mushroom and ham. Then the fish arrived in the company of tiny white potatoes and a plate of asparagus, all of which went down wonderfully with a bottle of cold Muscadet. It was, they agreed, one of the best meals they'd ever eaten—and they lingered over it, finishing with cognac and espresso.

When the waiter had gone, McBride held his glass out toward Adrienne.

"To us," he said.

She managed a little smile, held out her glass to his and touched it. They sipped their cognacs. "I wish this was real," she mused, meaning their dinner together, and the night in the fancy hotel. "I wish we were just here together." She looked down, as if she were studying the tablecloth.

"Hey," he said. "It is. And we are."

"I keep wanting to say 'forget it, let's just go somewhere—

Indonesia. Madagascar. Disappear.' Maybe nothing would happen—with Jericho, I mean. And maybe they wouldn't even come after us. Maybe . . ." She looked up at the ceiling and held the tulip glass of brandy against her cheek. He could see the tears glinting in her eyes.

"Adrienne . . ."

"And what are the chances, anyway—that we'll pull this off? It's not like the plan is so great. I mean, it's not even a plan, really."

"Yeah, it is," McBride insisted, sounding defensive even to himself. "It's just . . ." He didn't want to say "simple." "Elegant," he decided.

She replied with a funny look, and took a sip of Rémy Martin.

In point of fact, McBride thought, the plan was neither simple nor elegant. It was just basic. They'd gone over it in the room—though only for a minute, because that's all it took to explore the scheme's every nuance. Adrienne was to wait in the hotel while McBride went into the clinic, posing as a workman with a box of curtain rods for the director's office. Asking to use a telephone, he'd call Opdahl and, speaking as Lew McBride, tell him he was in Switzerland and on his way to kill him. That would flush the security team from hiding, and focus their concern on the clinic's exterior—from which the threat would be thought to be on its way. In the confusion, McBride would make his way to Opdahl's office, and put the gun to his head. If he got what he wanted, he'd call the police, and then Adrienne. If he didn't—and if she didn't hear from him within an hour—Adrienne was to call the police, tell them what she knew, and ask for protection.

"It's really just a mugging," Adrienne remarked. "Not so much a plan as an information stickup."

McBride didn't want to argue with her. "Yeah, well, it's all I've got," he said.

She ran her finger around the rim of her glass. A clear bell-like tone emerged, so loud that she clapped her hand over the rim and looked around guiltily. "I know."

"So?"

They sat there for a long time. Finally, she said, "Let's just go upstairs."

Polar Bears.

Every March at Bowdoin College, a contingent of crazies drove out to Popham Beach, a motley caravan of Saabs and Jeeps and junkers winding through the winter landscape. Once at the beach, they'd build a bonfire, toss back a shot of Jaegermeister and hurl themselves into the freezing surf. It was an homage to the school's mascot, and also, as someone put it, a chance to "give the finger to winter." There was only one way to do it—and that was *fast*, without thinking about it too much.

And that was how McBride covered the short distance between the Belvedere and the Prudhomme Clinic. Fast. Sprinting through the swirling snow, up the driveway onto the walk—and suddenly he was there, just outside the double doors. Where a simple chrome plate announced:

PRUDHOMME

He brushed the snow from the field jacket he was wearing, and slapped the watchcap against his thigh, as the automatic doors swung open on a skylit reception area. The space was remarkable for its uncluttered expanse, its odd angles, and the sheer minimalist luxury of the appointments: red leather Barcelona chairs, scrubbed pine floors, a scatter of small, jewel-like Persian rugs. He stepped inside, carrying the long brown box marked *Vorhang-Stangen*. Looked around. Smiled.

To the right, just past the entrance, he spotted a small hallway appointed with restrooms and a bank of three telephones. These were of the latest, sleekest Swiss design, futuristic cylinders of stainless steel that enclosed the caller in a space reminiscent of a landing pod. He was happy to see them.

A dour blonde in a soft pink uniform sat behind a circular, brushed chrome reception desk. Seeing McBride in his blue jeans, and watchcap, carrying a box full of curtain rods, she took him for a worker or deliveryman—as he hoped she would. *"Bitte?"*

With a boyish smile, he went up to the reception desk and, leaning toward the blonde, showed her the box. "Für Herr Doktor Opdahl," he told her, speaking in German.

"You can leave those here," she said. "I'll see that he gets them."

"Thanks, but—do you mind if I use one of the phones?" He nodded toward the ones in the hallway. "I'm supposed to call in."

The blonde didn't reply, at first. A frown flitted across her face—and then she smiled. "As you like," she replied, dismissing him with a flick of her fingers.

McBride glanced at his watch as he strode toward the phones. 10:35. He'd been up since dawn, but had forced himself to wait until the clinic would be busy with deliveries, visitors, staff meetings, sessions. It was, he felt, the most innocent of hours, the most unexpected time for a takedown.

Apart from the short hall which led to the public telephones and restrooms, he saw that two other corridors gave off the reception area. One led to a bank of elevators. Though he couldn't see them, he knew the elevators were there because of the noise and activity they engendered: the chimes when they arrived, the whoosh of doors opening and closing, the rattle of carts transitioning to the hall. Signs pointed the way to the pharmacy, a hydrotherapy room, and a gymnasium.

He could tell nothing about the other corridor. Since this was a residential facility, and patients must be housed somewhere, it was a good guess that it led to patients' rooms.

That the clinic was bigger than it seemed, he'd already determined. There were no cars anywhere, which suggested a sizable underground parking area. And from the vents that he'd seen from his room in the Belvedere, he guessed that there was more to the underground than just parking.

Walking over to the phones, McBride fished a phone card from his coat pocket and slid it into the receptacle. Almost instantly, the liquid crystal display told him that he had 23.7 Swiss francs worth of calling time left. Consulting a slip of paper, he punched in the clinic's numbers, and listened as the phone began to ring—and ring, and ring.

Actually, it was more a chirp than a ring—but still annoying. Turning, he saw that the receptionist was busy with a phone call of her own, talking animatedly into the receiver. Finally, her demeanor changed. She punched a button on the phone and said: *"Bitte?"*

McBride looked away.

"Bitte?" she repeated.

"Doctor Opdahl, please . . ."

Down the hall, an older woman in a pink uniform emerged from a doorway, flanked by a pair of severely emaciated young women. Each was carefully groomed, fashionably dressed, and fully made-up—the effect of which was ghastly, as if they were on their way to a fashion show in a concentration camp.

The phone began to ring in Opdahl's office as the nurse and her charges disappeared around a corner. Then the clinic's boss was on the line. *"Ja?"*

Opdahl's voice sent a spike of adrenaline through McBride's heart. For a moment, he couldn't speak.

"Ja—ist wer es?"

He cleared his throat. "It's Lew McBride."

There was a long silence at the other end. Finally, Opdahl said, "Well, hello!"

As soon as he heard the man's voice, McBride sensed that something was wrong. Or maybe not. "I'm going to kill you," he said.

"Are you, *really*?!"

"You're fuckin' right I am," McBride told him. "And soon."

Opdahl chuckled. "Now, Lew—I don't think for a second that you mean that. You're not the type . . ."

This isn't working, McBride thought. *There's something in his voice—or not in his voice. Something missing.*

". . . so why don't we get together—"

"We're going to!" McBride promised.

"—and talk it over?"

"There isn't that much to talk about," McBride began. Then it hit him—what was missing from Opdahl's voice. There was no surprise in it.

"Of course there is," the surgeon continued. "There's lots to talk about—it's a very exciting time for the Institute, as I think you know." He chuckled for the second time. "Why don't you let Rutger show you the way?"

Rutger? McBride stood where he was, stock-still, uncertain what was happening, but feeling, somehow, that things were beginning to slip away. Then his eyes drifted toward the ceiling, and he noticed the video camera for the first time, with the winking red diode just above the lens, and the lens pointing straight at him. Turning slowly, he caught a glimpse of the receptionist staring at him from behind her desk, and moving faster now, lunged for the box of curtain rods—

Only to be slammed against the wall.

"I see you've met Rutger—*and* Heinz," Opdahl observed, getting up from his desk to greet McBride as the latter was escorted roughly into his office. "Have a seat."

One of the security men shoved McBride into a chair across from the surgeon's desk, while the second guard tossed the curtain-rod box onto the couch.

"Gesetzt ihm in eine Zwangsjacke," Opdahl ordered, then switched to English as one of the guards left the room. "It's for your own protection."

"Fuck you," McBride spat, and instantly regretted it as the remaining guard clapped him—hard—on the ears, igniting a wall of sparks behind his eyes. Opdahl laughed— "Owww!"—as McBride came out of his seat, only to find the business end of a 9mm pressed against the nape of his neck. He sat back down.

The first guard came back a moment later, carrying a straitjacket. Seeing it, McBride shrank into his chair, but with the

Sig Sauer leveled at him, there wasn't anything that he could do. The second guard yanked him to his feet, and pulled the jacket over his arms. McBride took a deep breath as the guard made him cross his arms, then snapped the buckles shut at the small of his back. This done, the guard pushed McBride into the chair, and looked inquiringly at his boss.

"Ich nehme es von hier," he said, dismissing the guards as if he were brushing crumbs from the table. When they'd gone, he came around to the other side of the desk, leaned back against it and crossed his arms. "I said it before, and I'll say it again: you're a very brave man, Jeffrey Duran."

"Jeffrey Duran's dead," McBride told him.

Opdahl smiled. "My point, exactly." Finding a packet of Rothmans Silk Cuts, he lighted one, inhaling deeply. Then blew the smoke toward his captive, and said, "You're going to hate me for saying this, but you know what? This is the first place I'd expect you to come." He paused. "The receptionist had your picture on her desk."

McBride didn't say anything, just sat there fidgeting in his seat, hating the man in front of him.

Opdahl shook his head in mock confusion. "What were you thinking of? Did you think you'd take me by surprise? For God's sake, man, I've got a profile on you that's a foot thick—literally." He paused. "So there's really very little you could do—short of breaking into song—that would surprise me." He laughed to himself, and tapped the ash from his cigarette onto the floor.

McBride looked on, guts churning, face impassive.

Opdahl turned his eyes toward the ceiling. "So now what do we do?" He lowered his eyes to McBride. "I'm taking suggestions."

"Good. I'd suggest you go fuck yourself," McBride told him.

Opdahl roared his approval with a big, hearty laugh. Then wagged his finger. "That's funny, but bravado isn't going to get you anywhere. Then, again, nothing will, so—why not?" He paused, and scrutinized McBride. Nodded toward the box on the sofa across the room. "What are you supposed to be? A workman?" When McBride didn't answer, the surgeon's lips puckered in an effigy of awe. "How imaginative!"

It wasn't a conversation, really. McBride knew that better than anyone. Opdahl was having fun, playing with him—and that was fine. The longer the older man talked, the sooner Adrienne would come into play—though, in reality, McBride wasn't counting on a call to the police being much help. What he *was* counting on was getting out of the straitjacket.

"Obviously, we can't just let you go," Opdahl told him, "though I suppose I'll seem ungrateful when I don't." For a moment, the older man turned serious. "You did a terrific job with de Groot. I'm sure it wasn't easy. He's not like the others."

"How so?" McBride asked.

Opdahl made a dismissive gesture. "The clinic here—well, it's a cachement pond. On any given day, we have ten or fifteen young men and women with serious eating disorders—and/or a crippling dependency on drugs. Thanks to the charitable work that we do, quite a few of them come to us from foster care or state agencies. As you might suppose, this lack of family connectedness is convenient for the Program—as is the propensity of these poor creatures for generating distorted self-images of themselves."

"And de Groot?" McBride asked.

"De Groot was different. We needed someone with Henrik's expertise, so we made . . ." Here, the surgeon waggled his forefingers in the air. ". . . an 'involuntary recruitment.' " He smiled. "So Henrik doesn't fit the profile as well as we'd like."

"Expertise?" McBride wondered. The guy ran a company that installed fire alarms and stuff.

"It actually requires rather a lot of medication to make him the charming lad you know," Opdahl added. "So we're grateful to you. We really are." The surgeon hesitated for a moment, then furrowed his brows and leaned forward, moving his head from side to side, making a show of studying McBride. "My God, man," he said, "you're sweating bullets!"

It was true. McBride *was* sweating bullets, though not so much from fear as from his efforts to conceal the muscular adjustments he was making in an effort to get free. There was a trick to it, of course. Houdini had gotten out of straitjackets routinely and, as a kid, McBride had wanted to emulate him. He'd even toyed with the idea of asking his parents for a straitjacket on his twelfth birthday but, in the end, opted for a skateboard instead. Still, there was a trick—and it was one that he knew. In principle, at least—which he'd be the first to admit was a long way from actually doing it. Then again, he was highly motivated.

"I'm not going to kill you, if that's what you're worried about," Opdahl promised, flicking another ash onto the floor. "Though we'll have to do something." He paused, frowned, and thought about it. Then he looked up with a big smile. "I know! We'll replicate 'H.M.' You remember H.M., don't you?"

He did. And the thought of it made him look away, sickened at what Opdahl was suggesting.

The surgeon was suddenly incredulous. "Are you *trembling*?" He peered closely at McBride for the second time in as many minutes. "You are! Look at you!" And he laughed, a sort of burst transmission giggle, à la Dennis Miller.

And, in fact, McBride *was* trembling. He was losing motor control from the effort it was taking to free himself from the canvas jacket that pinioned his arms to his chest. The trick, which he'd read about in a children's biography of the magician, was actually pretty simple. At least, in theory. As the straitjacket was being put on, the wearer was to make himself as big as possible (which McBride had done), expanding his chest, flexing his muscles, and keeping his elbows as far from his sides as his handlers would permit. Then, when the jacket was in place and the wearer relaxed, he'd have the wiggle room he needed to get out. (Or so he hoped.) Houdini had done it dangling from a rope, ten stories above the street. Of course, that was *Houdini*.

"Industrial accident," Opdahl reminded him. "Textbook

case! Old H.M. wound up with a pole through his head—like one of those arrow jokes, but real. And, as I think you know, he survived the pole, though he wasn't what you'd call *intact*. Remember? He'd lost the ability to form long-term memories. So, every day, his wife would introduce herself to him and, every day, it would be like meeting her all over again. Same with his parents, same with his friends." Another chuckle. "We could tell you the same joke every day, and every day you would laugh." He looked delighted. "And you wouldn't be depressed about it. Not at all! You'd be a lamb. Because every day would be—" his face lit up "—brand-new!"

McBride's right arm was almost free. "What's 'Jericho'?" he asked.

Opdahl looked impressed. "My, you *have* been doing your homework, haven't you?"

"What is it?"

The surgeon took a long drag on his cigarette, and blew a stream of smoke into the air. Then he cocked his head at McBride. "Are you trying to get out of that thing?" When McBride didn't reply, he made a little moue, and said, "Well, good luck to you." Shoving away from the desk, he went around to the window, and looked out at the snow. Musing over his shoulder, he muttered, "Jericho," then turned around to McBride. "You'll just forget it in the morning, anyway," he said, and began pacing, moving in a wide, counterclockwise circle around the room.

"You don't know—you have no idea—what any of this is all about," Opdahl told him. "The Institute, the clinic—they're a lot more than they seem." He paused to consider. "Think of this place as . . . the crossroads of *Realpolitik* and *Realmedizin*. It's where they come together."

McBride's elbow was caught on the edge of a sleeve. Just a little bit more and . . .

"As a surgeon, it's my responsibility to cut out diseased tissue. The Institute has the same responsibility, except that its patients are states instead of individuals."

"In other words, you kill people."

"We remove cancers."

"Like Nelson Mandela?" McBride asked, sagging with relief as his right arm came free inside the straitjacket.

Opdahl paused in his circuit, and looked at his prisoner. Finally, he said, "Not just Mandela. Mbeki, too. And Tutu—too." He smiled at his own pun. "They'll all be at Davos—hobnobbing. Me, too. I like to watch."

Jericho's scope was suddenly apparent: the operation represented a clean sweep of South Africa's black leadership, eliminating at a single stroke the country's founding father, serving president, and moral conscience. "You're out of your mind," McBride told him.

"That's funny," Opdahl replied, "coming from a man in a straitjacket."

Only for a little while longer, McBride thought, using his right hand to begin freeing his left arm. "Why would you even think of something like this?"

Opdahl shrugged. "A patient has a boil—we lance it. That's all we're doing here." Seeing McBride's frown, and misinterpreting it, Opdahl elaborated: "Think of it as a 'preemptive bloodletting.' The country needs to be bled. De Groot will set it in motion." He paused again, and added, "What happens in Davos, explodes in Capetown."

"And Calvin Crane?"

Opdahl couldn't hide his surprise. "You *are* dangerous," he told him, returning to the chair behind his desk. "Mr. Crane became an obstacle. He had certain . . . *liberal* objections to Jericho's targets, and ethical concerns about some related investments. So he got in the way . . . for a while."

"What 'investments'?"

Opdahl shrugged, and looked away. "The Institute costs a lot of money—the clinic, too. Neither of them are self-supporting."

"So?"

"So we bought platinum futures—quite a lot of them."

McBride frowned.

"Just between you and me, South Africa's about to enter a

period of profound instability," Opdahl explained. "I think we can count on the fact that platinum's going to go through the roof. The Institute will benefit from that in a substantial way. And with those new resources, its influence will expand—so will mine, for that matter."

McBride shook his head. "Have you always been like this?"

Opdahl nodded. "I was a wicked child."

McBride withdrew his left arm from the sleeve of the straitjacket, and heaved a sigh of relief. Both arms were free inside the jacket, now, though still concealed.

Reaching for the intercom on his desk, Opdahl punched in a couple of numbers, and waited for the call to be picked up. "Frank? Gunnar here. I wonder if you'd come to my office for a moment. There's someone I'd like you to see." Hanging up, he sat back in his swivel chair, and began a series of slow turns, his head thrown back and eyes turned toward the ceiling. "Doctor Morgan assisted on your earlier operation. He'll be doing the surgery. I'd do it myself, but . . . Davos." He paused. "Which reminds me: how did you find out about Jericho?"

McBride shook his head slowly. If he wanted to, he could come across the desk before Opdahl knew what hit him—break his neck. Better, though, to find out as much as he could. "How's de Groot going to do it?"

Opdahl smiled. "Me first. I asked you a question."

For a moment, it occurred to McBride to tell the truth about Crane's papers—but no. If something went wrong in the next five minutes, Mamie Winkelman would pay for it. So he lied. "It came out in a session with Henrik—bits and pieces."

Opdahl frowned. "I'm sorry to hear that," he said. "The client isn't supposed to be aware—"

"He was way under."

"I'll bet . . ." A soft knock came at the door. "Come in."

McBride turned in his seat to see a powerfully built, handsome young man enter the room, wearing a set of blue hospital scrubs.

"Frank," Opdahl said, "you remember Jeff Duran, don't you?"

"Of course," Morgan replied.

"No need to shake hands," Opdahl joked. "I was just telling Jeff that you'll be operating on him this evening."

"Oh?"

"Yeah. You've been itching to replicate H.M.'s condition—and now's your chance. Jeff's become a disposal case, haven't you, Jeff?"

Morgan winced in mock sympathy.

"So? What do you think?" Opdahl asked, as if he'd just given the young surgeon a new puppy. "You like the idea?"

" 'Like' it!?" Morgan exclaimed. " 'Like it'!?" Coming to McBride's side, he touched a spot just below his hairline. "I'll go in here," he began.

McBride came out of the chair like a boulder from a volcano, driving his head into the surgeon's chin, then tearing off the straitjacket to lunge at the shocked Gunnar Opdahl. Who slapped a button on the edge of his desk, triggering a silent alarm, even as he shoved backward in his swivel chair, retreating toward the window.

McBride was on him in a second, scrambling across the desk to seize him by the throat. Lifting the older man from the chair, he drove the surgeon's face into the wall, yanked him back, and drove his head into and through the window, hoping it would cut his throat. And it might have, if Morgan hadn't taken out McBride's legs from behind, sweeping them with a karate kick that sent the younger man sprawling.

Opdahl staggered in a little circle, trying to breathe and shout at the same time, choking as McBride crabbed backward across the floor, driven by Morgan's kicks.

He could hear people running down the hall, now, shouting in English and German, even as Morgan tried to kick a field goal with his head. Catching the surgeon by the heel, McBride twisted, hard, and torqued him to the floor with a crash of glass from a toppling lamp. Lurching to his knees, McBride drove his fist into the back of the surgeon's skull, sending him sprawling, then dove for the box on the sofa. Tearing at the cardboard to get at the trigger, he succeeded at the very moment the door burst open and Rutger and Heinz came charging in, eyes wild.

"Ergreifen Sie ihn!" Opdahl screamed, fumbling in the desk for the Sig Sauer that he knew was there.

The guards blitzed, rushing the American even as he backpedaled with the curtain rod box in his hands—the box exploding as Gunther moved to brush it aside, sending a spray of blood and bits at the opposite wall. The fat guard, Heinz, stopping on a pfennig, eyes ballooning, hands in the air, as McBride swung the shotgun in an arc and Opdahl began blasting with the Sig Sauer, hitting everything in the room but his target. And McBride working the slide with real composure now, his left hand sliding back and forth on the barrel as if it were the fingerboard of a Stratocaster, pumping and firing, pumping and firing, taking Morgan out at the knees even as the surgeon bolted for the door—then turning on Opdahl whose mouth made a little O of horror in the split second that he had to think about things, just before McBride plastered his forehead on the acoustical tiles overhead.

Relative silence.

Heinz quaking, hands in the air, eyes shut. Morgan weeping in a pool of blood beside the door, his knees blown out, going into shock. Gunsmoke, and the smell of gunsmoke. McBride exhaling for the first time in a long time, the air sweeping out of his lungs in a single burst. Then a soft plop as a chunk of Opdahl's corpus callosum fell to the desk from the ceiling, landing like a load of birdshit on the financial pages of the *Neue Zürcher Zeitung*.

McBride turned to the guard. "Stay." Then he went to Opdahl's desk and, picking up the phone, told the receptionist to connect him to the Belvedere Hotel. Which she did. A moment later, he had Adrienne on the line.

"What's happening?" she demanded. "I heard—"

"Get the car out front," he told her.

"But—"

"Do it *now*." Then he hung up the phone, and turned to the guard. "Let's go," he told him, taking the man by the back of his collar, and placing the barrel against the side of his head.

Out to the corridor, where half a dozen birdlike patients fell back, gaping, as McBride and the security guard emerged from Opdahl's office. Moving with slow deliberation, McBride escorted the guard past astounded nurses, aides, and doctors, to the front doors. Which opened with a *whoosh* on what was now a dank, gray afternoon—with no Adrienne in sight.

Standing on the front steps of the clinic with the shotgun jammed against the guard's jaw, McBride considered his options—which were few. Either she'd come, or she wouldn't. And if she didn't, it was over. *He* was over. Because the police were on their way, or soon would be, and—

Suddenly, she was there, the BMW pulling into the courtyard, windshield wipers slapping back and forth, headlights blazing, the door flying open on the passenger's side. And Adrienne leaning toward him across the seat, eyes like saucers.

"Hop in," she told him.

41

Davos was a zoo.

Not the cozy alpine village that Adrienne had imagined, but a long and noisy strip of glitzy discotheques and bars, restaurants and ski shops. Concrete condo blocks rose up against the ring of peaks around the town, while a sprawl of cute chalets lit up the hillsides. Seeing it for the first time made her think that someone—it could only have been Satan—had decided to re-create Route 1 in Paradise. And it went on and on, stretching down the valley to the sister towns of Davos Dorp and Davos Platz.

Despite the commercialism, there was nowhere for them to stay. Besides the usual tourists, and those in town to ski, there were hundreds of support people for the World Economic Summit, an equal number of journalists, and crowds of demonstrators protesting everything from "Frankenfood" to cloning. They tried half a dozen hotels, and everything was booked—even the luxe Hotel Fribourg, which served as the Summit's headquarters.

High on a hill above the town, the Fribourg looked like a gigantic wedding cake, with each of its two hundred rooms boasting a balcony with white columns. Even before they got there, they could see that access was severely restricted. All the drives and walkways were cordoned off, and there were Swiss soldiers at checkpoints along the road. A crowd of protesters craned at the barricades lining the main drive, as an opening was made for a limousine. Polite shouts (it was a Swiss demonstration, after all) followed the limo in its crawl up the hill, the Mercedes's smoked windows hiding its occupants. Midway between the protesters and the hotel was a clutch of trucks and vans, servicing CNN, the BBC, and a dozen others. Cables snaked across the snow, feeding batteries of lights and microphones, cameras, and satellite dishes. Here and there a lone figure stood, bathed in a cone of white light, narrating the scene to millions of invisible observers.

Where de Groot was, was anyone's guess. If he'd taken a temporary apartment in the area—as he had in D.C.—he could be almost anywhere. In Davos or Klosters, or even in one of the smaller towns in the area: Wiesen or Langeise.

All Adrienne and McBride could do was look, going door to door from one hotel to another, poking their heads in the bars and restaurants, hoping to spy a tall and powerfully built Dutchman with a pelt of thick blond hair. It seemed hopeless—until McBride had a minor inspiration.

"Music . . . ," he muttered.

"What?" Adrienne rubbed her eyes. It was almost 2 A.M.

"De Groot's into trance music. He wanted me to go to a club with him. I had to tell him I didn't get out that much."

She looked puzzled. "What's trance music?"

"Big pants—DJs and raves. 'Special K' and light sticks. Very big in Europe."

"It is?"

He smiled. "I guess baby lawyers don't have time to dance."

"Oh? And how would you know anything about it?"

He looked embarrassed. "MTV."

Somehow, the loud monotonous music and thrashing bodies of the discotheques only served to emphasize Adrienne's fatigue. They wandered in and out of Club Soda, Trax, Rumplestiltskin, and the Kit Kat Klub. McBride's German came in handy as the inquiry was put to bouncers, bartenders, DJs, and the occasional fatigued dancer stumbling to the sidelines. At successive clubs, he honed his rap about the person they were searching for and by the time they hit the Kit Kat, he was fast and efficient: they were looking for a Dutchman, a big guy from Rotterdam, yellow hair cut short, good-looking, chain-smoker—ever seen him?

No, no and maybe, with half of the people they asked too stoned to remember. But the DJ at Rumplestiltskin helped them out by writing down a list of discotheques where "trance" was played, or failing that, a close relative—"house music." But no one at any of the places they visited knew Henrik de Groot by name or description.

"We could sleep in the train station," Adrienne suggested. "Or in the car. I'm whacked."

McBride nodded. "Okay, but just a couple more."

By the time he'd drawn a line through three more clubs on the DJ's list, the night was shading toward dawn and the discos were closing, disgorging rowdy clusters onto the streets, their laughter piercing the cold morning air. He was about ready to pack it in—and so was Adrienne who, game and un-complaining, was nevertheless dazed by fatigue, so tired that occasionally she failed to pick up a foot and stumbled.

"One more," McBride said, "and then we'll get some coffee."

And that's when he saw it:

TRANCE KLUB

and beneath those words, a circular sign displaying a dizzying pattern of silver and black concentric circles in the center of which a neon eye winked on and off. Chase lights zoomed around the circles like Pac-Men run amok. McBride stared so long and hard that when the eye blinked off, its af-terimage floated on the inside of his eyelid.

"Hey," he said, heading toward the sign at a trot, pulling Adrienne along with him.

"What?" Adrienne asked.

"He used to come here."

"How do you know?"

"He had a matchbook. On top of his cigarettes. Menthol cigarettes. I remember seeing it—when I was Duran."

She gave him a funny look.

Inside, the waitresses and bartenders were sitting at the bar, cashing out over cigarettes and coffee. *"Geschloten,"* one man said, a silver barbell bobbing on the end of his tongue. He gestured toward the dingy expanse behind him. A dark-skinned older man with a ponytail ran a huge vacuum cleaner over a grubby black floor stenciled with disinte-grating silver stars.

"I'm looking for someone," McBride said. A spiky-haired waitress with silver lipstick opened her mouth, and McBride cut her off. "No jokes. I'm looking for a Dutchman. Big guy. Blond hair. His name's Henrik."

"Sure," the waitress said. "I know Henrik. He's here a lot—unless he's traveling."

"Was he here tonight?"

"Yeah. He left an hour ago." She frowned. "Is he a friend of yours?".

"I'm his therapist," McBride told her.

She nodded, as if this made perfect sense. "Well, you got that right—Henrik is one sick fuck."

"You know where he's staying?" Adrienne asked.

The waitress gave them an evaluating look. "Maybe . . . is he in trouble?"

McBride made a sort of hapless gesture. "I wouldn't be here at seven in the morning if—"

"He's in the Alpenrösli flats—on the way to Klosters."

The man with the barbell in his tongue looked surprised. "And how do you know that?"

"Fuck off," she replied.

The Alpenrösli condominiums were in a half-timbered building on a hillside just outside of town. The structure housed four self-catering flats that were rented out by the week or the month, and a caretaker's flat below.

"We are complete," said the gray-haired woman who lived on the lower floor.

"We're looking for Mr. de Groot," McBride told her.

The woman shrugged. "Of course. Number 4—but he doesn't come home yet. All night, he's dancing, and then I think he goes to work."

"And where is that?"

The woman shook her head. "I don't ask."

They sat in the car in the parking lot outside the Alpenrösli and waited, turning the heater on and cranking it up whenever they couldn't stand the cold any longer or the windows steamed up. They took turns napping (there was nothing else they could do), and Adrienne went out for sandwiches at noon, walking halfway into town. By two P.M., the sky had darkened to the color of a deep bruise, and there was still no sign of de Groot. An hour later, the mountains were rumbling with thunder, and a soft snow had begun to fall.

"Maybe it's time for Plan B," McBride suggested.

"And what is that?" Adrienne asked.

McBride shook his head. "I dunno—I was hoping you did." In fact, Plan B was the police. It was their only option. But after what had happened at the clinic, no one was going to listen to them. By now, they were almost certainly the objects of a massive manhunt. If taken into custody, there'd be a million questions about the slaughter at the clinic, before anybody was going to listen to their theory about Jericho. And by the time they did listen, it would be too late.

Lights began to flicker on across the valley at 4:15 in the afternoon. Cramped and cold, McBride felt as if his legs were about to fall off at the knees, even as a carbon monoxide headache gathered at the back of his head. And then, quite suddenly, he was there—*de Groot was there,* head down, trudging up the street, wearing jeans, boots and a shearling jacket. In each hand, a plastic supermarket bag. "There he is," McBride said, suddenly sitting up behind the wheel.

They watched the Dutchman through a screen of falling snow, as he pushed open the gate to the Alpenrösli and tramped up the exterior stairs. Then he was out of sight, presumably inside Apartment 4—which was on the top floor in the back.

"Stay here," McBride ordered, pushing the button that unlocked the trunk, and opening the driver's door.

"Are you out of your mind?" Adrienne demanded. "I'm not going to stay here!"

He leaned toward her, and brushed her lips with his own. "Watch my back."

Not waiting for an answer, he got out and grabbed the shotgun from the trunk. Then he followed de Groot's footprints through the snow to the exterior stairs, and climbed to the top. There, he paused at the door to Number 4, took a deep breath, and rapped softly on the door. Then he stood back and waited with the shotgun in his hands, the barrel pointing at the floor. But nothing happened. He rapped again. Still no response. Frustrated, he pounded harder on the door, which swung open of its own accord.

Still carrying the shotgun, he stepped inside the doorway, casting his eyes left and right, listening hard. To nothing. If de Groot was in the flat, he must be standing stock-still, McBride thought, and holding his breath. And if he wasn't in the flat . . .

Entering the living room, McBride noticed a table with half a dozen lightbulbs scattered across it. Little lightbulbs, and all of them broken. Nearby, an electric drill and a glue gun. *What the fuck?*

A few steps took him into a truncated hallway—with one door on the left, and another on the right. Opening the door to the left, he found himself looking into de Groot's bedroom. Which was not so much a place to sleep as it was a sort of quacked-out racist diorama, with crude collages plastered to the wall. Pornographic pictures of black men and young blond women. Desmond Tutu's head on a chimpanzee's body. Some UFO photos, and a poster of Nelson Mandela with a circle drawn around his head in Magic Marker, the whole bisected by a diagonal red bar. Nearby, a third collage, consisting of Thabo Mbeki's head amid a bonfire of worms, with the nightcrawlers rising around the South African president's cheeks and ears like flames. On the floor beside the bed, a pile of strange and unpleasant zines: *The Odinist, Contre le Boue, Der Broederbond Report.* And on the far wall, facing the collages, simpy and idolatrous portraits of Adolf Hitler and Swiss ufologist Billy Meier.

It's a stageset, McBride thought. Prima facie evidence that the occupant's a "lone nut." But there was nothing imaginative about it. Like de Groot's screen memory, the scene in front of him was crude and trite, reminiscent of a cheap television show—a second-rate producer's idea of a racist's inner sanctum. If he looked around a bit, McBride was sure he'd find a diary filled with Freudian slips and parapolitical mumbo-jumbo. Maybe a picture or two, with de Groot holding a gun and a copy of *The Turner Diaries*.

But where was the actor himself? Where was the star? Heart thudding, McBride returned to the hallway and, holding the shotgun level at his waist, pushed open the door to what turned out to be the bathroom.

"Henrik?"

With the shotgun's barrel, he drew the shower curtain aside. But there was nothing. And no one.

Confused, he made his way back to the living room—and there he was, standing behind Adrienne, holding a gun to her head.

The Dutchman smiled. "Dr. Duran! I'm so glad to see you—"

"Look, Henrik, there's no need to—"

"Welcome to Davos! Really, it's a great place! Now, if you'll just put your gun down . . . I don't want to hurt you or your pretty friend."

McBride set the shotgun on the floor, never taking his eyes from de Groot. "Just let her go. She isn't—"

"Shhhhhh," de Groot said, finger to his lips. "We're with the Worm." He angled his head in the direction of the sofa. "Over there," he ordered, and gave Adrienne a gentle push. McBride joined her and, together, they sat down. The Dutchman stooped to the floor, picked up the shotgun, and removed the magazine. Tossing it into a corner of the room, he ejected the rounds that remained in the weapon's chamber, and threw it onto a nearby chair.

Going into the kitchen, he returned a moment later with a roll of duct tape. Tossing it to McBride, he ordered him to bind Adrienne's hands and feet, and tape her mouth. Seeing his reluctance, de Groot approached the couch and, without warning, hit McBride flush in the mouth with the butt of his revolver.

Stepping back, he watched with satisfaction as his erstwhile therapist did as he'd been told, tearing off a strip of tape to place across the terrified young woman's mouth.

"Now it's your turn," de Groot said, removing his shearling coat and hanging it on the back of a chair. Around his neck was a laminated ID, hanging from a beaded chain.

"Listen, Henrik—"

The Dutchman frowned. *"Not to talk,"* he ordered.

At that moment, the house shook with a sudden gust of wind, the lights flickered, and the gate below banged. Distracted, de Groot went to the window and looked out. "Storm," he said.

"Henrik, it's really important that you listen to me."

"I can't listen to you both."

" 'Both'?"

"The Worm," Henrik explained.

"I know what you're going to do, Henrik. And it's a very bad idea."

"Oh? And just what is it that I'm going to do?"

"You're going to shoot Mandela and the others."

De Groot shook his head. "Put six loops around your feet—tight." He paused. "I'm not going to shoot anyone."

"You're not?" McBride was confused.

"No. Now bind your *feet*, Dr. Duran. Around your ankles. Six loops."

McBride bent to his task, unspooling the tape and winding it slowly around his ankles.

"There won't be any firearms," de Groot promised. "Just fire." A snort of laughter jerked from his mouth.

McBride finished with the tape, and looked up. "What are you talking about?"

The Dutchman ignored the question. "Now, put your hands behind your back," he ordered. When McBride complied, de Groot grabbed the duct tape and began to bind his wrists. McBride's eyes swept the room, looking for a way out, something he could use. But there was only Adrienne—who seemed as if she were about to faint—and the table with the lightbulbs, drill and glue gun.

"What are the lightbulbs for?"

De Groot finished the taping, and came around to the front

of the couch. Glanced at his watch. Shrugged, and sat down in a leather easy chair. "The Worm is clever. He knows it's impossible to get at them with a gun. Even me, having a pass, working there. There's no way."

"Where? Where are you talking about?"

"The Fribourg. I've been upgrading the fire suppression system. Replacing the halon—because it's killing the ozone, you know? And with all the Greens in town, the hotel wants to make a gesture. It wants to be *compliant*, okay?"

McBride didn't know what to say. Didn't get it. "So what? What's that got to do with all the lightbulbs?"

"It's a retrofit. I've done lots. It's what I do."

"What is?"

"Getting rid of the halon. In the sprinkler system. Overhead, you know?" The Dutchman raised his hand above his head, and waggled his fingers. "You replace it with a mix of inert gases, and it doesn't cause any problems for the ozone."

"That's great, Henrik, but—"

"Only this time, the gas isn't inert. It's just gas."

"What?"

"It's petrol," de Groot told him. "I replaced the halon with petrol, so when the fire starts—"

"What fire? When?"

De Groot checked his watch. "In half an hour, unless they're running late. Don't worry, you'll be able to see it from here. The whole place will go up like a rocket."

"What place?"

"I've been telling you! The Fribourg. There's a gala for the South African delegation. Big banquet, lots of speeches from the *schwartzes*."

McBride shook his head. He still didn't get it. "What about the lightbulbs?" he asked. "What the fuck are the lightbulbs for?"

The Dutchman giggled, and McBride realized that he was on some kind of drug. "I keep forgetting . . . You see the bulbs over there—the little ones. They're for the podium. Or one of them is. When the speaker goes to the podium, he'll turn on the light behind the stand—so he can see his notes. Because it's dark in the ballroom. Very romantic."

"So?" McBride asked.

"It took me almost a dozen bulbs to get it right."

"Get *what* right?"

"Drilling a hole through the glass," de Groot explained. "Without breaking it."

"And why did you want to do that?"

"It's tricky. The glass is so thin—you need a special drill bit, or it shatters. Even then, the filament is fragile, so it kept breaking." The Dutchman sighed. "But I got it right—eventually."

"I still don't understand," McBride said. "What's the point of the hole?"

"For the starter fire," de Groot told him. "I fill the lightbulb with phosphorus and kerosene, so when it's turned on, the circuit's completed, and the mixture explodes. But it's just a small fire. Probably the speaker's shirt goes up, and maybe his hair—especially if he's using some kind of mousse."

"Then what?" McBride asked.

"Then? Well, there's a fire extinguisher on either side of the dais. One of the security guards will use it to put out the fire. Only . . ."

"What?"

"They've been altered, too."

"With what?" McBride asked.

"Butane."

McBride felt faint. "So when they try to put the fire out . . ."

"They make a bigger fire. Then the sprinklers come on, and the hotel—well, you'll see it from here."

"Henrik—"

The Dutchman tore a length of tape from the roll, and leaned toward McBride so he could place it over his mouth. McBride fell back, and out of the way.

"Henrik, listen to me. I want to tell you something about the Worm."

"No. There is already too much talk." Moving to the couch, he sat down beside McBride, the strip of tape in his hands. Suddenly, the lights flickered, then brightened so intensely McBride thought they'd blow. *A power surge,* he told himself, until the flash of light was followed by a boom of thunder, a crack of noise so loud that even de Groot jumped at the sound.

Then there was another flash of lightning, and another. McBride could feel the electricity in the air, the fine hairs at the back of his neck lifting away from his skin. The air shuddered with light. McBride couldn't remember experiencing a thunderstorm in the midst of a snowfall. The windows were opaque with snow, and the effect was extraordinary, an oscillation of light that was almost like a strobe.

De Groot sat there with the tape in his hand, poised to strap it over McBride's mouth, but blinking now, like a deer in the headlights.

It's the flicker, McBride realized. *He's conditioned to it, entrained by it.* Instinctively, McBride began to speak in the low, mellifluous tone that he used in his office when putting a client under. "Listen to me, Henrik. I want you to pretend that you're on an elevator . . . and it's taking you to your safe place. Deep in the earth." Another boom shook the walls, and McBride could see the lightning in de Groot's eyes. "The doors open. You step inside. The doors close. And now we're going down, deeper and deeper, to the safe place." The room flickered as lightning flashed, seriatim, beyond the window. "There's no Worm here, Henrik. Just a feeling of perfect peace."

De Groot's eyes were half-open, and seemingly unfocused.

"Now, we're sitting together on a rock, far from anywhere we've ever been," McBride confided, working hard to keep the strain out of his voice. "In a little harbor that no one else can see. Just you and me, the waves, and the birds. And a light wind that smells of the sea. Can you smell the sea, Henrik?"

"Yes."

"We're in a wonderful place, Henrik, but . . . my hands are tied. Do you think you can cut me free?"

The Dutchman didn't answer. And for a long while, he didn't move, but sat there in the flickering light, silent and blinking. Though his face was impassive, McBride knew that a battle was raging deep inside the Dutchman, in a part of the brain so primitive that words had no meaning.

Then the paralysis gave way, and de Groot got to his feet. Going into the kitchen, he returned with a boning knife in his hand. Looming above McBride, with a look of desolation and regret, he mumbled something unintelligible, leaned over, and cut the tape from his therapist's wrists.

Adrienne squirmed, but McBride held his hand out toward her until de Groot sat back down. He suggested to de Groot that he was exhausted and, soon, the Dutchman began to yawn. He probably was tired, McBride thought. He'd been up all night. He suggested that de Groot close his eyes and try to sleep. When he awoke, he was to contact the police and tell them about the Worm. Then he'd feel wonderful. Soon, de Groot was snoring quietly on the couch, his head thrown back, mouth open.

McBride freed Adrienne, then carefully lifted de Groot's ID from around the Dutchman's neck. Put it over his own.

"It won't work," she said. "You don't look like him."

"It's all I can do!"

"But—"

"Call the hotel," he told her. "See if you can get through. Tell them it's an emergency. Tell them the fire extinguishers are booby-trapped." He was at the door. "And get me a lawyer!"

"But—"

Then he was out the door and pounding down the stairs to the car.

It was three miles from de Groot's flat to Davos Dorp and it took him nearly fifteen minutes to cover the distance, crawling through the traffic, windshield wipers fighting the snow.

Even so, he couldn't get anywhere near the Fribourg—the access roads were in gridlock—so he abandoned the car by the side of the road and broke into a run.

De Groot's ID bounced on his chest as he charged up the hill through the slush and the snow. Arriving at a security barricade, he was stopped by a frozen-looking soldier. Waggling the ID, he cursed the cold, complaining loudly in German about having to miss the Wolfsburg Kaiserslautern match—just because someone thought there might be a problem with the fire extinguishers. "It can't be anything," he complained. "I just checked them this afternoon." The soldier peered through the swirling snow at the ID. "De Groot," he said. "I'll have to call."

A sort of makeshift shelter had been thrown up—a construction of canvas and transparent plastic—and the soldier retreated into this and spoke into his telephone. He tossed McBride an exhausted look, raising his eyebrows as he waited for a reply. It was difficult to wait. McBride kept imagining the round tables of banquet goers, the waiters clearing the plates, the speaker at the head table, checking his watch, sneaking a peek at his notes as he prepared to walk to the podium. The dinner had started at seven. How many courses were there? How long would it take? *Relax,* he told himself, but a glance at his watch sent his heart into his throat: 7:48.

Then the soldier poked his head out, and waved him through. McBride took off like a jackrabbit, leaving the soldier calling out with a laugh: *"Wo is das feuer?"* Where's the fire, indeed.

A figure dressed in lederhosen and an alpine cap was fighting a losing battle against the snow accumulating on the red carpet under the porte cochere at the entrance to the Fribourg. Also in sight were a man who looked like an admiral (the doorman as it turned out) and two soldiers. McBride launched himself in their direction, trying to remember the words for 'Fire security.' *Feuer*-something.

Then he was there. The doorman reached for the door's brass handle, suddenly frowned, and let his hand drop. One of the security men stepped forward, and took McBride by the arm.

"Feuersicherheit!" McBride yelled, grabbing de Groot's badge and jerking it toward the man, then wrenching free of his grip to plunge through the doorway.

"Stoppen Sie!"

He was running through the Fribourg's lobby, surrounded by crystal chandeliers, old wood and plush carpet, looking for a sign for the Ballroom. *What's the German for 'ballroom'?* People were screaming *Halt!*—which was German for 'Halt!'—but what was the German for 'ballroom'? Then he saw the sign:

BALLROOM

Three sets of swinging double doors, flanked by testosterone-types in dark suits, with little wires running from their ears. Nearby, a claque of smokers clustered around a standing ash-tray, and two ladies in African garb, with elaborate headdresses, made their way toward the restrooms. On a pedestal, a silver-framed sign:

WORLD ECONOMIC SUMMIT
SOUTH AFRICA RECEPTION

Seeing McBride, one of the security guards raised an arm to block the way. But McBride's impetus carried him past the guards and through the doors before anyone could actually stop him.

But he was too late.

The room—with its candlelit tables, and spiky flower arrangements, its white linen and gleaming crystal—was erupting in panic. Or if not panic, horror. Men in tuxedos and women in gowns, a handful of men and women in vibrant tribal costume, were getting to their feet and looking wildly around. The normal hubbub of three hundred diners—the clatter of dishware, the murmur of conversation, the burble of laughter—had given way to a primitive roar. A thin scream arced toward the spangled ceiling and it was as if the crowd was a single beast, with its eyes on the dais, where an elderly black man stood behind a blazing podium, slapping at the flames on his lapels.

The air was filled with a strange turbulence, a cannonade of gasps and shouts, as McBride sprinted down the aisle. Through the mass of people, he'd seen a waiter trotting toward the dais with a fire extinguisher in his hands.

"Don't!" McBride cried out, shaking off a security guard who was tearing at his shoulders—even as the waiter raised the fire extinguisher toward the burning man. Hearing McBride's shout, the waiter turned as the American bounded onto an empty chair, then onto the table, and launched himself at the dais, taking the waiter down with a flying tackle.

The fire extinguisher bounced free as McBride clambered to his feet, shouting, "The fire extinguisher's a bomb! Use your coats!" Tearing his jacket off, he began to slap at the flames, quieting the fire at the podium while another man rescued the speaker. Then someone grabbed him from behind, and jerked, and something crashed against his ear, driving him down to the floor.

Where he saw patent leather shoes on the blue carpeting— and felt a foot in the middle of his back. The face of one of the security guards appeared in front of him, so close McBride could see the pores in his nose, the stubble on his upper lip.

"Get everyone out," McBride shouted, suddenly so light-headed it seemed as if he were to float away. "The ball-room's a bomb," he muttered. "The ballroom's a bomb."

EPILOGUE

The only person to visit McBride during the week he spent in the Davos jail was a gentleman from the American embassy in Bern, and he was very straightforward.

There would be no publicity about the incident at the Hotel Fribourg. Henrik de Groot would be treated for his condition at a private sanitorium in an undisclosed country. Whether the Dutchman was ever to be released would depend upon how much—or how little—he chose to remember.

Meanwhile, arrangements had been made for McBride to pay a small fine for disturbing the peace at the banquet. He and his "girlfriend" would then be driven to the Zurich airport, where they would be placed on the first American carrier home. As far as the events in Spiez were concerned, cantonal authorities agreed that there was nothing to be gained by a public trial—which could only embarrass both countries.

"That's *it*?" McBride asked.

His visitor shrugged. "I'm just a messenger," he told him. "This isn't my brief. I don't know the details. But I can tell you this: based on the cables I saw—and the people who signed off on them—there's only two ways this thing can end."

"And what are those?"

"Well, my personal favorite is 'happily ever after'—that's the one we're shooting for."

"Great," McBride replied. "And what's the other?"

"The other? Well, the other is . . . *un*happily ever after.

That's the one where you decide to tell everyone your story. That's the one where you wind up in a Thorazine coma on the high-risk ward at St. Elizabeth's." He paused. "Don't go there."

He didn't.

When they finally got back to D.C., Adrienne's to-do list was three pages long, replete with categories and subcategories. The Odds and Ends section alone—a catchall for relatively trivial matters—had twenty-three items requiring her prompt, if not immediate, attention. These ranged from sorting out liability for the damage to the rented Dodge (finally returned after forty-two days, one paint-blistering fire and a rear-end crash) to reclaiming personal items left in her cubicle at Slough. That would be awkward, but after what she'd been through, she didn't mind, really. On the contrary, she was looking forward to hanging out her own shingle and practicing law, her way.

But first, she'd have to clean out Nikki's apartment, go through her belongings. She'd promised the Watermill that she'd have everything out by the end of the month—

And then, beyond this minor stuff, there was *Nikki* herself. Nikki's ashes still reposed in the "classic urn" and Adrienne felt it strongly—the need for some kind of ritual to commemorate her sister's departure from this earth.

McBride had his own list and most of it had to do with picking up the severed strands of an interrupted life. There were friends and colleagues—in San Francisco and elsewhere—he needed to get in touch with. He had a career to resume as a research psychologist. And there were dormant bank accounts and a small brokerage account with Merrill Lynch to reclaim. Maybe because he'd lived so close to Silicon Valley, his modest investments had been targeted toward the Internet. He remembered what he'd bought and at what prices; a preliminary look produced the happy news that during his walkabout as Jeff Duran, the value of his shares of Cisco Systems, Intel, and EMC had skyrocketed. He wasn't rich, but his fifteen grand had multiplied many times.

* * *

Lew couldn't take the idea of living in the apartment where he'd been "that robot." So until they figured out what they were going to do and where, they lived in the Bomb Shelter, enduring the disapproval of Mrs. Spears until Lew won her over by cleaning out the gutters, pruning the overgrown pyracantha and repairing her dishwasher.

"I didn't know you were so handy," Adrienne remarked.

"We were hard up," he explained, "when I was a kid. We couldn't afford to hire people to do things."

"Well, ditto. But I never learned how to fix anything."

"In Maine we pride ourselves on that Yankee can-do attitude."

"Can do, huh?" He was sitting on the edge of the bed, unlacing his shoes. She pushed him over onto his back and sprawled on top of him. She lifted herself up and looked down at him. She ran her thumb along his lower lip. "Does that extend to all areas of endeavor?"

"Absolutely."

She kissed him.

"We're famous for it," he said, coming up for air. "We also have Yankee ingenuity."

"Do you always talk so much?"

It finally came to her about two weeks after their return from Switzerland—how to send Nikki off in a style appropriate to her sister's lively and glamorous spirit.

She explained the idea to Lew and he helped her find the perfect vessel on the Web, a Challenger model yacht owned by a gentleman named Taz Brown. They communicated first by e-mail, then by telephone. "I hate to give her up," Brown said, "but my wife says I've got to trim the fleet and this one's named after the first wife."

Once a tentative deal had been struck, they coaxed Adrienne's Subaru back to life and, following Brown's intricate directions, drove the twenty-five miles to his nouveau brick mansion on the Potomac. The river was thawing, Adrienne saw, as they crossed it on Memorial Bridge; only a few patches of white, snow-crusted ice remained.

Brown was a dapper fifty-year-old wearing a blue blazer, khakis with a knife crease and tassel loafers. Once they'd introduced each other and Brown had cast a worried look at the scabby Subaru, he led them to the garage to show them the *Patricia*. The craft—and its siblings—shared space with a pair of Bimmers.

"It's big," McBride said. In fact, the mast was taller than he was.

"Fifty-seven inches in length, twelve inch beam, mast eighty-five inches from the deck. Comes in two pieces, with a carrying case that ought to fit right on top of your car. Good you've got a roof rack."

"It's beautiful," Adrienne said.

Brown grunted his concurrence. "Carbon fiber, composite hull—just like the America's Cup. And it comes with a suit of high-wind sails if you have a taste for ocean racing."

Adrienne asked him to demonstrate how to break the boat down and reassemble it, how to attach the keel, and how to operate the electronic controls.

"You're getting quite a bargain," he told her, as she wrote out a check for $1,250. "A new one would cost you five grand."

"I know it's a lot," Adrienne volunteered as they rattled back toward D.C., "but even the most 'economical' coffin would have cost five times as much. And, trust me, Nikki would like this much, much more."

The Mount Vernon Parkway is a beautiful twelve-mile stretch of road that follows the shoreline of the Potomac River south of Old Town Alexandria to the bend in the river chosen by George Washington as the site for Mount Vernon. The whole length of the parkway is paralleled by a heavily used bike and footpath and interspersed with parks, marinas, and roadside picnic areas. In nice weather, the riverfront is a lively place, with windsurfers and inexpert groups in canoes sharing the water with pleasure craft. On dry land, picnickers and fishermen share the terrain with joggers and cyclists, and families out for a stroll.

But it wasn't nice weather, and it wasn't daytime, so they had the shoreline entirely to themselves. The moon, fuzzy and indistinct behind the cloud cover, provided some light, but they had also brought powerful flashlights. It only took a few minutes to remove the *Patricia* from its carrying case and rig it, snapping on the mast, the keel and the rudder. Once it was floating in a protected little cove, Adrienne—fingers freezing—slipped the votive candles into the glass cups she'd affixed to the *Patricia*'s hull, one fore, one aft, for balance. After that, she settled the dish with Nikki's ashes in the rectangular depression amidship. Last of all, the flowers. She arranged them—rosebuds and jonquils, lilacs, and Queen Anne's lace—all around the hull.

And then it was time to light the candles and send Nikki on her way. Lew worked the radio controls and the boat moved sharply out of the cove. A breeze caught its sails and it began to heel over until he corrected the bearing to "a broad reach." She'd been a little worried that the weight of the candles and the ashes would make the boat difficult to maneuver, but it didn't seem to be affected by them. The votive lights winked and flickered, illuminating the white sails in a beautiful way as the boat moved out toward the center of the river. When it reached the channel, Lew maneuvered the sails so that it began to run before the wind. The tide was going out, the wind southerly—they'd checked beforehand.

"Bon voyage," Adrienne whispered, her hand raised in farewell.

Lew dropped the electronic control box into the carrying case, then put his arm around Adrienne. It was all up to the wind now, and to the water. The craft was moving nicely and within a few minutes, they could not see the hull or the candles at all, only the occasional, ghostly white of the sail as the craft rose up on a swell, only to fall back again. Lew put his arm around Adrienne's shoulder, and they stood together like that, in the freezing darkness at the edge of the shore, watching the sail wink out to sea on the black water.

And then, even that was gone.

Don't miss John Case's exciting novel

THE EIGHTH DAY

Available in bookstores everywhere

Here's a sneak preview. . . .

It was the mailman who reported it, calling 911 half an hour before Delaney's shift was supposed to end.

The missing man's pickup was sitting in the driveway and there were lights on in the house, so the mailman thought someone must be home. But no one answered when he knocked, and the mailbox was filled to overflowing. So maybe, he figured, maybe Mr. Terio had suffered a heart attack.

Delaney shook his head. He and Poliakoff were all the way to hell and gone, way out by the county line where civilization turned to kudzu.

Sitting behind the wheel, Poliakoff gave Delaney a sidelong glance and chuckled. "You want to use the siren?"

Delaney shook his head.

"The guy's probably on vacation," Poliakoff insisted. "We'll take a look around—I'll write it up. No problem."

Delaney gazed out the window. The air was heavy and still, thick with gloom, the way it gets before a thunderstorm. "Maybe it'll rain," he muttered.

Poliakoff nodded. "That's the spirit," he told him. "Think positive."

The cruiser turned onto Barracks Road and, suddenly, though they were barely a mile past a subdivision of bright new town houses, there was nothing in sight but vine-strangled woods and farmland. The occasional rotting barn.

"You ever been out this way?" Poliakoff asked.

Delaney shrugged. "That's it, over there," he said, nodding at a metal sign stippled with bullet holes. PREACHERMAN LANE. "You gotta turn."

They found themselves on a narrow dirt road, flanked by

weeds and at the edge of a dense wood. "Jesus," Poliakoff muttered as the cruiser crested a rise, then bottomed out with a thud before he could brake. "Since when does Fairfax County have dirt roads?"

"We still got a couple," Delaney replied, thinking the roads wouldn't be around much longer. The Washington suburbs were metastasizing in every direction and had been for twenty years. In a year or two, the farmhouse up ahead—a yellow farmhouse, suddenly visible on the left—would be gone, drowned by a rising tide of town houses, Wal-Marts, and Targets.

The mailbox was at the end of the driveway, a battered aluminum cylinder with a faded red flag nailed to the top of a four-by-four T set in concrete. A name was stenciled on the side: C. TERIO.

Next to the mailbox, three or four newspapers were jammed into a white plastic tube that bore the words THE WASHINGTON POST. A dozen other editions lay on the ground in a neatish pile, some already turning yellow.

When the mailman had reached out to 911, he'd suggested, "You should go in, take a look around the house, see what you can see."

But of course, they couldn't exactly do that. Under the circumstances, the most they could do was knock on the door, walk around the property, talk to the neighbors—not that there were any, far as Delaney could tell.

Climbing out of the cruiser, the deputies stood for a moment, watching and listening. Thunder rumbled in the south, and they could hear the distant hum of the Beltway. With a grin, Poliakoff sang in his cracking baritone, "H-e-e-ere we come to save the da-a-yyyy—"

"Let's get this over with," Delaney grumbled, setting off toward the house.

They passed an aging Toyota Tacoma at the end of the driveway, its rear end backed toward the house as if its owner had been loading or unloading something. Together the two policemen crossed the overgrown lawn to the front door.

The knocker was a fancy one—hand-hammered iron in the shape of a dragonfly. Poliakoff put his fist around it, drew back, and rapped loudly. "Hullo?"

Silence.

"Hel-lo?" Poliakoff cocked his head and listened hard. When no reply came, he tried the door and, finding it locked, gave a little shrug. "Let's go around back." Together the deputies made their way around the side of the house, pausing every so often to peer through the windows.

"He left enough lights on," Delaney observed.

At the rear of the house, they passed a little garden—tomatoes and peppers, zucchini and pole beans—that might have been tidy once but was now abandoned to weeds. Nearby, a screen door led into the kitchen. Poliakoff rapped on its wooden frame four or five times. "Anyone home? Mr. Terio! You in there?"

Nothing.

Or almost nothing. The air trembled with the on-again, off-again rasp of cicadas and, in the distance, the insectoid murmur of traffic. And there was something else, something . . . Delaney cocked his head and listened hard. He could hear . . . laughter. Or not laughter, actually, but . . . a laugh *track*. After a moment, he said, "The television's on."

Even so, there was nothing they could do, really. The doors were locked and they didn't have a warrant. There was no real evidence of a medical emergency, much less of foul play. But it *was* suspicious, and since they were already out here, they might as well take a look around. Be thorough about it.

Poliakoff walked back to where the newspapers were lying, squatted, and sorted through them. The oldest was dated July 19—more than two weeks ago.

A few feet away, Delaney checked out the truck in the driveway. On the front seat he found a faded and sun-curled receipt for a cash purchase at Home Depot. It, too, was dated July 19 and listed ten bags of Sakrete, 130 cinder blocks, a mortaring tool, and a plastic tub.

"A real do-it-yourselfer," he remarked, showing the receipt to Poliakoff, then reaching into the cruiser to retrieve his notebook.

"I'll check around the other side of the house," Poliakoff told him.

Delaney nodded and leaned back against the cruiser, going through the motions of making notes. Not that there was much to put down.

August 3
C. Terio
2602 Preacherman Lane
Oldest paper—July 19
Home Depot receipt, same date

He looked at his watch and noted the time: *5:29*. The whole thing was a waste of time, no matter how you looked at it. Delaney had responded to a couple of hundred calls like this during his ten years with the department, and nine times out of ten the missing person was senile or off on a bender. Once in a while, they turned up dead, sprawled on the bathroom floor or sitting in the Barcalounger. This kind of thing wasn't really *police work*. It was more like a janitorial service.

"Hey."

Delaney looked up. Poliakoff was calling to him from the other side of the house. Tossing the notebook onto the front seat of the cruiser, he glanced at the sky—there was a curtain of rain off to the south, which gave him more hope that Brent's game would be rained out—and headed off in the direction of his partner.

As it happened, there was an outside entrance to the basement—a set of angled metal doors that opened directly onto a short flight of concrete steps, leading down. Poliakoff was standing on the steps, the doors at attention on either side of him, like rusted wings. "Whaddya think? We take a look?"

Delaney frowned and inclined his head toward one of the doors. "That the way you found them?"

Poliakoff nodded. "Yeah. Wide open."

Delaney shrugged. "Could be a burglary, I guess—but let's make it quick." He was thinking, *Dear God, don't let there be a stiff down there, or we'll be here all night.*

Poliakoff ducked his head, calling out Terio's name as he descended the steps, Delaney right behind him.

The basement was utilitarian—a long rectangular room with a seven-foot ceiling, cinder-block walls, and a cement floor. A single fluorescent light buzzed and flickered over a dusty tool bench in a corner of the room. A moth beat its wings against the fixture.

Delaney glanced around. Nervously. He didn't like basements. He'd been afraid of them ever since he'd been a kid, though nothing had ever really happened to him in one. They just creeped him out. And this place, with its cheap shelves crowded with cans of paint, boxes of nails and screws, and tools, it was like every basement he'd ever seen: ordinary and evil, all at once.

Poliakoff wrinkled his nose.

"You smell something?" Delaney asked, his eyes searching the cellar.

"Yeah, I think so," his partner said. "Sort of."

On a shelf beneath the tool bench Delaney noticed a red plastic container marked: MOWER FUEL. "It's probably gas," he told his partner.

Poliakoff shook his head. "Unh-unh."

Delaney shrugged. "Whatever," he said, "there's no one here." Turning to leave, he started for the steps but stopped when he realized that Poliakoff wasn't following him. "Whatcha got?" he asked, looking back to his partner, who was holding a Maglite at shoulder height, its powerful beam funneling into the farthest corner of the room.

"I'm not sure," Poliakoff muttered, crossing the basement to where the flashlight's beam splashed against the far wall. "It's weird."

Delaney looked at the wall and realized Poliakoff was right: it *was* weird. At the north end of the basement, a corner was partitioned off by what looked like a pair of hastily built cinderblock walls. At right angles to each other, the walls were each about four feet across and went floor-to-ceiling, creating a sort of concrete closet, a closet without a door. "What *is* that?" Delaney asked.

Poliakoff shook his head and moved closer.

The closet—or whatever it was—was amateurishly made. Blobs of mortar bulged between the cinder blocks, which were stacked in a half-assed way that wasn't quite plumb. The deputies stared at the construction. Finally, Poliakoff said, "It's like . . . it's like a little jackleg *room*!"

Delaney nodded, then ran a hand through his thick brown hair. "It's probably what he did with the Home Depot stuff. He must have—"

"You smell it now?" Poliakoff asked.

Delaney sniffed. Even though he'd been a smoker most of his life, there was no mistaking the stink in the air. He'd spent two years in a Graves Registration unit at Dover Air Force Base and, if nothing else, he knew what death smelled like.

"Could be a rat," Poliakoff suggested. "They get in the walls. . . ."

Delaney shook his head. His heart was beating harder now, the adrenaline coursing through his chest. He took a deep breath and examined the construction more closely.

The sloppiest part was closest to the ceiling—where the top row of cinder blocks lay crookedly upon the lower course, mortar dripping from the joints. Delaney picked off a piece and crushed it between his thumb and forefinger.

"You don't think this guy . . . ?" Poliakoff let the sentence trail away as Delaney crossed the basement to the workbench and came back with a hammer and a screwdriver.

It only took a minute, and then the cinder block was more or less free of its binding. Hitting it one more time with the hammer, Delaney broke the block loose. Then he laid his tools on the floor and, reaching up, wiggled the block back and forth.

As it came free, a stench rose up, so pungent that Delaney could almost taste it—as if he'd touched the tip of his tongue to the place in his gum where a rotten tooth had just been extracted.

"Gimme a hand," he ordered, and with Poliakoff's help he removed the block from the wall and set it on the floor. By now, there was no doubt in either man's mind about what waited behind the wall, but they still couldn't see—the opening was too high. Taking up the hammer and screwdriver, Delaney went to work on a second cinder block, attacking it with a kind of desperation—even as he held his breath. Soon this second cinder block was free, so that there was now a window into the little room, just above Delaney's head.

Poliakoff was doing his best to keep his stomach still as Delaney looked around for something to stand on. He saw a straight-backed chair near the basement doors and dragged it over. Delaney climbed up on it and took the Maglite from his belt. Then he cast its beam through the window he'd created—and fell silent. From somewhere above, the laugh track surged.

"So what is it?" Poliakoff demanded. "What—"

Delaney swayed. "I'm gonna be sick," he said. And he was.